Revie...

'A smart, darkly funny tale ...
occasionally threaten to throttle us.'

Sara Cox – BBC Radio 2 DJ & author

'Free-range comedy. Poultry in motion!'

Dan Patterson – co-creator, *Mock the Week*

'Humorous and heart-warming. A great holiday read.'

Deborah Joseph – editor-in-chief, *Glamour*

'I woke up my very cross partner at 3.00am laughing. Adam Leigh has done it again – taken a rather unappetising premise and made it un-put-downable.'

Jonathan Margolis – author & journalist

'Besides making me think hard about a chicken salad for supper, I laughed a great deal.'

Jenni Frazer – *Jewish News*

Reviews of *The Curious Rise of Alex Lazarus*

'This is a very ambitious and dextrous take on a riveting world. Filled with a rich collection of characters, with Alex at its heart, it's very impressive. So much to like, great plotting and Alex's drive and ambition is intriguing.'

Abi Morgan – BAFTA/Emmy winning screenwriter

'Adam Leigh may well have created a new genre: the fictional business memoir. If you've ever wanted to know what it's like to start a new venture from the ground up, then let this inventive novel show you.'

Jonathan Freedland – *Guardian* journalist & author

'I genuinely loved this book.'

Steve Parish – chairman Crystal Palace Football Club

CHICKEN WARS

Adam Leigh read English at university and spent the next thirty years in a career in advertising, enjoying lots of long lunches and producing the odd campaign for toilet paper or dog food. His first novel, *The Curious Rise of Alex Lazarus*, was published in 2021. Adam has been married to his wonderful wife for over thirty years; she is his business partner and most uncritical fan. His three children are less forgiving.

Also by Adam Leigh

The Curious Rise of Alex Lazarus

www.adamleighwriter.com

CHICKEN WARS

ADAM LEIGH

First published in Great Britain in 2023 by
Adam Leigh, in partnership with whitefox publishing

www.wearewhitefox.com

ISBN 978-1-915635-29-7
Also available as an ebook
ISBN 978-1-915635-30-3

Designed and typeset by seagulls.net
Cover design by Dan Mogford
Project management by whitefox
Printed and bound by CPI Group (UK) Ltd, Croydon CR0 4YY

For Hannah, who last ate chicken in 1984

**A man should not eat meat
unless he has a special craving for it.**

Babylonian Talmud Chullin 84a

**Love does not begin and end the way we seem to think it does.
Love is a battle, love is war, love is growing up.**

James Baldwin, *Nobody Knows My Name* (1961)

**Were I not entirely aware of my duty to my family
and to my country, I would not have come
back tonight ... or indeed ever again!**

Audrey Hepburn in *Roman Holiday*

Prologue

Jack Fogel had a recurring dream about his funeral.

He imagined himself a bird soaring above the large grieving crowd. Proud of his popularity, he watched the mourners' procession shuffle sombrely behind his coffin towards the waiting grave. Even so high, he could make out the quiet chatter of their collective sadness, disbelieving he was gone. There were more people than he could have ever imagined paying respects. He tried to count aloud, but his voice could not get beyond ten, a *minyan* and the minimum number of Jews required to pray together officially. Even in his subconscious state, he was confused: had he just scraped by with enough people to honour his demise or was the legion of mourners real?

Like an avian drone, he swooped over the heads of the procession, an eclectic representation of his life that filled him with acute sorrow. He saw his ex-wife ensconced in earnest conversation with a disparate group of recent dates and putative girlfriends. She was shaking her head in admonishment of his many failings, and they seemed to be nodding sympathetically. His teenage daughters, indifferent to him at the best of times, stared blankly at the horizon, unmoved. Friends were silent, and he wondered if they too were feeling an imaginary sense of loss.

Behind the coffin walked his mother. Upright and immaculate, she was smoking a cigarette, flanked by his silently weeping sisters, dressed for work: a psychiatrist with a pad and pencil and a barrister in a horsehair wig and a gown. Nephews and nieces and other family followed, looking awkward, embarrassed and indifferent.

Then came the butchers, *shochets* and rabbis representing his business empire. Those that killed chickens wore blood-splattered aprons, leather galoshes and disposable blue gloves. They were sweaty and weary. The rabbinic authorities, the supervisors of the probity of his *kashrut* licence, had their heads buried in books of impenetrable learning. Everyone was irritable, brimming with disdain.

Right at the back of the slowly shuffling pack was a small group of his well-dressed friends from university. The non-Jewish men wore large black-velvet kippot, fiddling with them nervously as they walked. The women, elegant, professional and vibrant, wiped tears of real grief as they grabbed the men's arms for support in their unfamiliar introduction to the ritualised mourning strictures of Judaism.

Jack felt overwhelmed with confusion as he watched his departure into nothingness, realising that life would quickly return to normal for everyone supposedly grieving his loss. He was confident that he would not be reborn in a messianic age of eternal joy. A marble stone would mark his permanent home and it would be slowly covered with pebbles placed by a family member every time they visited. If they could be bothered to show up, that is.

Jack flapped his wings and weaved in and out of the crowd, desperate to be noticed. He tried to shout something, but his voice was a strangulated, helpless whisper. He swooped close to his family and could feel their breath on his feathered cheeks, but still they didn't notice him. Then he became aware of a commotion.

The butchers and factory workers were arguing vigorously with the *shochet*s, rabbis and authorities who sanctioned their trade. It was not just raised voices. Soon everyone was shoving each other, cuffing heads with angry slaps, kicking shins and raising fists like amateur boxers sparring in a gym.

Anger suddenly overwhelmed the mourners. Everyone was shouting. His mother was berating his sister who in turn castigated her husband, while he chastised their recalcitrant children. Friends turned on friends. Strangers confronted each other as if airing long-held grievances. He could hear snippets of rancour and several recurring phrases: *Why did you do that? What made you say that? What did you think you would achieve?* It felt like they were asking him to justify his disappointing life.

A surge of bitterness overwhelmed him as those supposedly grieving his loss descended into fistfights and expletive-filled name-calling. He was worth more than that, surely? He flew frantically through each argument and fight, trying in vain to shout 'Stop', but his pleas for restraint sounded like unintelligible farmyard grunts.

His coffin was slowly reaching its final resting place, a black hole that seemed to go on endlessly, a blank universe without hope. He felt impelled to restore order. With a flap of his eagle-like wings he soared into the sky, pirouetting and looping like an aeronautical display team. He saw the light of the celestial-blue heavens above him but pointed his beak towards the earth and began to dive.

The cold air smothered his face, and he was deafened by the wind. For a second, it was invigorating. Then he had landed by his coffin next to the empty grave. With a clear and theatrical voice, his capacity for speech returned.

'Stop your fighting and bickering. This is my funeral. A little respect is what I deserve.'

There was immediate silence. His hope that order would be restored quickly turned to dismay when someone started laughing at the back of the crowd. It was not from a rogue individual but a virulent infection that spread across the entire gathering almost instantaneously, cruel and mocking in tone.

His giggling mother stubbed her cigarette out and tossed it in the open grave. She produced a mirror from her handbag and held it in front of his face to show him the cause of the contagious mirth. He had thought himself a magnificent bird of prey. He was not.

They were laughing because he was wearing a pantomime costume. His face poked out from an elaborate headpiece. His body was tubby with outsized feet like the shoes of a clown.

He was dressed as a yellow and orange chicken.

PART 1

ORIGINS

Chapter 1

Jack grew up with the burden of expectation from his grandfather Solly that one day Fogel's Chickens would be his to run. Two shops and an enormous abattoir was the inheritance he was expected to embrace willingly by a chicken magnate and patriarch who was to be obeyed and never questioned.

Solly Fogel loved his nickname, 'The Godfather of Chicken'. In the seventies, he ran ads in *The Jewish Chronicle* in which he dressed like Marlon Brando chomping on a cigar with an enormous frozen chicken held aloft and the headline (his own creation): *Don Fogeleone. He'll pluck you a chicken you can't refuse!* When disputes for kosher licences became increasingly bitter and complicated, he was persuaded that revelling in mafia imagery was not that helpful for the family business.

Growing up, Jack adored his grandfather but was terrified by the mercurial temper of this man who had used his fists to settle arguments all his life. Proud of his pugilism, and with a handy jab even into his eighties, no one was safe. From a rival wholesaler trying to undercut him on price to an esteemed rabbi declaring an arcane religious judgement preventing the sale of a chicken. They would all feel his fury.

Solly had two children; Philip had gone into the business at sixteen and been his devoted if unremarkable lieutenant, while Sheila had married a dentist and decamped to a comfortable suburban life with two daughters and all mod cons. His four independently minded, ambitious granddaughters were evidently divine retribution for his disreputable behaviour as a youth and the many fights he had started thereafter.

Jack, his only grandson, was the future of Fogel's Chickens and from as early as he could remember, he received disproportionate love in comparison to his sisters. Long walks, regular trips to restaurants and an endless supply of surprise presents attested to his grandfather's devotion. Whenever Jack, a nervous child, entered a room, Solly's arms would be outstretched and his stern, unforgiving face would break into a welcoming smile. Jack basked in the warmth of this adoration, unaware of its accompanying expectation.

* * *

Shortly before Jack's bar mitzvah, his grandfather rang unexpectedly. Something must be wrong, and Jack's first instinct was a sharp fear that he had transgressed in some unknown way as, in his thirteen years, they had never spoken on the phone. Not one for pleasantries, Solly barked at him with the aggression of a courtroom prosecutor.

'You are coming with me on a trip on Sunday morning.'

'Why, *Zeyde*?'

'It is time you understood what you are going to become. I will collect you at eight thirty. Be ready or I'll get cross.'

For a second, Jack wondered if he needed to pack a bag or bring his passport. He had a foreboding this was going to be a significant event, but there was no chance of finding out more as his grandfather had already hung up.

Later that night, he asked his father if he had any idea what was going on. Phil Fogel was slurping a cup of tea in front of the television and looked up, irritated, from the episode of *Miami Vice* in which he was engrossed.

'How would I know? He never confides in me. He probably wants to buy you a present. Now if you don't mind, you're interrupting this programme and I am trying to learn about drug trafficking.'

Jack wandered back to his room unnoticed by his family, who were all too focused on their own needs. Maybe it wasn't a bad thing having such a close relationship with his grandfather. At least he was somebody's favourite.

* * *

Jack was up early, unsure how the sunny June day would unfold. At the allotted hour, his grandfather pulled up in his Moroccan Bronze Jaguar XJS and its passenger door swung open like the jaws of a shark ready to devour him.

'*If I was a chicken,*' Solly Fogel used to say, '*I would have remained at the back of the shelf unselected.*' A lean and wiry man with a pencil moustache and brilliantined grey hair, he was always impeccably dressed in a series of hand-made suits bought thirty years ago. That day, he wore a navy blue, thin-lapelled blazer with a yellow pocket square and a member's tie from the RAC Club in Pall Mall. He was not actually a member, but having called on them frequently to jump-start his battery on cold mornings, he felt somehow entitled to wear one.

'Don't look so scared, my boy. Today you learn about your past and your future.'

'Do we get to eat at least?' was the only comment Jack could muster as the noisy 3.4-litre engine of the Jag roared into life.

'What a *nudnik* you are. Of course you get to eat, but you'll have to work a little bit for your lunch.'

For a moment, Jack worried that he might have to pluck a chicken or make deliveries, but soon they were driving through the empty Sunday morning London streets in brittle silence. The first stop was a nondescript apartment block in a dingy inner-city street near Aldgate. Jack noticed that some of the windows were broken, and racist graffiti was scrawled on the walls.

'Do you know where we are, my boy?'

'Is this where you lived?' He was confused as it did not seem the kind of home that his dapper grandfather would willingly choose. Solly shook his head with sadness.

'This is where my home *was*. There was a terrace of houses here that were all bombed by the Nazis. This ugly thing was built in the sixties, and you know what, my chickens live in better conditions. Now, Jack, my boy, listen carefully to everything I tell you as this may be the last opportunity we ever have for such a conversation.'

Given they had dinner together every Friday night, it sounded a bit ominous for Jack's liking. All he wanted to do was return home and play with some of his bar mitzvah presents. The Sanyo cassette-radio ghetto blaster would have to wait a few more hours.

Solly inspected the building with disdain, muttering in Yiddish. Jack often heard his grandfather and father using archaic words from this long-dead language, as if everyone should know what they were talking about. They sounded like meaningless grunts or expressions of pain, but he was always too fearful to ask for a translation. '*Kschlipte Vstkenemeshbgge*' was what he thought he heard *Zeyde* declare, but it could just as easily have been another jumble of randomly connected consonants with the occasional vowel.

'Do you know the sacrifices that were made so we could live in this house? My bedroom was somewhere up there. Well, not just mine, I shared it with my brothers, Sidney and Nat. I have been in bigger broom cupboards. We never complained for a moment. That was what life was like for us, hardship without a grumble. Now get in the car and I will tell you about your family.'

Jack did as he was told, wondering if his face betrayed his boredom. The car was warm in the early morning sunshine, but Solly seemed oblivious to its stuffiness. Jack was immediately drowsy and wriggled in the chapped leather seat to try to muster enough energy to stay awake. His grandfather drummed his fingers impatiently on the steering wheel, like an austere rabbi waiting for silence before delivering the sermon.

'My parents came from just outside Białystok. Did you know that Białystok has been part of Germany and Russia and is now in Poland?' Jack shook his head, struggling to work out how a town was able to move countries.

'Your great-grandparents Yaakov and Sara left after the pogrom of 1905 when the Russians attacked the Jews. Yaakov sold chickens and lost everything. He came over here with nothing other than his wife and a bit of ambition. You see, Jack, Jews are always being attacked and that's why you have to fight back whenever you can. Your fists are your most valuable weapon. Not words. Punches.'

That philosophy was certainly not taught in Jack's Jewish school. Rabbis drilled into him that the way to get on in life was to study the Torah morning, noon and night. Even at twelve, he doubted that this was the only option available to him.

'My father traded chickens. He'd buy them from *goyische* farmers in Essex and Norfolk and sell them in the markets. You'd buy a chicken and then take it to one of the little *shecht* shops that were all around the East End. Not the nicely wrapped chicken off the shelf you buy today. A live bird, slaughtered while you wait.'

Jack was unable to feign the necessary engagement required and stifled a yawn, which his grandfather did not miss. He sucked air through a gap in his dentures, a clear sign of irritation, and his fist clenched subconsciously.

'Pay attention, young man, this is an important conversation, and you more than anyone in the family must understand why. So, let's play a game. How old do you think I was when I started working for my father?' Jack pondered for a moment, too scared to venture a guess in the event it made *Zeyde* even more grumpy.

'I'll tell you, *potz*. I was fourteen, about eighteen months older than you are now. No pointless Latin and physics lessons for me. I couldn't wait to start *schlepping* crates of birds and getting a few pennies in my pocket. And guess how old I was when I started picking up the crates of chickens myself in the lorry?'

Solly straightened his tie and smoothed down his oily grey hair, running a finger along the crease of the centre parting, preening in anticipation of the imminent revelation.

'I was fifteen years old, young man. *Fifteen*. Can you believe that I got away with such a thing?'

Jack shook his head and timidly replied, 'Wasn't that illegal, *Zeyde*? Couldn't you have got in trouble?'

'Trouble? As if. I always wanted to drive the lorry, but my father said that I wouldn't be able to reach the pedals. I'll show him, I thought. I went to the County Hall office and told a little white lie. Do you know what a little white lie is?'

Jack shook his head.

'It is telling something that does no harm to make you a bit more successful. They are very useful. Anyway, you didn't need to take a test in 1921. I told the fella I was seventeen and he believed me. Within a few weeks, I was driving a five-ton lorry carrying ninety crates and I couldn't believe my luck.'

Solly cackled, and Jack observed for the first time that his grandfather even laughed like a clucking chicken.

* * *

Bloom's of Whitechapel was Jack's least favourite restaurant, but to his grandfather it was the epitome of fine dining, quipping after every meal: '*If Michelin reviewed the restaurant, they would definitely give it three Stars of David.*' Established in 1920, it was unashamedly serving its antiquated menu of coronary-inducing cholesterol sixty years later.

Even as a child, Jack knew that waiters should not be rude to you. This was not the way they had been trained at Bloom's. If unable to finish a gargantuan portion of dry salt-beef, latkes the size of watermelons and carrots so soggy they must have been water-boarded, he was subjected to a barrage of criticism from disgruntled white-jacketed staff, who would remind you that if you did not finish your food, you might get diabetes.

They had adjourned for lunch after driving around the East End, Stamford Hill and Clapton, the history of Solly's business life a blur of detail that had overwhelmed Jack. Besides, he was starving, having not got up in time for breakfast, and his stomach produced a concerto of rumbles and gurgles.

His grandfather only ate roast chicken. That lunch, it swam in so much grease it reminded Jack of seabirds covered in crude oil from a grounded tanker that he had watched on the news recently. He stared at an overwhelming mound of salt-beef in front of him and anticipated the inevitable reprimand that the decrepit deaf waiter would hurl at him when he left it unfinished. Waving a fork anima-tedly, Solly talked as he ate, the remnants of masticated chicken still visible in his open mouth.

'Now we are sat down, I am going to explain the business to you. One day it will be yours. Does that excite you?'

Jack felt that had to be a trick question. If he said no, Solly would be incandescent. If he said yes, he would grow up and work in a soulless building where thousands of chickens were slaughtered every day. He did not need to answer because his grandfather was making a speech, not having a conversation.

'The word "*kosher*". Do you know what it means?' Jack nodded, realising it was much simpler than trying to speak. 'It means, among other things, "proper" or "correct". For Jews, keeping kosher means doing the right thing.'

The waiter appeared to clear the plates, stacking them on one arm while gathering the cutlery with his free hand. Solly's plate was empty bar a few chicken bones and a greasy glaze congealing by the second. Jack, however, had only managed to get through three-quarters of his salt-beef platter and knew censure was imminent. The waiter sighed with weary disappointment, staring venomously at Jack while muttering, 'You must have had a large breakfast this morning, young man, because a *mensch* wouldn't waste food like this without feeling terrible. So what do you want for dessert?'

Solly dismissed him with a diffident wave of his hand and glanced around the restaurant as if curious to see if people were tuning in to his lecture.

'Now, please tell me what's the word for unkosher.'

'It's *treif.*'

'Good boy, but let's look at the root of the word. It means *torn*. The rabbis teach us our faith is torn if we don't eat kosher. That's why what I do is so important. You are looking more confused than your father when I explained it to him when he was your age, and let's face it, he is no Einstein. Try to keep up. Imagine there is an invisible thread behind your back.'

Jack instinctively turned around and felt a fool, realising it was meant figuratively. Sheepishly, he twiddled the gravy-stained table-cloth, embarrassed that this time with his *zeyde* was proving such an ordeal.

'The thread is what links us to our past. Look, I am no philosopher, but I still have come to realise there is a reason I do what I do. What do you think that is?'

Jack knew he had to answer. He looked up at his grandfather and saw an old man, slightly hunched, looking momentarily vulnerable, and suddenly things became clear to him.

'You do it, *Zeyde*, because you think it is important for us to carry on the traditions.'

'Well, that's part of it. I mean, as Jews, we have certain responsibilities, sure we do. But that's not the reason, and remember this advice wherever you are.'

Jack leant forward instinctively.

'There is lots of money to be made from chickens. Lots and lots.'

* * *

When Jack looked back on that trip years later, it seemed he had undergone his own version of *A Christmas Carol*, in which he was a truculent Scrooge convinced to embrace his destiny by his grandfather, playing the role of all the ghosts. The past was represented by his former house in the East End, the present was lunch at Bloom's and his future the factory in Hackney they visited after lunch.

'Jack, my boy. You are now going to see what a modern chicken business looks like.' By now, all Jack wanted to do was be somewhere else. The heat in the car was as oppressive as his grandfather's love of poultry.

'No one knows more about killing chickens than me. It will come naturally to you too, it's in your blood.'

Jack shuddered and imagined some sort of hereditary virus with which he was afflicted.

'We Jews know how to kill an animal kindly. Did you know that? It's all about the blood. Before you eat a chicken, you must make sure you have drained it all. You must kill it quickly, with a slit of its jugular vein. The *shochet* uses a very sharp knife called a *chalef* and with one stroke it's done.'

Like a demented pirate, Solly dragged his finger across his throat to mimic the action, his eyes bulging with inappropriate excitement.

Jack felt his stomach churn and he burped, his mouth filling with the stale taste of salt-beef and gherkin.

'We have to check all the time to make sure there are no abnormalities. After the bird has been killed, it has to be washed and salted to get rid of any excess blood. When we are sure, it can be packed and sold.'

'Why does it matter, *Zeyde*, that there's a tiny speck of blood? Who cares?'

'God cares and you don't want to get in his bad books. What you need to remember is if you don't do it properly and according to the rules, they take away your licence and then no more good times for you and your family.'

To prove the importance of his wealth, he affectionately tapped the dashboard as if protecting the vehicle from bad news.

* * *

Solly held open the heavy steel door of the factory, which was wrapped in thick metal gauze with four locks and two handles. Metal bars also encased all the windows.

'You have heard of Fort Knox. Welcome to Fort *Clucks*.'

He chuckled at his witticism, which, like much of what he said, was beyond Jack's comprehension. Solly seemed to have so many things he needed to explain to his grandson and looked earnestly at him as he asked the next unrelated question.

'What do you know about vegetarians?'

Of course, Jack knew what a vegetarian was, although he had never actually met one.

'Vegetarians are our enemy, don't you ever forget that. Never trust a vegetarian. Imagine a world not eating chickens. How barbaric! God intended us to eat everything in the Garden of Eden, not just the fruit and vegetables. That's what the rabbis teach us. Your plate should always be filled with meat and vegetables. Are you following me?'

Jack was lost but nodded vigorously not to arouse suspicion, pretty sure by now that his grandfather's grasp of theology could at best be described as vague. As they entered the factory floor, the iridescent artificial strip lights made Jack blink. It was the end of the day and the *shochets* had departed, leaving several workers to hose down the floor and sweep up. Bloody feathers lay in desultory clumps across the cold stone, a memorial to the day's fallen chickens.

No one spoke, but they all touched their hairnets in salute, like soldiers greeting a conquering general. Without stopping to talk, Solly led Jack into his office in the far corner of the factory and motioned for him to sit down in front of his throne, an ancient, battered, leather swivel chair near collapse. Jack was disconcerted to see so many family photos scattered around the tiny room, which were mostly of him.

'Now, time for your most important lesson of the day. What I am going to tell you is the key to my success.'

He turned his back on Jack and rummaged in a filing cabinet, which slid open with a rusty screech. Eventually, after much foraging, he emerged with a torn manila envelope and, reaching inside, he produced various newspaper clippings, which he spread on the desk.

'I am going to tell you about some important battles I won. Each one made it into the papers. You could say I have a bit of a profile in the media.'

Jack looked at the fading newsprint and tried to understand what the strange headlines could signify. He did not know whether to be impressed that his grandfather was famous or embarrassed that the stories were all chicken related.

'This one is from *The Times* in 1933, when one of my drivers tried to swap my A Grade chickens for some inferior birds with a rival business who were paying him on the sly. I found out and do you know what I did?'

Jack shook his head.

'I decked him with a left hook and ended up in front of the magistrate, who let me off because he liked me and thought I was doing a service to the Jews by protecting their Friday night dinner table. I could have gone a few rounds with Jack Dempsey when I was younger, let me tell you.'

Solly was on a roll now, and picked up another crumbling newspaper.

'So, I am very proud of this story. In 1953, I heard of a new way to pluck chickens using machines and booked myself a passage on the *QE2* to visit the factory in Williamsburg, Brooklyn, because it would improve our efficiency by ninety per cent. I got it shipped back with me and assembled and then do you know what happened?'

'It plucked a chicken?'

'Don't be an idiot. I'll tell you what happened. My bloody workers thought they'd lose their jobs. This commie called Lou Katz organised a picket line and brought dockers, tailors and other workers to blockade the factory. Do you know what I did next?'

Jack had done tests at school with fewer questions.

'I fired lousy Lou Katz in front of the picket line and threatened to fire another person every day unless they came back to work immediately. They backed down at once and I was right all along about the machines. They learnt to use them without any trouble, and no one lost their job. The press loved this story because a good chicken dispute always sells papers. Listen to what they wrote about it all: "*A faint echo of a Luddite cry was to be heard in the East End of London. Late in the day, and perhaps inexorably, the Industrial Revolution reached the poulterers' trade.*'"

Jack's head was throbbing now from these relentless arcane anecdotes. *Zeyde* seemed to be at war with everyone and for the first time he realised that adult life may be rather complicated if it was made up of these constant battles.

* * *

In the car, after this exhausting family odyssey, Solly reached into his breast pocket and produced an envelope, which he handed to Jack.

'Go on, my boy, open it. It's your bar mitzvah present.'

Jack felt his pulse quicken, as he knew this was a moment of significance. The envelope had a slight bulge and contained a letter and a cheque for two hundred and fifty pounds, an eye-watering sum to Jack. He tried to decipher his grandfather's unsophisticated handwriting.

Our Dearest Jack,

Since you were a little boy, we have been so proud of you. You have a good heart, a great mind, and a brilliant future ahead. You must fulfil your promise even if it means fighting your enemies or the people closest to you. When you are older, perhaps you will look back on this journey we have been on today and realise that you are the future of Fogel's Chickens. In the meantime, take this other gift and always keep it close.

Your loving Zeyde,
Solly Fogel

Jack reached in the envelope again and pulled out a key ring. There were two silver letters, his initials JF, and a solitary key. Slightly bemused, he looked up at his grandfather, whose eyes had filled with tears.

Solly pulled him close and whispered, 'It opens one door. The door to the factory. And please God, you will use it every day when you are running the business.'

Chapter 2

For Jack, TV represented an escape from an indifferent family who found it so easy to ignore him. As a child, he had been an avid reader, but it was the small or big screen that fuelled his adolescent cultural curiosity. He devoured pretentious films on scratchy VHS tapes among the chintz of his family's mock-Tudor home in suburban Hendon. Kurosawa, Fellini, Bergman and Herzog, the more obscure the better as far as his fledgling artistic mind was concerned. Above all, he loved television, dramas, comedies or documentaries, anything so long as it was edgy or provocative. He was obsessed with all aspects of production and knew there was only one career to pursue when he eventually managed to extricate himself from the expectations of his grandfather.

There was only one TV, nestled in the corner of an aquamarine-coloured living room that would give you a headache if you stared too long at the walls or carpet. As a child, Jack wondered if his mother was colour blind or just had no style. He hated everything about the room, from the gilt mirrors and faux Monet prints to the framed photos of his bar mitzvah, nestled between dusty bottles of undrunk advocaat. The sofas were abrasive velveteen, and the central heating was always turned on, making TV viewing both sweaty and uncomfortable.

The problem was that he rarely had free rein over the remote and was always forced to give way to someone else's viewing demands. His father, Phil, was devoted to sport and had an ability to stare morosely at any competitive game, which baffled Jack. Snooker, crown green bowling, speedway, wrestling – Phil lapped them all up, particularly when there was no football or cricket available. The physical exertion he watched exhausted him, and he would frequently fall asleep at climactic moments in the action. Significantly overweight, a full ashtray on his ever-growing belly, his exercise routine involved little more than a lugubrious trudge to the loo every once in a while.

Phil Fogel also adored American police dramas and would often quip as he settled into his battered leather recliner that '*If I had my time again, I'd be a police inspector, not an inspector of poultry*'. He was obsessed with solving fictional crimes and would absorb in reverential silence the trail of clues and then confidently but incorrectly announce the murderer. Jack once tried to bond with him, joking about his inability to recognise a smoking gun by stating, '*You know, Dad, you are more Shylock than Sherlock.*' His father winced and turned the volume up, despairing that he had produced this bizarre child he could not understand.

Phil was despondent his only son did not share his passions. '*Chelsea is in your blood,*' he would shout regularly, as if the game was a Jewish tradition dating back to his *shtetl* origins. Surely preferring a book to a soccer match did not make him a freak? But his father had hoped to share a deep-seated hatred for Tottenham and Arsenal with his only male ally in the house. How Jack disappointed him.

It was not much better with his mother, Stephanie. As a child, Jack saw her as a normal, if sullen parent, worn down by domestic drudgery and always complaining that no one understood the monotony of her responsibilities. When he looked back, he realised she must have felt trapped by marrying a man she had met at sixteen, who had not got more interesting with time.

His mother embarked on her own journey of self-improvement and the TV became its focal point. She watched BBC Two assiduously, believing it to be a symbol of intellectual aspiration. When Channel 4 began, she pretended to be thrilled, although the alternative comedy and edgy new drama in truth left her cold. Jack sensed her consumption of subtitled documentaries about the Aztecs was more a declaration of intent than a genuine passion. Like her husband, she would often drop off to sleep and awake with a jolt, declaring that shutting her eyes was just a sign of intense concentration. She made little effort to share Jack's tastes, declaring instead that he was needlessly pretentious and calling him 'my son the intellectual' with a conspicuous absence of maternal pride.

She was rarely affectionate. Rather, she saw Jack as a future provider of her financial security, a message she repeated for as long as he could remember. His filial responsibility was to give up his own dreams to look after her as she got older. She had a premonition that her marriage to the chronically overweight chain-smoking Philip would not endure for ever and would bemoan his unhealthy lifestyle after every fat-rich-carb-full dinner she served him. And despite Jack's undemanding good nature, she displayed little curiosity in understanding who he wanted to be in adulthood. He was like a familiar meal in a local restaurant. You knew what you were getting, but it never made you that excited.

Jack was sandwiched between two sisters, Tracy the Elder and Karen the Younger. They acted as if these descriptors were royal titles, which explained their sense of entitlement. After all, whoever bowed down to King Jack the Middle One? Tracy was the self-appointed leader of the siblings, and everyone had to follow her dictatorial edicts. Karen exulted in her position as their mother's favourite and was determined to be best at everything. For Jack, who hadn't the energy for all-out war, it was simply exhausting to be ordered around by one and manipulated by the other.

Even with a four-year age gap, the girls were very close and Jack's attempts to hijack the TV schedule by watching what he wanted was another manifestation of his unnecessary presence. Despite Phil's significant girth, the Fogel patriarchy carried little weight as far as decision-making was concerned. Jack would be comfortably settled on the sofa watching a classic film, trying not to upset anyone. His sisters would snatch the remote control, change channel and carry on their conversation as if he wasn't even in the room.

Tracy and Karen outperformed him academically as they breezed through school. With busy, boyfriend-filled social lives, they were engaged in an impressive array of extracurricular pursuits, which made their mother inordinately proud. Tracy excelled at both sports and drama and Karen was an extremely accomplished pianist and a public debater incapable of losing an argument. Jack possessed no equivalent skills and being pleasant and academically competent did not sufficiently differentiate him from the ordinary sons of Stephanie's ordinary friends.

The girls didn't hate their brother, they just struggled to include him in the conversation. With a sisterly telepathy and their own made-up language, they were oblivious to any of the components of his adolescent life. Sometimes they would fall out with combustible theatricality and their fights would be accompanied by the throwing of shoes, hair-pulling and elaborate profanity-laden insults. The schism would not last long and invariably the reconciliation would serve to exclude Jack further from their self-contained world of mutual dependence.

Poor old Jack. He was like the lonely ghost in a stately home, compelled to haunt the corridors but rarely observed. When he got older, he would tell his friends that he did not grow up in conflict. Conflict requires people to care. No, for Jack it was an upbringing spent in the cloying inertia of his family's disappointment that he was not someone else. It was not surprising that he wanted to make a name for himself in TV. It might get him noticed.

* * *

'Jack, why didn't you tell us that you are going to be the next big thing in Hollywood?' Karen shrieked as she triumphantly waved a clump of paper she had just stolen from Jack's bedroom.

He felt his stomach muscles tighten with anxiety as he anticipated the inevitable humiliation. What should have been a quiet family dinner on a drizzly evening during Jack's final year at school had been hijacked by his sixteen-year-old sister's egregious theft. Surreptitiously foraging in his bedroom, she had found a draft treatment for a TV drama, which was far more than she expected to uncover. She was thrilled.

'Karen, you absolute bitch, give it to me now.' To Jack, she possessed the moral code of a particularly immoral serial killer and he tried to snatch the papers back but was restrained by the flabby forearm of his father.

'We are eating,' Phil declared with a roar that disintegrated into a pitiful wheeze. Karen retreated a step and stared at Jack with mocking defiance and then glanced at her mother, because she knew that as her favourite there was no scenario in which she would not receive her support.

'Don't call your sister that, Jack. Apologise immediately,' Stephanie barked as she shovelled tinned fruit into plastic bowls, waving the ladle as if it was a weapon. A rogue segment of mandarin flew across the kitchen and landed in the textbook Tracy was reading. As a first-year medical student, she felt entitled to total respect, particularly from Jack, who was yet to emulate her exam success. Picking out the fruit, she looked accusingly at him.

'Oh, very funny, Jack. You are so mature. When we study the brain next term, I'll be sure to tell you what's wrong with yours.'

Jack attempted to remonstrate, but Karen now saw she had managed to turn the whole family against him and pressed on with her assault.

'Why don't you share your writing with us some more?'

Her smile was demonic, and he could not understand the pleasure she was taking in his discomfort.

'Karen, you should stop now,' Tracy told her sister with little conviction and a grin that suggested she wanted her to do the opposite. Even Stephanie folded her arms in a way that said '*this is fun*'. He slumped in his chair, overwhelmed by frustration, and wondered if he should answer their questions to end the ordeal and then run off and join the French Foreign Legion.

'All right, what do you want to know?'

'What's it called?' Tracy asked.

He paused, overwhelmed with embarrassment.

'*No Clue to Love.*' It did not sound impressive, and the girls sniggered.

'Are there any coppers in it?' added Phil, believing the word 'clue' could be used only in a detective series.

'No, Dad. It's a drama and I suppose a love story.' His father growled like a bear and picked up a newspaper to avoid listening to his son's nonsense any further.

'Written from your deep well of experience, no doubt?' Karen had a precocious ability for sarcasm, used indiscriminately to slaughter the innocent. Fortunately, Tracy sensed Jack's vulnerability and seemed to take pity on him. For a moment, he wondered if she was an ally.

'What's it about? I'd love to hear.'

Soothed by her change of tone, he decided to share his idea with his unforgiving family audience and began to pitch the concept like there were real television executives in front of him.

'It's a six-part drama about a brilliant psychiatrist who cures all his patients but can't make his own love life work. In every episode he helps a patient through a clever diagnosis, which is contrasted with a new personal relationship that fails because he doesn't understand his own emotions.'

Tracy gave an involuntary snort of disapproval, riled by this silly plot that undermined her ambition to become London's most eminent psychiatrist. Her sad little brother, a wannabe English student who knew nothing about shrinking heads, was muscling in on her patch. Picking up a knife, she pointed it at him accusingly and then began to cut an apple.

'Go on, Carl Jung. What are the cases he cures?'

Jack wanted to sound impressive, but since Karen had stolen a loose synopsis rather than a fleshed-out script, this was going to be highly unlikely. Why was this happening to him now? All he wanted was to eat quickly then get back to his essay on the poems of W.H. Auden, unnoticed, when Karen embarked on this cruel campaign of humiliation. His throat suddenly felt sore as he attempted a final explanation.

'It's more the themes I have focused on – you know, things like alienation, isolation, the nature of love.' It sounded ridiculous. Karen had never looked happier as she began his final cross-examination.

'So, no plot then?'

'Well, not fully worked through.'

'And the episodes haven't been written.'

'Not in any detail.'

'Managed to sketch any characters?'

'One or two,' he lied.

'But lots of themes? Impressive, Jack. ITV will certainly want a second series.'

His face flushed beetroot with shame and inadequacy as he muttered in defeat, 'It's early days, I suppose.'

The girls got up from the table having satisfactorily dismantled his self-esteem. Their work was done. He was going to have to toughen up considerably to survive this role of disappointing middle child. As if to emphasise the need for resilience, his mother decided to provide her own assessment.

'I am sorry to tell you, darling, you may need to consider doing something else with your life. If this is anything to go by, the thought of you becoming a writer is quite frankly ridiculous.'

Jack looked forlornly out of the kitchen window to the darkness of their small garden and wondered if it was too cold to sleep in the shed.

'That's a bloody understatement,' added Phil, helping himself to a third slice of apple pie. 'Thank heavens we have other plans for you, or you'd end up starving and penniless.'

Chapter 3

Solly died the day Jack finished his finals at university.

Aged eighty-eight and widowed, he had been in robust physical health, his mind sharp as ever, and although long retired he was a constant irritant for Phil, now trying to run the business as his successor. Solly would get dressed in a blazer and tie, and in between his long walks and bridge games, he would phone his son three times a day to monitor the performance of Fogel's Chickens. He would begin each conversation with '*It's none of my business*', before launching into a tirade of frustrated abuse that suggested he thought the complete opposite.

A quiet death was the most peaceful gesture of his entire life. One night, he went to bed in ancient monogrammed silk pyjamas, shut his eyes and drifted calmly into the world to come. His daughter, Sheila, concerned at him not calling on the dot of nine thirty as always, found him lifeless, with an unfamiliar crooked smile and a crumpled *Daily Mail* next to him. Jack drove home immediately to begin the week-long mourning period, foregoing parties and post-exam celebrations without complaint. He was sad and wistful to lose his *zeyde*, a constant source of love and a wiser influence than his insipid father.

But as he sprinkled earth in the grave at the end of the funeral, he guiltily realised his grief was diminished by enormous relief. He was sure the hundreds of mourners were all staring at him, wondering if he was going to be the future ruler of the chicken empire. As the dry summer earth thudded against the pine coffin, he knew he would now be spared the imaginary conversation with his grandfather, rehearsed in his head so many times, in which he would be forced to reveal his life plans.

'Nu, *Jack, when are you joining your father in the business? You have your degree. Stop with the books and learn to kill a chicken.*'

'*I am sorry,* Zeyde, *I don't think I can.*'

'*What do you mean? Don't make an old man angry.*'

'*I don't think the business is for me.*'

'*The business is only for you. What do you think I have been telling you since you were little?*'

'*I want to do something else.*'

'Else?'

He imagined Solly roaring the word like Mr Bumble shouting at Oliver asking for *more*.

'*OK, Mr Bigshot, before I give you a hiding, tell me what you want to do.*'

At this point, Jack anticipated his voice cracking feebly in the face of his grandfather's credible threat of violence.

'*The thing is, and I am so sorry, I mean I would never want to upset you.*' Jack imagined the rapid onset of a stammer.

'*Just say it, you* schlemiel.'

'*Wh-what I w-want … to do with my life is to … w-work in TV.*'

* * *

'What I want to do with my life is to work in TV.' It was his second year at university and Jack was desperately trying to impress the extremely attractive girl he had hesitantly approached at a party.

'Repairing or selling them?'

'No, writing and producing. It's my destiny.' It sounded ridiculous and he felt a sharp pain in his stomach, as if his body was rebelling against his conversational ineptitude. He tried to change the subject, but all he could manage was the inane question, 'So what's your destiny then?'

'To avoid blokes who use the word *destiny* at parties, for a start.'

'Sorry. I've got off to a poor start, haven't I? I don't know why but you're making me nervous.' He knew exactly why. She exuded a confidence that was as sexy as it was intimidating. Jack's relationship experience to this point was perfunctory. He always felt slightly invisible when he tried to impress a girl he liked. His sisters' indifference to him, growing up, had dented his self-worth and he anticipated that the pursuit of love might require more tenacity than he could easily produce. He'd be pretty much single throughout his student days.

'Then it's a good job you'll be behind the camera, not in front of an audience,' she quipped, her eyes fixed on him as if in a blinking contest.

'I like to see myself as more cerebral rather than a big charismatic personality.' He bit his lip as he said this. Had he just admitted to lacking charisma? This was proving a more excruciating attempted pick-up than normal.

'Quick tip. If you're trying to flirt with me, you may want to work on your technique a bit. Try to talk yourself up if you want to make an impression. I missed your name, by the way.'

He hated his name. It made him sound more Jewish than he wanted. Often, he imagined he was called something that suggested a spy or a rogue cop rather than the son of a kosher poulterer. *Jack Fellows? Jack Francis? Jack Fist?*

His mind was clearly distracted by these musings when he inadvertently answered, 'The name's Fogel. Jack Fogel.' *Oh, my Lord, where did that come from*, he almost added aloud.

'Very 007, I'm sure. Hello Fogel, Jack Fogel. I'm Ali. I haven't got a clue what I'm going to do with my life, which is what I think you were clumsily asking. But I do intend to excel in everything. Does that sound a bit arrogant? I hope not, I think I'm a little drunk. Maybe you should just prattle on about your dreams and I'll listen or walk off discreetly if they are particularly dull.' She made an imaginary toast with her plastic cup filled with warm, sweet white wine and he clinked his bottle of Budweiser, a little too enthusiastically as it fizzed up, spilling over her hand.

And that was how Jack met his future wife, Alison. Even their first encounter reflected the subsequent nature of their relationship. Her wit was incisive and her attractiveness disconcerted him. With immaculate hair cut in a chic bob (not that Jack could have named the style), her brown-black eyes sparkled with mischievous intent in the pallor of a dingy student house, although in truth it took him a few years to remember their colour. She was by far the most sophisticated girl he had ever tried to impress with his nebulous promise of TV fame. It seemed unlikely that he was going to succeed, and further ridicule was surely imminent.

However, after several hours of intense conversation, he persuaded her to go on a date with him. She did not make it easy and mocked his timidity by telling him, 'Well, since you stuttered the question so nicely and I've had a couple of cancellations, we'll give you a chance to audition for the role.'

'What role is that?' He tried to sound diffident, but it just came out as over-eager.

'A decent boyfriend. Can you play that part?' She was staring at him with a confidence that he found simultaneously terrifying and arousing.

'What a stroke of good fortune for you. I think I was born to play that part.'

The following day, they went to see the Tom Hanks film *Philadelphia*, chosen because it was sufficiently mainstream for a date, but also serious enough to suggest he was not a feckless, immature student. It was an inspired choice. They both wept without inhibition, and she held his hand tightly throughout. Though just twenty-one, Jack was smitten; a gentle soul, he could not stop his mind racing forward to a life of unfettered excitement and romance. And this life certainly did not involve selling kosher chicken drumsticks and five-pound family roasters to the Jews of north-west London.

* * *

Jack discovered in his relationship with Ali a side of him that he had not realised existed. As a teenager, he always felt compelled to apologise for nameless mistakes he was unwittingly making. Everything was a struggle: to be respected by his parents, to be noticed by his sisters, to be free from his grandfather's expectations. Now he was adored without reservation. Ali loved his obsession with TV and the arts, his dislike of sport, his sense of humour and intensity. Despite her predilection for gentle mockery, she never asked him to change.

Alison Roth came from a very different background to his. She was brought up in St John's Wood, the daughter of a lawyer and the most polished woman Jack had ever met. Her father, Jimmy, had a client list made up of actors, entertainers and writers, and was so urbane he could engage in conversation with anyone. Roberta was a couples therapist and Jack was always fearful that she would continually spot small fissures in his relationship with her daughter. She had a love of sparkling conversation and ran her home like a literary salon, entertaining lavishly.

If Jack had been terrified in trying to seduce their daughter, he was tongue-tied and incoherent the first time he went to their house to meet them. Their style and sophistication were completely unfamiliar traits, schooled as he was in dinner-time conversation between his father and grandfather about the iniquitous fees levied on the business by the kosher authorities. Nevertheless, they made him feel very welcome. He was Jewish and that was an improvement on Alison's previous boyfriends. Jimmy knew lots of powerful people in television and seemed enthusiastic about Jack's aspirations, which was more than could be said for his own parents, who doubted his ability to prosper in such an amorphous career.

They were married four years later. As a couple, how mature they felt next to their friends, still fumbling around with casual dalliances post university. The first to settle down, they moved into a grown-up house with curtains they had chosen rather than inherited from a landlord. This was Ali's driven world view and for the time being, Jack was an obedient follower.

When their parents met on their engagement, it was an uncomfortable moment for Jack. His father was withdrawn, whereas his mother was liberated by their elegance and became worryingly garrulous. Stephanie Fogel was bitter that her education and independence had been curtailed by a youthful marriage and was obsessed with self-betterment, although to Jack it was more a case of craving social status. At dinner, she launched into an unexpected lecture on a variety of topics about which she knew very little, creating high levels of bemusement.

Their wedding was lavish. The ceremony took place at the oldest, most beautiful synagogue in London, Bevis Marks, followed by an 'intimate party' for three hundred people at The Savoy. Jack felt a passive bystander at the event, which was like an enormous TV production with many meetings about wardrobe, catering and music. He acceded benignly to whatever was expected of him and observed that Ali was in her element, genetically programmed for this moment.

The joyous party overcame the incompatibility of their respective parents. Everyone behaved immaculately and Stephanie buzzed energetically from table to table, introducing herself to an array of the Roths' colourful friends. Phil Fogel was more circumspect and spent much of the time chatting to his business colleagues and clients, who had been adroitly positioned at the back of the room, as close to the exits as possible. At the end of the evening, uncharacteristically tipsy, he pulled his son off the dance floor to declare, '*I am very proud of you, Jack, but I hope you know what you are doing.*'

Their careers took flight. Ali had got a job at a Swiss investment bank on graduation, realising quickly that her true vocation was indeed oiling the grubby wheels of capitalism. Her rapid success was a source of pride for Jack. They were young and enjoying the trappings of her ridiculous salary.

His ascent was steady, if unlucrative. After graduating, he got a job as a runner for a TV production company and while Ali was flying off to be trained (that's what they called the minimal lectures and full-on partying) in New York, he was proving adept at multiple-coffee-ordering and taxi-booking.

It did not matter because they really loved each other and viewed their future as an uninterrupted ascent. Promotions and wealth for Ali. Creativity and fame for Jack. They talked about children and how they would raise them and planned a life of comfort, luxury and philanthropy. The investment bank would help them accrue rapid wealth. Jack's tenacity would propel him into a global entertainment hub, be it London, New York or LA.

He progressed quickly from runner to researcher to junior producer. Within three years, he found himself in de-facto control of *What Choice Do I Have*, a sort of game show that required contestants to debate, often vociferously, an audience-generated moral dilemma. It was a simple blend of comedy and amateur philosophy, and clever marketing from Channel 4 had created a growing passionate following and ensured that the format was generating significant international interest. Jack was gaining real traction as he began selling it to prospective broadcasters.

Some five years after meeting, they couldn't have been happier. Glamorous holidays, expensive restaurants and undiminished passion for one another. Jack and Ali made their friends a little nauseous with their affectionate canoodling and their evident self-belief. They avoided conflict because they only did what made them happy.

Shortly after Jack's twenty-sixth birthday, his overweight father went in to work one day and found himself arguing aggressively with a particularly obstructive representative of the London Council of Kosher Supervision. That morning, an argument over fees soon evolved into prodding, pushing and name-calling. A junior colleague observed an unfamiliar vein throbbing on Phil's puce and sweaty face. Suddenly, he clutched his chest and crumpled to the floor as his legs buckled. Phil's heart attack at the age of only fifty-seven was fatal and changed Jack's life forever.

War was declared on his happiness.

Chapter 4

'It has to be you. I can't believe you are being so difficult.' Stephanie stubbed her cigarette out in the overflowing ashtray with staccato jabs. She was chain-smoking to alleviate her irritation with her son. 'This business was always going to be your responsibility.'

A month had passed since Phil's funeral and the family were gathered around Stephanie's worn dining-room table to consider their future. The siblings sat on one side, and their mother and Mr Gledhill, their accountant, faced them. The room had hosted many boisterous family occasions, but there was a distinct absence of levity as Jack anticipated his imminent punishment.

Solly Fogel was adamant that financial advice had to come from gentiles, not his fellow Jews. The more English and aloof the advisor, the better. Gledhill Cooper, based in dingy offices near Holborn, had been the financial brains behind the business for decades. No one knew Mr Gledhill's first name. His age was unfathomable, but by now he was in his eighties, stooped and almost entirely deaf. The Fogels were his only Jewish clients, and despite a forty-year relationship, their business and its antiquated customs were a total mystery to him.

'The business is your responsibility now, Jack,' he declaimed, clearly not having heard Stephanie say the same thing.

'Why does it have to be?' Jack pleaded.

Stephanie did not want a debate with her recalcitrant son.

'I don't care if they have asked you to present the *Nine O'Clock News*. You are going to have to put your TV career on hold. The family needs the business to carry on. There are a lot of people depending on it.'

'You mean you, Mum. If we sold it, you'd be fine.'

'You ungrateful monster!' she howled. Jack knew she was putting on a show to get her own way. He looked at the blank expressions on his sisters' faces, steadfastly avoiding eye contact, and realised he was bereft of allies. Stephanie turned to Mr Gledhill and implored, 'Please explain his duty and his grandfather's wishes.'

The decrepit accountant looked bemused, having no recollection of such a conversation. Maybe it was one of those inexplicable Jewish principles that no decision could be taken unless it was guaranteed to evince guilt or despair in another family member? Jack shifted uncomfortably in his chair, suggesting he would rather be anywhere other than participating in the extinguishing of the bright future he had planned.

Tracy and Karen were not unsympathetic to his plight but had no intention of being any help. Tracy was also married and ensconced in her nascent medical career as a psychiatrist. Karen had qualified as a barrister and was happily dating a corporate lawyer. They had broken free from the antiquated kosher world of their father and grandfather. Whatever love they had for Jack was overridden by selfish self-preservation.

Jack knew he was in trouble. The problem was that the business had stagnated under Philip's stewardship and was not robust enough to command a healthy sale price, assuming there was a demand from anywhere to buy a kosher chicken wholesaler. Its heritage and resilience had provided security for the family for many years and Jack could not abandon it now. There were also a few practical considerations to remember.

Solly had not trusted anyone to be his successor other than, rather reluctantly, his only son. But there were additional beneficiaries of his largesse who could not be forgotten. Auntie Pearl, for example, was Solly's youngest sister, who had been widowed at forty and left penniless. Jack thought of her as the 'Miss Havisham of Edgware', stuck in her crumbling house, unable to move on. In the meantime, the business paid for her household expenses and fruitless addiction to the National Lottery. In addition, there were sundry cousins who received cheques because of some long-forgotten debt Solly felt compelled to pay.

As for Stephanie, she had a clear view of what needed to happen in the aftermath of her husband's demise. Her grief could, at best, be described as superficial, and while always a loyal wife, she had outgrown the narrow world of Philip Fogel. She wanted to travel and sample new cultures without having to worry about money. Jack was not going to stand in her way. The business needed to be in safe hands, and it was going to take some time to steady the ship. Fortunately, she was helped by the peculiar conditions of her husband's will, which had been written by Solly many years previously. He had made it clear the future custodian of the business could only be Jack and consequently had devised a Machiavellian strategy to ensure this happened.

Fogel's Chickens was to be carved five ways between Jack and his mother, sisters and aunt. Stephanie, Tracy, Karen and Sheila all received fifteen per cent. Jack's portion was forty per cent, but on condition that he guaranteed not to sell the business for at least seven years. Solly may have boasted limited Torah knowledge, but Jack nevertheless felt he had been set a biblical challenge. Jacob had to wait seven years to wed his true love, Rachel, after being tricked into marrying her sister Leah by their father, Laban. Joseph dealt with Egyptian hunger by storing seven years' worth of grain to contend with the next seven years. Jack was compelled to support his family for seven years to achieve potential liberation or redemption.

That afternoon, he needed a valid argument (other than his own future happiness) not to do what was expected of him. His sisters were unbothered by the slight of fewer shares, thrilled to be absolved of any involvement. Stephanie was on a determined mission to embark on a new life that she had previously deemed impossible. The annual dividends would keep her financially extremely comfortable. There was also significant rental income from a portfolio of family property that had been built over the years as part of the business. She just required Jack to do his bit, work hard and pop the cheques in the post.

Poor Jack. He felt the constrictive pressure of responsibility and his heart raced with anxiety and fear. The years of lectures from his grandfather had led to this moment. He remembered one phrase that Solly would always call upon if he thought Jack looked disinterested: '*Remember what the Talmud says. Sometimes in life you must choose between what is right and what you want.*' Of course, this was just another of his made-up sayings, used to get his way. Where in the Talmud does it say you have to give up a flourishing TV career to slit thousands of chicken throats?

Mr Gledhill was getting impatient by now. It was late afternoon, and what he needed was a large G&T. Instead, he was having to listen, with impaired hearing, to this unusual family argue over an unwanted inheritance.

'Jack, I am afraid that the wishes of your father and grandfather are quite clear. Seven years of hard graft to support your mother and delightful sisters. Are you going to be so difficult as to ignore them?'

Jack felt everyone turn their focus on him, desperate for his assent, so that they could all get on with living their independent and much more interesting lives. He shook his head but managed to mumble his surrender.

'What choice do I have? It is what I must do.'

'Don't be a *potz*, of course you have to do it,' Mr Gledhill declared emphatically. He looked pleased with himself for finally recalling Solly's most frequently used Yiddish insult.

* * *

'Why does it have to be you?' exclaimed Ali in desperation later that evening as she propped herself up on her elbows in bed. It was nearly midnight, and she had only just come back in from work, having grafted for days solidly on another meaty corporate transaction that had subsumed her for the last few months.

'You know this isn't what I want at all, don't you?' Jack replied in exasperation.

He had been terrified about this conversation. While they had discussed the expectation for Jack to take the reins of the business, he had maintained a blithe optimism that there would be another solution, so Ali had not properly considered its reality. They were happy and on the trajectory she had always imagined. She was making silly money, which would give her choices, and Jack was meeting interesting people in TV who seemed to like him. Alison Roth had a clear vision of the life she wanted: money, stimulation, and lots of beautiful children. A butcher for a husband was not an acceptable alternative.

She was always respectful to Jack's family. While she found little in common with his parents, she understood that duty sometimes has to prevail over one's inbuilt prejudices. Jack was a loyal son and she loved him for this. She liked his younger sister, Karen, a lot and had introduced her to a work colleague who she was now dating. Her relationship was frostier with Tracy the ambitious psychiatrist and her husband, Clive. He was also a psychiatrist and Ali found their company joyless and intense. '*Why? Why? Why?*' she would rail, '*they always want to know why. It's bloody exhausting.*'

She had deliberately not changed her name from Roth when they got married through fear that it might outwardly link her to Fogel's Chickens. That wish was now under serious threat and despite her work-induced weariness, she felt a surge of adrenalin as she confronted the reality of Jack's situation, pacing briskly around the bed, deep in thoughts of escape.

'You'll just have to tell them "No", Jack. I fell in love with the loser who told me he was going to be something big in TV. There was no mention of poultry. You are going to have to sever this hold that your dead grandfather seems to have on you.'

Jack was sitting on the bed and subconsciously clutched a pillow to his chest, as if for protection.

'It's not that easy. I wish it was. There is no one to run it and no one to sell it to. I can't abandon a seventy-year-old family business on which lots of people depend for their livelihoods.'

'What, you mean your selfish mother, a mad old aunt and some random cousins? Oh, come on, Jack, wise up.'

'You're being unfair, Ali. There's value in the business and why shouldn't I preserve for our children the inheritance that has been created for them.'

Jack couldn't quite believe that he was defending his earlier acquiescence. He had done his best to be sulky and truculent in his mother's dining room. Now, several hours on, while numb at the thought of leaving his cool Soho office for a Hackney slaughterhouse, he was strangely calm about the decision. Ali paused for a moment, sensing that Jack seemed to have made his plans without her.

'Wait a minute. I'm beginning to think this is not a discussion but a declaration. Are you interested in what I think?'

Jack jumped off the bed and stood in front of her. He put his hands on her shoulders in an ill-advised gesture of affection. She took a step back, tripped over one of his shoes and stumbled on to the bed. On a happier day, it might have been funny, but she was now seething with unfamiliar anger. She threw the shoe at him, missing by some distance and knocking a photo frame off the wall. There was a funereal silence.

'You've made your mind up, haven't you? You're becoming a bloody kosher butcher.' Her incredulity was now accompanied by tears. She seemed to be grieving for the ending of her fairy tale.

'Yes, I'm going to have to run the business for a while. I don't want to, but I'll try to make it successful, and I'll get out as soon as possible with as much money as I can get when it's sold. I'm going to try to write and see if I can keep a second life going in TV. It must be possible in some way. I'm doing this for our future, you know. Why does it change anything? We love each other and will have a great life, I promise. Your career is unaffected. Our children, you know the ones we always talk about, might even have a better life because of my sacrifice.' It was a passionate declaration, although he had quite deliberately left out the seven years' minimum sentence stipulated in the will. Enough bad news for one day, surely.

Ali slumped on the bed and wept into her hands. As her shoulders sagged and her body unclenched, Jack wondered why she was being so unsupportive. After all, he was the one with a new and unwanted job. She did not really want to talk any more, but briefly looked in his direction and shook her head.

'It changes everything, you idiot.'

* * *

Ali tried to carry on without resenting his new job and to avoid conflict they threw themselves into work. She continued to be paid exorbitant bonuses that calmed her suppressed anger. Jack was learning an unfamiliar business while trying to unravel the failings of his father's management, and they bumped along only by avoiding discussion of his new career. She had been fascinated by the shenanigans of his TV life and wanted to know all the events of his working day. Now they only talked about the pressures of deal-making (hers), family (hers) and perhaps, if there was time, friends (mainly hers). Then she got pregnant.

They had frequently discussed their vision of family life. Jack had few requirements, so long as the kids were not too ugly, while Ali imagined a beautiful, curated home that would have graced a magazine. In the event, they were blessed with two daughters, born twenty months apart. First came Natalie, with thick dark hair like her mother, followed by Isobel, strawberry blonde and blue-eyed and clearly a Fogel in appearance. A couple of years later, the family unit was completed by a yappy little cockapoo called Felix. For a while, the excitement of parenthood compensated for the strains in their relationship.

Ali had never been happier, slipping energetically into her new role. She stopped working after Isobel and her patience with the children was limitless. Indeed, Jack marvelled at her ability to remain focused during any activity undertaken: reading a story, a four-piece farmyard jigsaw or an impromptu game of hide-and-seek. She was discovering the world afresh through the innocent eyes of her perfect children.

Jack was a less confident parent. Of course, he was besotted with his wide-eyed, gorgeous girls, who reciprocated with uncon-ditional affection. It was so much simpler than the other stuttering female relationships in his life. The problem was, they were just a bit boring. Lying on their bedroom floor playing with dolls and imag-inary unicorns was penance for him. He could not wait to discuss films, books and TV programmes when they were older. Ali would cheerily remind him that '*by the time they are interested in that stuff, they most certainly won't be interested in you*'.

Ali gradually fell out of love with him, and he was too distracted to notice. Her self-contained world of tutus and iced biscuits was all she needed, and the house felt calmer when he was at work. When he arrived home from a sixteen-hour day, she would resent his moody and exhausted presence. He would try to engage in conversation and wished she could muster some interest in his business, beginning to transform under his guidance. His initial seven-year commitment to the business had passed and he was now handcuffed to it with no possibility for escape. Meanwhile, Ali would have rather discussed a train timetable and had no need for chicken-related conversation, other than to give the occasional freezer order.

His marriage deflated like a sad party balloon. She could not even be bothered to bombard him with a barrage of put-downs and slights. When they were falling in love, he revelled in the banter that symbolised the continual spark of their passion. Indifference now rendered her polite but diffident, which felt far worse. It was the three girls in their perfect dressing-up world and silly old Daddy. Sometimes he would sit in the kitchen helplessly watching them ignore him.

It was not that Ali did not need a husband; she just wanted a different one. Shortly before Natalie's sixth birthday, she made him a cup of tea when he got back from work and calmly suggested they had a chat. He did not imagine his day would end this way when he left before dawn to go to a job he did not want but felt compelled to make a success. Slumping into one of the ludicrously uncomfortable designer chairs, her pride and joy, he awaited his execution.

'I am in love with someone else, Jack, and I want a divorce. I don't need anything from you other than your signature.'

Jack felt his body temperature drop several degrees. It was an unexpected physical reaction accompanied by a palpable wave of nausea.

'I've only been gone fourteen hours,' he replied, feebly wondering how on earth she could have met someone when she spent so much of the day as Europe's finest mother.

'Please let's do this with some dignity. How much more obvious did I need to make it that I was unhappy? Even the dog knew.'

'Look, I know we're a little bit disconnected these days, but I thought that was just what happens at certain times to everyone. Surely it's just a phase?'

'Well, I'm ready for a new one,' she cut back. Jack stopped for a second. Why was he apologising for not getting on better with her when she had just admitted to an affair? He should be the angry one. A most awkward silence followed, in which Jack stared at his half-drunk mug of tea.

Eventually, he could not stand her coldness any longer, so he mumbled, 'Who? Who on earth have you found?'

Ali shrugged her shoulders and casually replied, as if ordering coffee at Starbucks, 'Simon Felix.'

'You named the dog after your lover?'

'No, the dog came well before. Perhaps there was a subliminal thought in my head that Simon and I had unfinished business. I am sorry, but that is just how it is. We'll both be happier apart and I want nothing from you other than a sensible agreement on how we raise the girls.'

Simon was the boyfriend before him at university. His name was really Alan Simons, and he was an actor. To join Equity, he chose the surname *Felix* because it meant happy and Simon was a cheery soul, although Jack always thought *Simon Dull* would have been a much more accurate character assessment. He was, however, very good-looking, something Ali always mentioned when they went to watch him in various small parts in regional theatre. He did the odd commercial and walk-on in the soaps, but had never played Hamlet at Stratford. Jack thought him a loser, but Ali always vigorously defended his talent against these attacks.

Failure or not, Simon managed to secure the role of Casanova in his marriage and a casual coffee had turned into Ali confessing her unhappiness with Jack, followed by an intense affair. Her parents increased their babysitting considerably, asking few questions. It was all over.

The separation and divorce were conducted with civility and efficiency. He knew he had lost her, even though his feelings were undiminished. The financial settlement was made easier by Ali's prosperous years in the City and Jack's willingness to avoid conflict. She did not want much from him in return, and access to the children was agreed without argument.

The girls reacted with a mixture of bemusement and equanimity. In well-rehearsed speeches, Jack and Ali lovingly reinforced the benefits of two bedrooms, two set of toys and double presents on birthdays and Chanukah. They had few other questions, assuming thereafter that a mother looks after you, while a father supplies treats and cuddles but is good for little else.

Six months after the conversation in the kitchen, they were divorced. Jack moved into a new flat and shortly afterwards, Ali casually ended her relationship with Simon Felix the night before he shot a new commercial for a floor cleaner.

PART 2

BATTLE LINES

Chapter 5

February was Jack's worst month of the year. Always cold and dark, it was punctuated by Valentine's Day, a phoney and cruel reminder that he remained chronically single, ten years after his divorce. It was particularly bracing that morning, when Jack left his Hampstead flat and sank into the heated leather seats of his Jaguar F-Type coupé. Since Ali divorced him, his life had combined professional success with personal unhappiness as he struggled to reconcile its warring factions. His car was an ostentatious purchase he had recently made when feeling particularly lonely and each journey in it reminded him of his grandfather's Jag, which Solly had loved more than his own children. '*In such a car, you've arrived before you get there*' was a famous aphorism that Jack remembered him proclaiming, as if he were the motoring correspondent of the Talmud.

Five a.m. was a brutal hour to travel to work every day, but somehow its awfulness was a punishment he felt he deserved. The journey to the factory outside St Albans took half an hour. Soft jazz music from a playlist filled the car from the pin-sharp quadraphonic sound system. Jack imagined he was nursing a whisky in a smoky Greenwich Village basement club in the early hours of the morning, holding hands with his lover, anticipating the unlimited potential of their future life. But that was not the case. It was the soundtrack to his daily journey to the state-of-the-art factory he had built to supervise the killing of thousands of birds every day.

He was quite the poultry magnate now. A wholesale business providing twenty-five thousand chickens each week, five butcher shops scattered around London and Manchester and two flourishing restaurants was the tangible proof of his business acumen. Employing over a hundred people, he wanted for nothing financially, and in his quiet, unobtrusive way, he was respected as an innovator and entrepreneur. These achievements were tempered by personal sacrifices and disastrous relationships; he had abandoned his TV career and Ali, having dreamt of a hacienda in the Hollywood Hills, not an abattoir just off the M25, had long since abandoned him.

The work was hard. No long lunches and evening drinks in Soho House, like his friends who still worked in creative industries. He was the anomaly in his social group. His first call each morning was often to a lorry driver to check the chickens had been picked up on time from the farm. The day was then spent supervising production, stock control and developing new product for his shops. He had built a strong team of lieutenants, but he still had to make the decisions no one was confident enough to take without him.

That morning, he had spent a couple of hours checking in with his team before he could take a break for a quick coffee, shutting the door of his office against the cacophony outside. It always struck him as odd that the factory's predominant noise was the industrial roar of machinery rather than the symphonic chorus of chickens, screaming and groaning in anticipation of their imminent execution. When the kids were little, Jack had made them laugh with his different impersonations of clucking chickens. But when thousands of birds are facing their death, they don't sound like those on Old MacDonald's Farm. No cluck, cluck here. Just a muted drone of fearful chirps. Jack tried not to think about it too much or he knew he'd feel even worse about the profession he had not wanted to pursue.

It was shaping up to be a difficult day, beset with frustrating problems. The conveyor belt that took the birds for washing and salting had broken down for forty-five minutes, resulting in production halting. It was a Tuesday, one of their busiest days, and by the time the engineers had replaced the broken belt (for the third time in a month), the shift required overtime and thus additional cost.

Then there was the late arrival of Mordechai the *shochet*, indifferent to the inconvenience his long study session with his rabbi that morning had caused. Managing the *shochets* was the hardest part of the job. No one else was allowed to kill the chickens in their absence. They didn't work for him but the London Council of Kosher Supervision, although in truth they really answered to God. Jack was most definitely not divine in their eyes, just very irritating, and if he angered them, they could arrive late or go slow.

While there were not many abattoirs that could boast standard-issue iPads for stock control, it was still a very basic operation where things often went awry. First you had to pick up the chickens. In his grandfather's day, the farms were within a reasonable radius of London. Now his suppliers were scattered from Devon to Yorkshire. The drivers often needed to complete twelve-hour journeys, which just pushed up his costs. His grandfather didn't believe in drivers taking a rest; however, Jack was fully compliant with rest and recuperation requirements between journeys, no matter the inconvenience. That morning, one of the deliveries was over two hours late.

He had also had a very tetchy conversation with Stacey Blor, who managed his two thriving restaurants, Clucks, along with her chef husband, Gadi. Jack was always looking for new ways to diversify his interests, and the increased popularity of kosher eating-out had prompted him to act. He had paid a fortune to a marketing consultant with a goatee to come up with the insight 'Be Innovative with Chicken', and a vibrant dining experience with a strong take-away business was the subsequent result. The talented Israeli, Gadi, saw the menu as an opportunity for immortality by naming most of the dishes he created after himself.

You could choose between Gadi's Beautiful Burgers, Gadi's Oriental Wings and Gadi's Spicy Thighs. His signature dish, Gadi's Chicken Aleppo, reflected his proud Syrian heritage, creating a recipe allegedly dictated by his dying grandmother. In truth, it was an experiment with aubergines, dates, pomegranate seeds and green peppers undertaken in the tiny kitchen of his flat in Kilburn. Aleppo was once home to tens of thousands of Jews, but by the time the first restaurant opened, it was cruelly destroyed by civil war. Jack felt this might be inhibiting, but conversely the romantic allure of a lost culture created enormous appeal and Gadi's mystery dish developed its own cult following.

As good as Gadi was at dousing a chicken in a combination of random spices and vegetables, the success of the restaurants was largely due to the tenacity of his aggressive wife, Stacey. A New Yorker, she had met Gadi while backpacking in Thailand a few years previously. Working every hour possible, she was a curious blend of charming and belligerent. To customers, she was like the manager of an uber-cool metropolitan eatery, treating customers like celebrities. At the same time, she would hector the staff to ensure that the restaurants were smooth-running operations and they all lived in fear of her displeasure.

To Jack, she was rarely polite. Before moving to the UK, she had been a film and television agent and, smitten by the swarthy Gadi, she treated him like precious on-screen talent. In particular, she resented Jack for failing to recognise his brilliance and support him in his career. Instead, each day before opening, she would pace the restaurant in her AirPods, snarling loudly in a variety of conversations seeking out potential opportunities for them to find a bigger stage.

All she really wanted was to make Gadi a star with a newspaper column, a publishing deal and a cookery show on primetime television. Somehow, her failure to deliver anything more substantial than a monthly column in the *Jewish News* was all Jack's fault. Stacey's ambition was not just the pursuit of fame, she also wanted to expand the business rapidly, with Jack funding the growth. She demanded more restaurants in the UK, New York and Tel Aviv, and thought that Aleppo Sauce had a major future in grocery retailers as a staple of every well-stocked pantry.

On the call, Stacey struggled to conceal her impatience with Jack's cautious approach. They had been having the same argument for weeks now and like peace in the Middle East, the dispute was proving unresolvable without threats of bloodshed. Her deep nasal voice sounded like pebbles being ground in a food mixer and she terrified Jack. Her onslaught was particularly vituperative that day.

'Don't be a drag, Jack, the site in Marylebone is perfect. You know it is. How many more times do I need to spell it out to you? We will develop a whole new lunchtime trade. All those property tycoons and their wives. We can up our prices twenty-five per cent and they won't even notice. Charge them for tap water and serviettes and they won't complain. Why are you so negative?'

Jack always tried to be as supportive as he could to his abrasive junior partners, but this was clearly not enough. He tried to remind her that they had an agreed strategy.

'Honestly, Stacey, why are we having this conversation now? What is the point of a business plan if you want to rewrite it daily?'

'I don't want to rewrite it. I want to rip it up, you *doofus*. The world is moving fast, and we are in danger of standing still because you are too scared to get out your chequebook. You are in Gadi's way, and I won't allow it.'

Jack wanted to point out that Clucks was just a glorified fast-food joint and she should not get carried away, but this would have provoked another tirade he did not have strength to endure. He tried, therefore, to placate her.

'Stacey, you know how much I value you both. Should we have a chat to try and make sure our expectations are aligned?'

'Jack, you can shove your aligned expectations up your *butthole*. I tell you what is going to happen. You are going to open some more restaurants and you are going to help me give Gadi the profile his talent deserves. Or you can find a new chef and a new person to name your dishes after. You got it?'

'Are you threatening me?' He could not control the irritation in his voice, but she was too focused on making her own argument to notice.

'And while we're talking names, "Clucks" is a *fricking* stupid name. We've thought about it, and we want to rename them "Gadi's Grill". It's a no-brainer. People come to the restaurant because of Gadi. I am getting some papers drawn up.'

He realised she had a point about the name. 'Clucks' had seemed funny at the time, but was hardly going to get serious attention. It was also evident that a fight about intellectual property was imminent. The discussion was, however, over for now because Stacey had hung up before Jack could even utter '*Let me sleep on it and please stop shouting.*' How had that got out of hand so quickly, he wondered, fearful of yet another battle looming. It was still only ten thirty.

* * *

Lunch was normally made up of whatever he could find in the fridge and today it was a stale bagel, so solid it could have been used as a murder weapon. He was lazy when it came to looking after himself, exemplified by the culinary extravaganza of a cream cheese, carrot and sweet pickle sesame bagel that was currently in danger of breaking his jaw.

Yet despite the inedible food, the hour he took for lunch was the most important time of the day. He made it clear that he wasn't to be disturbed unless several thousand chickens escaped and needed to be recaptured on the M1 heading north. Eating was ancillary to the real purpose of his break. He was working on a treatment for a TV comedy and making excellent progress, having refused to abandon his original dream of creating something that would make him famous in the world of entertainment.

He feared he had become a distorted version of the promise he had shown at the start of his marriage. Granted, he was a very good businessman making an excellent living, but it was at the expense of hiding his true self. To his employees, he was consistently polite, precise in direction, yet not really loved because of his aloofness. His sharp sense of humour rarely surfaced, and no one felt comfortable making small talk with him. Jack worried that if he appeared happy in his role, he was somehow validating its permanence and he yearned to escape. He just didn't know how.

Frustration had calcified into resentment and brooding anger. The unrelenting monotony required an outlet for his stifled creative energy, and he would sit at lunchtime in his cubicle office, gazing at the wall, trying to find a way to escape. And then one day he had a sort of sitcom epiphany and the treatment arrived instinctively. His routine was now punctuated by a joyous hour of writing in which he took charge of an alternative reality, the characters, their dialogue, and their destinies. It was the perfect antidote and for the first time in many years he felt a romantic idealism that maybe things would change.

The premise of the comedy was blindingly obvious in its derivation. Called 'Widgets', it was the story of a man named Zack who really wants to be a writer but is unexpectedly left the family plastics factory when an uncle dies and forced to keep it going. Every time he has some success in his private or personal life, the business, like a relentless enemy, interferes with his plans for escape.

* * *

Jack threw half the remaining bagel in the bin, and it landed with a clang that sounded like cymbals crashing. He stared at the laptop in front of him with satisfaction. The first six episodes were finished, after several drafts, and presumptuously he had written plotlines for a second series. The characters were now real people for him. Zack's family – a materialistic wife, two irresponsible sons and an ageing hippy uncle living off the proceeds of the business – dragged him back every time he thought he could free himself from the burden of the factory. His staff were a chaotic chorus, dim, hapless, but with an integrity that contrasted with the venality of Zack's family.

The project was moving forward. Jack had a small but loyal coterie of friends from his time in TV, whose careers had flourished. Mike Gibson, his most active supporter, could not have been more influential, having produced some of the most popular comedies and dramas of recent years. He knew Jack had given up everything to support his family business and thought his idea was genuinely interesting, which is why he wanted to help. To Jack's delight, Mike had called him a couple of days earlier to tell him that they were ready to start pitching the idea to a broadcaster. '*Don't tell them your day job*' was the only other guidance he received.

Jack was immersed in crafting a joke when an email pinged up on his screen that shook him from his writing reverie.

Frank Stone – Age Discrimination

The email was from a lawyer at a large West End firm, and it outlined the significant case that Fogel's Chickens longest-serving employee was preparing against them. Sixty-eight-year-old Frank was one of Jack's foremen and had been in the firm for almost all his working life. Still a huge bear of a man, he could unpack a lorry willingly, but he was beginning to stoop and his movements were slowing.

Jack had recently seen him doubled up in discomfort, rubbing aching joints. They had chatted amicably, and Frank had complained about his chronic pain. Jack wondered if perhaps the job was getting too hard, and he might want to think about winding down to retirement, which Frank seemed to appreciate. Jack thought he was simply being a concerned employer, as well as a decent human being, and had followed up again with Frank, agreeing that he would indeed retire in three months.

The email was from Frank's son-in-law, an aggressive litigator, and repurposed the narrative to suggest Jack had told Frank he was too old and not strong enough to work any more. Apparently, Frank was a regular at his local gym and had recently competed in a 10k run, which attested to his physical competence. Moreover, an administrative error years ago had left Frank without a proper service contract, which, according to the rottweiler son-in-law, was another flagrant example of his victimisation. The email talked about 'substantial damages'. It was outrageous. Jack often joked to his friends that he never discriminated against any of his staff because he disliked them all equally, but now this false allegation was going to cost him lots of money to make the problem go away.

Jack shut the laptop, realising that his creative muse had to be subsumed once more to the demands of his ridiculous business. Years ago, kind-hearted Frank Stone would have taken a bullet for Solly. Now, when there was money to be made, the principles of loyalty disappeared. The day was turning out to be another catalogue of misfortune and Jack felt alone. Surely nothing else bad could happen.

His phone rang. It was his mother.

Chapter 6

'Hello, darling. I had a spare ten minutes, so I thought I'd check in. How are you?'

'I'm fine, Mum. Where are you?'

'We've just docked in the British Virgin Islands or maybe it's the US Virgin Islands, I can't quite remember. These virgins all look the same to me.' Jack peered out at his view through the narrow porthole of his airless office. Blood and feathers would be how he described his current vista.

'How's the trip?' He really didn't want to hear about it in exhaustive detail. Not with the day he was having, but he knew he had little choice.

'Wonderful, such a lovely boat and delightful people. You know when they are smaller, you get a much more intellectual crowd.' She was now an expert on the differences between cruise ships, given they were her second home for so much of the year. Jack did not pay much attention to her assessment of individual boats as he had no intention of ever going on one himself. Instead, ever the dutiful son, he politely enquired about her partner of the last couple of years.

'How is Kurt?'

'Oh, everyone loves him. I'm scared one of the lonely widows might try and make a play and push me overboard. He's doing two talks and they are all oversubscribed. The first is on the history of ballet and the other is on Alexander the Great.'

'I thought he was a physics professor?'

'Well, that's what he used to teach at university. But he is what they call a polymath. Do you know what that is?'

'Of course I know what that is, Mum. Even if I didn't, you'd tell me again because it is impossible to mention his name without you describing him that way. I'm very pleased that you have someone with such a breadth of knowledge. It must make up for the years with Dad.' The last comment sounded more barbed than he had intended.

'Jack, please don't talk to me with that snarky tone. We are not going to argue; I'm phoning for a catch-up, not a fight. Why are you always so aggressive?'

He took a deep breath and tried to muster some inner calm. For the last twenty years, his mother had provoked a reaction in him that had not been present before his father's death. From that moment, she had felt an enormous release from the constraints of Fogel's Chickens, while Jack became chained to it for life. He hated her expectation of ongoing financial support by dint of his hard work and as the years passed, her reliance on him grew inversely to her gratitude.

Her new life initially began slowly. She went to classes, immersed herself in the cultural life of London and did a bit of travelling. The change came when she met her first boyfriend, a retired property developer. Suddenly, life was transformed into the best of every-thing: restaurants, business-class flights and top hotels. She loved the trappings of the world he inhabited, although their incompati-bility meant the romance soon floundered.

Jack was introduced over the next few years to a succession of disparate partners, each more unpredictable than the last. There was Terry from Essex, who worked in 'scrap metal' and was most likely a gangster who buried his enemies under tons of concrete just outside Romford. He was followed by a year with Len, a retired football manager, half-Jewish and a successful radio pundit. Unfortunately, Stephanie's poor grasp of the offside rule irritated him after a while, so she got kicked into touch. Next was 'Scruffy Ray', nicknamed because of his threadbare charity-shop clothes, who turned out to be Sir Raymond Green, a prominent retired civil servant.

All these relationships petered out because it seemed to Jack that his mother was looking primarily for stimulation rather than love, as if she had plotted the furthest point from her marriage and was following a zigzagging trajectory to get there. She never seemed upset when a romance ended and would make Jack feel worse by criticising his failure to enjoy the unpredictability of life like she did. It was fine for her to be so carefree. He was the one stuck inside a fluorescent-lit factory, killing chickens while she took her cheque and phoned the travel agent.

Kurt was twelve years younger and a Swedish academic with an unwillingness to volunteer much biographical detail. He was apparently a big noise on the cruise lecture circuit, and she happily followed him from boat to boat, paying her own way, properly smitten by his Nordic charm and brilliant mind. Jack did not like him at all and was reminded of a serial killer on one of the Scandi crime programmes he watched, assuming his motives to be dark and opportunistic.

'Is Kurt looking after you?' he asked, concerned for his mother's vulnerability. He could not shake the thought that his hard work was somehow benefiting her dodgy boyfriend.

'Don't you worry. He is quite charming and has old-fashioned manners that are delightful.' The years had changed Stephanie. Manners had not been a big preoccupation for her when Jack was growing up, but now she sounded like she had just graduated finishing school in Switzerland. She changed the subject.

'How are the girls?'

'They're fine, I think. I mean, they don't exactly confide in me.' Natalie was now seventeen, a drama-loving social gadfly with a succession of boyfriends, and Isobel fifteen, brooding and deeply industrious, with a penchant for staying home and songwriting.

Jack had dinner with them every week and would spend at least one night of every other weekend with them. When they were little, they were a happy enough gang, based on his simple strategy of bribery, indulgence and treats. They had grown into unfathomable young women who answered his questions but provided little insight into their lives. He dreamt of adult conversations and craved some understanding of what they were thinking, who their friends were and what were their dreams. He got nothing back. Even more irritatingly, this was not the case for his mother.

'Natalie sent me a photo of her latest boyfriend. Very handsome but a bit too old for her if you ask me.' Jack did not know what she was talking about. There was a real bond between his daughter and mother, a lust for life and short attention span were their common DNA.

'I wouldn't know. If her leg fell off, she'd forget to tell me.'

'Teenage girls are not meant to discuss their feelings with their fathers. Do you think Tracy and Karen told Dad anything?' That was just it; Jack wanted to believe he was different from his father and grandfather, who were mired in the antiquated patriarchy of the *shtetl*. His daughters, it seemed, saw him as a chicken pedlar, not an interesting bloke.

'I do my best,' he replied lamely.

'Well, darling, you may need to do better. Natalie finds you impossible.' She may have been thousands of miles away, but boy could she make him feel miserable with effortless ease. There was no point asking for an explanation of why he was an inadequate father as he did not want to know the answer. Years of his mother's disrespect had made him adept at changing the subject when things got this difficult, so he shifted the conversation on to safer ground.

'Talking of my sisters, have you spoken to Karen? You know she's been selected to stand as the next candidate in the Dudley South by-election?'

'Of course I know, who do you think she called first?' She was still Stephanie's favourite, her greatest pride and most common topic of conversation. Karen had become a successful barrister, one of the youngest QCs in the country, a Conservative councillor and now putative MP with the prospect of a safe seat. Married to an equally successful lawyer, Richard, they were a power couple with a house in Notting Hill and an even bigger one in Provence.

'She'll be in the cabinet by the time you get on the plane home,' Jack said with admiration. He had a less complicated relationship with Karen these days, so long as he did not question her enthusiasm for Brexit or tell her that he still voted Labour. In return, she rarely asked about the business as it bore no relevance to her flourishing career other than the quarterly dividends she cashed.

'I could not be prouder of her. She is inspirational. What she has made of her life in such difficult circumstances is remarkable.' Before Jack could ask her to explain what those might have been, the line went suddenly dead.

He did not call back.

* * *

'Hello, little bro,' Tracy said, chomping as ever on a lunch on the run. 'To what do I owe the pleasure of this midweek call? Have the girls gone off the rails emotionally and you are unable to cope? Or it's not that dream where you're dressed as a chicken and Mum stubs a cigarette on your coffin? I'm thinking of writing that one up as a case history for my students.'

'I hope you're more tactful with your patients?'

'Depends how irritating they are.'

Jack needed to speak to his elder sister to compensate for the wave of self-loathing that normally followed an interaction with his mother. After the early years of Jack being an unwanted presence, the dynamic of the sibling relationships had changed. The sisters grew apart, not dramatically, but enough to allow him some space to become particularly close with Tracy.

She was a consultant psychiatrist specialising in children and adolescents. Her husband, Clive, had the same specialism and worked with geriatrics. They lived noisily with their three children in a large terraced house in Tufnell Park, always filled with laughter and chaos. Messy and homely, it was the sort of place where you would sit at a newspaper-strewn farmhouse table, drinking tea, eating toast and jam and discussing how to heal a fractured world.

Tracy saw everything as a therapeutic problem, and this could make conversation sometimes challenging. Nevertheless, she recognised the sacrifice Jack had made for his family, having built her well-respected career as he abandoned his dream. Guilt and compassion therefore made her now an attentive sister. She had never got on with Ali, whose world view she found too materialistic, which kept her apart from Jack when they were married. Now they spent lots of time together and talked constantly, as if their fractious childhood did not exist.

'I just wanted to vent, if that's OK.'

'I'll put the meter on. It's time and a half on my lunch break. What's up?'

'You name it. The factory is a pain, it keeps going wrong. My partners in the restaurant are impossible to manage. My girls don't talk to me. Mum rang to tell me that she is in paradise with Sweden's next Nobel Prize winner and our oldest employee wants to sue me because he thinks I'm ageist. Every time I try to work on my TV idea, something goes wrong in the business. I am forty-six, single, and it all feels like too much hard work.'

There was a pause as Tracy considered her response.

'Bloody hell, Jack, I'm a child psychiatrist, not a bloody miracle worker. Have you tried a rabbi or a trip to Lourdes?'

'Very droll. I didn't think you'd have an answer, but I just wanted to hear a friendly voice and they were out, so I called you.'

'Come for dinner on Friday night with the girls if you've got them. I promise I'll try to listen to your woes, although I'm always knackered at the end of the week, so can't guarantee to stay awake.'

'That will be lovely. I'll talk very loudly.'

'You always do these days. Why are you continually so angry?' It seemed that even their casual conversation needed to conclude with an assessment of his irritability.

'I'm not that grumpy, am I?'

'Nice try, Jack, for some free therapy, but I have a much more needy teenager with separation anxiety in my waiting room. Tell you what, I'll have a nap before you arrive on Friday and then I can really demolish you over dessert.'

'Sounds like a perfect evening.'

He hung up and stood by the window, which looked on to the car park. The murkiness of the slate-grey winter's afternoon sapped any residual energy he possessed. He was relieved to have made this arrangement with Tracy. Despite the mocking, she had a way of making him see things from a more optimistic perspective.

He had forgotten to tell her the worst thing that had happened. Yesterday, he had briefly spoken with Lionel Gutterman, owner of Gutterman's, one of his main customers but also a rival with his own chain of shops, who had asked if they could meet urgently on a matter of supreme importance to their collective futures. Despite the palpable insincerity of the call, there was little option other than to arrange a date.

Jack's fragile stomach started to tighten, as if the thought of seeing Lionel up close had produced a very physical reaction. His body was preparing for attack.

Chapter 7

If you tried to pick a match from a Dulux colour chart for Lionel Gutterman's tan, the closest descriptors would be 'Rich Mahogany' or 'Deep Burgundy', and Jack always assumed it had been painted in a beauty salon rather than acquired by sitting in the sun. As he entered, Lionel was sitting in the far corner of the café, his thick dapple-grey hair blow-dried into a wind-resistant clump and his brilliant-white smile exposing a set of teeth filed to symmetrical perfection. Dressed casually in pressed jeans and a salmon-pink cashmere cardigan, an extra button was rakishly left open on his shirt. Jack saw the gleam of a chunky gold chain nestling in a profusion of wiry chest hair and thought he resembled a cruise-ship crooner his mother would probably date.

They had agreed on the neutral territory of an Israeli café, Yoffee Coffee, on the Golders Green Road, and Jack prayed the meeting would not take long. As he approached, Lionel got up and opened his arms as if greeting a distant relative at the airport and pulled him forcefully into his chest for a consent-free hug. Jack was overwhelmed by disparate smells ranging from pungent aftershave to Deep Heat muscle relaxant and possibly even fried fish.

'Jack, my boy. You look thin. You need someone to care for you. If you're not concerned about your appearance, let me tell you I am.'

'You needn't worry about me. I'm in immaculate condition. I have the body of a man at least two years younger.' Lionel ignored the joke and instead shook his head wistfully.

'You know, your beloved grandfather would want me to tell you that you don't look so hot. Your health is always more important than business, don't you ever forget that, *boychik*.'

Jack clenched his fists below the table in frustration. How he dreaded his interactions with Lionel, and this was on course to be a squirm-fest of massive proportions. Indeed, he could not believe that Solly's memory had been invoked with such insincerity, given Lionel had never actually forgiven his grandfather for firing him thirty years ago.

* * *

Lionel was the son Solly had hoped for instead of mediocre Phil Fogel. Starting in the business at sixteen, he soon caught Solly's eye with a combination of a commitment to hard work and a ruthlessness in dealing with less motivated colleagues. A subscriber to his boss's mantra of 'kill chickens, work hard and you'll get paid', by the time he was twenty-six, he oversaw production in the factory, managing a staff of forty people with impatient intolerance.

Solly confided constantly in Lionel, seeing him as his *consigliere* and calling him 'my dear boy' whenever they talked. It mortified poor old Phil, ten years his senior, who was given a portfolio of lesser responsibilities and earned a reputation for incompetence within the business. His resentment of Lionel kept him awake most nights, but whenever he tried to discuss these feelings with Solly, he was ignored.

Fortunately for Phil, Lionel's ambition pushed him too far when he demanded that Solly make him managing director and give him significant equity in the business. The discussion degenerated quickly, causing Lionel to make ill-advised threats about publicising some of his employer's '*less than legal accounting manoeuvres*'. An incandescent Solly cornered his protégé on the factory floor at the end of the day, with pushing, shoving and obscenities soon followed by Lionel's immediate dismissal. Phil Fogel took enormous pleasure in escorting him out of the factory with an enormous smirk that did not disappear for weeks.

Lionel decided revenge would be to sell chickens in gleaming modern shops and build a catering business that would make him Fogel's Chickens' largest customer. That way, he would make Solly's life permanently uncomfortable and be an unpleasant rash that no ointment could remove.

His empire grew to six shops, and a huge slice of the bar mitzvah and wedding catering market. At the same time, he became an extremely wealthy, philanthropic pillar of the Jewish establishment – the Master of his Masonic lodge, Life President of his synagogue, single-figure golfer with a beautiful villa in Sotogrande. Father to three brilliant children and grandfather to seven prodigies, he had married three times. His childhood sweetheart, Barbara, was jettisoned after thirty years of marriage for a minor actress, Jessica Bloom, a couple of years older than his daughter, who quickly left him for a cameraman she met on set. He was now happily married to Irene, an age-appropriate widow with a love of champagne and a commitment to wearing a wardrobe of mink as often as she could. He feared no one.

* * *

'What's up, Lionel?' Jack asked as his coffee arrived. He intended to drink it quickly and minimise the time spent in Lionel's presence, but unfortunately Lionel had ordered breakfast and he had to politely watch him chomp his way through his 'Full Israeli', waving his fork half in admonishment, half in threat.

'How are your girls, Jack? Must be hard being a father to two teenage daughters on your own. And girls today, so different from when I married Barbara. They want to make something from their life. I could never cope like you have had to do.'

Jack tried to ignore the distraction of Lionel's specious small talk and its political incorrectness. These were barbs clearly intended to rile him because he was single and a bad parent. He refused to rise to the bait.

'What do we really have to talk about?'

Lionel pushed his half-finished plate away and leant forward, resting a large liver-spotted hand on Jack's. Instinctively, Jack wanted to pull away but did not want to show weakness, although the touch of Lionel's leathery skin did precipitate an involuntary shiver.

'Jack, my boy. We need to carve the chicken up a bit more fairly.'

'I wasn't aware we were eating one together?'

'Don't pretend this will come as a shock to you. What I mean is, there is not enough business to go around, and you need to give up some of your interests to me.'

'You are bonkers, Lionel. Why would I do that?'

By now, their hands were no longer touching, and Jack contemplated either getting up to leave or launching a tirade of swear words that would give him enormous satisfaction if he could manage to get four good ones out in a row.

'You will do it, young man, because otherwise I will stop buying chickens from you, set up my own factory and watch Fogel's Chickens, that wonderful family business set up by your crooked grandfather, collapse. And I will love every minute.'

Lionel's motives could not have been more obvious. Biblical wrath had been fuelled over many years by the memory of useless Phil Fogel, shooing him out of the factory with a triumphant smile. Jack had no knowledge of what had really happened other than his father's version of the dismissal, but he imagined Lionel leaving the building and looking dramatically up at the heavens as he shook his fist and vowed to destroy the Fogel family at some future point. What did any of this have to do with him now?

'Sorry, Lionel, are you threatening me or are you going to make me an offer I can't refuse? I don't really understand how you think you can call me to a meeting and suggest I give up bits of my business. And what did you have in mind? I might as well be entertained as well as irritated.'

Jack was often criticised by his family for being phlegmatic and unemotional. He didn't know why because most of the time he suppressed a simmering anger, which was rising now, ready to spray like projectile vomit all over this odious self-satisfied man.

'Calm down, Jack. I'm trying to be reasonable here. I want your shops in Golders Green and Hendon. Your leases are due for renewal. You are going to sell the business to me for a very low price. It's all in this offer letter, which I think you should accept.'

Jack hadn't noticed that there was an attaché case on the floor, which Lionel pulled on to his lap and opened. It was of course made of mottled alligator skin, the perfect accessory for its reptilian owner. He produced an envelope, which he slid across the table. Jack did not pick it up or even glance down but took a slow and deliberate deep breath before replying.

'Please don't tell me to be calm when you are talking such nonsense. They are my two most profitable shops. I am not getting rid of them because you have invited me for a coffee and told me to.'

There was no way the shops were going to be handed over on such a capricious request, yet Lionel, who had waited years for this moment of retribution, was undeterred.

'I am not telling you; I am suggesting you strongly consider doing what I say. If not, I'll buy fewer chickens from you and make your life uncomfortable with the kosher authorities. Perhaps I'll chat with your disgruntled partners in the restaurant – you see, I know all about your refusal to expand the business further. There is so much fun I can have at your expense and if you are worried I'm going to play dirty, you're right, I will.'

Jack wanted to respond but his mind was clouding with a mixture of rage and disappointment. Why had his life become endless conflict deriving from a business he hadn't wanted to run in the first place? Lionel looked at him curiously as if feigning compassion, then motioned to the waitress for another coffee for them both. This ordeal was on to its second cup.

'Let me explain something to you, my boy. Do you play golf?' Jack shook his head wearily.

'Well, I do. Imagine it's a beautiful summer's day. Not too hot, the sky blue, and the course is empty. You're playing with a dear friend, well matched with a similar game. Eighteen holes of wonderful competition, you're up, you're all square, he's up. It's all down to the last. You drive. He drives. You are level on the fairway. You both pitch to the green. You are the same distance from the hole. You get down in two and he leaves his putt a bit short. Nothing too far, let's say a two-footer. You have had a wonderful round. A drink beckons on the clubhouse terrace. Do you give him the putt and call it a halve or do you still try to win? What do you say?'

'I'm sorry, you lost me at "*Do you play golf?*".'

'I'll tell you, Jack, for nothing, that you don't give him the bloody putt! You never give anyone anything for free, you try to win. You always try to win. And I'm afraid, Master Fogel, I am going to defeat you many times over.'

Jack watched spittle form in the corner of Lionel's mouth as the crescendo of this pointless anecdote unleashed a crooked snarl. The surprising nature of the encounter was magnified by a commotion taking place on the street outside. Jack, sitting by the window, became aware of a person in an enormous chicken costume positioned in front of them, distributing flyers to the innocent public passing by. Some people were trying to avoid the scene, scurrying gingerly across the road, fearful of poultry assault. Lionel was delightedly hopping from one buttock to the other on his seat, thrilled that he knew what was going on while Jack looked bemused.

'Oh, you'll be wondering who that is.'

Jack was defiantly mute, determined not to give him the satisfaction of asking.

'That's "Chaim the Chicken", my new brand ambassador – at least, I think that's what they call it these days. He's handing out offers to potential customers. Very effective, I am told. And do you know what this one says? This week, all our chickens are twenty per cent cheaper than yours. That's what I call a good promotion. He's on his way to stand in front of some of your shops. You're going to be seeing a lot of him, I'm afraid.' Lionel took a slurp of his fresh cappuccino and tapped on the glass, trying to catch the chicken's attention, waving with uninhibited exuberance.

'Chaim the Chicken' reminded Jack of his recurring dream in which he appeared in a similar garish costume by his own graveside, evincing laughter from the assembled mourners. He was in no doubt now that Lionel would willingly be a pallbearer at the funeral of Fogel's Chickens. As he rose to leave, he exhaled a deep sigh of regret and self-pity. It seemed his life was going to get far worse very quickly, and who looks forward to a long and feathery war?

Chapter 8

Tracy and Clive's house reflected the chaotic brilliance of two consultant psychiatrists with a competitive need to be more successful than their partner. Books and papers were strewn everywhere, and their loyal cleaner had long since given up trying to introduce order, simply hoovering any free floor space, dusting lightly where a surface permitted and drinking copious cups of tea the rest of the time. They had two dogs to compound the mess. Max the Dachshund seemed to suffer from an anxiety disorder that made his toilet training a little erratic. Maggie the Labrador exuded canine disdain for her mentally fragile housemate and so fights, barking and howling were the soundtrack to everyday life.

Natalie and Isobel loved dinner at their aunt's, finding the disordered fun so different from a night on their own with their father as well as spending time with their three cousins, the eldest of whom, Benjie, was Natalie's age. That night, as always, they had roast chicken for dinner. While the girls ate little red meat and rarely touched fish, there was an unspoken loyalty to the humble chicken. Poultry slaughter had quite literally put food on the table for the different branches of the Fogel family, and no one was brave enough to rebel against its place on the menu.

Tracy specialised in asking the kids about feelings and emotions in the most natural way possible. Jack marvelled at her ability, knowing that if he broached a sensitive topic with Natalie, he would be accused of reactionary opinions he was sure he did not possess. He had of course got things wrong as usual when trying to participate in the debate. Tracy had been nonchalantly asking what they thought was important in a relationship. Clearing plates as she spoke, she announced: 'When I was your age, Nat, I had fallen in love. Not with useless Clive here, with a boy who taught me to appreciate that love and sex can be two very different things.'

'Must we, Tracy?' Jack asked with surprise at the direction of the conversation. 'I may be an old fart, but is this appropriate?'

He knew that was not the right response and his daughters stared at him with irritation. Clearly, he was an old fart.

'I resent that statement,' interrupted a cheerful Clive. 'Don't listen to your aunt, I am not in the slightest bit useless.'

Jack envied their easy manner with the kids, who were both by now completely engaged by their aunt's candour.

'Who was it, Auntie Tracy?' Isobel asked as she scooped some sorbet into her bowl. Jack often assumed her silence to be a sign of unhappiness. Tonight, however, she seemed lighter and more joyful than he had seen for some time.

'Yeah, who was it, Tracy?' Jack demanded, realising he'd need to join in to avoid further rejection. 'I'd have remembered if there was anyone remotely interested in you hanging around the house. I thought useless Clive was the only boyfriend you ever had.'

'Given I didn't speak to you until you were at least twenty-one, how would you know? Anyway, I am asking Natalie what she thinks. No one here is interested in your view.'

'Too right,' his elder daughter added, just in case he had any self-esteem left. 'Now, I happen to agree with Auntie Tracy about sex and love. In my experience, two very different things. Right now, I think I prefer the sex.'

Jack nearly choked on the piece of melon he was eating, and he could not quite believe his seventeen-year-old daughter's woman-of-the-world bravura.

'Natalie. This is not for the Friday night dinner table, young lady, despite what your aunt Germaine Greer over there says. And besides, your sister is only fifteen. I'm not ready to hear your views on relationships. She most certainly doesn't have to.'

Jack knew he was going to be in trouble as soon as he spoke. He had no idea where his puritanical indignation and antiquated idiom came from.

'Oh, Dad. Wise up. Whatever you do, don't call me "young lady". This is not 1950 or whenever it was you were born. I am not your baby girl any more, and who the fuck is Germaine Greer?'

'Well, you're behaving like a baby now,' Jack countered, not entirely sure of what he was saying. Beneath the rapidly descending cloud of irritation, he knew it was unfair to punish her for trying to sound adult.

'You are literally, like, the most embarrassing father any girl could, like, wish for?'

Jack could not help himself.

'Which one is it, darling? Am I literally the worst or am I figuratively the worst? It's just since you say "like" every other word, I am bound to get confused. I suppose that's why you don't talk to me much and I had to find out about your latest boyfriend from your grandmother.'

He'd gone too far now without a doubt, confirmed by Tracy's exaggerated head movements imploring him to stop talking. His fractious relationship with his daughter needed little to ignite the flames of her disappointment and he had poured a jerrycan of petrol on it and lit the match. Natalie threw her napkin on the table and glared at him with an identical fury to her mother at the end of his marriage. Jack was engulfed by remorse and shame.

'It's no wonder I can't trust you, Dad. You are so weak, and you don't understand women. I'd rather tell Auntie Tracy what I'm thinking from now on, if that's OK. It's just one big fight with you. If you'll excuse me, I am going to leave the table.'

She got up and gave a controlled nod to her aunt and uncle, like taking a curtain call, and walked towards the living room, followed by her loyal cousin and sister. It seemed she had been terribly wronged by her father; he just could not work out how it had degenerated into the deficiencies of his character so quickly.

Isobel peered over her shoulder as she left the room and shouted, 'Honestly, Dad. Look what you've done now. You really are useless sometimes.'

There was a moment of sublime awkwardness, followed by Tracy clapping her hands to indicate it was time to change the subject and forget his emotional ineptitude.

'Well done, Jack, I think you handled that very deftly. Perhaps you'd better tell me what Lionel Gutterman had to say instead.'

* * *

Jack didn't feel in control of either his body or his mind. The strains of the day, coupled with an enormous dinner, had left him producing a disarmingly loud symphony of uncontrollable gurgles and rumbles and he sipped an enormous mug of peppermint tea, hoping its soothing properties for an unsettled stomach would help. Ibuprofen and paracetamol hardly touched the sides for him these days.

Jack had just got to recounting the unexpected appearance of Chaim the Chicken when the bell rang. Several seconds later, the door flew open, and their sister Karen skipped into the dining room, a bottle of champagne in her hand and an ebullient smile spread across a heavily made-up face. Tracy and Jack were surprised by her unannounced entrance, it was so rare they were all together. The kids followed her back into the room, equally bemused by the arrival of their aunt, the aspiring politician who they rarely saw.

Dressed in an immaculate Tory-blue suit, evidently purchased on one of her biannual shopping trips to Paris, she looked as if she were going to give her maiden speech in Parliament.

'I am here, my darling family, to celebrate my elevation as candidate for the incredibly safe seat of Dudley South. I have just hotfooted it down from the constituency party meeting and wanted to share the news with you all.'

'Why aren't you with Uncle Richard and the boys?' Natalie asked. Her burgeoning left-wing idealism made her quite hostile to her aunt's politics, and she began to pace a corner of the dining room as if marking out her ideological territory.

'They're away for the weekend, so where else would I want to be?'

Jack glanced at Tracy and their eyes flickered a sense of collective disbelief at her sincerity.

'Wow, Karen, Dudley South must be the furthest up the country you've ever been. Lucky it wasn't Dudley North. Anyway, Mum told us that she wanted help placing the ads of congratulations in *The Sunday Times*.'

'Very amusing, Jack. You really are the funniest butcher I know.'

There was a reason the siblings were rarely in the same room together and Karen had stopped smiling now in the face of the perceived assault. Given it was her home, Tracy tried to defuse the tension by embracing her sister in a spontaneous hug, declaring to everyone, 'Let's cut the banter, please, and celebrate Karen's success. A Fogel in government. Who'd have thought it? *Zeyde* Solly would be so proud. Congratulations, little sis, it's an amazing achievement and a real honour. Promise me when you become Secretary of State for Education, you will mandate every child has to eat chicken every day at school.'

'Of course I will, and when I become Chancellor, I'm going to introduce a tax on all vegetarians. But please let's not count those chickens yet. The election is months away and I do have to win the bloody thing.'

She was interrupted by the pop of the champagne cork, which flew across the room as Clive clumsily opened the bottle and proceeded to pour everyone a drink. In their chaotic home, glasses were in short supply, and they saluted Karen by clinking an array of tumblers, brandy glasses, mugs and espresso cups.

'To the Fogels,' Jack declared as self-appointed family patriarch. Natalie was happy to participate, particularly lubricated by a generous helping of booze, but refused to sanction her aunt's politics, shouting: 'All hail the revolution. May you all be lined up and shot.'

'Charming, darling,' Karen said with little warmth. She had always been fond of Natalie, seeing in her the values she had loved in her former sister-in-law. Tonight, though, she barely tried to hide the condescension in her voice as she closed the conversation.

'Not for discussion now, sweetheart, but we must go out for lunch very soon and you can allow me to put across my side of the story. Now, I think that's enough politics for this Shabbat dinner. What other family news is there?'

Tracy looked at Jack, spurring him to continue with the narrative he had begun as Karen arrived. She knew Jack was desperate to discuss the situation and perhaps it would engender a bit of family unity for once.

'Well, our hapless brother was just regaling us with the tale of a top-level business meeting with his nemesis Lionel Gutterman, who, it seems, wants to destroy our family empire with the help of Chaim the Chicken.'

Karen swigged from her mug, slightly befuddled. No one had noticed that in the random crockery allocation, it had the two words 'Control Freak' emblazoned across its front. Karen sought clarification.

'I'm sure I should understand what you said, and I even recognised some of the words, but I really don't know what you are talking about.'

Jack looked at the kids and, with a dismissive wave, ushered them out of the room. He knew the detail of his professional life would evince contempt from them and right now he felt too fragile for the resigned disinterest that Natalie would struggle to conceal. It would be like staring at Ali and being reminded of his previous deficiencies as a husband.

'You lot can carry on doing whatever it was you were doing. I need to tell Auntie Karen some stuff that will probably just bore you.'

Natalie and Benjie needed no prompting to escape and were half out the room as he spoke, but Isobel lingered, reluctant to depart. She was always interested in the business and had a vicarious pride in its longevity. It was also the only way she found herself able to engage with her father.

'Can I stay, please, Dad?' Jack nodded but was not really listening, clearly formulating a brief overview of his challenges to share in this impromptu family board meeting. He recapped the story of his day for Karen's benefit, summarising all his challenges in five minutes, and for the first time in the house that evening, there was calm as no one interrupted him.

'So, my absent business partners. What do you think?'

Karen, a combative barrister by training, automatically assumed it was only her opinion being solicited.

'I think you do nothing. Absolutely nothing. You carry on trading. You sell him chickens and you ignore his threats. He is bluffing and he needs you as much as you need him. There is little he can do, and he is just looking to avenge the fact that Dad punched him and threw him out of the business all those years ago.'

'I think Dad may have exaggerated his role a bit, but you're right, I think he wants to cause us pain more than he wants to make money.'

'I agree with Karen, and that's a rare sentence these days,' Tracy added. 'Don't be bullied by him and his lanky accomplice in a chicken costume. We are better than that.'

Jack was momentarily buoyed by the unfamiliar sisterly support and realised that even if Lionel had opened hostilities, there was no need for him to fire back just yet. He was about to thank them for helping him at the end of an extremely irritating day when Karen continued as if her position was the only one worth considering.

'I understand the pressure, Jack. Really, I do. But you must promise me that after the commitment I have just made to the good people of Dudley South, you won't embroil me in your conflict with a rival. Right now, I really regret that I didn't take Richard's dull surname when we got married. *Smith* is so much less Jewish-sounding than *Fogel* and come election time, I don't want a google search linking me to a kosher chicken dispute in Golders Green.'

Jack was incredulous. How had his troubles become a potential issue for her political career?

'Point taken. I'll have a word with the Chinese and see if they can have all mention of your family taken down from the internet.'

Karen was not in the mood for being challenged; her brow furrowed, and she shook her head.

'I would appreciate a little consideration for me, Jack, at this sensitive time for my career.'

'And perhaps,' he hissed back, 'you could support me. Let's not forget you are the ones doing what you want to with your lives.'

For once, both sisters were silent.

Chapter 9

Jack lay in bed several hours later, struggling to sleep as his mind unpicked the exhausting events of the evening. He'd gone to Tracy's in search of support but had left with a profound regret that he and his younger sister had managed to turn on each other so quickly. The evening fizzled out and he returned home with his girls, who were clearly furious but unwilling to explain to him his crime.

Staring into quiet darkness, he felt sorry for himself. Forty-six years old and unfit, his hair was reassuringly thick but with a creeping greyness that matched his current horizon. He contemplated his future. What did he have to show for the endeavours of the last twenty years? A significant business, fraught with mounting problems, and two unfathomable children with their instruction manual long since lost. His family seemed unwilling to stand by him and his closest friends were ensconced in their own dramas and unavailable. He was so lonely.

Being maudlin was unhelpful and would simply escalate over the weekend into tetchiness with his daughters and too many KitKats. He had never wanted to be single but had been consistently unsuccessful in trying to replace Ali. He recalled a particularly excruciating Sunday lunch as a teenager when his grandfather decided to explain how chickens mate. It was a strange topic of conversation, but Solly was an autodidact when it came to all things poultry and had a perverse respect for the species, even if he was their executioner on an industrial level. Cockerels apparently 'crow' as they perform a dance of love. They are capable of impregnating hens anywhere between ten and thirty times a day, it only taking a few seconds. The hens become 'broody' and the cockerels strut around them to deny the romantic approaches of younger rivals.

Jack was no cockerel, even if the opportunities for meeting women were significant for an eligible divorcee with a healthy head of hair. He often found himself paired with eligible women, but he had no idea what was expected of him. He refused to treat each date as a casual encounter in pursuit of sex, and having experienced only one serious relationship in his life, this was his yardstick for future ones. Craving companionship, yet terrified of genuine commitment that ended in pain, he held back emotional intimacy from every date in case he found himself too close to what might be considered a relationship.

The result was a series of short and unhappy liaisons. The average length was about three months and sometimes he would find himself alone for up to a year at a time. He managed a few weekends away with these partners but the moment a complication emerged – their children, his children, their need for commitment, his inability to express love – the parting was swift and amicable.

There was one exception. A few years after his divorce, he encountered Elizabeth Higgins at a fortieth birthday party and embarked on something more substantive. She was eight years younger than him, resolutely independent and conveniently not Jewish. For Jack, this was an aphrodisiac more powerful than chocolate or a Barry White CD. She was a successful web designer from Lincoln who knew very little about the machinations of his north-west London background. Working long hours for a global advertising agency, she travelled and was ambitious. With low expectations of his duties as a boyfriend, she was perfect.

He wondered why she liked him so much. Partly, the less he tried, the better company he was. They shared a love of cinema and date nights always consisted of a film and dinner, followed by an uncomplicated sleepover, normally at her tiny Notting Hill flat.

She did not want to meet his children and he had no interest in meeting her parents when they came to town. Every other weekend and the occasional midweek date were sufficient for them both and their conversation, while crackling with enthusiastic affection, rarely included any mention of their emotions.

After a trip to see a grim French film about the affair between two eighteenth-century aristocrats, they sat in a fashionable Soho restaurant, and Elizabeth casually ended the relationship. Jack had been prattling on about cinematography, oblivious to her distraction, when she announced, 'You know what, I think we can both do better.' They finished their meal amicably as he realised he could not disagree with her assessment. He hugged her sheepishly as she got in a cab and said farewell to his low-maintenance attempt at happiness.

That was two years ago, and he had not managed to find such uncomplicated contentment since. He did not miss Elizabeth, but he ached for the simplicity of their dating. Now he tussled with an incipient anxiety that he needed to find someone with whom to spend the second half of his life. As a child, his family had viewed him as some sort of uninvited lodger in their affections. As a husband, he had not been sufficiently interesting to sustain the marriage beyond its first ten years. He was a disaster.

* * *

It must have been 2 a.m. by now and he really couldn't sleep as his restless mind created unhelpful scenarios for his sad future. The ping of his mobile phone stirred him from this miserable musing. It was a text from an unhappy Ali.

> What on earth did you say to Natalie? She wants to come home tomorrow as you have really upset her. When will you ever learn?

Ali was still angry with him, even if they had not been together for over twelve years. He sometimes felt the focal point of all her frustration for life's disappointments. Initially, she had found new love quickly. A year after their divorce, she hooked up with uber-charismatic James Harrison, who offered a glimpse of the future Jack was spectacularly unable to provide. He was a publicity-seeking criminal barrister on trajectory to become a QC and was often on TV as an opportunistic commentator on all matters legal. Recently separated, he had one son roughly the same age as the girls. Ali went back to work at her investment bank, and everyone got on beautifully. Jack was consumed with envy for her perfect world.

They quickly moved in together. It was everything Ali wanted: an elegant, worldly existence with the constant promise of more excitement to follow – travel, entertainment, dynamic new friends. But after six years together, it fell apart unexpectedly when James left her without warning for a young barrister in his chambers. His apology was the insincere gesture of a man who had found happiness elsewhere. To compound Ali's humiliation, he married her replacement soon after, the baby bump clearly visible on the photos Ali unfortunately saw on Facebook. She crumbled, physically and emotionally, losing significant weight, as her eyes sank into the black pools of sadness that had formed around them.

Jack tried to help her by being the best father he could. For a few months, the girls lived with him full time as her grief bloomed. She convinced herself that Jack was enjoying her pain in revenge for his abandonment years before. 'Kosher karma' is what she told her therapist had befallen her. When she emerged from the despair, she was filled with uncontainable anger unleashed at him, the girls, her parents, friends, colleagues, shop assistants and random members of the public. She was just so sad.

Time partially healed and Ali did what she could to repair the damage she had inflicted on her poor children. They pootled along comfortably, the flimsy calm occasionally destroyed by Jack's perceived failings as a father. But she did not want him to be happy if she could not be and was reassured that his life consisted of long miserable days in an abattoir without a loving partner to mitigate the tedium.

The night dragged on as he tried to flee the pain of the day. His sleep was fitful, punctuated by his recurring funeral dream, with a slight variation. This time, he stood over his open grave dressed as Lionel Gutterman's new mascot, 'Chaim the Chicken'. People seemed to be laughing at him with even more intensity and even in his subconscious state, he felt ashamed.

* * *

The next evening, he attempted to soften Isobel's hostility towards him. Natalie had long since fled back to her mother's house on parole from her father's incompetent care, so Jack made a special effort with his other daughter to spend quality time doing what she wanted – schoolwork and virtual conversations with school friends on social media channels rather than chatting to him.

Saturdays were problematic. Shabbat was of course a day of rest and the only time his business could not operate. There are thirty-nine rules observant Jews have to follow stemming from the need to separate the Sabbath from the rest of the week. The prohibition to create fire has been interpreted over centuries of rabbinic discourse to ensure the day is without electrical sparks of any sort. For modern life, this means eliminating all its manifestations, from switching on lights to text messaging, and while Jack liked the separation of Shabbat as a concept, he was unwilling to do everything required to ensure full compliance with its strictures.

The snag was that as the owner of a business answerable to the Beth Din, a rabbinic court, he had to avoid flouting its rules too overtly. He had deliberately moved to Hampstead, which was slightly less populated with orthodox Jews, and was careful, if he did drive on Shabbat, not to be spotted in his car. He hated the necessary hypocrisy this entailed but soothed himself that he had not chosen to run his business but was simply the last Fogel standing. Surely he had compromised enough that any divine presence (if there was one) would cut him some slack, given the amount of kosher chicken he provided for the community?

The girls hated his cautious approach to going out on a Saturday and this gave further ammunition to their enormous data bank of his failings. That day, he had tried to suggest to Isobel watching a classic film together as a bonding tactic, which sometimes worked if he could find a movie that transcended his daughter's intolerance of anything made more than ten years ago.

Breakfast at Tiffany's was not going well. Jack had hoped the combination of sixties' New York, Audrey Hepburn's Givenchy style and her plaintive rendition of 'Moon River' would do the trick. Isobel was not so impressed.

'Watch her strum the guitar. It's ridiculous. They haven't even made it look like she can play. It's like the rest of the film, completely phoney.'

'Don't you think it's a tiny bit romantic?'

'No, I think it's completely wrong. She's basically some sort of prostitute wanting to marry a man with lots of money. And that bloke in love with her is a rubbish writer being kept by an older married lady. What kind of lesson are you trying to teach me here?'

She had a point. He had not seen the film for years and his memory of it was influenced by his honeymoon, which started in New York with a trip to see it playing in a small Chelsea cinema before they walked to Tiffany on Fifth Avenue to take Ali's picture in front of one of the windows. Watching it with Isobel, he realised it was just the dubious tale of 'two drifters off to see the world' who were amoral chancers.

His phone rang, interrupting a potential argument. It was his brother-in-law Clive, something of a surprise as they rarely communicated directly.

'What's up, Clive? Everything OK?'

'Why should it not be OK? Tracy has not left me and Karen has not tried to sue us for the emotional distress you caused yesterday. I'm calling because I forgot to discuss something with you. What are you up to now?'

'I'm trying to complete Isobel's film education but not having much success.'

'What are you watching?'

'*Breakfast at Tiffany's.*'

'Hmm, poor choice from you, Jack. Is she struggling to see Audrey Hepburn as a symbol of male idealised beauty in need of a dominant partner to protect her from her own fragility?'

'Well, that's not quite how she put it, but I think she prefers her heroines to be handy in a knife fight.'

Isobel by now had switched to watching a dystopian series on Netflix and her father's conversation made her shout out at him: 'Shut up, Dad, you have no idea what I'm thinking.'

He moved to the kitchen to carry on the conversation and avoid further abuse.

'Anyway, to what do I owe the honour of this rare call? What do you want to discuss?'

'Actually, it's appropriate you're watching something romantic because I have a proposal for you.'

'You're not my type, and it would kill Tracy, but it's flattering you ask.' Quite witty, he thought, and he looked around the empty kitchen in search of someone to validate his sense of humour. Clive did not seem in the mood.

'I may have someone interesting for you to meet.'

'What are you talking about?'

'Jack, you're an unhappy disaster. Your anger is ill concealed beneath the surface of your discontent. You struggle to have close relationships with us all and you are not exactly blessed with a surfeit of friends.'

'Blimey, I hope that's not how you described me to her. Not exactly a ringing endorsement.'

'Listen, my friend. If we don't tell you, how are you going to move on with your life? Right now, you're engaged in a great war of unhappiness.'

'I really do appreciate your pep talks, but they are not that helpful. Some time ago you mentioned you wanted to fix me up with someone. Was there actually something you were going to tell me?'

Jack had poured himself a large whisky as they spoke, feeling the need for the numbing calm of his mandatory daily dose of single malt.

'Her name is Sonia Lewis. She's the cousin of my tennis partner, she's thirty-eight and looking for a relationship. That's all I know. I have her number if you want it?'

'What does she do? Why would she want to meet me? Have you done any due diligence?'

'No. She's apparently very nice and a bit different.'

'Different good or different weird and bonkers?'

'We try not to use the word "bonkers" any more in the psychiatry business. I'm afraid I know nothing more, other than her cousin thinks she's lovely. But then, can you trust your family?'

'Not currently. How did this come up in a tennis match?'

'He came for dinner last week. Tracy went off on one about how worried she is about you. They all got quite excited about the possibility of you meeting her. Tracy made me ring now because you'd dismiss her out of hand.'

Jack felt disappointment once more that someone close to him did not trust him to be able to have an open conversation. He'd much rather have spoken with his sister than her husband, who was proving himself to be the least cuddly psychiatrist since Hannibal Lecter. A brief silence was punctured by Clive's clear irritation.

'Tracy says don't think of trying to discuss this with her. Just bloody call the woman and ask her out. Now, do you want her number or not? She's expecting your call unless she has decided to flee the country because someone tipped her off about you.'

'OK, text it to me. I mean, if she's the enigmatic cousin of your tennis partner, who am I to say no?'

Clive hung up and two seconds later texted Sonia Lewis's telephone number. He sat, unable to move, and glanced at the kitchen clock, listening to the loud ticking of its second hand marking the passing of another unsatisfactory day. Still, it had ended with a vague promise of change.

Maybe.

PART 3

SKIRMISHES

Chapter 10

Jack thought of the exotic and brilliantly coloured fish of the Maldives. He and Ali had been married a couple of years when she received an unexpected bonus after inhuman sixteen-hour daily shifts working on the sale of a French utility company. To celebrate the windfall, they immediately booked an indulgent escape to a luxury villa perched on stilts above the translucent Indian Ocean.

Every day they swam for hours, surrounded by butterfly fish, barracudas, green sea turtles, bluestripe snappers and whitetip reef sharks. Jack would listen to the tinny rise and fall of his breathing through the snorkel as he glided effortlessly above the stunted cream coral reefs. He and Ali also learnt to scuba dive and by the end of the holiday they were blowing underwater kisses to one another and holding hands as the dayglo fishes brushed obliviously past them.

When not in the sea, they holidayed in spectacular style. Their villa had a terrace facing the limitless azure horizon, which at dusk would explode with endless firework combinations of burnt oranges, reds and yellows. They lay on loungers, fawned on by attentive staff, who would appear like benevolent genies with exotic cocktails and elaborate French-themed meals served on china plates and revealed with a theatrical flourish from beneath gleaming silver domes. They had an outside jacuzzi shaded by lush green coconut palms and they watched the twinkling of a million stars as they sipped their nightcaps. Intoxicated with happiness, they made unfettered plans for a glorious future.

And now it had come to this: a soggy, rain-splattered Tuesday, sitting on an orange plastic chair in an anteroom in Willesden Magistrates' Court. Through the dusty blinds hanging half-heartedly above a window covered in Health and Safety notices, all he could see was a dark grey sky and fast-moving clouds, promising enduring rain.

A month ago, he could never have envisaged that he would be forced to attend a hearing, hoping three faceless magistrates would exonerate his shop manager charged with common assault. This unexpected turn of events had been a result of Chaim the Chicken's attempt to leaflet outside Jack's Golders Green shop. The ensuing argument between his loyal lieutenant Lawrence Klein and a man in a pantomime costume quickly degenerated into an unpleasant brawl. When he lay indolently on his Maldivian lounger, he saw an uninterrupted pathway to contentment, but this idealism had been gradually superseded by pettiness and conflict.

It all happened in an instant. Lawrence had initially followed Jack's instructions and ignored Chaim, believing it to be a harmless, if very irritating, stunt. However, it soon became clear that customers were intimidated by the chicken's overzealous distribution of Gutterman's promotional material and were avoiding coming into the shop. Lawrence was Jack's most trusted member of staff. He'd worked for the business since leaving school and was a curmudgeonly but decent man with great pride in his work. The ridiculous creature outside his shop made him snap and he rushed out to put an end to the nonsense.

The fracas was hard to describe accurately, despite the many eyewitnesses. Lawrence had audibly shouted both 'I am calling the police' and 'I'll knock your beak off if you don't move'. Mrs Feigenbaum, a frail octogenarian with a walking frame, was trying to enter the shop to buy a pack of Chicken Supremes and told the police that it was Lawrence who had thrown the first punch. Chaim, allegedly, shoved him quite hard in response, despite the limitations of his plastic wings and enormous foam clawed feet. Removing his headpiece, a gurning nineteen-year-old Aaron Levy eyeballed Lawrence.

The grandson of Lionel's closest friend, he was on a gap year, trying to earn a bit of travelling money. With youthful impudence, he shouted at his foe, 'Call that a punch, grandpa?' and slapped Lawrence across the face as they fell into a frenetic clinch, like two heavyweight boxers intertwined on the ropes.

At this point, a Polish electrician, Marek Zielinaski, emerged from the gathering crowd to act as a peacemaker in this most unlikely fight. Unfortunately, in his attempt to separate the foes, one of them accidently punched him in the face. As he regained his composure, he found his hand bloodied from a nasty gash above his eye that had suddenly appeared. The police were called, and statements taken from enthusiastic bystanders, for whom the fight was an unexpected distraction from a mundane Wednesday morning's shopping. Mrs Feigenbaum felt like Miss Marple as she described the events in painstaking detail. Eventually, Lawrence and Aaron were both charged as the police struggled to establish who had hit the innocent Marek.

Now, in the court's anteroom, Jack sat silently a few seats away from Aaron and his anxious parents. Despite his pugnacity, Aaron looked like a disgruntled teenager dragged to an adult social event against his wishes. He only took the stupid job for a few weeks and now his overindulgent, super-protective parents were terrified that his future was going to be blighted by a criminal record. Jack tried not to catch his mother's stare, which he sensed was directed at him in quiet fury. He looked at his shoes, gazed out of the window and pretended to read a poster about court procedures, but he couldn't escape the discomfort of her unblinking scrutiny and eventually she exploded with spluttering rage.

'You should be ashamed of yourself,' she began, pointing at him with her finger like an angry Lord Kitchener. Lawrence had nipped into the car park for a nervous cigarette and Jack felt the need to correct her mistaken identity.

'I think you don't mean me,' he replied lamely, still reluctant to look her directly in the eyes for fear of being turned to stone.

'I certainly do mean you. I know exactly who you are, Jack Fogel. Your henchman didn't assault our son without following your orders.'

Why did every situation mutate into something unexpectedly worse? *Take a deep breath, take a deep breath*, he told himself, attempting not to get embroiled in another pointless argument. All he really wanted to do was to drive home, but he knew that free will did not exist in his life.

'You are giving me too much credit for a non-existent master plan. Lawrence politely asked your son to stop blocking our business and he was met with an appalling lack of respect.'

'I'll tell you what your mate Lawrence did. He hit my son, and I am going to tell everyone you made him do it.'

'That's upsetting. I mean, the other children in the playground may not want to play with me if that's the case.'

This was now escalating from a petty scuffle to a truly puerile squabble and the raised voices had provoked Aaron's father into action. He stopped scouring the sports' pages and stood up as if poised to ask Jack to step outside. Jack was not intimidated by his latest adversary, who was squat and round, remembering he'd won his last fight, although in truth it was in primary school and involved conkers.

'You shouldn't speak to my wife like that,' Aaron's father raged in a voice that was squeakily inadequate.

'I'd rather not speak to her at all if I had my choice,' Jack replied, and he took out his phone and stared at its locked screen. He wasn't sure why he thought this act might make him invisible, but any further need for name-calling was prevented by the Clerk of Court calling them back in for the magistrates' verdict. His relief the ordeal was nearly over dissipated when he realised that to retrieve Lawrence, he had to walk past his antagonists. He could smell the pungent body spray of Aaron, who had been observing the exchange with an infantile grin.

'Roasted by Mum. You must be so embarrassed, little man.'

'Oh, piss off, you irritating little shit!' Jack snapped back. Sometimes it was hard to be witty and elegant when facing an onslaught of idiocy.

* * *

Lawrence pleaded not guilty, but sadly the magistrates did not agree, and he was fined £500 plus costs as well as a victim surcharge to the wounded Marek. He sat in brooding silence in the car on the way home, unwilling to engage in conversation. Even though he was paying the fine, Jack felt he was being blamed for Lawrence's uncharacteristic violence. Once more Jack had the uncomfortable sensation of being a guilty man without any knowledge of his crime.

The day had been made worse by the ticket he got when he forgot to extend his stay in the car park. As he had pulled it from his windscreen, he had to contend with another skirmish with Aaron's aggressive mother. Her son had been let off by the magistrates, who had fallen for his veneer of youthful naivety, applied artfully when questioned in court. Mrs Levy approached Jack as he was preparing to drive off. Tapping his window, she bellowed like a firebrand at a political rally, 'Justice was served today. Justice was served.' Jack contemplated running over her foot, but in the end nodded vaguely and started the engine.

He drove Lawrence home and watched him trudge up the path to his front door, where his wife was waiting as if welcoming a wounded hero returning from years at war. She gave him an enormous hug and they stood motionless in their embrace for several moments. Jack felt his loneliness rise as he wondered why there was no one in his corner.

'Move on. Move on,' he declared emphatically to his empty car. 'This has got to end.' He had often wondered if there would be a moment of clarity when he could see his way through to a happier life. He could not quite imagine what this would feel like, but perhaps a starting point might be to end hostilities with his recently acquired new enemy. He scrolled his phone for the 'G's. Lionel Gutterman was sandwiched in his contacts between his lawyer, Antony Grossman, and his GP, Dr Harvey. He might need the help of both to calm him down if the call went badly.

* * *

'Lionel, enough already. We need to stop all this nonsense immediately.' Jack adopted a firm tone, having decided there was no point making small talk with the small-minded.

'We certainly do, Jack, and it might be nice if your man Lawrence apologises to Aaron Levy and his family for what he has put them through.'

Jack immediately regretted making the call from his car rather than his office. He needed room to pace to lessen the frustration that any conversation with Lionel created and reminded himself not to be deflected from his mission, irrespective of the provocation. A couple of teenage boys walked past the car and stared at him in the gloom. It must have looked like he was talking to himself and he could see them point at him with derision. Unperturbed, he pressed on.

'You have to stop trying to disrupt my business so crassly. Surely you have higher standards?'

Lionel did not respond for a moment and when he did, his normal disingenuous bonhomie was replaced by aggression.

'I will not be lectured by a Fogel on morality. Your grandfather would use violence and intimidation on his enemies. It's not surprising it's hereditary.'

'Stop mentioning my grandfather. This is not about what happened in the past. I am sorry you feel wronged, but this is not some ancient Sicilian vendetta. Can we be a bit more constructive?'

'OK, Jack, I'll call off my imaginary assassins. Now, have you thought about my proposal?'

'Which one?'

'The one where you sell me your two shops for a knockdown price.'

So much for rational debate.

'It's not so much a proposal really, Lionel, is it? Rather, a ludicrous ultimatum. The shops are not for sale. I am willing to consider all options, but I suggest we ground our expectations on planet Earth if that's OK.'

Was that a growl he heard from Lionel? It sounded like an animal in pain.

'You need to show me a bit more respect, young man. Your temper will be your undoing.'

Jack was not aware he had lost his temper, but restraint was proving tricky, and he felt an unpleasant taste fill his mouth. Bile was the ancient humour of anger, he remembered from his medieval history. Lionel seemed able to facilitate gallons of its production every time they spoke.

'Lionel, I am at a loss to know what you want from me.'

'Well, let me elaborate. I am going to need far less chickens to start with.'

'What do you mean?'

'I think since our relationship is so poor, I am going to try some other wholesale options. So, from next week, our order with you is going to be seriously reduced. Probably by about a half.'

'But your only other choice is Thornsteins in Manchester. The extra transportation alone will cost you a fortune and, without being disrespectful, you know the quality is inferior.'

'That's my problem, not yours.'

There was another long silence as Jack contemplated the implications. The teenage boys walked back past the car and, for some unfathomable reason, made the 'Loser' gesture he had seen his daughters do in his presence many times. He thought of chasing them down the street, but remembered he was embroiled in a serious, if unhinged, business discussion.

In this bizarre commercial relationship, Lionel was his largest individual customer. Losing half a weekly order was a big financial blow, but as his mind quickly calculated its implications, he also felt a duty to stand up to bullying. After all, Lionel was behaving so erratically. Surely common sense would dissolve the festering resentment Lionel had nurtured for Solly Fogel for all these years and he'd calm down when he realised it was costing him money to still be angry. Jack knew he had to show unshakeable strength.

'Lionel, do what you want. I have no idea what's going on, but if you want to lessen your order, that's your prerogative. But can I ask you to call off your comedy chicken from performing outside my shops? It demeans us all.'

Jack wondered if this conversation might form the basis of a truce. It would be so good to move on from this incident, even if he was selling Lionel fewer chickens. He would take the hit if it meant no more of these confrontations.

'Consider it done, young man,' Lionel replied chirpily. 'This was, I suppose, what you'd call Phase 1 of my campaign. I have other plans for Chaim the Chicken. Exciting plans, you'll see.'

Chapter 11

'Is that Sonia?' Jack asked later that evening.

His heart was beating much faster than normal. It had been several weeks since his chat with Clive and he had considered phoning most days, but fear of rejection had prevented him.

He thought about her a lot, which was ridiculous, given he knew scant detail about her life. It was her old-fashioned name, Sonia, that had piqued his interest, somehow suggesting she would be different from other women he had ever met. He couldn't track her down on Facebook or Instagram, not that she would have been able to find him if she had tried. Social media was for people who wanted to share their faux happiness and his misery meant he had little he wanted to broadcast.

He did find an out-of-date LinkedIn profile with no profile photo, which revealed little more than that she worked in marketing in the not-for-profit sector and spoke Spanish. He tried to build a narrative for her life but was struggling to give it much depth or vividness. What he did realise was that this introduction seemed to have taken on a significance for him that belied the casual way in which it had been made.

The nastiness of his argument with Lionel galvanised Jack to make the phone call. Still in his car, he stared at the logo on the steering wheel and remembered his grandfather's XJS. If he didn't want to be like his grandfather, why had he bought the same car? The thought made him shudder and he felt the need to speak to Sonia from the safety of his flat.

Later, in his kitchen, he dialled her number and counted the unanswered rings. One, two, three, four ... he had got to eight and was about to hang up, relieved she was not there, when he heard her voice.

'Yes, I am Sonia. Who are you?' She sounded in a rush.

'I am Jack Fogel. I was given your number.'

'I'm sure you were, otherwise how would you be calling?'

'You make a fair point. My brother-in-law Clive plays tennis with your cousin, and he told me that I should phone.'

It sounded desperate when he said it aloud and she burst out laughing.

'Well, that clears everything up. When shall we get married?'

'I'm pretty free next week. But I won't have the criminal checks done by then. Can you wait a bit longer?'

'It's a blow, but it's probably for the best, given you may be a plonker. Anyway, Jack, lovely as it is to plan my future like this, I must finish up at work. Do you just want to ask me out for dinner, and we can get on with the day?'

Jack's heart was thudding noisily against his ribcage. She was so uninhibited and confident.

'Would you like to go out for dinner, Sonia?'

'Oh, that's why you called.' She seemed to be enjoying his awkwardness. 'Of course I would, Jack. I know very little about you other than your brother-in-law Clive has a weak backhand, but I trust my cousin would never give me a dud introduction.'

'I hope I'm more dude than dud.' He was tongue-tied with anticipation and wondered what had impelled him to say something so ridiculous. Sonia's initial spark was replaced with a business-like briskness.

'I'm sure you are, Jack, but I'll have to check that out for myself. Let's make a plan. Do you mind meeting near Shoreditch, it's handy for me? I know a nice place to meet where I can position myself by the door, in case I need to make a quick escape. Next Wednesday at eight o'clock? I'll text you the details.'

'Perfect,' he replied, without even checking if he was free.

'Well, goodbye then, Clive the tennis player's brother-in-law.'

'Most looking forward to meeting you, really I am.'

Adrenalin was making him incoherent and he was now speaking like Yoda. The line went dead as he was in mid-sentence. He was definitely out of practice.

* * *

The intervening week disappeared in a flurry of stress. His excitement at a first date in over six months was dissolved by a mounting to-do list of problem-solving. Jack could not remember another time in his life when he'd had to spend so much time triaging disputes. As he awoke each morning, he would feel the dormant muscles in his flabby abdomen knot and intertwine as if trying to protect him from the inevitable barrage of punches he was about to receive.

The day after his call with Sonia, his mother re-emerged from her ocean voyage and agreed to meet for an early dinner at a local trattoria. Since her husband's death, she had avoided feeding her family as much as she possibly could. Married young, she had been forced to observe the demanding Jewish dining calendar: Friday night dinner, lunches on the festivals and frequent family celebrations. Widowhood heralded the end of this domestic enslavement and Jack's children were raised in the expectation of seeing their grandmother only if a nice restaurant was involved.

When Jack entered Signora Fraquelli's, he was struck by how young his mother looked. Tanned, with russet-dyed hair coiffed to perfection, she was disarmingly happy to see him, immediately arousing his suspicion of an imminent lecture or a financial demand. He often struggled to define their relationship as it had been built on conflicting foundations of love, respect and tension. He admired her enthusiastic interest in friends and family, who saw her as a pragmatic advice-giver on relationships. Indeed, freed from the old-world values of Solly and Phil, she revelled in new connections with interesting people, previously denied to her. As a grandmother, she improved when the children got older. She lacked patience to read stories about moo-cows and disappearing moons to toddlers, but their adolescence made them worth spending time with, and she proved excellent company to her teenage brood.

Jack, however, saw her as an increasingly selfish woman. He had become her provider and she made him feel like a business manager rather than a son. More empathetic to the emotional needs of her daughters, she treated him like another male Fogel, tarnished by the chosen profession of butchering. Indeed, the moment she found her freedom, she forgot that he had lost his. She adored his girls but was increasingly indifferent to his growing feelings of loneliness. Her maternal instinct, as far as Jack was concerned, was little more than financially motivated tolerance.

As it was only 6 p.m. the restaurant was almost empty, and he assumed she must have some other pending social engagement, making this a necessarily quick dinner. That summed up his mother – always something better to do. He was used to her staring over his shoulder mid-conversation, anticipating someone more interesting entering the room.

'Have you asked me here because the early bird supper is cheaper?' he asked as he sat down.

'Actually, Jack, I'm a bit jet-lagged and want an early night. You must remove that enormous chip from your shoulder. I am your mother and why can't I just enjoy being with you instead of you acting like you want to be somewhere else?'

Jack shuddered with a cold blast of guilt. Had he himself become so selfish and forgotten that a social encounter could take place without a questionable motive?

'I'm sorry, Mum. I'm just a bit stressed. The business is not that easy and it's making me tetchy.'

For an instant, Jack contemplated the possibility of nonjudgmental support from his mother, something he had craved since the moment his father died. He relaxed a little and decided to let her regale him with tales of her recent cruises without complaint.

The calm was momentary and, like a needle scratching across a record, he was jolted out of this strange sensation of love. Staring at him suddenly with a gaze of acute disappointment, she asked, 'So why have you upset Lionel Gutterman?'

If he had been chomping on one of the bread sticks from the basket, he would have choked.

'What are you talking about? When have you been talking to him?'

'I've been playing bridge with him and Irene for the last few years now. We have become rather friendly.'

'And you didn't think to tell me?'

Jack felt tears well up in his eyes like an eight-year-old boy being scolded unfairly by an unreasonable parent. He stared behind his mother at a poster for the famous Fellini film *La Dolce Vita*. His life did not feel that sweet right now and his mother was oblivious to how upset he felt.

'Why would I need to, until now?'

'Well, for one thing, his contempt for Dad might have merited a bit of loyalty from you.'

She looked briefly at the menu as if keen to change the subject and then carried on with her mission.

'You know you have really upset him.'

Jack wondered if you were allowed to punch your mother in public. They all live in thrall to their mums in Italy, so probably not, but he did contemplate giving her a discreet kick under the table.

Instead, he put his head in his hands and carried on talking to the tablecloth.

'Are you mad? I know *he* is. I mean, he's just asked me to give him two of my shops and put a kid in a chicken costume outside their entrance to intimidate my customers. Why would you listen to what he wants to say? He has declared war on us, and he wants me to be miserable.'

His mother was unmoved and, instead of softening, she carried on her advocacy for Lionel.

'You know, I feel sorry for him. Your grandfather and father treated him terribly. We owe it to him to make amends. He told me everything when he phoned me today.'

Jack marvelled at Lionel's tenacity in trying to find new angles of attack. *Et tu, Mum?* Betrayed by the woman who bore him. His mind was pirouetting from one random irritated thought to the next. Maybe he would have to kidnap Lionel's grandchildren and brainwash them in retaliation. Reasonable discourse was an increasingly unrealistic option in this unfolding nightmare.

'Did he send you here to bargain with me? Please tell me the truth.'

Jack leant back as casually as he could to try to suggest that he didn't blame her for her treachery if she confessed the truth. He thought of ordering a new birth certificate and claiming he was an orphan.

'Don't be silly, darling. I'm here because I've missed you. But you need to make peace with Lionel and give him at least some of what he wants. You have to put right the injustice that was done to him by your family.'

'Mum. You need to make some choices about where your loyalty lies. Do you need a clue? Your children are a good starting point.'

Stephanie scrunched up the linen napkin that was lying pristine on her plate. Now it was her turn to get angry.

'Jack, don't lecture me, there's a good boy. As I see it, you owe your business rival some recompense for how he has been treated by the Fogels. It's well within your power, so get over your pride. You are not your father, please don't behave as he would have done. Now, enough of this. I want to tell you about my cruise and all about Kurt's new book, which I am helping him publish.'

She began to tell a circuitous story about Kurt's new academic study, the seminal treatise on the history of Bridge. There was little interesting independent research on the subject, so she was going to help him publish, which in turn was an overt request to Jack to help secure the funding for the project. Jack was trying to process that his mother's new friendship was another flank on which he could be attacked. It was clear that she was not keen to revisit the fractious conversation and was by now looking for photos on her phone, keen to show Jack where she had enjoyed the best cocktails on her trip. He smiled obediently, wishing he was elsewhere.

* * *

Parents' evening the next night was not much better. He and Ali were committed to showing unity in front of the girls and attended concerts and celebrations with an amicable veneer. The girls were not entirely fooled by their act but played their part in maintaining the appearance of family togetherness. Recently the facade had started to crack under the strain of teenage anxiety and Jack worried this simple trip to Isobel's school to select her A levels would become another opportunity to question his parental competence.

This was the first time Isobel had accompanied her parents. Previously, she had heard separate accounts of her good reports; now she had to sit between them and worry if their latent anger with each other was going to unravel in front of Madame Moreau, her French teacher. The evening started unfortunately with a petulant spat as Jack met them a fraction late at the entrance to the school. Ali, clearly on edge, avoided giving him her customary polite kiss on the cheek.

'Couldn't you have been on time?' she snarled. Jack looked at his watch and shook his head.

'I am a minute late. I'm sure the teachers haven't gone home yet.' He turned to Isobel, who was looking down the street as if waiting to be rescued. 'Hi, sweetheart, ready to be embarrassed by your parents?'

'Jack. It would be best for us all if you try to keep your talking to a minimum tonight.'

Before he could remonstrate with Ali, they strode off without him towards the dining hall. Jack decided it was best thereafter to do very little other than listen to the rhapsodic praise of the teachers wowed by Isobel's academic prowess. Each in turn felt that she could study their subject to the highest level at university. It was all going so well until the last conversation, with Dr Dexter, Isobel's physics master, whose handshake was so limp it could be described as wilting. Jack could see from Ali's strained expression that she had already dismissed him because of the dull subject he taught.

'You know, Isobel is the best physicist in the year. She has a remarkable gift for the subject,' he began with surprising enthusiasm.

It was as if he had waited all night for this moment and felt a duty to the Physicists' Guild to accurately convey the specialness of her potential. Isobel smiled awkwardly, seemingly excited by the revelation. The news was an inconvenience to Ali, who had decided her daughter was destined to be a linguist at Oxford and the Sorbonne. She needed to shut this nonsense down.

'Well, that's wonderful to hear. If only she could do seven subjects! She has her heart set on language and literature moving forward.'

Jack was sure he could sense Isobel's confusion and intervened.

'I think Isobel should think really hard about what she wants to do for herself. She clearly has an equal ability with the Sciences and the Arts.'

Dr Dexter's face lit up with hope that she would not be lost to pointless literature and might spend meaningful days contemplating black holes. He was about to try and make the case when Ali turned angrily on her ex-husband and declared, 'Isobel knows what she wants. Don't contradict it and cause her stress.'

'Isobel has a plan? Or do you have a plan for Isobel?'

'What does that mean?'

'It means we are blessed with a clever daughter. Let's have the decency to allow her to consider her future without our prejudices.'

Jack was arguing so much these days that he had lost all sense of whether he was shouting. Clearly, he had raised his voice because the people in the queue behind had stopped talking, eavesdropping on this much more interesting conversation.

Dr Dexter, unused to evincing such passion when discussing physics, turned to Isobel and cautiously asked, 'Will you at least give what I have said some thought, please?'

She nodded and rose from her chair, desperate to flee the scene. Ali trotted after her without looking back, leaving Jack compelled to say something polite to the petrified teacher.

'Well, that went well, I think. Same time next year?'

Dr Dexter smiled wanly, and Jack sat briefly in silence before trudging out of the hall, his pride replaced by another reminder of his parental ineptitude. They were not waiting for him anywhere and he walked alone to his car. He was only trying to do the right thing for Isobel, but wondered if that was how it would be remembered the next day. He sighed in anticipation of the angry text he would inevitably receive from Ali and started to compose in his head an equally petulant response.

Pulling out of the parking space, his reverie was obliterated by the sound of his front bumper grazing the car in front and the tinkle of breaking glass. He looked around furtively to see if there were witnesses to what had happened. The pavement was empty and with a mixture of shame and resentment, he drove off, refusing to round off a bad evening with a hefty garage bill.

* * *

'Good news, Channel 4 may want a meeting to discuss "Widgets".' Jack tried to hear what his friend Mike Gibson was saying, but factory noise made conversation difficult.

'That's fantastic,' he shouted above the collective shriek of terrified chickens.

'I can't hear you. It sounds like you're on a battlefield,' Mike replied. 'Call me back when you've done your slaughter for the day.'

His old friend's production company, Smash & Grab, was helping him with its development, and they were ready to progress the project to the next stage, much to Jack's excitement. He would not normally take a call while prowling the production line, but he had grown increasingly anxious for news on the progress of his TV project. Jack marched back to his office and shut the door, but Mike's phone went straight to voicemail. He left a message and then swore out loud, knowing it might take another two days to finish the conversation with one of the busiest producers in TV. His writing was a crucial release from the quotidian grind of his business and personal misfortunes. For Mike, it was just one of many exciting projects and sometimes Jack wondered if all the help was simply a philanthropic gesture with no expectation of success. Still, Channel 4 had been their agreed first choice broadcaster, so maybe he was about to receive some unaccustomed good fortune.

Jack was desperate not to be stressed. He had ensured a relatively light work schedule so he could get home and prepare himself for his first date with Sonia. His expectations had grown, like Japanese knotweed, dangerously out of control, and he had a bizarre sensation that positive change was imminent. The condition of his stomach was always a reliable gauge of his state of mind. Cramping knots had temporarily been replaced by the fluttering wings of invisible butterflies in anticipation of his evening.

There were still some jolts of reality to contend with. He had received another letter from Frank Stone's lawyer telling him that he had evidence of 'systemic discrimination within Fogel's Chickens'. Who, apart from the chickens themselves, had been discriminated against, Jack wondered? It was all a ploy for a compensatory payment for Frank, who had been signed off work due to the 'emotional trauma of premature retirement'. Jack could not believe that such flagrant fiction could result in a potential damages settlement and his resolve hardened not to succumb to opportunist blackmail.

He had a stack of other issues. His accountant wanted a meeting, there was a problem with his tax return. One of the lorries needed replacing quicker than he had expected. He had found out from Isobel that Natalie had split up with her boyfriend and was devastated. His supplier of beef products wanted to talk about putting up his prices. Gadi and Stacey wanted to meet to discuss their plans for the restaurants and had ominously informed him that they expected 'a resolution or a release from their contracts'. He sent them yet another stalling email, knowing that avoidance was not a sustainable strategy.

By early afternoon, he was exhausted by the pettiness of all these arguments and decided to drive home and have a go at meditating to acquire some inner peace. After attaining nirvana, he would enjoy a long bath and begin the tricky decision of wardrobe and aftershave selection.

He was about to log off for the day when he noticed that an email from Lionel Gutterman had arrived in his inbox, titled '*Thought you'd want to know*'. Jack considered ignoring it, but what if it contained the joyous news that he was retiring to his mock-Tudor hacienda in Marbella and wanted to apologise?

Sadly, this was not the case, and the draft of a newspaper ad filled his screen. Chaim the Chicken was making his debut in *The Jewish Chronicle* as a cartoon character with bright yellow feathers and a lopsided grin that made him look in need of urgent dental work. He was holding a placard explaining that all Gutterman's chickens were 20% cheaper than Fogels. The headline was similarly unsubtle.

TO BRING OUR CUSTOMERS THE BEST, SOMETIMES WE NEED TO RUFFLE A FEW FEATHERS

He stared at the ad in disbelief. What on earth was the idiot doing now? It seemed the phoney war was over, and Lionel had begun his blitz. Jack couldn't understand how he suddenly had an enemy with such determination to create pointless mayhem. Now, however, was not the time to confront this moron. No, he was going to go home and practise deep breathing so that when he met Sonia Lewis, this beguiling new presence in his most mundane life, she would see him as the person he wanted to be. Not the poor bastard being stalked by a vengeful chicken called Chaim.

Chapter 12

The evening did not begin well as he sat waiting for Sonia in New Leaf, a Danish vegan restaurant in Brick Lane. The steampunk chrome chandeliers emitted a watery magnolia light, and he struggled to read his newspaper. Craning forward to absorb the illumination of flickering tea lights on the table and engrossed in a TV review, he sniffed a charcoal smoky smell, quickly realising that the pages had caught fire. A single, growing flame was making its way toward his hands.

Instinctively, he dropped the smouldering paper on to the antique wooden floor and threw his glass of water on it, managing only to douse his khaki chinos with a damp patch that suggested a major incontinence problem. By now, a waiter was stamping on the smoking *Evening Standard*, extinguishing its tiny flames and releasing charred black remnants of carbonised paper that floated upwards like storm clouds. People on the adjacent tables were snickering and Jack half expected sarcastic applause. For some reason, he decided to take a small bow to hide his embarrassment. As he straightened up from the theatrical gesture, Sonia Lewis was standing in front of him looking slightly confused.

'Was there an article in there you didn't like?' she enquired with a broad smile. Jack tried to compose himself by inhaling deeply. He sucked in the smoky remnants of his newspaper barbeque and coughed, wondering how much of the incident she had seen.

'Hello, you must be Sonia. I'm Jack the Arsonist. As a matter of interest, how long have you been here?'

'Long enough to enjoy the floor show. I don't think the fire brigade are going to be recruiting you any time soon.'

Jack motioned towards their table, not knowing what the protocol was at such a moment, he was so out of practice. He leant forward to give her a kiss on the cheek, which she did not expect, and her nose grazed his eye as she pulled away.

'Shall we start again then?' she asked as she watched him place a napkin on his lap to hide the damp patch spreading like an oil slick across his crotch.

'Yes please. I was hoping to make you laugh with my conversation, not my clumsiness.'

Sonia looked at him without saying anything. For a moment, they stared across the table, evaluating each other in the dusky pallor of the poorly lit restaurant. There was an intensity in the moment that made Jack optimistically wonder if she was also excited about the potential of this liaison.

He was not very observant, but he tried in his head to list the merits of her features, even if he could not describe the deep-blue pools of her eyes like they would in a book. She was dressed casually in skinny jeans, boots and an orange roll-neck woollen sweater; her hair was black, ringleted and shoulder-length. Most importantly for Jack, she seemed to be constantly smiling. He drew a hasty conclusion that his date for the evening was down-to-earth and kind, given she was looking back at him with an expression of mild confusion rather than contempt. His mind was now racing out of control, and he got lost in a narrative in which he found a lifetime of joy with her and a gingerbread cottage in the woods to boot. Sonia cleared her throat with a stagy cough to wake him from his fantasising.

'Have I lost you to your thoughts?' she asked gently.

'Sorry, Sonia. I was composing myself after a recent near-death experience. It really is lovely to meet you and I hope that doesn't sound too forward.'

'No, it's very nice to hear. Shall we look at the menu and order so we can get on with finding out a bit about each other?'

'Lovely idea. I hope it's plastic. I'd hate to start the pyrotechnics again.'

* * *

'You need to know I can't abide liars. I value being true to your feelings above everything. What about you?' Sonia asked quietly as she sipped her pink gin and tonic, garnished with what looked to Jack like potpourri.

This bold statement was delivered so casually, she could have been asking if he liked the restaurant's decor. Jack was unprepared for such forthrightness, still deliberating what to choose from the complex and inhospitable menu in front of him. He was a conservative eater and felt a mixture of panic and incredulity at the esoteric options. Nervous and starving, a slab of succulent red meat would have suited him rather than the agonising deliberation between a main course of 'Green bean, bronze fennel, beurre blanc' and 'Corn pearls, grilled corn and liquorice' with a side of either 'soy meringue' or 'yakitori beetroot'.

'Then let me start with an admission,' Jack ventured carefully.

'And what is that?'

'This may not be my ideal choice of restaurant.'

Sonia nodded, unfazed, as if appreciating his plight.

'I'm sorry, I should have told you I was a vegan.'

'Well, with you being so honest and all. It would have given me a chance to have a bigger lunch. I hadn't really looked closely where we were meeting.'

'You're a carnivore, I presume?'

Jack wondered if she was toying with him and was terrified the evening would now end before his plant-based starter had even arrived. Sonia had told him two things – her life contained no meat or dairy and was underpinned by a commitment to telling the truth. Unfortunately, he was a butcher for whom many aspects of his life were something of a lie. He didn't want her to find this out before she had at least experienced some redeeming qualities in him, even if he couldn't remember what they were. Surely a successful relationship could be based on her acceptance that his profession was not who he was as a person.

'I can't fib, I do eat meat from time to time.'

He sounded like a sinning Catholic in the confessional. He'd never sought absolution for his diet before and for a moment remembered his grandfather's imprecation that you could never trust a vegetarian. Solly would be throwing left hooks angrily if he was sitting with him now in trendy East London's finest vegan restaurant. Ironically, it was about a hundred yards from Solly's original *shecht* shop where, ninety years ago, he would slit chicken throats while his customers waited.

'Don't worry, Jack. I'm not a militant vegan. I would never lecture anyone who had a different view to me on what they eat. Everyone must do what they want to in life as long as they are true to themselves. That's my mantra. Anyway, it's not meat eaters who bother me. It's the way in which it's produced that I find really upsetting. Well, what would you expect me to say? I mean, I have a vegan café and love talking about food. I don't even know what you do, Jack. I bet it's something worthwhile. You look like a really good bloke.'

Jack's heart started to rumba in excited response to the positive character assessment he had just received. The adrenal surge forced a panicky reply that came from the furthest point away from his conscience.

'Oh, I'm very dull. I run the family property business. Not worth talking about. But I'm also developing a TV series. Yes, TV production has always been my first love.'

So much for the truth then.

* * *

'I was married for five years. I wanted children. He didn't have the heart to tell me that he didn't want a family. He also forgot to tell me the bit about being more attracted to men. Came as a bit of a shock when he left me for a social worker called Stephen.'

'Oh, I'm so sorry. I can only imagine how distressing that must have been. Mind you, my wife left me also, for a terrible actor, just in case you wanted to claim all the glory tonight.'

Jack had just taken a mouthful of his starter, which looked like it was made from a rain forest and tasted like a lettuce dipped in custard.

'I'm sorry too. How did that work out for her?' Sonia asked solicitously.

'Not well. He never improved as an actor.'

'Are they still together?'

'No, she's had several more unsuccessful relationships. We're just about OK, so long as I let her remind me of my inadequacies as a father. Did your failed marriage make you so open and honest?'

'*Failed* is a bit strong, if you don't mind. "Misaligned expectations" is how we like to refer to it these days. What can I say? I just want people I care about to not hide things or avoid difficult conversations. I suspect it's because my liberal Jewish Dad always taught me to be true to my beliefs.'

'You tell me about your liberal Jewish background and then I can tell you about my staunchly conservative one,' he heard himself say, immediately worrying he had made a mistake alluding to his family in a way that would require explanation. He tried to qualify this last statement. 'You are much more interesting than me, I assure you.'

'Well, if that's the case, this is going to be a short-lived relationship,' Sonia replied with what he thought was a defiant look in her eyes, but maybe was just squinting caused by the poor light.

'All right. I'll make something juicy up if that's what it takes.'

'You're not really getting the hang of this "tell the truth" principle of mine, are you?'

'Give me time, Sonia. Give me time.'

* * *

Suddenly it was 11 p.m. as Sonia ordered an Uber, and the waiter brought the bill in what seemed a biodegradable hessian ashtray but was apparently chicory, lime and mint chocolate shavings. Three hours of wonderful conversation and the date had exceeded the huge expectations that he had created.

'Do you think you can eat the bill as well?' Jack asked, reaching for it instinctively. Sonia frowned and hurriedly produced her purse from her bag.

'Don't blow all that effort you've made, Jack, by a crude display of chauvinism. We go Dutch on this meal.'

'What do you take me for?' he rebutted. 'I was just going to make sure I didn't overpay for my dessert. I think some of the strawberry foam had evaporated by the time it arrived and I don't want to pay full price. Of course we're going Dutch, even though I forgot my clogs.'

His confidence had been loosened by the gin and tonic and bottle of wine they had enjoyed with the meal, and he managed to find plenty of topics about which he didn't have to lie: his daughters, his sisters, his mother, and his struggles to understand who he was alongside these powerful women.

She was particularly sympathetic when he acknowledged his lack of emotional connection with the girls. He adored them but couldn't crack the mystery of their respective genetic codes. Natalie seemed a perfect clone of her mother, combining charm and intelligence with a driven vision of her future. He worried she saw him through the eyes of her mother, and the lens was distorted. Isobel was more enigmatic. He sensed they shared a similar outlook, he just could not quite prove it yet. Sonia was fascinated by these parenting dilemmas and listened without giving an unsolicited opinion.

He spoke about his mother and sisters with a loving if irreverent affection. He described Tracy as a wise older sister engaged in a competitive 'who's the best shrink' marriage with the equally brilliant Clive. He mocked the Tory affectation of his formidable younger sister, Karen, who used her barrister's debating skill in her quest for political power, making it clear he had little time for her world view. As for his mother, he tried to maintain some balance in describing her affectations, choice of boyfriends and need for continual funds. Sonia laughed when he explained that for his mother, social mobility was moving her table nearer to the captain's each time she went on a cruise.

Finally, he told her about his latest idea for a TV sitcom, neglecting to mention that it was his first foray back into that world for twenty years. He was fortunate that, as a teenager, she had loved the Channel 4 programme he worked on, *What Choice Do I Have?* He intimated there had been further work in television before conceiving the idea for 'Widgets', eliding the details of the intervening years through a series of vague references to some of his property business interests. On reflection later, he concluded that he had adroitly ushered the conversation away from revealing what he really did for a living. For the first time in ages, the word 'chicken' did not crop up.

He tried to listen more than he spoke and his reward, significant biographical detail, made him like her even more. Witty, modest, perceptive, independent, resilient, compassionate, kind. Jack had adjectives aplenty to tell Tracy when she inevitably called first thing in the morning to find out how things had gone.

Sonia was an only child. Her mother had tragically died when she was very young, and she had been raised by her father and her maternal grandmother. Robert Lewis was a headmaster who had become a senior official in a national teaching union. He had a sense of rectitude that while liberal in outlook was also fuelled by a self-belief that he was always right. Growing up, he doted on his daughter, but also lectured her continually to stick up for what she believed in and be true to herself. Her grandmother was a much more calming influence whose homespun wisdom was a balance of insight and malapropism, her favourite advice being: *Remember, sweetheart, to smile because life is not always a piece of cheesecake.*

She grew up in West London, away from the North London ghetto of Jack's childhood. She studied psychology and Spanish at university and sang in a band, which carried on semi-professionally for a couple of years after they graduated. It was called 'Painting Liberty' and they released a single, 'She Stoops to Nothing', which once got played on Radio 1. She lived with the lead singer for a couple of years until he became a solicitor and moved to Manchester. She worked for over ten years for various charities and NGOs in the UK, a couple of years in Barcelona and eighteen months in Chile. She taught yoga, wrote a food blog and made jewellery, which she sold online.

She was married and divorced. She was close to her father and saw him and his new wife regularly. Proud of her Jewish heritage, she was not that interested in religion. At eighteen she became a vegetarian, in her mid-twenties a vegan who celebrated the infinite possibilities creative cooking could provide. To mark her thirtieth birthday, she published a vegan dessert cookbook. When she turned thirty-six, she decided to leave her marketing role and put all her available money (a small inheritance from her beloved grandmother) into opening a café in Shoreditch.

Open from 7.30 a.m. to 5 p.m., it was intended to be a second home for its loyal customers. Everything produced on the premises, all ingredients naturally sourced, it wasn't just a place to eat, you could work there and even book a small anteroom for meetings. At lunchtimes, musicians gave recitals, entrepreneurs took part in debates about ethical business challenges, authors read from their new books. It was a community for like-minded individuals to demonstrate that her grandmother was right. Smile at your customers and you might sell a bit more vegan cheesecake.

She worked long hours, starting at 5.30 a.m., and made little money, though she hardly cared. For Sonia, life needed purpose and meaning and she had finally found its conduit in her fledgling business. Her friends worried that she might be lonely, but she would tell them that she had coffee with hundreds of lovely friends every week. And she charged them for the privilege. The café was called Sally's and was named after her grandmother. When she told him this, he wondered if the one-letter difference in names between her grandmother Sally and his grandfather Solly was some sort of cosmic sign of their compatibility?

She had little time for dating, but there was something mysterious about how Jack had been described that had created irrational expectation for her too. Her cousin had told her, '*I don't know what he does, but he is apparently a really good person*'. She loved this description, although its vagueness stemmed from her cousin deliberately omitting to tell her the truth about Jack's business, which he knew. Sonia was therefore intrigued by the prospect of this supposedly worthy person, who she hoped was also funny and interesting. She was delighted that he seemed warm, homely and self-deprecating and was charmingly cute in his desire to impress.

As they moved outside the restaurant and walked toward Sonia's waiting Uber, she took his arm. Jack tried to stay calm but felt compelled to make a declaration at the same time.

'Sonia, I'm forty-six, you know. Hard to believe, but I use a very expensive moisturiser.'

'Jack, I'm thirty-eight and my moisturiser is made in Brighton by a commune of Druids. Why are we talking skincare regimes?'

'Because I think I'm too old to muck around hiding how I feel. I've realised that now.'

'How do you feel then?'

Jack stopped and turned to face her.

'Like I really want to see you again. I've had the best evening in ages.'

'We're not hanging around, are we? All right, Romeo, I have loved meeting you and would love to see you again too.'

'Excellent. When can I see you again? This weekend, before you change your mind?'

'Sadly, I'm working. I have to cater a party on Sunday, and I'm very nervous as I've never done one before. Not that I told the client that.'

Jack, swept away with excitement, did not see her work schedule as an impediment, but rather an opportunity to impress her further.

'Do you need some extra help? I can be a waiter if you like. When I was a student, I worked one summer at The Savoy. I was pretty good at it, I seem to remember.'

The lies were tumbling out now in the pursuit of another date. His wedding reception had been at The Savoy but he'd never waited on a table in any establishment. Some unconscious impulse was making him invent a backstory that would somehow mitigate his current disappointment in how things had turned out.

'Are you sure? I thought you had a life?'

How had he convinced her of that, he wondered.

'Nope, I'm free on Sunday and can even bring my own corkscrew.'

'That's fine. We'll provide you with everything. Just a black T-shirt and black jeans, please, and a steady hand.'

'I rock that look. I'll slick my hair back and might even burst into a couple of choruses of "Greased Lightning".'

'I'm regretting this already.'

'You have nothing to worry about. *Professional* is my middle name. Well, its Nathaniel, come to mention it.'

He was talking rubbish now and he told himself to shut up. As she opened the cab door, she stared at him with a slightly perplexed look.

'Can I trust you, Jack Fogel? Can I trust you?' She leant forward and kissed him gently on the lips. It was too short to signal intent, but it caused Jack's heart to perform a vigorous dance of expectation once more.

'Of course you can,' he whispered unconvincingly.

Chapter 13

A much happier Jack uncharacteristically overslept after his successful date. As he stood in the shower, he realised that his stomach was not cramping in anticipation of the day's miserable exertions. Perhaps his life was going to improve, and he could finally resolve its disparate conflicts? As he was putting on his sweatshirt and jeans, a shaft of spring sunshine snuck through his curtains and danced across the bedroom wall, lightening his mood further. Sonia liked him. He liked Sonia. Everyone else could go away.

Having told her that he was too old for games, he decided to text immediately, unable to contain his excitement. He found a picture of a young, handsome Elvis Presley in black jeans and T-shirt.

HAD A GREAT TIME.
THIS IS WHAT I'LL LOOK LIKE ON SUNDAY xx

Jack pressed send, believing the message was a perfect continuation of the amiable flirtation from the night before. He remembered her gorgeous smile as she pulled off in the taxi, confident she felt the same way as him.

By 6 p.m. he had reached for paracetamol in a forlorn hope that the stabbing gut pain would lessen. Things had not panned out as he had hoped, both in terms of the time it had taken her to reply and the nature of the response. He realised that running a thriving café would make her too busy to banter during a normal working day, but was nevertheless disappointed to have heard nothing back. Maybe he had misread politeness for enthusiasm? Eventually, in the late afternoon, he received the brief message:

NOT SURE?

What was she not sure about? Him or his joke? He replied immediately, unwilling to guess the appropriate delay required to make up for his poor opening salvo.

I CAN PUT LESS GEL IN MY HAIR.
DON'T WORRY I WON'T EMBARRASS YOU.

Then, as an afterthought, remembering a conversation with one of his daughters in which emojis were designated mandatory for any meaningful chat, he sent one more text.

 x

As soon as he pressed send, he worried he was coming across as an idiot, although when did SMS constitute a meaningful insight into the inner workings of your soul? Clearly, Sonia was not deliberating with the same anxiety, as she texted back instantaneously.

I AM SURE YOU WILL BE FINE. BTW, I HATE EMOJIS. Sx

Curt and admonishing but with a kiss, he couldn't decide if he had made things worse. This is why he hated modern dating; it was like an elaborate game of chess in which you had to plan your moves with guile. While a pragmatist not a romantic, the feeling that he had to control his emotions in case they caused a bad reaction just made him feel sadder.

He had spent the day trying to fight back against Lionel, emboldened by his post-date optimism. Sitting at his desk, he had studied the Gutterman's ad about to appear in *The Jewish Chronicle*.

It was an open declaration of war. Jewish newspapers used to be a hub for communal debate that often resulted in *broigus,* a Yiddish word to describe the bitter discord that only Jews could inflict on one another. By now, Lionel obviously wanted a *broigus* and Jack intended to give him one of such rancour it would be talked about for generations to come.

He could hear his grandfather whispering from the afterlife some mangled form of scripture in his ear: *The lord giveth and you must give a hiding to whoever tries to taketh it away.* The more he stared at the ad, the angrier he became. Leather-skinned Lionel was trying to disturb the fragile equilibrium of his existence. Why should he have to accept this? Jack fancied himself as a bit of a copywriter, and what limited marketing the business had done in the past was the result of his clever penmanship. *To hell with this petty war of words*, he thought, *time to get down in the mud*.

He called Ray Collins, another loyal lieutenant, into his office. Nicknamed 'Professor Poultry' in the business, he was the go-to person for any questions about chicken production, an expertise rarely lauded outside the factory walls. Jack had a hypothesis he wanted to test.

'Look at this outrageous ad from Gutterman's. They're trying to attack us, and I won't stand for it any longer.'

Ray, a laconic man, merely shrugged his shoulders, indifferent to the significance of an offer for cheaper chickens from a rival. He was always wary about interactions with his boss. As professional as they were, he could sense Jack's continual disappointment at having to talk about the intricacies of kosher slaughter. Struggling for a reply, he muttered, 'I'm not sure how you think I can help? How you run the business is your choice.'

Jack was not listening and paced his cramped office as if pondering some complex philosophical issue. Ray stared at his filthy rubber boots and wished he wasn't there, finding this social interaction unnecessarily uncomfortable. Eventually, Jack stopped shuffling back and forth and outlined his argument.

'So, as you know, Lionel is ordering less chickens from us and has gone to Thornsteins in Manchester, and what is it that you always say about their chicken?'

Before Ray could answer, Jack carried on with his enthusiastic rhetoric.

'You always tell me that their birds are not left to spin as long as ours after they've been washed and salted. What does that mean? I'll tell you what that means. It means we have got him.'

Ray was thoroughly bemused and wondered why Jack was talking to himself. Got who? For what? And why did he have to be involved?

With the enthusiasm of a child showing a parent his latest artwork, Jack turned over the A4 pad of paper on his desk, to reveal a rectangular layout of a press ad. In black biro, dot capitals, he had written:

WITH A FOGEL CHICKEN, YOU GET 20% LESS WATER THAN OUR NEAREST RIVAL

'All I need you to tell me is whether it's true.'

Panic rose like a geyser, and Ray did not know how to respond. On the production line, he supervised his team calmly and knew what he was doing. But Jack seemed obsessed with attacking not just Lionel Gutterman but a rival business, and this felt serious. He knew his birds were less watery, but was it by five or fifty per cent? Not even the Almighty knew the answer to that existential question. Professional pride made him unwilling to admit uncertainty to Jack and in the end, he gave up resistance.

'Yes, it's true, Jack. Bang on.'

Ray just wanted to get out of the tiny office, whose walls seemed to be closing in on him. Besides, he thought, peeking at the ad again, the headline was terribly complicated. Jack was oblivious and carried on outlining his strategy as if in some revenge-fuelled trance.

'The thing is, Ray, in a war there are always going to be unintended casualties. The genius of this ad is that it will encourage Gutterman's customers to ask for our birds in his shops. That will piss him off no end. And do you know what, even if it's a bit exaggerated, by the time they complain, we'll stop running it. Well, thanks, Ray, you've been an enormous help.'

Alone and triumphant, Jack sat down at his desk, cracked his knuckles and, with venomous enthusiasm, began to draft some accompanying copy.

* * *

The next morning, he received a call from the advertising manager at *The Jewish Chronicle*. Overnight, he had briefed a designer to create an ad that was 'graphically arresting, modern and unmissable', as if commissioning a major piece of artwork. The designer duly obliged with a clever use of orange and black typeface, giving the ad the confidence that Jack was looking for. Delighted, he booked a page within a few minutes of the copy deadline.

He didn't catch her name as she spoke so quietly, but it sounded like Karen, Sharon or maybe even Darren. Whatever it was, she was clearly very young and nervous of confrontation.

'How can I help you?' he asked brusquely.

'It's about the ad you've just booked,' she mumbled.

'You know, I would never have guessed.'

'Well, I'm sorry if I have surprised you,' Karen-Sharon-Darren replied politely in response to his petulant sarcasm. 'I don't want to upset you, but I'm not sure we can run it, I'm afraid.'

'Whyever not? It's rather good, don't you think?'

Why was he being such a git? He didn't want to be that sort of person.

'The thing is, we have an ad from a similar business and I'm not sure that it would be ethical for us to take it, on the basis that you booked yours second.'

'I assume you are referring to Lionel Gutterman's unprovoked assault on my business.'

Jack was aware that he sounded very self-important.

'I am not at liberty to disclose our other advertisers,' she replied with as much defiance as the squeak in her voice would allow.

'Of course I know it's a Gutterman's ad. That's why I've booked mine in response. Now, please can we just run it without any more discussion.'

'The thing is, Mr Fogel, the editor has made his decision and he can pull any ad he's not happy with. He doesn't believe in causing communal arguments.'

'But he is happy to ruin my business at a whim?'

Jack was standing, fists clenched, feeling the bilious release in his long-suffering stomach. By now, he didn't really care about what impact his ad would have; it was rather the pain of defeat in a skirmish with Lionel.

'I am sorry, Mr Fogel, really I am.'

'I bet you are.'

'We just can't afford to offend any of our important shareholders.'

'Who are you talking about?'

Of course, Jack knew the answer without having to wait to hear it from this unfortunate emissary, unfairly given the responsibility for revealing this latest Gutterman triumph. The bastard had bought shares in a paper to spite him now. The ensuing silence was punctuated by Jack's pompous retort.

'Well, *The Jewish Chronicle*'s loss will most certainly be the *Jewish News*'s gain.' Could he have sounded more ridiculous?

Chapter 14

Thursday night was always the most popular night in Clucks, with two full sittings guaranteed as a largely Jewish clientele celebrated the end of the working week. For Jack, this promised to be a most unusual gathering, surrounded by his mother, two sisters and younger daughter, Isobel. Indeed, the concept of a family conference was very rare and had not really taken place since the disastrous afternoon at his father's will-reading twenty years previously when his future happiness was eviscerated.

Karen had called him in the afternoon and announced that a meeting was needed to discuss her political future and its implications for the family. Attendance was not optional. She suggested Clucks as a venue because '*I am unlikely to be spotted by any political enemies there*'. Jack knew this was an insult of some sort, but couldn't be exactly sure why, given that she had never been to either of his restaurants. He was meant to be having a quiet dinner with Isobel and didn't want to let her down. She was, however, thrilled to be included in the family debate.

He arrived last. To get to the table, however, he had to negotiate another confrontation with Stacey, who he tried to avoid at the door. She saw him immediately and strode towards him with menace.

'Whoa there, jittery Jack. You weren't trying to avoid me, were you?'

'As if, Stacey. A trip to Clucks wouldn't be the same without being attacked by you. Look, I've just come for a quiet family catch-up. Can we speak tomorrow?'

'Well, that depends if you're going to actually come back to us on any of the issues you're so carefully avoiding. I'm prepared to wage email and text *jihad* against you if that's what it takes to get an answer.'

Jack said nothing, thinking the best strategy was to carry on moving as she spoke, and he tried to weave between the tables as quickly as he could. Unfortunately, he brushed a customer's coat off her chair as he passed, so he had to stop to apologise. Stacey stood close to him, smiling at his unsuccessful attempt to escape. She touched his elbow lightly to move him on.

'Come on, Mr Fogel. Let's leave these nice people to enjoy their meal. Now, we don't want you running off again. I'll show you to your table.'

Her face rearranged into a beatific smile, and he felt her grip tighten and the sharp pain of her steak-knife-sharp nails digging into his arm. When they got to the table, she transformed into a different person for his unsuspecting family.

'Well, a huge hello to the Fogel clan. What a huge pleasure to finally meet you all together, and let me welcome you to Clucks. I am Stacey Blor, the manager, and my lovely husband, Gadi, is our brilliant chef.'

Jack hoped that this wouldn't be a long conversation, but Karen unfortunately felt the need to respond on behalf of them all, as if a visiting dignitary.

'It is so nice to be here. I'm Jack's sister Karen, and you have our deepest sympathy. I mean having Jack as a partner in a restaurant. I don't know how you don't try to poison his food.'

Jack didn't have the energy to defend himself. Instead, he rubbed his wounded arm, which Stacey had just released from her fierce grip. She was carrying on her offensive while maintaining a veneer of syrupy charm.

'Now, now. I'm lucky to work with such a considerate person as Jack. He always has our best interests at heart.'

She patted his arm in what seemed a gesture of affection but was really the opportunity to pinch him quickly once more. Before Jack could say anything, Karen made things worse by asking Stacey another question.

'Honestly, you and Gadi have done such a great job here. What a buzzing restaurant this is. But tell me, Stacey, why has it got a ridiculous name like Clucks, which can only have been Jack's idea? You should call it Gadi's, or something like that. Give it some personality. Let him have some recognition.'

Stacey smiled knowingly at Jack as she replied, 'It's funny you should say that – it's exactly what Gadi and I think. We're trying to persuade Jack, but he doesn't seem to agree, and we don't want to cause any upset.'

Stephanie did not want to be left out and turned to him, wagging a finger in admonishment: 'Jack. Jack. Jack. When will you ever learn that you don't always know all the answers?'

Stacey's work was done, and she had been given a further glimpse of Jack's vulnerability. This battle was not over. She went round the table and shook everyone's hand, placing her free hand on a shoulder or an arm to accentuate her friendliness.

'I'll leave you to discuss this without me. Whatever you lovely people think is best will be good enough for me and Gadi.'

When she had gone, Tracy said to Jack, 'Well, she seems lovely. You must feel lucky to have someone like that running your restaurant.'

There was momentary lull and then Isobel looked at her father and said, 'Dad. Don't be a tosser. You should do what she says.'

* * *

The Fogel family, secreted at the back of the restaurant, were sitting round a large table, groaning with salads, Iraqi flatbreads and a large tray of sauce-smeared and sticky Chicken Aleppo. For a short period of time, the conversation was free from barbs or put-downs. Jack felt it safest to remain silent and let the discussion of mundane family life carry on around him without risking an intervention likely to cause offence. When the plates had been cleared, Karen decided it was time to begin the formal agenda for the evening.

'So, I'm sure you'll be wondering why we are here tonight,' she began, and was immediately interrupted by Tracy.

'Is it because you want us to vote for you? It'll be tricky, as we don't live in the constituency.'

Stephanie made a strange sucking noise through her teeth that signified irritation whenever anyone tried to criticise Karen.

'Can you please afford your sister some respect. She is trying to do something great here. Go on, darling, and Jack, for God's sake, no attempts at humour.'

'As if I ever could be funny, Mum. Karen, I am ready to receive my instructions. Would you like me to stamp pro-Brexit messages on every chicken, if it helps?'

'That's just it,' said Karen icily, 'we need to keep the chickens very much in the background, if you don't mind.'

'Surely you're not going to smack the chicken thigh that feeds you, Karen?' said a mischievous Tracy. 'You should be proud that the business has given us all freedom to get where we are today.'

'I wish that were true for me,' bemoaned Jack, prompting his mother to snap, 'Oh, stop wallowing in the self-pity. You have a very nice life, thank you very much. You've made more money than if you'd carried on working in TV.'

Karen turned to her mother in a conspiratorial whisper that they could all clearly hear: 'You know, despite the tedious protestations, I think this is what he always wanted to do after all those years lording it over us as *Zeyde's* favourite.'

Familiar sensations of victimisation and being misunderstood washed over Jack. However, he was surprised to see Isobel look visibly upset by the cruelty of these last comments. She smiled at him and, with a little wink, made it clear that for the first time, she was on his side. His happiness was interrupted by Karen clapping her hands and calling the family to order for a second time.

'Guys, please put down your weapons. I really need your help.'

'Are you all incapable of being nice to one another?' Everyone turned to Isobel, who was twirling a spoon in her fingers, looking serious now. 'I mean, from my perspective, all you do is try to say something clever, but rarely show each other much respect.'

Jack felt a surge of pride and nodded in agreement. She was right. He had spent the last twenty years trying to tell everyone how much he resented their expectations of him.

'I agree. We each try always to have the last word. Why is that?' he asked.

'As a highly respected psychiatrist with a six-month waiting list, I can honestly say I haven't a clue. I am sorry, Karen, for what I said. I think it might be just because we have different politics that I can't celebrate your success.'

'Don't worry, Tracy, I know you love me. And besides, your lot will never get into power anyway. Now, we should listen to the incredibly clever Isobel, and all be a bit more supportive to one another.'

Isobel gave a thumbs-up to the table.

'Look at me. I'm the glue holding this struggling family together.'

Stephanie, who had been slightly bemused by the sudden onset of honesty, patted Isobel's hand and said, 'Well done, darling. It's good to know the next generation has a bit of sense.'

'My turn to make peace,' Jack began. 'Karen, I'm very proud of you and all you have done. I will not hold you personally responsible for us having to queue in a different line in passport control in

Spain. Now, some time ago, you mentioned you needed our help. What can we all do?'

Karen rummaged in her bag and produced a manila folder. She was about to speak when the lights went off and an upbeat version of 'Happy Birthday' flooded the restaurant through the sound system. Gadi and several sweaty cooks emerged from the kitchen with a cake covered in sparklers, banging assorted drums and cymbals as they converged on a large table next to the Fogels. Everyone seemed very happy in the boisterous carnival atmosphere, except Karen, who looked like she was having to deal with hecklers before a major political speech. The other diners joined in, clapping and cheering, but the Fogels sat motionless, realising that Karen was in no mood for levity.

She produced various sheets of paper and handed them to her siblings and mother when the restaurant had quietened.

'I need you to fill these in as quickly as you can.'

Tracy, naturally suspicious of authority, had put on her glasses and was shaking her head as she read the form.

'What on earth is this?'

'My insurance for the election.'

'Is someone trying to blackmail you, darling?' Stephanie asked, looking confused.

'No, Mum, of course not. These are declarations of anything in your life that could harm my election prospects. This is standard policy from Central Office for any new person standing. Labour want this seat and their researchers will work hard to find my weaknesses.'

'I prefer to call myself your brother rather than your weakness.'

'That's not what I mean, Jack, and you know it. I just need you to think hard about anything in your life that, if revealed, could affect my chances.'

Tracy frowned. 'What sort of stuff do you mean? I don't know where to start, as my life could be a nightmare for you. What with the medical negligence charge and all my investments in blood diamond mines, the local paper will have a field day.'

'I thought we were having a truce, Tracy? Look, I'm not expecting there to be any major surprises, but I do need you to rack your brains for any vulnerabilities that could be exploited.'

This did little to assuage her sister's visible anger.

'You invited us here for a dinner just to check we wouldn't embarrass you and then inform us we make you potentially vulnerable in your political career. Karen, we are your family, not part of your election manifesto. It's so insulting to us all. Isn't that right, Jack?'

Jack froze in the turmoil of another family row. He shared his sister's resentment of Karen's expectation that everyone would do what she wanted all the time to further her own interests. For now, however, he was troubled by the form she had given him to complete, which requested huge amounts of personal information that seemed unnecessarily intrusive.

One of the headings read: *Please outline any potential commercial or business interests that could impact the candidate.* Where would he start? Should he mention the litigation with a trusted employee claiming discrimination? What about the imminent conflict with Stacey, who had been staring at him malevolently for large parts of the evening, and her husband, who always seemed to be wielding a meat cleaver? And then there was 'Chaim the Chicken', who was no longer intimidating customers entering his shops but about to become his advertising nemesis. Above all, if he was being truthful, he would need more than a small box on an A4 form to describe the ongoing assault from Lionel Gutterman on his business. For a second, Jack was paralysed by indecision, unsure of the right thing to do.

He produced a pen from his jacket pocket and started to fill in the form quickly, shutting out the noise of his two bickering sisters. When it came to the box about business interests, he wrote a single word: *None.*

Chapter 15

'You must be *Jack*?'

Never had his name been pronounced with more disdain. The door of the café was opened by a very tall, extremely handsome man, also wearing black jeans and T-shirt, rounded off by a short white apron. The look suited him much better, and Jack felt completely inadequate as he was scrutinised suspiciously by this Adonis.

'Yes, I am Jack. Hi. How are you? Who are you?'

'I am Alexandru, Sonia's partner. Nice to meet you.'

His voice suggested there was nothing nice about meeting Jack and he put such emphasis on the word *partner* that for a second, Jack wondered if he meant it in a personal rather than business capacity. He shook Jack's hand with a grip as muscular as it was unnecessarily tight.

'That's a Romanian name, isn't it?'

Alexandru nodded, clearly still unimpressed. He stayed silent for a few moments to enhance Jack's discomfort and eventually muttered, 'Yes, I am from Bucharest.'

'My great-grandparents are from Romania. Botoşani in the north, I think.'

Alexandru looked at him, perplexed, and Jack wondered why he was sharing family genealogy with a stranger outside a vegan café on a Sunday morning. His grandmother's family had fled pogroms in Moldavia a hundred years ago, but this hardly seemed relevant to Alexandru, who was blocking the doorway, reluctant to let him enter. He pointed his finger accusingly.

'Sonia tells me you are a very good waiter. This is a very important event for us. We have worked so hard to get here. Don't *fuck up*! Do you understand?'

Jack by now was starting to feel irritated to have encountered this level of hostility from the outset. Normally, this happened only when people got to know him.

'I will not drop a single pulse or nut canapé, I promise. Now, please can I come in?'

They stared at each other for a few more antagonistic seconds and then Alexandru moved out of his way and, with a facetious wave of his arm, bade Jack enter.

'Welcome to Sally's. Finest café in East London.'

Sonia was busy loading cellophane-wrapped plates of food into giant wicker baskets. She looked up and saw him, her face breaking into a smile of genuine pleasure.

'Oh, Jack, you came. Thank you. It's great to have you here.'

She was too busy to stop what she was doing, so he took off his coat, put it on a chair and saluted like an army cadet.

'Reporting for duty, boss. I'll do anything except clean the loos.'

Like Alexandru, she also looked him up and down as if checking his uniform was dress-code compliant. He had a pair of black Levi's in his wardrobe but had to go out a few days previously to buy a slightly larger T-shirt as the ancient one he possessed fitted a little too snugly around his untoned midriff.

'Thank you for raiding your dressing-up box to come and help me. Have you met Alexandru? He's my work husband and I'd be lost without him.'

'We've just been chatting like old friends about our proud Romanian heritage.'

Alexandru disappeared into the kitchen, allowing Jack to speak more freely. 'Actually, I think he hates me. Please tell me he hasn't gone in there to get backup.'

'Yes, sorry about that, he's very protective of me. He doesn't like anyone who can get in the way of us running this business together. He was my first employee and now he has invested all his savings to have a small share of the café. Boy, did he go mad when I told him that a bloke I met on a blind date was helping us today. So that's why you didn't get a hug.'

'I'd better not let you both down.'

'Not if you want to see your daughters again. Now, do you know how to slice a lemon?'

* * *

Jack was much defter in the kitchen than Sonia had expected. For the next couple of hours, he threw himself into his culinary duties with meticulous diligence. He didn't want to tell her he was adept with a knife because as the owner of a chicken factory and butcher shops, he had been trained in how to cut, pare and slice. When he inherited the business, he was required to understand all its manufacturing processes, so had worked on the factory floor in different roles to secure a grounding in basic slaughtering. At the end of the day, he would wash his hands meticulously to eliminate any trace of his new career and return home to an increasingly disgruntled Ali.

All those blood-splattered strokes with a cleaver were at least now earning him kudos with Sonia as she watched him fan an avocado like a Michelin chef.

'Where did you learn how to do all that?' she asked as they sat with a cup of coffee during a quick break. Jack thought it best not to say *an abattoir*.

'I used to be high up in a knife-carrying gang back in my youth. I didn't like the fights, so I'd volunteer to do the red peppers and aubergines for the salads when we got back from a rumble.'

'Do you have many other hidden qualities?'

'I would like to think so. The trouble with hidden qualities is that you don't know where you've left them.'

Jack instantly regretted sounding like a badly written fortune cookie. He changed the subject.

'Anyway, why does Alexandru dislike me so much?'

While his work had secured a few begrudging grunts of approval, Jack sensed that he was being stared at constantly by Alexandru to somehow prove to Sonia his unworthiness.

'He doesn't dislike you. He's just very protective of me.'

'Is he in love with you?'

'If he is, it'll come as a blow to Lucca, his boyfriend.'

'I didn't realise.'

'Why would you?'

'I wouldn't.'

'Exactly.'

'Sorry.'

'For what?'

'I'm not sure?'

The stilted exchange lapsed into awkward silence and Jack couldn't tell if he had upset or disappointed her. To his relief, Sonia tapped his hand affectionately as she got to her feet and said, 'But it is adorable watching you try to say the right thing to me.'

'I'm nervous. It's my first vegan catering function.'

'You'll be fine as long as you don't wear leather trousers. Now, come on, back to work. Don't worry, Alexandru will grow to love you and it will be me who is jealous.'

Buoyed by the nuggets of encouragement coming his way, Jack needed to stay calm, continue chopping and be helpful. This was an important day for her, and she was placing a disproportionate trust in someone she had just met. He picked up his knife.

'OK, chef. Ready for more chopping drudgery. By the way, whose party is it we're doing today?'

Sonia was walking towards the kitchen and turned to him to reply.

'It's an eighteenth party for a girl called Lily. She's a strict vegan and loves the café and comes in here often with her dad, who's something big in TV. I think he has a production company. His name's Mike Gibson, I'll try to introduce you. Maybe it will be helpful?'

* * *

'What on earth are you doing here?' Mike said when he saw Jack several hours later. 'Have your chickens all run off and you need a bit of extra cash?'

Jack put his finger to his lips, invoking silence, as he guided Mike to the corner of the room, his head bowed as if that might make him invisible. They had just arrived to set up the party, and glasses and dishes were being unloaded by Alexandru and two other people, while Sonia attended to the food in the kitchen.

'It's quite a story and if I didn't believe that there was a cosmic power shaping my destiny, I do now,' Jack began.

'What are you talking about? I mean, I've seen some elaborate ways to gatecrash a party, but if you'd wanted an invite, you could have just asked. Getting a job with the caterer seems a bit desperate.'

'We're on a date.'

'What, now? Are you going to need to borrow my bedroom?'

'No, but I am going to need your help.'

'Don't you always?' Jack felt panicky. He didn't want Mike's enjoyment of his discomfort to destroy things with Sonia.

'Seriously, mate. I may need to give you a script. Do you think you can stick to it?'

'Jack, what do you take me for? I'll have it produced and it'll probably win an Emmy. Now, please can you tell me why on earth you're hiding furtively in my living room, eyeing the kitchen nervously.'

'I met Sonia, who you have hired to do the party, on a blind date and it went so well I agreed to help her out today. It's just I haven't quite told her everything.'

Mike stared at the ceiling as if an explanation was written there. Eventually, a sadistic grin spread across his face.

'You haven't told her about the chickens, have you. She's a vegan and you didn't want to put her off.'

'Well done, Sherlock. All that cocaine you did in your twenties has not affected your mind palace one bit. But you can't say anything.'

'So, what does she think you do?'

'Something in TV. Plus, I have a lot of property.'

Jack had always liked Mike, although success had made him more arrogant over recent years. He needed the support of an old friend. Mike's next comment was, however, unnervingly accurate.

'Why don't you just tell her the truth? Surely you want to start the relationship on an honest footing?'

'I suppose I don't want to show her the side of me I hate: the angry businessman with lots of nonsense to deal with. I will tell her, but I want her to like the good bits of me first.'

'You've lost me. I don't like any bits of you. You tell her whatever you want, your happiness means nothing to me.'

Mike put his arm round Jack affectionately and continued, 'So what are my lines, then? I'll tell her you wrote *The Sopranos* if it helps you get your leg over.'

Before Jack could reply, he became aware of someone standing close to him and he turned to see Sonia with a quizzical look on her face. He didn't know how long she had been there or what she may have heard.

'Do you two know each other?' she asked.

'I should have said something to you when you told me whose party we were going to, but I didn't want to worry you. Yes, I've known Mike for years. We've worked together.'

At least that statement was true, Jack thought. Sonia was not smiling.

'I thought I explained to you about always being truthful?'

Jack couldn't tell if she was joking or angry, but he noticed Mike's expression stiffen. He clearly felt vindicated in his criticism of Jack's dangerous behaviour. The moment passed and Mike launched into his designated part with the professionalism of a top actor.

'Hi, Sonia. We've not really met, although I've eaten in your wonderful café many times with Lily, who told me that if you didn't cater her party, she'd vote Tory now that she's of age.'

'Well, we wouldn't want that. And you know Jack – perhaps I can ask you for a reference?'

'I've known this plonker for years. We worked together in our twenties, and we're now working on his marvellous sitcom.'

Jack felt relief that Mike was not lying, except perhaps for the endorsement of the sitcom.

'How's the project going?' Sonia looked from one to the other. She was clearly still not convinced.

'It could be huge. Really. It's very funny.'

'That's a relief,' Jack joined in. 'I'll be able to give up this crummy job.'

'Easy, tiger. You're still on probation.'

Sonia's tone was inscrutable. It was Mike's turn to look from one to the other. He wasn't sure if it was sexual tension or the destruction of a future relationship he was watching. Wanting to move away, he said to Jack, 'Back to work now, slave, but I'll be needing you later.'

'Why is that?'

'Because as your luck would have it, Neil Yeats from Channel 4 is coming. You can make your pitch to him today rather than having to wait for a meeting.'

Jack stood in silence next to Sonia as Mike left the room. He was in no doubt that he was telling the truth about Neil's attendance. His stomach reacted to this news with an evacuation of gas that could be heard in the street. Sonia laughed at his awkwardness and took a step towards him, taking his hand in hers.

'Are you nervous, Jack?'

* * *

Jack was considerably more relaxed when he got back to Sonia's flat in the early evening. The party had been an enormous success. The food was devoured by Lily's friends, who took it for granted that in civilised society, a function would be meat and dairy free. The only dissent came from Mike's ninety-year-old father, Colin, a retired army man baffled by the platters of multicoloured salads with vegetables he didn't know existed. With each new one that emerged from the kitchen, he would bark out, *Surely this one has got some bloody chicken on it?* Jack had been pouring him a drink and drew the old boy aside to console him.

'I understand how disappointing it must be for you, I love chicken too. You could say without it, I'd be destitute.'

Colin seemed delighted to have found an ally and gave him a knowing wink as he whispered conspiratorially, 'Are you some sort of double agent? I do hope so. Teach these silly children a proper lesson in nutrition. Now, be a good fellow and see if you can get me something to eat that was slaughtered rather than picked.'

'I'm sorry, sir, I don't think that will be possible. Lily has made it very clear that it's vegan only today, on pain of death.'

'Well, if I have to eat more of those green leaves, I think death can't come too quickly.'

Mike now sidled over to join them, holding out his glass for Jack to refill.

'So, Dad, you've met my old friend Jack, who with completely libidinous motives is moonlighting as a waiter today.'

'You know this man?' Colin asked in surprise.

'Believe it or not, we're actually working on a programme together at present. We've been friends for years.'

Jack put his bottle down and the three of them stood in a huddle.

'I was just extolling the virtues of chicken to your father.'

Colin nodded earnestly. 'I like this chap. I think he's some sort of quisling trying to infiltrate the veggie nutters.'

'Vegan, Dad, not veggie. You'll upset Lil on her birthday. And Jack, you should be careful with what you say around here about poultry.'

'Don't worry. Lily can't hear us.'

'I wasn't talking about Lily,' Mike replied, staring directly at Sonia, who was approaching with a tray of mushroom, chestnut and dill dip. 'You know what they used to say in wartime. *Careless talk costs wives.*'

Colin started to laugh, a phlegmy cackle that soon produced a bout of coughing. Mike slapped him on the back and took his glass from him, but his father brushed him off.

'You bloody idiot, Mike. The phrase from the Second World War was *Careless talk costs lives.*'

Sonia was now smiling and Jack's heart beat a little bit faster, partly in fear but mainly with desire. Mike looked at Jack, enjoying the situation comedy of the afternoon.

'No, Dad. I was right the first time. Don't you agree, Jack?'

* * *

Sonia's flat was a one-bedroom on the first floor of a Victorian house in Hackney. Jack did not know anyone who lived in the area but was struck by the irony that two generations ago, his family lived in adjacent streets, desperate to flee the inner-city squalor and reach the promised land of Hendon and Golders Green. Now, the area had been cleansed of its grime and was magnetising the trendy youth of the capital with its coffee shops and artisanal charm.

Sonia had gone for a shower to wake herself up and wash off the smells of the kitchen, leaving Jack to inspect her small living room. She had simple taste – a comfy sofa and two armchairs with bright cushions arranged symmetrically. On the walls were a couple of modern paintings, one a still life of flowers in a jug and the other an abstract in dayglo colours, and disparate sculptures, vases and photos sat on pine shelves alongside books, candlesticks and some wilting tulips in need of fresh water. Jack was not sure why he was making an inventory of her possessions. He seemed to be looking for more validation for a growing fascination he was struggling to contain.

Sonia emerged from her bedroom in jeans and a T-shirt, drying her curly hair with a towel. Jack had been flicking through a photo album he found on the shelf and flipped it shut in embarrassment, feeling he had violated a golden rule of dating privacy. Sonia smiled, sensing his discomfort.

'Checking for evidence I had a life before you swept me off my feet?'

Sitting down on the sofa, she let the towel fall to the floor. Jack put the album back on the shelf and, without saying anything, picked up the damp towel and folded it neatly, placing it on the arm of the sofa.

'Well, there won't be much feet-sweeping going on if we leave a mess around the place.'

He wasn't sure what he was doing, but he needed to buy a little time to contemplate the significance of what she had just said. Could it be that she really liked him? He sat next to her, trying to maintain an appropriate non-touching distance. Sonia curled her legs up and faced him. She let out an enormous, exhausted sigh.

'That was a tough day, but I think it went well. What do you think? Your mate Mike seemed happy. And everyone seemed to enjoy the food, except his father, of course. But the joys of veganism may never resonate with his generation.'

'You did brilliantly, Sonia. You will have built up your fan base considerably after today. Besides, it wasn't your fault that Lily's friend went into anaphylactic shock when she had the nut roast. Still, who knew it would be so much fun to stab someone with an EpiPen?'

There had been no such incident, of course.

'Very droll, Jack. As you know, food safety is no laughing matter. And while you're being such a numpty, let me remind you, Mr Carnivore, you are much more likely to pick up something nasty from a badly prepared slab of meat.'

The conversation was veering in a direction that Jack was keen to avoid, so he changed tack.

'How did I do in the end with Alexandru? Surely he wants to work with me now. I was a bloody brilliant waiter, if I say so myself. Nothing dropped or spilt and a constant smile, despite a lack of feedback from that difficult man I was trying so hard to please.'

'Worry not, Jack. He told me that you did very well for a socio-pathic loser he thinks is completely wrong for me.'

'He could tell all that by not speaking to me? He's got some intuition. The only interaction I really had with him was when he came and interrupted my chat with Neil from Channel 4. It was quite embarrassing to be told to go fetch the brownies from the fridge when I was mid-pitch.'

Jack was exaggerating, but Alexandru had caused the conversation to end abruptly, when progressing well. Mike articulated a genuine belief in the project's potential as a traditional sitcom with compellingly rounded characters and dialogue so witty that it would appeal to multi-generational audiences. Hearing him declare this to a third party had meant a lot to Jack, whose self-belief when it came to his creativity had been emasculated by his years running a business he did not want.

'Did your pitch go well?' Sonia asked sincerely. 'I mean, I know it was hardly the right place, but sometimes serendipity needs to be grabbed with both hands. At least, that's what I read last time I checked my horoscope in the *Daily Mail*.'

Jack held back from making a comment about meeting a tall dark handsome stranger, feeling it might fall flat and obviously not be true. Instead, he placed his hand on her arm, which was resting on the sofa. It felt like the right time to show intent. Intent for what, he wasn't sure.

'Yes, it was a good conversation, I think. He's invited us in for a meeting and was very polite. Maybe he is interested, because he kept saying things like *that sounds clever* and *that could work*. Anyway, he was a lot nicer to me than Alexandru.'

There was silence. Sonia was so tired that her eyes started to flicker and droop, but not before she took his hand in hers, interlocking fingers with comfortable familiarity. Jack felt more contented than he could remember being for a long time and watched her drift off into sleep. He wanted to stroke her hair but remembered that Ali hated it when he would try, as if his caresses might ruin her look.

The flat was quiet, but he could hear the footsteps and muffled laughter of Sonia's neighbours above, which he was not used to in his modern purpose-built Hampstead apartment. For a second, he contemplated shutting his eyes too, because a day of being on show was taking its toll. The serenity was shattered by the intrusive klaxon of an incoming text. Sonia shot up as if she had been doused with cold water.

'What on earth was that?' she squealed, as if in pain.

'Sorry, that was my phone. I should have put it on silent. It's ruined the moment a bit, hasn't it?'

'I suppose it's saved the day, actually. I was in danger of quite literally sleeping with you on a second date.'

She sat up and stretched. The romantic promise was disappearing rapidly. Jack did not even have time to absorb the quasi-sexual suggestion as he read the text that precipitated the evening's denouement. He turned the phone to Sonia and all he could think to say was, 'Welcome to my world, Sonia.'

It was a curt, unpunctuated, emoji-free message from his older daughter, Natalie.

Need break from you got shit to deal with and cant take being near you sorry x

Sonia began to say something and then paused. Jack's head was shaking in his hands. She stroked his back. It felt very nice, and he looked up at her. He was so disillusioned with his life, even though Sonia represented a possible antidote to its poison.

'Sonia. Why does everything have to be such a battle?'

'I don't know. I'll consult my shaman and get back to you. I suggest you kiss me now and then go back to your clearly miserable life. I am so shattered, and I'd like to be more awake the first time you stay over.'

Jack felt the caress of her lips and as he briefly shut his eyes, he realised that she had brushed her teeth when she showered in anticipation of this moment. She really was very considerate.

Chapter 16

The new week started with a coffee in his office and the compilation of a massive to-do list. Jack had always viewed himself as a practical and expedient individual who could juggle a busy workload while remembering to take the washing out of the machine. Now, he thought, it was all happening too fast, as he sipped from the mug Tracy had bought him on his birthday years ago with the words *Grand Executioner* emblazoned in blood-red on its chipped china. The elation of his new relationship was not going to be enough to make his problems disappear.

As soon as he drafted his list of tasks, he scrunched it into a ball and threw it away, dissatisfied. He had to find a strategy to settle these disputes mounting up like unpaid parking tickets. The problem was that his view of the future was unclear, other than hankering after the adulation that 'Widgets' might bring. All he wanted was to escape the profitable millstone of his family business and the little personal pleasure it afforded.

Sonia, whom he had met twice and kissed properly once, was swamping his thoughts with the possibility of joy so long absent from his life. Amazingly, she liked him more than he could have expected, and they had agreed to spend a significant part of the next weekend together with an implicit understanding that it included an uninterrupted Saturday night and Sunday morning. Why was he not telling her the truth, given that the longer he withheld it, the worse the consequences? The rationale was his need to hide from her the person he had become through no choice of his own. He knew he would have to confess eventually but hoped by then they would be so in love it would not matter.

Unfortunately, his wonky moral compass was further revealed when he tried to find out what had precipitated Natalie's text the night before. His only option was to ring his ex-wife in search of an explanation.

'Ali, I got the weirdest message from Nat last night. What is going on?' There were few pleasantries these days between them, and her initial froideur suggested to him she knew what might have happened.

'Well, what do you think is going on?'

'If I knew what was going on, why would I be asking you?'

'There must be a reason. Can't you think?'

Ali could effortlessly blend condescension with menace.

'No. It's like your love for me, I have drawn a blank. Now, we can do this all day, but I'm sure we have better things to do, so please can you help me out a bit here.'

'Bethany thinks it's for the best that she doesn't see you for a bit.'

'Who the hell is Bethany?' he barked, wondering if she was some poisonous friend of Nat's he hadn't met. Maybe she was her favourite YouTuber or latest hairdresser? Logical discourse seemed impossible when discussing family matters these days.

'Bethany is her therapist. She is very highly regarded, and we are lucky we got her.'

'Natalie has a therapist. Since when?'

'For about six months now.'

Ali sounded triumphant delivering the news of his second-tier parenting status. Jack's stomach contracted and his world yet again began to close in. It wasn't a reaction to his seventeen-year-old daughter having a therapist, rather his incredulity he had not been told. He stared at an old picture on his desk of the girls with him on one of their first holidays without Ali. They stood at his side at a Mallorcan beach restaurant in brilliant sunshine, golden skinned, with arms draped round him and instinctive adoring smiles, now long forgotten.

'Was anyone going to tell me?'

'We agreed we'd wait until Bethany thought it was the right time.'

'*We?*'

'Yes. Me and the girls, of course.'

'Isobel is involved too?'

'Well, we often meet to do family therapy.'

Ali must have loved firing that last bullet. He wanted to point out that fathers were often considered part of a family too, but felt she was so in control of this narrative he had little choice but to let her tell him what was happening. An explosion of his rising anger would end the call, so he tried a more conciliatory approach.

'Ali, please tell me why you haven't shared that Nat is having such a hard time.'

She paused for a moment. Their conversations about the children over the years had mainly been civil and constructive. When Ali was angry with him, it was usually an outpouring of internalised frustration that would not last long. After a moment of reflection, she continued with an unexpected apology.

'I'm sorry, Jack. This conversation has got off on the wrong track. Let's start afresh. The situation is that Natalie has been having an awful time of late and is really struggling. I'm very worried about her, so I arranged for her to get some help, primarily to give her some coping strategies. The problem is her unhappiness is more entrenched than I first thought.'

Jack felt a dread of what was coming next. He was acutely aware of the viral spread of mental illness among teenagers, especially the girls, and had heard some terrible stories from friends about the suffering inflicted on these poor young minds by the twin evils of social media and overanxious parenting. His mind hurtled towards terrible thoughts as he imagined various frightening outcomes for poor Natalie.

'What is it? What's happened that I don't know?'

'That's just it, Jack,' Ali replied in a voice as gentle as she could muster. 'It's you. You are not just the cause but the focal point of her unhappiness. That's why we all get so angry with you.'

'What ...'

He felt he had been punched incredibly hard by a bodybuilder with a knuckle-duster. He couldn't finish the sentence.

'I know this will be difficult for you to hear, and we need a coffee so I can tell you what Bethany thinks you should do. Let me simplify a complex situation. I suppose Natalie is just disappointed by you, and can't process the emotion, which is obviously a major challenge for her emotional well-being.'

'What on earth have I done?' Jack tried to think rapidly how he might have inadvertently slighted her. He knew they lacked the intimacy he was beginning to have with Isobel, but he was not a monster and thought he just needed to navigate these bumpy teenage years to engender adult closeness thereafter. He was completely wrong.

'That you don't know is why we are in trouble.' Ali answered elliptically. Jack wanted to scream.

'Ali, help me out here. I am clueless as to how I've caused so much unhappiness.'

'OK, Jack, you asked. Please accept that while you have not done anything other than love our daughter, the sad reality is that you have caused her lots of misery. In a nutshell, and I am paraphrasing Bethany, Natalie feels that you don't love her because she reminds you of your mother, with whom you have a strange relationship based on your resentment of her financial dependence on you. Natalie thinks Isobel is your favourite. Natalie hates that you treat her like a young girl when she wants to be seen as a woman and Bethany thinks that has something to do with you equating her early years with when we were happy as a family. Bethany thinks you should give Natalie space and not see her for a bit while she processes her own identity, and then you and Natalie will need to spend a lot of time in sessions with Bethany. I am sorry, I know this must be hard for you to hear.'

She did not sound smug as Jack tried to process his failings. His hand flicked the silver frame with the picture in Mallorca so that it fell face down on the desk, and he struggled for a coherent response.

'Well, this Bethany is certainly opinionated.'

'No, Jack, she is objective and good at her job.'

'What do I have to do?'

'You have to grow, Jack. You have to face up to some truths you have tried to avoid.' This was becoming a common refrain.

'But what prompted her to send me such an angry text last night?'

'Oh, I forgot to add the biggie.'

'There's more?'

'I'm afraid she's really embarrassed by you and what you do. She knows you hate your business, and she thinks you're a coward not doing something else if it makes you miserable. Plus, she wants to be cool and hip to her friends and slaughtering chickens is for her a gross and grubby profession. And then there's this ridiculous thing with Shlomo the Chicken.'

'It's actually Chaim the Chicken.'

He wasn't sure why he felt the need to correct her. Ali had clearly passed on her prejudices to Natalie.

'Whatever. There's some silly conflict going on, isn't there, and this character now has a Twitter account and is saying stupid things about you. Did you know? Someone at school somehow saw it and she got teased. It's so humiliating for her.'

'It doesn't do much for my self-esteem, let me tell you.'

There was a protracted silence, as if further conversation was impossible for them both after such an emotional declaration. Jack listened to the metallic groan of the production line outside his office. This was the harsh reality he didn't want Sonia to see. He was a terrible father stuck in a cold and noisy abattoir, hardly the stuff of romantic dreams. Eventually, Ali spoke in what sounded a teary voice that betrayed affection he thought had been extinguished by years of separation.

'Jack, believe it or not, I still have love for you. You are a good man. You and I have raised two lovely girls and I know that you love them and would keep them safe at all costs. But you are oblivious to the effect of your frustration on the rest of us. I know you have made sacrifices. We all know. But just because you are fighting on all fronts, don't drag us into your misery.'

* * *

He immediately called Tracy, but it went to voicemail. When she rang him back an hour later, she was neither surprised nor reassuring. She told him it was indeed probably for the best that he kept some distance and suggested he send a loving text to Natalie explaining that he understood the situation and would wait until she was ready to speak to him. Tracy was in a rush and promised him a longer conversation, but it was clear she was primarily worried for her niece, not him. Her parting words were very direct: '*Have some emotional resilience and focus on supporting Nat before her misery becomes hardwired like yours.*'

He did as he was told, and to his surprise received a solitary-word reply to his text of '*ok*' with no kiss or emoticons to convey if she appreciated his message or hated him further. As the morning wore on, he grew slowly calmer, resolving to press on with forging something meaningful with Sonia, unsullied by the skirmishes around him. Until he knew what he wanted to do with his life, how could he reveal its ugliness to her? He had just found out that his daughter was extremely unhappy and in need of major therapy to deal with him. It was hardly a character reference for a potential life partner.

For the time being at least, Sonia had to see a one-dimensional version of Jack that was unlikely to cause her to run away.

Chapter 17

He was still embroiled in a parochial media battle with unhinged Lionel. As he suspected, their respective ads had run to resounding indifference in the community. Sales for the week had been fine in the shops and his customers were unbothered by the shenanigans of his rival. Funny word, shenanigan, he thought, which made him look up its etymology on his phone. Apparently, it's from the Gaelic, meaning 'I play the fox', a wholly appropriate description for his rival. And no one should allow a fox in the chicken coop.

When he looked at the Gutterman's ad again, however, he noticed in the copy a Twitter handle, *@chaimthechicken*, which he had missed before. Why was it there? After all, Lionel spent more time in the tanning salon than he did on social media. Jack was not a social media fan, believing it the cause of his daughters' inability to sustain a meaningful conversation for more than five minutes. He had similarly been reluctant to promote his business through these channels, believing that it was not needed to stimulate sales of extra chickens. Sadly, his freedom to remain anonymous was evaporating.

He spent ten minutes trying to recall his Twitter login, eventually remembering his ironic password of *iwanttoescape*, and to his surprise found Chaim the Chicken had already amassed over three thousand followers. Scrolling through the threads, he did not feel unduly worried by the puerile conversations unfolding. There were tweets about Chaim's philosophy on life ('*I cluck therefore I am*') with a few poultry pun comments in response, worthy of a 1970s sitcom. Every couple of days there was a chicken-related joke, clearly selected from a Google search. One had elicited a particularly long and engaged debate.

> A man runs to the psychiatrist and says:
>
> 'Doctor, you've got to help me. My wife thinks she's a chicken!'
>
> 'How long has she had this condition?'
>
> 'Two years,' says the man.
>
> 'Then why did it take you so long to come and see me?'
>
> The man shrugs and replies, 'We needed the eggs.'

Jack knew Woody Allen used this line at the end of *Annie Hall* to describe the addictive irrationality of relationships. The thread evolved to random examples of why people fall in love and had little to do with chickens.

It was all so irrelevant. Even the slew of incongruous and tacky promotional messages that intermittently appeared were harmless. One tweet read:

> Why did the woman cross the road? Because she was in a rush to get to a Gutterman's Chicken.

There were random tweets that knocked him and his business directly and were surely unfathomable to anyone reading them.

> What do you call a chicken that has seen better days?
>
> A Fogel's chicken.

Jack found it impossible to understand what Lionel hoped to achieve. Rationally, he knew he needed to be the bigger person, but it was hard when all he wanted to do was sue him for libel and make sure he was sentenced to hard labour in a maximum-security prison. He thought of the old cliché of *There's no such thing as bad publicity* and wondered if the person who wrote it had ever had to put up with an unfunny talking chicken posting online insults.

He stared vacantly at the plain white walls of his office for a few minutes, in search of inspiration. Ever the pragmatist, he concluded that to move forward, he had to find an intermediary who Lionel might respect. Since their collective purpose was to provide Jews with kosher food, there was only one place to go. He was taking it upstairs.

* * *

Rabbi Isaac Furstein was a third-generation Orthodox rabbi with what his older female congregants called 'matinee idol good looks', who dressed like George Clooney in beautifully tailored suits and immaculately polished Italian leather shoes. His erudition, expressed through a series of brilliant books, made him an increasingly respected philosopher and media personality who could combine Talmudic study with the plotline of a popular television series to make a profound observation on the nature of the modern human condition. He was also one of Jack's oldest school friends.

They met for coffee next day in his office in London's largest synagogue, nicknamed 'the Chief Rabbi's Waiting Room' as it tended to nurture future candidates for that role. The desk was piled with papers and the bookshelves ran floor to ceiling, encircling the room with the breadth of his learning. Everything was arranged with meticulous care and the books were alphabetised with a geometric precision that could only be achieved using a spirit level.

He poured piping hot coffee from a silver pot into a Rosenthal china cup, one of the few possessions his grandparents had brought with them when they fled Nazi Germany.

'Oh, it's just like tea with the vicar,' Jack observed as he took the cup, carefully aware of its unquantifiable value.

'When did you last have tea at the vicarage? Did you get some cake? I bet it was a lovely moist sponge. We have some *kiddush* cake left over from last Shabbos, but you'd chip a tooth on it if you're not careful.'

'I'll pass, thank you. I mean, that's your reputation all over. Great sermons. Crap pastries.'

The rabbi smiled at Jack as he poured himself a coffee. He had an ability to meld into any social setting – from ultra-orthodox gatherings to banter with a childhood friend. But his time was not limitless, and he tapped his cup lightly with his spoon as if calling a formal meeting to order.

'So why do you need to see me urgently, Jack? I'd love to believe it was a crisis of faith, but I suspect it's something else.'

'Psychic as well as learned. No wonder you have such a big office. I don't suppose you know Lionel Gutterman.'

Rabbi Furstein's face was impassive.

'A little. President of his *shul*. Generous communal giver. Big in chickens. What of him?'

'I don't suppose you can have him killed?'

* * *

As dispassionately as he tried to explain the situation, it still sounded like the ridiculous plot of a bad book: Solly Fogel fires Lionel and now he wants revenge on his grandson years later by demanding two of his shops and waging a terror campaign through Chaim the Chicken. Despite their friendship, Jack tried to avoid expressing his commercial fears to the rabbi, who was part of the official establishment that provided his business with a trading licence. He finished by reading some recent tweets to give colour to the madness, including the most recent bizarre message:

I dream of a world where chickens cross the road
without their motives being questioned.

'Who on earth would want to follow this rubbish?' Jack asked, noticing five hundred new followers since he had looked the day before.

Rabbi Furstein sat for a second with his hands interlocked on his lap and then stood up regally, touching Jack lightly on the shoulder as he walked behind him as if to reassure him in advance of his response. He took a book from the shelf and returned to his chair, flicking through its pages in silence. Jack could see that it was a volume of the Talmud, a chunk of Aramaic text surrounded by blocks of ancient commentary and arcane debate. How on earth could this possibly help him with a Twitter campaign being waged against him by a fictional chicken?

The rabbi shut the book and placed it on a small table next to his chair. His voice was soothing.

'So, Jack, of course you know the word for peace in Hebrew.'

'A bit insulting to ask if I can recall "*shalom*" from a schooling sat next to you copying your homework.'

The rabbi smiled and wagged his finger.

'Ah, but can you tell me how many times it is mentioned in the Torah?'

It was like guessing the number of sweets in a jar for Jack and he hadn't a clue.

'It's not something that has troubled me too much over the years. You're the published author on matters rabbinic. How many?'

'How would I know? I'm not sure anyone has ever counted, but what I can tell you is it gets mentioned a lot and do you want to know why?'

Jack nodded wearily; all he wanted was the answer to his own problems, not a lecture.

'Our collective challenge,' Rabbi Furstein continued, 'is to think about the wider meaning of the word. I won't bore you with deconstructing its roots, but you know that Hebrew has a very deliberate way of redeploying the components of one word and making it appear as the root of another to amplify the meaning of the former. "*Shalom*" can be found in the roots of other words meaning "well-being", "it was worth it", "perfect" and "whole". So, the peace we talk about is more complicated than ending a battle with a truce. It suggests a well-being and a serene completeness not just for nations but for individuals too. Maimonides tells us, "Great is peace, as the whole Torah was given in order to promote peace in the world."'

Jack marvelled at his friend's effortless erudition but had no idea where it was leading. He did not want to be disrespectful but needed to have some more practical business guidance.

'Isaac, you're not telling me that the answer is to study more Torah, surely? I can't see that worrying Lionel too much.'

'Of course not, I can recognise a lost cause when I see one. No, I think you're missing my meaning. You have outlined a dispute that needs resolving. You must find your "*shalom*" and what I have explained is that peace does not come with mediation and negotiation over a specific conflict. It is the *wholeness* you need to find from addressing all aspects of your life. It's clear to me that Lionel Gutterman is just the tip of an iceberg of misery you have run into. It's not what you have explained, it's what you've left out that is telling. We've known each other since we were kids. Do you not think

I know how you feel about your business that was thrust on you? And I assume you're still single? You have never asked me to do any matchmaking on your behalf and I'd even be prepared to talk you up, despite what I know. I am trying to tell you that this malaise is more widespread than your parochial battle with a business rival.'

Jack knew he was right but could not bring himself to acknowledge the enormity of the task. It felt like asking an overweight occasional runner to train for a marathon. Knowing his time with the rabbi was coming to an end, he tried to push for a more immediate solution.

'I know. I know. I really am a bit of a mess. I wish I had more time to share the rest of my miserable existence with you because you would be able to help me, I suspect, like few can. But in the meantime, what do I do about Lionel? I need his vendetta to stop before I can tackle the rest of it all.'

Rabbi Furstein shook his head and shut his eyes, seemingly frustrated that Jack was ignoring the substance of what he said. He walked to the door and opened it, suggesting the meeting may now be over.

'Lionel Gutterman is easy. I'll give him a call to suggest he thinks about the pointless nature of what he's doing. Men like Lionel love it when I pick up the phone and seem interested in their lives. No one likes to argue with a rabbi with connections to the Almighty and the BBC.'

An assistant came in briskly with a pot of fresh coffee for the rabbi's next meeting and some clean cups. As he was leaving, Jack turned to him and asked, 'What if Lionel isn't up for making *shalom* with me? Will I need to find a shady bloke at the pub with a baseball bat?'

'Well, don't look at me. I am clergy.'

* * *

To his amazement, his mother's partner, Kurt, was waiting for him when he returned to his office. Standing with his hands clasped behind his back, he turned towards Jack and, with enormous effort, produced an inscrutable smile that could more accurately be described as a wince.

'I am sorry to trouble you in your place of work. I hope you have a minute for me.'

'What is it, Kurt? Is Mum OK?' Jack's pulse was racing, as the only explanation for Kurt's presence must be something serious.

'I am sorry if I alarmed you. Your mother is most well, and her health is as you know quite robust.'

Kurt Johansen spoke flawless English like he'd learnt it from an eighteenth-century textbook, and his manners were even more old-fashioned. Jack looked at him in the bright gleam of the halo-gen strip light, which did little to change his complexion. In his youth he must have had strawberry-blond hair and a rosy outdoor complexion. Now, in his early sixties, his thick wavy hair was grey, and his once ruddy cheeks had a haunted pallor, offset by arctic-blue eyes that were now staring at Jack with little warmth. Immaculately dressed in a single-breasted grey suit, white shirt and navy-blue knit-ted tie, his shoes were so brightly shined that Jack could see his bemused expression reflected in them as he shook Kurt's hand.

'Then what brings you here? Are you researching kosher chick-ens for your next lecture series?'

The muscles in Kurt's face tightened further and the constipated smile looked now like an expression of disdain. Despite speaking at least six languages, irony was not one of them.

'Most certainly not. I am preparing a series of engaging semi-nars on who was the most violent monarch, "Eric the Red" or "Ivan the Terrible". It promises to break new ground.'

Jack tried not to snigger at what sounded like the keynote address at a Serial Killers' Convention. Kurt cleared his throat with a mechanical cough, signalling a more formal intent.

'I have come here on a significant personal matter, and I will not delay further. I am here to tell you that this evening I will be asking your mother Stephanie to marry me and I would like to ask your blessing and consent. It is most important that the Fogel family patriarch endorses this union.'

Jack did not know how to begin to deconstruct the ludicrous sentence.

'Stephanie, oh *that* mother!' was all he could muster as a delaying tactic as he grappled with the notion of being the family patriarch. His sisters would have found the misconception of his sibling authority quite hilarious. What was much more troubling was his growing distrust of this charlatan, who seemed to have bamboozled his mother with a vampire-like charm and no discernible source of real income.

'Why now, Kurt? You don't even live together, and my mother gave me the impression that she was very happy with the current arrangement.'

He was stalling to come up with an objection, realising the metaphorical cruise liner had left the port and was well on its way up the fjord. He did not trust this man, who had captured his mother's heart even though they had so little in common, and they knew nothing about him other than the flimsiest biographical detail provided by a smitten Stephanie.

Jack sat in his chair and started to swivel it from side to side in jerky movements as he considered hiring someone to kill Lionel who could give him a good deal on polishing off Kurt as well. His soon-to-be stepfather continued outlining the future, oblivious of Jack's rising irritation.

'I do not believe in living with your mother until we are married. It sits uncomfortably with my religious beliefs. And, on that very subject, of course your mother's Jewish faith and my Lutheran observance require a civil ceremony to avoid the discomfort that can be caused by the mixing of religions. Indeed, given we met at sea, I will be suggesting to your mother that we are married by Captain Stiles, with whom we have grown close, when we next voyage on the *Ocean Princess II* in three months. I believe she will look very favourably on this proposition. I do hope that you and your charming family will join us then. It is a most lovely boat, you will find.'

The image of this horrific prospect flashed before Jack: walking his mother down a run of red carpet on the deck of some massive ship, saluted by staff in white uniforms and cheered by clinically obese Americans whooping in delight as they returned for the third time to the all-you-can-eat breakfast buffet, dressed in Hawaiian shirts and baseball hats. He had never been near a cruise ship but was confident this was how his mother's wedding from hell would unfold.

'This is a lot for me to process. I appreciate you coming to see me, it's just unexpected.'

Jack wondered if Kurt had misinterpreted his last statement as his assent, which was not the case. He had not yet asked the principal question that Professor Creepy needed to answer.

'But tell me, Kurt. How do you intend to support my mother?'

Kurt's frozen smile melted to nothing. Silence. It reminded Jack of one of the bleak Scandinavian films he used to devour in his youth. No one said much, but every utterance was laced with a darker meaning. Eventually, Kurt replied in a chilly monotone.

'I believe that to be a strange question, since it reveals your distrust. Let me assure you in the spirit of openness, Jack, that while my means are modest, my intentions are noble and fuelled by love and admiration for your mother. We will, I assure you, lead a good life based on foundations of mutual support. And, of course, it is a relief for me to know that this most impressive commercial operation provides us with a very comfortable income that will sustain us for years to come.'

Kurt finished this declamation with a stiff and unexpected bow. There was little deference in his voice, only defiance.

'That does not make me happy to hear, I'm afraid, Kurt. I don't work this hard to fuel your future well-being. This is my family's business, and it has not been built to fund your lack of a proper work ethic. This sounds to me like opportunism on your part.'

He was shouting now in anger.

'"*Wealthy widow with a fortune earned from kosher chickens is befriended by a shyster.*" It's the oldest play in the book, Kurt.'

'I have come here in good faith and now I must leave insulted.'

'Not insulted. Challenged.'

'No, Jack. Insulted. I love your mother. I shall make her extremely happy in the winter of her years. You, on the other hand, seem a very unhappy man who begrudges her a stable future. I will not be judged by such standards.'

Kurt left the office without another word, shaking his head and staring at the floor. Despite the protestations, Jack did not believe a word he said. There was something completely disingenuous about the man and there was no way he was going to fund his parasitic, peripatetic lifestyle. He would have to coordinate an intervention with his sisters.

He wondered how he would describe him to Sonia when they spoke next. Kurt the chancer? Kurt the sociopath? Kurt the curt? The last one was only a letter off.

* * *

He read the email from Rabbi Furstein before leaving the office.

From: Rabbi Isaac Furstein
To: Jack Fogel
<u>*Re: The Irascible Lionel Gutterman*</u>

Hi Jack,

Apologies for sending you this note but I am rushing around, and I thought you'd want to know the results of the half-hour call I have just had with Lionel on your behalf. Here are the disappointing highlights.

1. *He spoke for 90% of the call and didn't want to be interrupted.*
2. *He explained the historic anger he has towards your family. Your grandfather agreed to give him 25% of the company and then reneged. That is why he thinks you have a moral obligation to 'hand over' the shops to him. He wouldn't tell me what, but he has 'a grand plan' to make it impossible for you.*
3. *He knows that the rivalry, the ads in the paper, the social media and all the stunts may seem grubby, but according to Lionel, 'business is a war, and these are legitimate weapons' at his disposal.*
4. *He doesn't think you care that much about the business and that annoys him.*
5. *He invited me and Deborah to his house for dinner. Don't worry, I haven't accepted yet.*

So, I am afraid I have not really helped you find a resolution. You do have a very determined foe and while I am on the side of your happiness, I can't really take sides in what is just a commercial dispute.

Jack, to make peace, you may need to give up something.

That's it, I am all out of clichés.

Isaac

Jack, though disappointed, was not surprised. Rabbinic involvement was a distraction not a directive for Lionel, who had no interest in a truce. He obviously wanted to make Jack suffer, and it seemed there was more pain coming his way. His stomach beat out a couple of noisy rumbles, like distant thunder threatening a nasty storm. Time for Plan B. Not that he had much of a Plan A. Or maybe he should go straight to Plan C?

It was so confusing.

Chapter 18

Jack began to see Sonia often and each time was better than the last. When they were together, he ignored the growing fissures in his business and tried to be an alternative version of himself. He began to stay over every time he saw her, and there was something about their unspoken expectations for the relationship that made their physical intimacy match their enjoyment of each other's company.

His strategy was not to have an agenda. There was no rush to introduce her in person to the complexity of his family. Natalie was not talking to him, and he was trying to establish an independent relationship with Isobel, so it seemed best to compartmentalise his life at this stage. For her part, Sonia for now seemed happy not to plan as well. She was often exhausted, working fourteen-hour days, six days a week, so time with Jack was a balance of recuperation and romance.

Sundays were spent in a variety of simple pleasures: lying in bed reading the papers, long walks with café stops for coffee and cake, watching TV snuggled together on Sonia's squashed sofa. And talking: about a separate past, an entwined present and the tantalising possibility of a shared future. It was all happening so quickly, Jack thought a month after he helped her at Mike's party. He did not want to do anything to disrupt the contentment.

Occasionally, he had to steer conversation away from what a court of law might have described as the truth. Mostly, they chatted about their upbringings and family relationships. A slight adjustment was required when discussing his grandfather's influence, Jack transforming him from butcher to baker, the owner of Fogel's Bagels and Buns, an apocryphal East End bakery. How much more fun that would have been, Jack thought, if he had become King of the Sour Dough rather than Prince of the Headless Chickens. When she asked him how he lived such a comfortable life, he referenced the legacy of the family property empire he was managing. And that was partly true. He just made it all sound dull so she would not want to discuss things in too much depth, and he became adroit at changing the subject without making it look like there was something he was trying to avoid.

The rest of the time, the conversation spread out like an ocean of discovery: previous partners, travel plans, books, plays, TV, films, songs, first concerts, political discourse, religion, parenting, divorce, hopes, disappointments and friendships. On those subjects, Jack stuck to a more honest narrative. Above all, he could not quite believe that the surge of affection he felt for Sonia was reciprocated.

One Sunday in June, a squally electrical storm made the prospect of leaving their bed for the day impossible and they lay entangled, with the remnants of breakfast and the papers around them. They were laughing about a story they had read together in a supplement about a Kensington pseudo-therapist, formerly an investment banker, who was persuading middle-aged long-married couples to embark on a journey of exploration of their sexual experiences in past lives through a combination of hypnotherapy and ketamine.

Sonia propped herself on her elbow and looked at him. For the first time in years, Jack felt lucky. His mind cascaded poetic thoughts, but he held back from sharing them. He tried to find the right words to compare her unadorned beauty to the natural food she served in her simple café, but if he tried to articulate the thought, he knew it would come out wrong. Who wants to be told so early in a relationship that their eyes remind their lover of an avocado? Snapping out of the desire to declare his joy in verse, he realised that Sonia was also distracted. She was clearly deciding whether to say something.

'What's up, Sonia? Do you want to go visit the guy we just read about? He looks very expensive, and I'm not sure I want to spend all that money to be told that I was a libidinous gorilla in a former life.'

'Unlike you, I don't spend my day thinking about sex gurus. I just need to ask you something, even if it kills the buzz. It's not a big deal. Or maybe it is, but it's driving me mad. Here goes. Are you ready?'

Jack nodded like an obedient puppy. She seemed to have become worked up in a matter of seconds, making him panic he had unwittingly done something wrong. Her question was not what he expected.

'Why do you eat meat, Jack? It's been really troubling me, and I have to know.'

His stomach tautened in anticipation of a test for which he had done no revision and he feared this random question could precipitate a conversation in which he would have to spill the beans on what he really did. Well, spill the entrails, more like. He considered his answer carefully before speaking.

'OK, I didn't see that one coming and I'm not sure what to say. I eat meat because I always have, and I like its taste. Is that really such a big problem?'

'I don't know. It's weird. Perhaps I'm just worried that our different choice in food suggests we might not be suited long term. Is that mad?'

The casual intimacy of the morning had been replaced by something more ominous. He wondered what on earth was happening.

'I'm at a loss. When we met, you told me that you didn't care. And besides, I have not eaten a mouthful of anything dead in your presence. You're not someone who criticises the choices other people make, are you?'

She stood up and went to the window. On cue, the rain thudded against the glass and the wind rattled its aged wooden frame.

'No, I'm not. It's just different. With you, I think I need to have higher standards. You're right, I'm not self-righteous at all, I hope. I'm a vegan because I believe animals should be treated well. It's funny. I don't even want a pet at the moment. If you offered me a dog, I'd say no. It would drive me mad cleaning all the hairs off my lovely sofa. I just believe that what I eat reflects my view of a fairer world. And so, I am wondering what this means for my ...'

She looked at the ceiling, searching for a word. Jack had got a bit lost with her logic.

'Sonia. What is going on? You're rambling on about food and our relationship and a hypothetical dog that moults imaginary fur. I can eat any fruit in the forest so long as it's with you. Look, I'm not known for my emotional intelligence, but even I suspect this is a conversation about something else. Why are you torturing yourself about our diets?'

Something changed, and she sat back on the bed. To his relief, she took his hand and kissed it tenderly. He kissed hers in return. He thought the episode might now be over, and he was ready to attribute it to a low blood sugar that impaired rational conversation. To his surprise, however, she made an unexpected declaration.

'I'm asking you all this because it may be important in the future. And I hope we have a future because I really, really, really like you, Jack. I may even love you. OK, I said it, there you go. And to a carnivore. I'm living in the moment here and feeling vulnerable.'

His heart began to beat fast, and his mouth felt suddenly very dry. If this was elation, it was quite an uncomfortable sensation. He had not expected that she would be the first to say those words. He pulled her towards him, and they stayed silent in an embrace.

Eventually, he replied, 'If it's any consolation, I really, really, really like and may even love you too. And I think we could be so happy together. I'm so glad we're having this conversation.'

Could it be so easy to articulate a truthful emotion with no fear of being rebuffed? He was nevertheless disconcerted that her declaration followed on from a conversation about his eating habits. Given he had omitted to tell her the role that meat really played in his life, he was treading a narrow path across a steep ravine.

He scrabbled in his head to formulate a crude plan to remedy the situation. First, resolve the commercial conflicts and then decide the professional life he was going to have thereafter. He would take Sonia on holiday and being together somewhere sunny she would surely fall in love with him for eternity. In case the end of time was too far off, he would pick the right moment to tell her the truth and make the logic for his harmless deception seem compelling. How hard could it be to resolve, given that the difficult part was getting her to fall in love with him in the first place? The rest was logistics.

Sonia disengaged from his arms to say, 'So, you'll give up meat then. Thank you. Well, that's my takeaway from the conversation.'

'I am really sorry, Sonia,' Jack replied earnestly.

'Sorry? Come on, Jack, "*Love means never having to say you're sorry*". You know the line from *Love Story*. I adore that film, by the way.'

'No. I really am sorry, Sonia. In all the emotion, I've just knocked my cup off the bedside table. There's coffee all over your duvet.'

* * *

Miraculously, there was an unexpected lull in hostilities. Jack wondered if Rabbi Furstein's call with Lionel had not been such a disaster after all and the mediation had somehow worked. His enemy appeared to have retreated to his bunker or otherwise gone on holiday. The advertising assault abated, and the curious attacks stopped running in the Jewish press. Even the mobile advertising van that Lionel emblazoned with the line 'When it comes to chicken, Gutterman's Good and Fogel's Fairly Fair' stopped parking in front of Jack's shops. There were sporadic tweets from Chaim the Chicken, but as several weeks passed, Jack hoped that his enemy's energy for battle had dissipated.

Gadi and Stacey were also distracted, particularly after the chef broke a couple of bones in his foot when the staff of Clucks took on Signora Fraquelli's Italian restaurant in a friendly football match. It was not that amicable a sporting occasion and after being fouled by the dessert chef Aniello, Gadi tried to remove both his legs with a crude tackle that resulted in an eight-hour trip to A & E to diagnose his ligament damage. Gadi's limited mobility seemed to temporarily halt any aspirations for global domination and Jack avoided the couple, hoping they were having second thoughts.

Business muddled on without him having to worry excessively. He met with his accountant for a review and was encouraged by how strong his cash reserves were. There were a few clouds on the retail horizon as problems emerged with the two shops that Lionel coveted. He was trying to renew the leases and the landlord was behaving unreasonably, which made Jack suspicious.

Somehow, it could all wait. There were always going to be problems: staff issues, broken-down vans, machinery in need of replacement, disgruntled customers, unreliable suppliers, pedantic religious supervisors, bird flu outbreaks and unscrupulous business rivals. It was just so much easier to deal with when his heart fluttered in anticipation of a next encounter with Sonia.

He also decided to avoid further confrontation with his family for the time being. Kurt, as promised, had proposed to his mother, and she had gathered the family together for an impromptu celebration. Jack thought it best to feign happiness and not make waves. His mother behaved as if the icy Swede had lit a flame of burning passion well beyond overweight Phil Fogel and Kurt continued as if the argument in the factory with Jack had never happened. When he proudly lifted the sleeve of his new Armani suit to reveal a Cartier watch on his hairless wrist, an engagement gift from a smitten Stephanie, Jack even managed to restrain himself asking why Kurt was showing off his bling when his mother had no engagement ring.

Natalie texted to say it was too difficult facing the family and was absent, leaving Isobel and her cousins to make a fuss of their grandmother. In truth, they felt Kurt was very creepy, but like their parents, it somehow seemed easier to do the right thing and ask lots of enthusiastic questions about the wedding, hoping it would not take place at an inconvenient time for their social calendars.

Jack spent the afternoon trying to be invisible. It reminded him of his teenage years of co-existence with a family who did not really get him. He chatted amiably with his brothers-in-law in a corner of the room, but he wondered how long it would take anyone to notice if he put his coat on and walked out.

There was a time when his dissatisfaction with supporting such an ungrateful mother would have produced a resentful anger that would prevent him properly digesting food for weeks. It was different now. As the Fogels celebrated the uncomfortable union of his vain mother and this money-grabbing opportunist, Jack felt strangely serene. After years of discomfort, Sonia was going to be the antacid that cured his family indigestion.

PART 4

ATTACK

Chapter 19

Jack thought that the waiting room for the Choice & Resolution Wellness practice in Camden Town was clearly designed by a very unhappy person as he surveyed its bleak minimalism from the discomfort of a chrome-framed sofa. Alone and contemplative, he shifted uncomfortably on its taut leather cushions and felt a foreboding gloom descend on his newly acquired optimism.

He had been asked by Ali to book an appointment with his daughter's therapist, Bethany, to begin the 'long and painful journey' necessary to bridge 'the canyon of unhappiness' that now existed between them. Ali seemed to revel in the language she used to describe the state of his relationship with Natalie. Painful journeys to build bridges across a huge canyon did not sound so much a holiday as basic training to join the SAS.

He stared at the black-and-white prints in front of him: reportage images of what seemed to be war, political protest and grief. Jack was perplexed why someone would choose to fill a reception area with such bleakness, unless it was a subtle plan to ensure no one entered a therapy session in a good mood. He got up to look at the photos in closer detail to see if perhaps he was missing the point, oblivious that someone had entered the room and stood next to him.

'They're ghastly, aren't they. I mean, who wants to see a fourteen-year-old Somalian pirate with a gun right before baring their soul. Unfortunately, my bloody partner in this practice believes they are great art and that decorating decisions should not be democratic. Anyway, enough about the decor. You must be Jack. Welcome, I am Bethany.'

She was not who he expected. He had assumed her to be a worldly woman ten or fifteen years older than him since every time Ali quoted her, it was with a reverence normally reserved for someone with much greater life experience. Bethany, however, was indeterminately young and dressed in a billowing purple tie-dye dress with Doc Martens boots. As she shook his hand vigorously, Jack stared unsubtly at the tattooed trail of stars between her thumb and forefinger. He was supremely embarrassed when she responded by asking, 'Don't you like my lovely stars? Shame, because they are very important to me.'

Jack couldn't think of a reply that would not incriminate him further, so he just shrugged. She was unfazed by his awkwardness.

'Stars, let me tell you, are a symbol of success and ambition. A fixed point for a journey. Somewhere you'd like to reach but can often seem too far away. Not a bad metaphor for what we all go through in life, don't you think?'

Never one for homespun philosophies, Jack was nonetheless impressed and tried to relax.

'Apparently, I need to go on journey with you. I'm just hoping it's not going to take light years.'

She smiled and placed her hand softly on his shoulder to usher him to her consulting room.

'Hard to say, I'm afraid, but I'll put the kettle on because you'll definitely need some refreshment along the way.'

* * *

'Why do you think you're here, Jack?'

He had expected this opening question but was still flummoxed how to answer. Jack was normally not bothered by silence, but his delay in replying became an excruciating reminder that from his perspective, he was ignorant of his parenting crime.

'I'm not entirely sure, if I'm being honest.'

'And are you being honest, Jack?'

'I try to be. It's complicated.'

He wondered if he was thinking of Sonia rather than Natalie when he said this.

'What's complicated?'

So, therapy is simply having your last sentence repeated back to you as a question. No wonder he'd been keen to avoid it through all his years of unhappiness. Still, he knew that whatever he said would be regurgitated in a future session with his wife and daughters, and his only choice therefore was to take it seriously.

'I suppose I never imagined my life would be full of these difficult choices. When I first married Ali, everything was easy. I had my dream job, and we loved our life. But I had to give it up to run the family business just as I became a father. Since then, things haven't exactly gone to plan.'

'How so?' Bethany asked. He was glad he wasn't paying her by the word, or he would be getting irritated now. Also, why did her head tilt in concern every time she asked a question? Maybe you learn the gesture at therapy school and must incorporate it into each appointment thereafter?

'Well, for one thing, my elder daughter isn't talking to me at present – but then you knew that, of course. I haven't felt happy for years and I seem to be disappointing lots of people, though not as much as I'm disappointing myself. Does that sound self-pitying? I suspect it may and I'm sorry to come across a bit desperate. It's just that as bad as things have got at work and with my kids, I've recently met someone, and I'm hopeful that something is about to change for the good. She's all I can think of at present.'

Bethany leant forward conspiratorially. Did this signal a breakthrough or just that she wanted a good gossip?

'Tell me all about her, Jack. You seem to really want to.'

She was spot on, and the compulsion to confess his unfamiliar romantic elation was overpowering.

'I don't know. She makes me happy. She's very lovely.'

'I'm sure she is. But why?'

Jack had listed Sonia's virtues so many times in his head that he knew them off pat.

'Where do I begin? She's kind. She's funny. She doesn't judge me. She believes in love and long-term relationships. She wants a partner. She thinks I'm interesting, for some reason. She's affectionate. She's compassionate. She's a vegan. She runs a vegan café. She doesn't know I have a kosher chicken business. She wants kids. She's very attractive. She has similar cultural interests to me and doesn't like sport.'

Jack looked up, having made this declaration to his shoes rather than to Bethany's face. It felt good to list what he loved about Sonia to someone who did not really know him. He had not wanted to discuss her with his family for fear of a negative comment about his behaviour.

Bethany was chewing her pen and seemed perplexed.

'Can we back up a bit, Jack? You've given me a lot of information.'

'Is it irrelevant to my relationship with Natalie?'

'No, it's extremely relevant. However, I have a more important question for now.'

'I'd be disappointed if you'd run dry so early in our session.'

He had resorted to weak humour because he knew what was coming as Bethany pointed the pen accusingly at his face and asked:

'Why does your vegan girlfriend have no idea that you kill chickens for a living?'

* * *

Can you perjure yourself in therapy? Jack wondered, as the hour of torment drew to an end. When he explained his relationship with Sonia, he pretended his big secret was no big deal and he intended to tell her imminently. Bethany possessed a PhD in inscrutability and he could not decide if she was silently judging him or genuinely empathetic to his problems.

At the outset, she explained the session was an exploratory conversation to get to know him and help formulate a plan for Natalie. They discussed candidly his relationships, with the girls, with Ali, with his mother and his sisters, and his perceived failings as a father. He admitted to overcompensating with treats and indulgences when first divorced from Ali but as the girls got older and his guilt diminished, he struggled to find common ground with them.

'It's interesting, Jack, that you feel deficient as a father to your daughters,' Bethany said in the last five minutes. He had hoped that he was nearing the end of his discomfort and she would exonerate him with a basic pass in entry-level parenting. Unfortunately, she had kept a real zinger up her hippy-chic sleeve.

'It seems you have been surrounded throughout your life by strong women. What impact do you think that has had on you?'

He digested the question for several seconds, reviewing the peculiar dynamics of the Fogel clan. His grandfather had taught him an antiquated form of masculine behaviour that often involved physical violence to resolve disputes. He had struggled to engage with a father he seemed to disappoint. While he loved them both, they represented an upbringing he did not want to replicate. The women in his family were complicated in their behaviour but so much more impressive. Eventually, he managed to respond in an embarrassed whisper.

'It's so hard to understand why I am like this today. When I reflect on it, I suppose being forced to make a choice I didn't expect has made me live with low-level anger ever since. And if you grow up feeling you are different from the expectations that have been set for you but don't do anything about it, you lose your self-respect. I think what I resent about my mother and sisters is that they are doing what they want. And if I ever seem happy, then Ali seems to resent me. No wonder I haven't a clue what to tell the girls.'

To his surprise, his eyes moistened. He never cried and spontaneous emotion normally eluded him. This time, the self-examination prompted a feeling of intense sadness. Like the incessant knocking of a woodpecker, he couldn't escape the next thought: *Why would Sonia want to stay with a bloke like me?*

Bethany said nothing but stared at him, expressionless. He was beginning to understand that the purpose of therapy was to help you make decisions by providing the platform for self-discovery. It was a total nightmare. He wiped the tear away and saw from the clock to his side that his time was up.

'Am I cured?' he asked, desperately trying to gain some composure. Bethany smiled and stood up and placed her two hands on Jack's. Was she going to bless him or give him a slap, he wondered?

'Let's focus on Natalie, shall we? She's going to need you to resolve these conflicts to help her on her journey. Do you think you're up for that level of honesty?'

He nodded, unsure if it was some sort of trick question.

* * *

'Guess where I have booked?' asked Jack.

He had gone straight from Bethany to Sonia's flat and they were sharing a giant salad from the café with chilli-coated vegetables he couldn't name. He was desperate for the comfortable familiarity of red meat and carbohydrates but that was always going to be impossible when he was with her. His hunger reflected the dilemmas of his life. How could he make his own choices to get what he wanted?

Drained by the demands of work and the session with Bethany, this was the bright spot in his day: to be with Sonia made everything so much better and he could see the possibility of happiness, not failure. He told her loosely about the therapy, focusing on the part where he discussed his relationship with the girls. She listened but did not comment and her gentle empathy was another reason he considered her up there with Mother Teresa in the sainthood stakes.

That morning, he had booked a weekend away. Their first together, he wanted it to be the perfect way for her to see him at his best before the next part of his romantic master plan, when he explained the true source of his wealth.

'I'll give you a clue. It's your favourite film and you have never been there.'

'*Apocalypse Now*. OMG we are going to Vietnam. A bit of a long way to go for the weekend though, isn't it?'

'Nice guess, have another try.'

'Of course I know the answer. I mean, it's not as if I don't check your phone every time you leave the room to find out who you really are.'

The quip made Jack's hypersensitive stomach pirouette and, for a second, he feared he'd regurgitate the turnip or kumquat or whatever else was in that salad. Did she really spy on him, in which case he might as well get his coat?

Sonia was toying with him. A couple of weeks before, they had watched *Roman Holiday* together. Despite Jack's prodigious cinema knowledge, for some reason he had never seen the classic movie. While he preferred black-and-white films to be existential and subtitled, he was charmed by the whimsical romance between beautiful princess Audrey Hepburn and cynical journalist Gregory Peck, who falls in love with her. She escapes from her gilded royal existence and is whisked through the sights and sensual pleasures of Rome by the opportunistic hack in search of a scoop, who lies about who he really is. The truth inevitably separates them, and it struck him as an inadvertent reflection of his own relationship with its unexploded secret at its centre. Hopefully, he would not end up alone like the film's protagonists.

'Will we meet the Pope?' Sonia asked as she kissed him.

'I'm hoping so. I've found a tout who says he can fix up an audience for €300 cash. If not, I've lined up a couple of nuns who said they'll show us round the Vatican after work. I've even found a vegan *gelato* café so we can have ice cream by the Colosseum.'

Sonia's smile was enormous.

'I am so excited. Our first holiday together somewhere I've always wanted to visit. I'll break the news to Alexandru that he's in charge for a few days. I can't wait.'

'A fortnight and we'll be there. The plane was full, I'm afraid, so I hope you don't mind sitting by the toilets.'

'It will be perfect wherever I sit. I just can't wait to be alone together to learn everything about you. There feels like there's so much more to find out.'

Chapter 20

If only I could go on holiday without worrying about my business, lamented Jack as he opened an email from his landlord. Not for years had he been so excited about going away and it was beyond irritating that there was no sign of his commercial disputes abating. It seemed a quiet life was for monks and librarians, but not chicken magnates.

The leases of the two disputed shops were close to expiry and a drastic increase in rent that bore no relation to basic reality was being demanded. The shady landlord had bought the properties three years previously, trading via an opaque Jersey-registered company. With one director, a Mr Eshtov, and correspondence conducted through a local lawyer, Jack had hitherto encountered few problems.

The email was threatening and legally dubious. His own lawyer drafted a lengthy reply demanding that the integrity of the leases was respected and requesting a market rate rent solution. Jack could sniff the overpowering cologne of Lionel Gutterman in the background and was up for a vicious fight, supported by aggressive lawyers defending his commercial probity.

Any vestige of professional dignity, however, went out the window the following day with the unexpected resignation of Lawrence Klein, the manager of his Golders Green shop, and two other members of his retail staff. They had all been in the business for many years as similar roles elsewhere were impossibly rare. Unless, that is, you joined Lionel Gutterman.

He was virtually speechless during the call from a stammering Lawrence, who explained they had all been made an amazing offer by Lionel that was impossible to turn down. Lawrence spoke as if they were prize footballers being lured to a bigger club and his efforts to justify himself served only to provoke Jack's indignation.

'So let me get this straight. You appeared in court and were found guilty of common assault because you fought a boy in a chicken costume disrupting your shop. And now, despite that humiliation, you want to work for the man who was behind it all?'

'I know it sounds strange, but he has apologised and has been extremely generous. I must think of my retirement, you know, Jack.'

'I don't want to be rude, but I think you've lost your marbles.'

Maybe he had pushed it too far with that last comment. Given everything that had happened recently, he wondered if it was likely to be misconstrued as discrimination against people with mental illness and another legal action against him would begin. Instead, Lawrence got angry.

'There's no need to raise your voice at me. I am leaving your business and so are the boys. I want to make a bit of money before I get too old, and Lionel has given me lots of assurances. Thanks for the good memories, Jack, although you'll have to remind me what they are. I am leaving in a month, and there is nothing you can do.'

The conversation ended abruptly before it turned even more unpleasant, if that was possible. Jack was bemused how Lionel had so many openings for new staff in his current shops. He had found Lawrence moody and morose over the years and would not miss him personally. Nevertheless, he had been loyal and hard-working, and these departures were disastrous, because losing three staff members would make his daily retail operation very tricky. For the first time since the conflict began, he worried that Lionel was winning.

* * *

To his amazement, Karen called to discuss their mother and he wondered if it was connected to the looming general election and the demonic energy she was expending to win over the Dudley South community. She was clearly trying to control her narrative and had no time for small talk, speaking brusquely to Jack as if to a lowly employee.

'I've been worried about Mum marrying Kurt. Especially after the private investigator's report.'

'You hired a private investigator – Magnum or Columbo? My word, Karen, Dad would be so proud of you. I really hope there are no compromising photos of them *in flagrante*, and if there are, I don't want to see them.'

She ignored him.

'I have a growing reputation to protect, so it was the only sensible thing to do. He has a colourful past, it turns out.'

'And yet his complexion is so grey.'

'There's more than meets the eye about our mysterious Swede.'

'Was he once in ABBA?' Jack could not resist trying to provoke a rise as a cathartic revenge for the years of disdain Karen had shown him. He could not tell from her reaction if he was succeeding.

'He was a lecturer at the Blekinge Institute of Technology. It's the twenty-third best university in Sweden, so not exactly Harvard. He was asked to leave after complaints of improper behaviour from several female students, who alleged he repeatedly commented on their appearance in a way that made them all very uncomfortable. He also frequently offered additional supervision and support in his flat, rather than in his office in the university. It's all a bit opaque, but the students' descriptions of him make him sound a real creep.'

'He makes my skin crawl, so I can only imagine how their skins must have felt. I just can't understand how Mum can bear to be with him.'

'There's more.'

'You're not going to tell me he's Jewish after all?'

'Enough nonsense, Jack. If I wanted to have a conversation based purely on pointless sarcasm, I'd sit down to dinner with my children. This is important and it relates to the business you run. I'd hate to hear you complain even more about your life and then accuse me of not having warned you.'

'I'm sorry, Karen.' Like hell he was.

'He's not got a penny to his name. It's amazing what you can find out about someone's finances with a bit of underhand investigation. He hasn't got any income coming in and yet he seems to be intent on living a rather expensive lifestyle, don't you think? It's clear he's going to bleed Mum dry, which I suspect means that she will just keep coming to you for money.'

'Not going to happen, Karen. Not going to happen. I am going to mash that Swede!'

'Very witty, Jack – how long have you been thinking of that line? Now listen to me properly. Action needs to be taken, do you understand? I suggest you get Mum to sign a prenup or something like that.'

'It would be great if you helped. You are her favourite, after all. Maybe you'll be able to loosen the weird hold that Kurt-the-Flirt seems to have.'

It didn't seem an unreasonable request; nevertheless, it was met with a froideur used whenever Karen wanted to frighten other people into doing her bidding.

'Jack, I am terribly busy trying to build my political career and I can't focus on this right now. You control the family money, therefore this is for you to resolve.'

'This is something all three of us should resolve with Mum. If you can't see that then I'll leave you to march on Parliament and we'll do the dirty work for you again.'

In her hurry to get off the phone, she missed his irony.

'I knew you'd understand, Jack, and I appreciate you taking the lead. Oh, and one more thing, brother dearest.'

'There's more?'

'You must keep this discreet. Very discreet. I need to keep my campaign all about the policies.'

Jack very much doubted anyone would care in the slightest about her personal life and a whiff of scandal might make her seem a more interesting candidate. Still, given the barbed tone of the conversation, he had very little desire to prolong the pain of talking to her.

'Mum's the word!' he replied and then realised what he had said, so quickly added, 'Actually, she's the bloody root of the problem.'

* * *

As the trip drew near, Jack's mood was controlled by the texts he received. He ran large parts of his life remotely, perfect for someone who seemed to disappoint people when he met them in person. He yearned to see Natalie in person after many weeks apart, reliant entirely on sporadic terse messages. With the approval of his relationship *consigliere* Tracy, he sent his daughter a short message, cramming all his love into a few inadequate words.

Hi Nat. Just checking in. I miss you and am thinking about you. Here if you want to chat x

The next day, he received a dispiriting reply.

No Dad. Not yet.

He knew his paternal instinct to fix the situation was not going to work, confirmed by a text from Ali that arrived simultaneously.

> Give her space Jack. I have spoken to Bethany, and
> she has asked that you minimise contact.

The suspension of contact released a wave of dark emotion he assumed to be his own form of grief. He had no choice but to wait for Bethany and Ali to help Natalie reconnect with him, however long that took. It was as if she had been kidnapped and the ransom demand kept changing. All he wanted to do was pay up.

Still despondent, he thought he should do something constructive and protect his mother from the charlatan she intended to marry. Tracy had been much more of an ally than Karen and they agreed they would tackle this difficult conversation together. Stephanie was on a short ten-day cruise to support Kurt in his latest lecture tour, wowing the widows no doubt with some arcane talk on something like 'the history of sex pests'. Jack sent her a carefully composed text, attempting to convey their concern without causing panic.

> Hi Mum. When you are back can Tracy and I meet you?
> We want to discuss the wedding and make sure you
> have thought through financial logistics and that you
> are protected etc x

To his dismay, he got an immediate terse response.

> Nothing to discuss. Kurt and I bemused by your
> message.

To make matters worse, as he stared at his screen wondering whether to reply, another message followed on.

> Kurt and I are thinking of moving to somewhere
> bigger. I will need to talk to you about the business to
> arrange finances.

He forwarded the text to his sisters and Tracy responded first.

> FFS. We will have to read her riot act together when
> she is back. Or poison Kurt. Or both.

A few hours later, Karen joined in the sibling conversation.

> Maybe you'll have to take some money out the
> business for her Jack. It's her inheritance too.
> Make sure this is sorted.

He texted Tracy back.

> Make sure this is sorted? Will she have us arrested,
> if we don't?

By the end of the day, all he wanted to do was leave the office without further incident. Sonia texted him a picture of piles of neatly folded clothes beside an empty open suitcase.

> Can't decide. What do you fancy for the trip?
> Nun's costume or gladiator? x

A surge of excitement and desire defused the stress of dealing with his mother.

> Well, when in Rome, Sonia Maximus! Can't wait to see
> you later x

He had one more thing to do as he had not heard from Mike Gibson for a week or so about 'Widgets'. After his daughter's party, Mike had sent Jack some notes and he had revised the pilot script in anticipation of the meeting with the commissioning editor. As a date had not been confirmed, Jack sent Mike a quick text.

Any news from Channel 4?

He didn't expect a reply, but this time it was in seconds.

Yes, every night at 7 pm – thought you knew that.
Now leave it with me worry pants. Kind Uncle Mike is
on the case. Hopefully in a couple of weeks.

Not a disaster then, and something to look forward to on his return. The prospect of progressing, however slowly, with his TV project somehow justified his current behaviour with Sonia. He intended to tell her the truth and maybe he would do it in Rome, after all? An inevitable moment of tenderness would make it much easier for full disclosure of his actual day job.

This clarity was clouded once more with a text from Stacey. He had hardly spoken to her for weeks but a few words, punctuated unnecessarily aggressively, reminded him that his business challenges were not lessening.

MUST speak next week. MUST resolve our future and
you have a CHOICE to make. Hope you are feeling
bullish ... I know we are!!!!!!!

What more do they want, he wondered? A shouty showdown was imminent and he was not confident of a happy outcome. How on earth was he going to broker peace to protect his valuable restaurant assets? Still, as he shut his computer, he resolved to use the next few days to find inner peace. Sonia was his future, and these were a few inconsequential obstacles blocking a vista of happiness.

His phone pinged with another text, this time from Isobel.

Dad. Check the Chaim the Chicken tweet.
It's bonkers x

* * *

For a few years, Jack had used the famous 1946 Louis Jordan song 'Ain't nobody here but us chickens' as the telephone hold music for the business. After all, there are not many chicken-related songs, and the tale of disgruntled hens trying to sleep while Farmer Brown stomps around noisily would raise a smile for a waiting customer. When Jack checked Twitter, he had to sit down in disbelief at the elaborate effort Lionel was now making to discredit him. Chaim the Chicken had recorded his own version of the song with an accompanying video, animated to quite a sophisticated level.

In the video, muscular Chaim, a luminous-yellow bird, holds sway over a scrawny, limping Fogel chicken, smacking the rival bird around in a display of poultry abuse. The rewritten lyrics were an assault on Jack's business as well as the rules of poetic scansion.

There ain't no good in Fogel chickens
There ain't no real taste at all
So, calm yourself and take the bus
To buy your juicy bird from us
At Gutterman's our birds taste swell
And also cost half the price as well

Chaim struts arrogantly past a Dickensian Fogel's shop into the shiny, modern Gutterman's establishment. Fireworks explode as the music reaches its crescendo and a logo is emblazoned across the screen with the tag line: 'You get a better bird at Gutterman's.'

Jack put his head in his hands and groaned like a wounded animal. An intelligent man, he could not understand what Lionel was hoping to achieve from this nonsense. He had supplied him chickens to sell in his shops for years and there had been no drama. Now, you would think they were competing for the next moon landing.

His incredulity gave him hope that despite this effort, it would be to no avail for Lionel. In the unlikely event Jack's customers saw the film, they would be bemused by its desperate attempt to discredit him. He played the clip a couple more times and felt his equilibrium return. It was hardly having much of an impact as only a few thousand people were following the thread and it was not being shared. Soon it would be buried in the digital graveyard of unwatched content.

Jack celebrated that he was a better person than Lionel. Besides, this was nothing more than a parochial commercial spat that could be resolved quickly. He drove to Sonia's knowing they were going to have the most incredible few days of his life in Rome, perfect in every way. And somewhere, in the sulphurous pits of hell, or his dingy office in Edgware, Lionel was going to be running his hand through his bouffant hair, wondering why no one was interested in pathetic Chaim the Chicken and his puerile pop video.

Chapter 21

Early-morning Heathrow bustled with the energy of disparate travellers embarking on stressful business trips or well-deserved holidays. Jack surveyed its kinetic movement from a café stool, sipping a pre-flight coffee and clenching Sonia's hand as if worried she might run off.

'Do you think anyone in this airport is as excited as I am?' he asked.

'I don't know, but if you loosen your grip, the blood may reach my brain again, so I can think about it.'

'Sorry. This holding hands in public is still a novelty for me.'

He let go and Sonia wiggled her fingers exaggeratedly to restore their circulation.

'Are you happy to be seen out with me then, Jack? We've not exactly gone public with our relationship to date. Surely I'm not that much of an embarrassment?'

She tore off neat pieces of her vegan almond croissant with surgical precision. Jack had already devoured his more traditional buttery version and the table was a carpet of untidy crumbs.

He didn't know if she was serious, but there was an element of truth to what she said. As his contentment had grown, he had prevented anything external impinging on the relationship. Hiding the aspects of his life that made him miserable made it increasingly complicated to find reasons for Sonia not meeting his family. The strategy was unsustainable, and she was beginning to make jokes about his imaginary sisters, daughters, and total absence of friends.

None of this was an issue now. They had canoodled from the moment they got in the cab to choosing paperbacks in the departure lounge they had no intention of reading. As their flight was called, they strolled to the plane and Jack felt his years of frozen happiness beginning to thaw.

Sitting at the gate, his daydreaming was interrupted by the sight of a dishevelled individual standing next to them. Jack stared at the tall man wearing jeans so loose that his faded black Calvin Klein pants were almost entirely on display. He was wondering how someone so scruffy would not be embarrassed in public when he realised it was in fact Tom, an electrician who repaired machinery at his factory. His surprise was quickly replaced by panic that he might reveal something unfortunate in front of Sonia. Tom's stubbly face broke into a broad grin of recognition.

'Hello, Jack. Small world seeing you here. You off to Rome then?'

He was always very cheery, and Jack liked him, but now was not the time for a conversation.

'I hope so, or we're about to get on the wrong flight.'

He could feel Sonia looking at him in expectation of an introduction he did not want to make. Sensing his reluctance, she extended her hand towards Tom, stepping in front of Jack as she did so.

'Please forgive Jack. He's obviously not had enough coffee this morning and is still half asleep. I'm Sonia.'

'Tom. Lovely to meet you,' he said, grabbing her hand and shaking it with unnecessary enthusiasm. It was torment for Jack to think Tom might let slip his true role at the factory without appreciating the consequence, especially as Sonia was settling in for a nice pre-flight chinwag. In different circumstances it would have been a source of pride that he was going out with someone so open and charming, but right now it was a major inconvenience.

'What are you doing in Rome?' Jack interrupted, trying to take charge.

'Visiting my girlfriend. She teaches English there. I've told you about her, I'm sure I have.'

'Jack was probably too busy thinking about his next TV script to listen properly, I'm afraid.' This reference to Jack's secret life in television blindsided Tom, but Sonia carried on talking before he could ask for clarification.

'So how do you two know each other?' she asked.

Jack's guilty secret left him no choice other than to boorishly interrupt the conversation to wrench control.

'Tom's a brilliant electrician, who does a lot of work for me at my properties. Tom, this lovely woman, Sonia, is remarkably my girlfriend, and this is our first trip away together. Now if you don't mind, I don't want to burden her with tales of bad wiring.'

Jack consoled himself that it was a statement both truthful and incomplete: the abattoir was his property and its fuse board had been repaired only a couple of weeks previously. Tom was by now unnerved by the strange facial expressions and behaviour of his client, but there was something about Jack's tone that made him hesitant to ask anything further. A short silence was broken by a heavily Italian-accented airline announcement: '*Prego. Rows 8–16 nowa boarding.*'

'That's us!' Jack shouted as if he had won at bingo. He leapt to his feet and grabbed Sonia's arm. To his relief, Tom stayed put.

'You must have paid lots more for your seats, as I'm at the back of the plane. Safe flight and I hope the first holiday is a big success. Don't let Jack bore you with his freezer problems.'

The comment was lost over another seat announcement, but Jack could take no chances and frogmarched Sonia to the safety of a throng of people standing in line. She looked over her shoulder and shouted back to him, 'Nice to meet you and have a lovely weekend yourself.'

There was no reply and Jack observed Tom was tapping on his phone as if deliberately trying to avoid their gaze. As they took out their passports and boarding passes, Sonia said mockingly: 'OK, Jack, let's stand in this enormous queue for no reason. It's not going to make the plane take off any quicker, you know. What a charming little worrier you are.'

A few minutes later they were in their seats, Sonia's head on his shoulder, both succumbing to early-morning drowsiness. Jack felt calmer now the danger had passed; after all, a chance encounter like that could easily have unravelled his fragile narrative. For now, he was safe. Just as Sonia was drifting off, she whispered with gentle admonishment:

'Really, sweetheart. If you're happy to be seen in public with me, you're going to have to work on your manners a bit. You really were quite rude back there.'

* * *

The advantage of a trip to Rome in July was that they were guaranteed azure skies and brilliant sunshine, but as they left the air-conditioned comfort of Leonardo da Vinci airport, the heat blasted them like a demented hairdryer.

'Bugger me, if it's going to be this hot, I may not have packed enough T-shirts,' Jack exclaimed as he put their bags into a waiting taxi.

Sonia was in a loose summer dress that was unlikely to do much billowing in the breeze-free sunshine. She pointed to a small sweat patch that had appeared on Jack's white cotton shirt.

'You may need an extra spritz of deodorant when we check in, if you want to keep nuzzled close to me.'

Jack sniffed his armpit instinctively, realising immediately this was not an attractive thing to do.

'Sorry, not exactly the romantic start I was hoping for,' he apologised as the cab pulled off.

'No, really, it's lovely to watch you inhale your own scent. Very primeval.'

After that, they quietly observed the city unfolding in front of them. The ochre and terracotta apartment buildings, the pavement cafés, the fountains and the piazzas fringed by classical statues was everything Jack had imagined. As the taxi approached Piazza Venezia, they gasped as the city's full magnificence became clear. The Victor Emmanuel National Monument dominated a vista that included their first glimpse of the Colosseum, Trajan's Column and the Forum.

'There's so much to see. This place certainly couldn't have been built in a day,' was the best Jack could muster. Sonia's face was framed by an enormous smile, as she ignored his feeble joke.

'I can't believe it's taken me thirty-eight years to get here.'

'You just needed the right Gregory Peck.'

'In your dreams, matey boy. And let's be honest, I am no Audrey Hepburn. Have you seen me dance?'

'You will always be my princess. Even if you have been around the block a bit.'

She punched him affectionately on the arm and drew a bit closer to him.

'Anyway, are the next few days going to be your homage to *Roman Holiday*? I mean, you've seen the film once and as sweet as it was, you spent half an hour telling me that Fellini captured the essence of post-war Italy far more evocatively. You quite ruined the mood, I must say.'

'I'm just trying to give you a basic education in European cinema, but I'll save that for dinner tonight. Still, since I know how much you like the film, I've managed to introduce a few references to it as part of my grand seduction plan.'

'What are you talking about? Are we going dancing on the Tiber, or do we simply get to split up at the end of the weekend?'

'Neither, of course. It's actually a rather nice coincidence. The hotel, which I've been keeping a secret from you, is at 19 Via Margutta.'

Jack gave a little nod as if to say, *How clever am I?*

'Am I meant to know the significance of that?'

'Well, I did sneakily watch bits of the film again when planning the trip and was tickled to hear Gregory Peck announce his apartment at 51 Via Margutta, a few houses up from where we are staying. Kismet or what?'

Sonia was nonplussed.

'I think it qualifies as "or what". Also, I hope the hotel is nicer than his flat, which was the size of a cupboard. That bit I remember.'

'You won't be disappointed. It's so cool and hip, I'm surprised they let me in. As for number 51, I did sneak a quick peek on Google. It's a building site, I'm afraid.'

'I'll cope with the disappointment. All I care about is that the hotel has plenty of oat milk for my breakfast cappuccino.'

Jack smiled, trying to mask his concern. He had completely forgotten to phone up and ask if they catered for vegans. It was too late. The cab had pulled up outside a beautifully restored yellow building with giant modern doors revealing the boutique hotel inside. And like an excited child at Christmas, Sonia was striding towards Reception.

* * *

The temperature each day nudged an unbearable thirty-three degrees, and the streets were congested with so many tourists that it was hard to walk more than a couple of paces without slaloming around someone hunched over a guidebook. This made intensive sightseeing less desirable, and they reduced their planned itinerary to adjust to the conditions. Jack had been uncharacteristically organised and booked a guide to help avoid queuing at the Colosseum, Forum and Palatine Hill, but it had still been a feat of endurance rather than pleasure. While they were both genuinely interested in ancient civilisations, the avoidance of dehydration and sunstroke became their primary objective.

The elegance of the Spanish Steps and Trevi Fountain was shattered by the hordes of selfie-stick-wielding, overheated tourists jockeying to take the perfect picture of a landmark while a thousand people obscured its view. Jack and Sonia did not bother hanging around, realising there might be more comfort to be found in the marbled halls of an ancient building such as the baroque art collection of the Palazzo Colonna. It was still rammed, but at least it was cool.

When it came to the Vatican, Jack had been given the sensible advice to book the early morning first-viewing tour of the Sistine Chapel, which required a seven o'clock arrival. Naively, he had assumed there would be about ten people, joined by the Pope in his dressing gown to show them around. It seemed, however, that all the people they wanted to avoid had the same idea and a fleet of coaches disgorged enthusiastic multinational armies ready to do battle with the Swiss Guard.

Nevertheless, they had a bit of good fortune and Jack's group was the first to be let in with a staggered start. Their guide, an overexcited student called Toto, stressed how lucky they were to be at the front of the grid and broke into a trot to keep them in that position. As the sweat poured down his face, he kept shouting at the stragglers at the back to keep up. Jack felt sorry for two octogenarian Spaniards who were getting gradually lost and in danger of a coronary incident as they shuffled behind in despair.

Jack and Sonia were sufficiently fit to maintain a light jog and were rewarded by being the third and fourth people to enter the most famous site in Rome. They walked hand in hand, staring upwards in silence at *The Creation of Adam*. He did not want to ruin the moment by saying anything crass or pretentious, knowing he was capable of both. In truth, he found churches a bit boring, and this was just another one, albeit with an excellent decorator. He would, however, have visited twenty more that morning, so long as he was with her.

It was a trip of contrasts, because when they weren't stuck in the chaos of an overcrowded city filled with sightseers, they found themselves in their own world of passionate joy. The hotel was elegant and their chic suite, with its effective air conditioning, was a much more enjoyable place to be in the afternoon. Sometimes it was hard to leave their bed and return to the crowds.

Jack may have forgotten to check the oat milk supplies in the hotel, but he did his research on where to eat. It had been a happy coincidence that probably the best vegetarian restaurant in town was a hundred yards from the hotel, and it was so good they ate there twice, Sonia devouring the potato gnocchi the first night and a cauliflower risotto the next. Jack only cared about her food needs and would have eaten the flowers on the table if Sonia asked him to.

They had lunch one day in the Jewish quarter and went to its best restaurant, devouring *carciofi alla giudia*, which was simply a giant plate of fried artichokes but sounded so much more glamorous when ordered in Italian. And they drank endless cups of *espresso*, Italian beer in chilled glasses and late-night negronis in various cafés and bars, watching the drift of disparate people as Jack made up his own commentary to imagine glamorous and unlikely backstories.

On their last afternoon, they jumped in a cab and headed to the church of Santa Maria to see the Bocca della Verità – the ancient marble mask of an angry face whose mouth, according to legend, will snap off the hand placed inside of anyone not telling the truth. It was the setting for the most famous scene in *Roman Holiday*, when Gregory Peck and Audrey Hepburn, hiding the truth of their identities, slip their hands into it nervously, half expecting something terrible to happen. Sonia insisted on visiting it, even though Jack felt extremely uneasy at being close to an edifice dedicated to truthfulness.

There was a longish queue, but because the path was shaded, Sonia was quite happy to wait. By now, Jack had formulated his plan to tell her about Fogel's Chickens, praying the inevitable anger would hopefully blow over like a tropical storm. His idea was to return to London and head to her flat for the grand reveal. Still flushed from the excitement of the last few days, he would confess everything over dinner and explain all his reasons for not being able to do so earlier. It was risky, but the reward was his sustained future happiness.

As they edged toward the Bocca, Sonia was reading on her phone about its history. Her face screwed up in horror at what she discovered.

'This is the site of an ancient cattle market, apparently. And one interpretation is that it was originally a drain cover that the blood from slaughtered cattle flowed into. Oh, that is so revolting. Blood running down the streets into a hole in the road. Yet again it makes me wonder how you still eat meat. It's unfathomable. How many more examples do you want that it's barbaric to slaughter animals?'

Jack felt a sweat on top of the sweat that had already made his T-shirt damp and sticky. Why did all roads in Rome lead to the truth he was hiding: that his real job was running a massive abattoir and chain of butchers? Getting sucked into a serious conversation now was definitely not a good idea, but there was something about Sonia's rant that seemed to demand a reply. He chose his words very carefully.

'I'm sorry. I can understand how seriously you feel about this and how upset I make you, which is the last thing I want to do. I really love you. You know that by now and I'll do a deal. If we don't talk about it for the rest of the trip, we'll address the subject properly when we're back at your flat tomorrow night.'

Maybe things were beginning to coalesce into a natural course of events. And now Jack had not simply to tell the truth but confront what a new life with Sonia might mean for his old carnivorous one. It was far too hot for emotional intensity, and Jack was relieved that she backed down.

'I love you too, you fricking animal murderer. You've got yourself a deal.' They were declaring their feelings spontaneously, without hesitation.

As they edged towards the scowling marble mouth, it suddenly became clear to them both that the movie's sophistication was not reflected in the snaking line of smelly and unkempt tourists in search of another clichéd picture. There were about ten people in front of them and Sonia turned to Jack and announced, 'Oh, sod this nonsense. Can we go for a drink somewhere glamorous rather than hang around here?'

He nodded and wordlessly they stepped out of the queue and walked briskly towards a taxi rank. Jack still could not stop himself commenting on the situation.

'Delighted to scarper, but I thought you wanted to see if I passed this ancient polygraph test. I was ready to lose a hand for you.'

'I hope not, Jack. As I always tell you, I like my men with two hands and the ability not to lie.'

'I'll drink to that,' Jack replied glibly. What an idiotic thing to say. *Shut up or you'll destroy all the good work that got you to this point.* He regained his composure and asked the driver to take them to the Hotel Russie. Time to sip some cocktails on the elegant terrace of the famous Stravniskij terrace bar, where the romantic mood would be rekindled. One more night of staring at Sonia's lovely face in a beautiful setting, making love in a luxurious hotel room, and then in twenty-four hours, with a carefully rehearsed declaration of the truth and explanation of his reasons, Jack would be set free from the burden of deception. He was so nearly there.

Chapter 22

Richie Johnson had always loved chicken.

Brought up by his grandmother in the 1980s in a small town just outside Atlanta, his diet was almost entirely fried and focused on the body parts of poultry. Wings, legs, thighs – it didn't matter so long as it was doused in breadcrumbs and battered in oil. Fruit and vegetables were as rare as dodo eggs in his daily menu.

By the time he was fourteen, Richie was six foot three and weighed two hundred and twenty pounds. In high school, he became a promising linebacker in the football team until a knee injury put an end to any commitment to exercise. Instead, innate verbal dexterity and a powerful baritone voice provided a new route to fame and fortune as a rapper. When it came to creating an identity that would be truly distinctive, his relentless desire to devour chicken proved a source of inspiration.

And so began the global ascent of Drumstx in the world of rap. His 2007 album 'Ain't No Chicken' sold over four million copies and won a couple of Grammys and its follow-up, 'Wingin' It', did nearly as well. His rap tackled themes of love, violence and the establishment, but if there was a chance to reference his food of choice, he would gladly incorporate it somehow into the song or its video. In his early career, he even fronted a global ad campaign for KFC based on one of his songs, cancelling his endorsement when he decided to launch his own restaurant.

All of this was unknown to Jack as he spent his last night in Rome with Sonia. Having left the Bocca della Verità, they decided that for twenty-four hours they would switch their phones off and cut themselves adrift to enjoy each other's company, undistracted by texts, emails or the news. Jack rehearsed his speech for the next evening in his head in between eating great food, sipping cold white wine, and retiring to the intimacy of their bed.

At the same time, a bored Drumstx was scouring his social media channels in his LA hotel suite before leaving to shoot a commercial for his new hot chicken sauce. He was savvy in how he communicated with his fan base, and for many years had shared every waking thought on Twitter, amassing a following of over seven million people worldwide. His ability to channel humour in a rhyme and his liberal agenda, coupled with a restless ambition for success, made him an unconstrained commentator on any subject.

Jack's life was often shaped by the randomness of the universe. He had little faith in the divine to bring him comfort, believing bad things happened because life was basically rubbish. He had no luck. His father's weak heart saddled Jack with the business when he dropped dead, and his mother and sisters were more interested in their own lives so did not want to help him. As a father, he had done his best, but for some unknown reason, his elder child blamed him for her unhappiness.

It was therefore just another cruel coincidence that Drumstx's social media team had recently added new monitoring tools to his Twitter account to pick up interesting chicken-related content. He was about to drag himself into the shower when he came across the animated film of Chaim the Chicken singing and dancing 'There ain't no good in Fogel chickens'. The first time he smiled, and by the fourth time he watched it, he was laughing out loud. The parochial spat of two butchers in London fascinated him, even though the limited thread of comments suggested he was in the minority.

Unfortunately for Jack, Drumstx was no stranger to kosher chicken, being managed by Freddie Hirsch, unique in the music industry as not simply a Jew but an observant one. Freddie's *haimische* home had been frequently visited on a Friday night by his client, who would devour Debbie Hirsch's chicken soup/roast chicken combo with relish.

This Fogel guy was therefore insulting the honour of his Jewish brothers and sisters. Drumstx stared at the blank white walls in his minimalist suite and began to compose a response to make Chaim the Chicken famous. Inspiration came quickly and he typed his poetic response.

'*If it ain't real kosher, you just say no sir ...*'

To reiterate whose side he was on, he added:

'*Yo Chaim, you're cool.*

See, Fogel you fool.

You don't mess with the betterman.

Go buy chicken from Gutterman.'

He signed off with his regular hashtags of *#lovechicken* and *#drumstxhotandspicy*, the latter being the sauce he was in LA to promote. After all, every random tweet he crafted still offered the chance to sell more product. Letting out an enormous burp, he rolled his hefty frame out of bed to start the day. By the time he was soaping himself under the jet of boiling water in his enormous multi-nozzled shower, his mind had wandered to a thousand more pressing things.

Jack lay with Sonia nestled in his arms in a hotel room in Rome, drifting into peaceful sleep. The evening had been the perfect conclusion to an idyllic trip. Satiated and deeply in love, he was completely unaware that millions of people across the world were now siding with Lionel Gutterman in their dispute, courtesy of this most unexpected intervention.

Chapter 23

As the plane touched down on the tarmac at Heathrow, Jack's stomach began to knot in anticipation of the conversation he was going to have in Sonia's flat in a few hours. They had been silent during the flight, reading their books to give them a break from the happy intensity of the previous three days. Sonia was caught up in her novel and barely looked up for two hours, while Jack stared at the jumbled words of his, scrabbling for the right way to tell her the truth and evaluating different approaches in his head.

No, he realised, as the plane came to a halt by its stand, you cannot prepare and control a sensitive conversation; you must just get on with it and hope that the real love between them could accommodate his mistake. He was so certain of their future together, he even wondered if he should do something mad like propose to her straight after revealing his full life story. Tempting as it was, he knew that patience and calm was what was needed right now. He looked out of the window as the passengers began to disembark. The brilliant Italian sunshine had been replaced by the industrial grey drizzle of a miserable English summer's day. The holiday was over.

* * *

There is nothing nice about getting out of an airport. Even though it was a Monday afternoon, it was mobbed, and they walked for what seemed like miles to get to passport control. Industrial action meant there weren't enough immigration officers on duty and the queue snaked like an oversized boa constrictor through the Arrivals hall. As they inched forward, Sonia switched on her phone and rang

Alexandru to see how the weekend had gone, relieved to be told takings had been particularly strong on Saturday. Jack held back from doing the same. The moment he turned his phone on, he would be sucked into the chaos of his life, relinquishing the pleasure of Sonia's company for something gloomier.

They collected their bags, the last it seemed, off the carousel, and walked to the train station to take the Heathrow Express to Paddington. It would be late afternoon by the time they got back to Sonia's flat, and Jack would confess immediately. He would make a cup of tea for them both and say whatever came into his head to relieve the tension. His declaration would be sincere and passionate. He yearned for the truth.

There was not long to wait for the train and as they walked to the platform, Jack grabbed a free copy of the *Evening Standard* from a stand. The carriage was busy, but they found a couple of seats next to each other. Opposite them, two American tourists, clearly new to Europe, stared with wonder at the unfolded Tube map on their laps. Jack and Sonia smirked at their attempts to understand how to get from Paddington to *L-c-y-sest-ar Square*.

The train pulled off with a flurry of pre-recorded announcements. Jack stared out of the window as Sonia idly started to scan the paper. After not very long, Jack became aware that her arm, resting next to his, had tautened and her knee, pressed against his, was now rocking frantically from side to side. She was reading an article, her face contorted in an unfamiliar grimace. He read the words too and a flash of pain in his stomach was so intense he thought he might faint. There was an ancient photo of him accompanying the piece, from an old website. She did not look up from the paper as she wailed, 'What the fuck is this all about? What haven't you been telling me?'

* * *

CHICKEN WARS DECLARED IN THE BATTLE
OF THE KOSHER BUTCHERS

A local business disagreement between two butchers has attracted the attention of the Grammy-winning rapper Drumstx and has now become a global battle on Twitter, thanks to his intervention.

Lionel Gutterman, owner of six kosher butcher shops in North London and Manchester, has been engaged in a turf war with Jack Fogel, owner of Fogel's Chickens, a poultry business including an abattoir in St Albans, five London shops and two restaurants, 'Clucks'. The dispute revolves around the ownership of the Fogel's shops in Hendon and Golders Green, which Gutterman claims belong to him in recompense for his illegal dismissal from Fogel's Chickens in 1988.

The commercial disagreement spread on to social media when Gutterman began a Twitter feed for his brand ambassador, 'Chaim the Chicken'. Gutterman produced a short animated film, recording his own version of the famous Louis Jordan song 'Ain't nobody here but us chickens', which proclaimed the superiority of his chickens over those of his rival.

Yesterday, Drumstx shared the film and endorsed Gutterman's chickens. Over the last 24 hours, his tweet has been liked by 356,000 people and shared over 100,000 times.

Lionel Gutterman commented: 'It is an honour to receive such support from Mr Drumstx. Our business is based on religious and ethical principles. Sadly, Jack Fogel gives those Jewish values a bad name. He was recently sued for age and disability discrimination, has fallen out with his restaurant partners and clearly has an unfair monopoly of the kosher market. He has even resorted to violence, arranging the assault of a 19-year-old student, Aaron Levy, who was dressed as my mascot, Chaim, and was innocently handing out leaflets raising money for charity.'

Rabbi Isaac Furstein, who was asked by Mr Gutterman to intercede, issued a statement via the London Board of Kosher Supervision: 'We would hope that peace can quickly prevail between these important businesses in our community. It behoves both of their leaders to find an acceptable compromise. There is plenty of chicken to go round.'

Stacey Blor, co-owner of the restaurant chain 'Clucks', told the Evening Standard: 'We cannot comment on the issue of the shops, but while Mr Fogel is still our current partner, we are in discussion as to whether it is still appropriate for us to be commercially aligned.'

Jack Fogel was unavailable for comment.

* * *

The train was pulling into Paddington and Sonia had been staring out of the window in silence for a couple of minutes. She took deep breaths and tried to compose herself but was struggling to staunch the flow of tears. Jack's head was spinning in the chaos of what had happened. His world had not simply unravelled but been destroyed by a nuclear explosion. Vilified in the press as an unscrupulous businessman, his relationship was about to disintegrate through the revelation of the enormous lie he had told. If he tried to defend himself, he might make things worse, but he had to say something. He tried to touch her arm, but she recoiled as if he had given her an electric shock.

'Sonia. I love you and I have done you a wrong, which I was going to try and explain to you tonight.'

As he made the declaration, it sounded weirdly stilted, as if the denouement to a Victorian melodrama. He carried on, not sure what to say.

'Now you know my business. I am completely perplexed how this bizarre battle has made the papers. It's all nonsense ... it's all ... I don't know what to say?'

Jack could not give an adequate explanation and despite the onset of adrenalin, words began to fail him. Sonia's expression was an unfamiliar mix of anger and misery.

'How? How has this happened? All I asked for was the truth. Wasn't that what I told you the evening we met, you arsehole? And now you are a different person than the one I fell in love with. I don't know who you are, in fact. What have you done to us? You own an *abattoir*? You're a butcher, you have a property business and I bet you are nothing in TV. Did you not think I might have wanted to know some of this?'

The Americans opposite had abandoned their attempt to find a route from their hotel to Westminster Abbey and were making little effort to hide their fascination in the massive argument taking place. They knew it had something to do with the newspaper discarded on the floor and the wife was clearly contemplating picking it up to make sure they had the full context. Jack could hardly speak, his mouth felt so dry.

'You have to let me explain what's happened, I beg you. You may never forgive me, but maybe you'll understand.'

The train doors opened, and Sonia grabbed her case from the overhead rack without saying anything. It was clear that she wanted to leave on her own. As she edged towards the door with the other disembarking passengers, she muttered to no one in particular, 'You are an idiot, Jack.'

Pushing her way through the crowd, she disappeared onto the platform. Jack felt that he should run after her, begging forgiveness. As he got up to follow, the American woman shook her head like a disappointed headmistress about to discipline a pupil, indicating he should stay put.

He slumped back in the seat and wondered if Lionel was satisfied now.

* * *

Wheeling his case to Starbucks in the station, he ordered a coffee and sat at the back of the café, staring at the black screen of his iPhone. Unable to delay further, he pressed the side button and waited for it to come to life and the assault to begin. Within seconds, repetitive pings formed an atonal concerto, reminding him of the extent of his troubles. On it went.

Ping. Ping. Ping. You're buggered. Ping. You're finished. Ping. She hates you. Ping. Your business is over. Ping. Natalie will hate you even more. Ping. You've lost. Ping. Loser. Ping. Ping.

35 text messages

27 WhatsApp messages

24 voice messages

64 emails

Ping. Ping. Pingety-fucking-ping

* * *

It took him several hours to go through most of them and his head felt like it might explode from the complexity of the jigsaw of angry messages. A day off the grid and somehow he was a fugitive who had fled the scene of the crime. He grabbed a pad to jot them down by category, level of vitriol and urgency.

First the media enquiries. It seems the story had run in the *Evening Standard* after it had appeared that morning in the *Daily Mail*. He had calls from *The Times*, the *Daily Mail*, *The Daily Telegraph*, *The Jewish Chronicle*, *Jewish News*, *The Times of Israel*, BBC

News, Sky News, The New York Times. Was there anyone in the media who did not want a quote? Jack wondered if, because it was July, people were on holiday so there was no news elsewhere. If only a natural disaster somewhere in the world could replace his own personal one.

Then came his family. Inevitably, his harshest critic was his mother.

> **What have you done – this can't be good for our business.**

The ludicrous absence of maternal compassion stemmed obviously from fear that her plans with Kurt were under threat.

His ever-dependable sister Tracy was more compassionate.

> **Are you ok Jack. Call me.**

An hour later she had tried again.

> **I am panicking now. Please call asap just to let me know you haven't done anything drastic.**

Karen was initially sympathetic.

> **This is mad. Be strong and tell Lionel where he can stick his Chaim the Chicken. You've got this xxx**

Self-interest quickly replaced her benevolence and the next text reverted to her traditional use of capitals to convey commands to be obeyed, not questioned.

> OMG the press has found out about me being your
> sister. You MUST sort this NOW.

Ali was kinder, but evidently intent on protecting her daughter ahead of her ex-husband.

> Jack. We are worried for you. This all seems so
> unfair. I hope you are coping. Please don't call Natalie
> though. She is too upset at the moment and the press
> attention has been a big setback for her.

The thought that Lionel was causing such fissures in his relationship with Natalie compounded Jack's anguish. Thank heavens for Isobel.

> What has happened? I know you have done nothing
> wrong. That Lionel is horrid. Love you Dad and sending
> huge hug. Call when you can. #drumstxsucks xxxx

He sent a few quick texts to say he was OK and trying to process what had happened. More pressing were the messages from his management team, store managers, accountant, lawyer, suppliers all wanting to know what was going on. All this interest was the result of the random intervention of a global rap superstar to a song on Twitter and had nothing to do with the daily operation of his very uninteresting business.

Jack expected his supply chain and loyal customer base to remain unaffected by this nonsense. He made some calls to reassure everyone that mad stories in the news tend to blow over once they hit the headlines and no one would be interested within a couple of days. Crisis management for Jack had hitherto been nonexistent. Now, with his luck, it was only a matter of time until Kim Jong-un and the Dalai Lama waded in with an opinion that he would have to deal with.

He tried to follow some of the Twitter threads but disappeared down rabbit holes of irrelevant comments from all over the world. They evolved from simple 'likes' of the song to musing on the nature of who we are as people, what we eat and what it says about us as global citizens. A few months ago, Lionel had asked for the keys to a couple of shops and now, in the bizarre social media ether, Jack Fogel was somehow responsible for climate change, food poverty and the inequality of Western capitalism.

There were several voice messages from Stacey, acknowledging Jack's humiliation with the sincerity of an undercover assassin. She was insistent they meet immediately and asked if he'd come to the restaurant tomorrow afternoon. It was impossible to find an adequate excuse to delay the confrontation further, but since he was now such an adept liar, he might think of a good one overnight.

Mike Gibson also called, seemingly ignorant of Jack's media exposure. He sounded flustered, informing him something serious had come up, asking him to call as soon as he could. Jack shuddered at the prospect of further rejection and was sure now that nothing positive would happen in his life for quite some time.

Rabbi Furstein left Jack a soothing message, wanting to talk as soon as possible. He referred to Jack as 'my friend' several times, and his sign-off was clearly a request to Jack to spare further communal embarrassment: *As my grandmother used to tell me when I complained my big brother hit me: sometimes you just need to be the bigger person. I can give you a back-up quote from the Talmud if that helps too, but I thought I'd keep it simple as you must have a lot on your plate.*

Inevitably, Lionel Gutterman could not resist leaving a self-congratulatory message and Jack imagined the Cheshire-cat grin fixed on his mahogany face, wondering how hard it would be to get hold of those undetectable Russian poisons and meet him for coffee.

How do you think you are doing in this little battle of ours then Jack? My friend Drumstx the rapper seems to have helped me rather a lot. This has got to stop now however for the sake of our businesses. You need to stop being so stubborn. I have won the PR battle and as they say, to the victor must go the spoils. Call me and we can make this go away.

Jack hardly touched his coffee and two hours of listening to messages and making phone calls left him exhausted. He knew that to avoid spiralling into despair, he needed to maintain the conviction that there was a way forward with Lionel. All he could really see, however, was loneliness and grief if Sonia was absent from his life.

His phone, almost out of battery, pinged one last time.

Come to the cafe at 8pm to explain. S

No kiss. No reminder of their affection of the previous three days. This was not how it was meant to be.

Chapter 24

Alexandru, opening the door, glowered at him like he was a mass murderer who ate kittens in his spare time. The café was empty, save another man staring at him with equal contempt. Jack guessed it was Alexandru's partner, Luca, who had been drafted in to ramp up the levels of loathing. There was no need. Jack could not have hated himself more at that moment.

They sat in menacing silence for ten minutes, until Sonia emerged from the kitchen, wiping her hands on her apron. She saw Jack and froze. He could not believe that only twenty-four hours before they were clinking glasses in a bustling restaurant in Rome. She walked to the counter and poured two glasses of water and then sat opposite him, her expression quizzical. He had no idea of her mood and when she spoke, her voice sounded stripped of any affection.

'Well, I certainly didn't see this coming,' she began.

'I'm sorry, Sonia. I am so, so sorry.'

His anguish was greater than when Ali announced she was leaving their marriage. Despite the clammy evening, he was shivering, his pain so much more intense because it was self-inflicted. The café had an eerie stillness, intensified by Sonia's two brooding bodyguards sitting in silent judgement and refusing to look away. He noticed the daily specials menu board of pulses, grains and wholefoods, vegan dishes reminding him that perhaps he had no place in Sonia's world.

'You may be sorry, Jack. You may be sincere. I'm just not sure that is enough.' Alexandru nodded vigorously in agreement. It was not helping Jack that these two unwanted bystanders were sitting so close to him.

'Do we have to have an audience for this conversation?'

'You can ask them to leave, but I don't rate your chances. And if you don't mind me saying, Alexandru and Luca are the least of your current problems, if what I've read in the *Evening Standard* is anything to go by.'

'I'll cope with their scorn. Yours is much harder to bear. And frankly, my current business problems are a sideshow. All that matters is you.'

He was begging too hard, and his pleas sounded so stilted that Sonia started drumming her nails on the table with irritation. His attempt at sincerity was making things worse.

'What did you think was going to happen, Jack? I knew you'd planned a major discussion of some sort. I thought you were going to tell me that you were ready to meet my dad and introduce me to your girls. Do you know, for a second I even wondered if you were going to do something daft like propose? But no, you'd run out of road, hadn't you? That chap Tom we met at the airport was going to give you away, which is why you were so weird with him. You were too nervous that I was going to find out your secret. Am I right?'

'Of course you are. I was terrified Tom would make a comment about the business by mistake. Full disclosure, he's an electrician who fixes the freezers and fridges for me in the factory, by the way.'

'Your factory? Ah yes, is that the one where the chickens are killed?'

'It's the only one I have, I'm afraid.'

Sonia stood up and stretched her arms and shoulders in small circular motions, clearly exhausted by the day's revelations. Outside, a group of young people on a night out walked past the café window, laughing boisterously. One of them, for some reason, shouted 'What a wanker!' very loudly. It seemed to Jack that he could only be passing comment on him.

Sonia returned to her seat and took a couple of deep breaths before speaking.

'Jack, who on earth are you? I mean, we've been so intimate and have discussed our lives in such detail. Yet you misled me, controlling the conversation for your own ends. That's a shitty thing to do.'

'It's not my finest moment. Can you believe it was an act of love?'

'It's a strange one, if it is. Do you realise I was excited about us maybe having a child together one day?'

'We still can.'

'Yes, and if it's a boy we'll name him Pinocchio after you.'

'I lied to you. I am not a liar.'

'Very clever distinction, but not sure I agree.'

Now it was Alexandru's turn to get up, noisily scratching his chair against the wooden floor as he did. He walked slowly to the door and checked if it was locked, like a cowboy in a deserted saloon preparing for a fight. Returning to his table, he rested his hand on Luca's and resumed his disdainful staring. The interruption irritated Jack.

'Maybe Tweedle Glum and Tweedle Glummer on the next table will stop looking at me like that.'

'Maybe you will leave, and they won't have to.'

'Sonia, I don't want it to end without you understanding me better.'

'That's not for you to decide, I'm afraid. Anyway, over the last couple of hours, I've done my own research to find out about you. It's quite a business you run, no wonder you can afford nice hotels. But in the end, do you know the mad thing about all of this?'

'What, madder than finding myself hated globally because a rapper I've never heard of shared a song from my rival trying to destroy me? A new level of bonkers, if you ask me.'

She smiled briefly at the absurdity of what he said.

'I'll grant you that must hurt. I was, however, referring to something much more important. No, the mad thing is I would have fallen for you if you'd told me the truth in the first place. Do you think I'm so narrow-minded that I can't differentiate you from your business? I fell in love with the funny, pretentious, caring and ever-so-lost Jack Fogel. I liked you from the moment I walked in the restaurant, you moron.'

Alexandru interrupted her with a derisive snort. Clearly, he did not think that Jack was loveable in any way.

'Sonia, I didn't mean to lie. It was all a bit of an accident. I was so excited to have met you and was worried that you wouldn't want to carry on the date because I'm the enemy of the vegan community. And then when we hit it off so well, I wanted to delay exposing all the crap in my life in case you changed your mind.'

'That's a bit self-serving, isn't it? I'm a vegan, Jack. It's a lifestyle choice, not a fundamentalist religion.'

'I'm so ashamed of myself. You're the best thing in my life and now I've risked everything.' He was almost shouting now. He didn't care, he had to unburden himself, no matter how trite his despair sounded.

'This is the truth I should have told you two months ago. The thing is, I've done very well with the business. Much to my annoyance, I'm good at running it and have made it very successful. This tied me to it even more as it got bigger, which in turn just made me more miserable. Then you came along and showed me I didn't have to be the angriest and most resentful person in the room. God, however, chose this moment for Lionel bloody Gutterman to announce a ridiculous vendetta against my family and has waged a ludicrous war against me ever since. It's been so demeaning. I now realise that I've been terrible in all my relationships. I seem to be failing as a father and this made me desperate not to be an equally bad boyfriend. I hoped, somehow, you'd be blinded by your love for me. That's not worked out too well, has it?'

He slumped in his chair, overwhelmed by a sensation of imminent loss. Sonia touched his shoulder briefly. He didn't know if it was a good sign or a gesture of farewell.

'Good speech, Jack. I mean it. However, there's so much I don't understand, and however awful things have been for you, I can't really get past the bit where you sort of withheld some vital and relevant information. "*Jack, please always tell me the truth. OK, Sonia. Thank you, Jack. You're welcome, Sonia. What do you do, Jack? I have a property business, but let's talk about something else.*" Am I being unfair? Because that's how I remember the conversation.'

He had never heard her sound so caustic, yet what right did he have to complain?

'Sonia, I can't lose you.'

She didn't reply, but started to collect the glasses and trudge towards the door to the kitchen, leaving him fearful that their relationship was perhaps beyond repair. He gave it one last go.

'Sonia. We can be happy. Please, give me another chance.'

'Why should I give a chance to someone who can't be honest about their life? Why should I?'

She disappeared out of the room to the sound of his failed pleading. Alexandru moved with purpose to the front door once more, this time to unlock it and hold it open. As Jack walked past him, he spoke in an unexpectedly gentle voice, given his last twenty minutes of sneering facial expressions.

'You really have destroyed a wonderful woman, Jack, with your weak behaviour. It was so unnecessary. This is not just about you. We really love her too, you know, and can never forgive you. I hope she doesn't.'

Chapter 25

Jack had struggled to sleep after the tumult of seeing Sonia, his mind yo-yoing from one desperate thought to the next. Eventually, he fell into a deep slumber accompanied by a horrible dream in which he was lying on the floor of a derelict factory as a long queue of people took a ticket from a deli counter in its corner. Once their number was called, they would take their turn kicking his supine body while shouting *No one likes you*. Yet again he was dressed as a chicken, although this time his feathers were black and matted with blood. Even in his subconscious state, his grief was palpable, and it was a relief to be woken by a call from Tracy telling him an interview with Lionel and Drumstx was about to start on the BBC.

He turned on his radio to hear Lionel coveting fifteen minutes of fame by mimicking the cut-glass diction of a wartime newsreader. In LA, it was the early hours of the morning for Drumstx, who was evidently speaking from a party that was in full swing. Their interviewer, Phil, a journalist more comfortable grilling politicians than discussing grilled chicken, sounded particularly annoyed at being given this trite story to cover.

Lionel was asked why he had recorded the song and took the opportunity to outline the importance for the Jewish people of keeping kosher, rather than answering the question.

'*Allow me to elaborate, Philip, on the unbreakable bond of the Jewish people with their God's commandments for upholding specific dietary laws.*'

Phil's attempt to ask about his rivalry with Jack stimulated further pomposity, as if Lionel thought he was running for public office.

'*Sometimes one is compelled to put aside the quest for financial advancement to uphold values of commercial decency and integrity. My nemesis is a fellow poulterer, Jack Fogel, who I am afraid seems to be intent on dragging our noble butchering trade into the Dark Ages. We shall prevail over such deplorable behaviour.*'

By now, Phil was desperate to be interrupted by news of a boy band splitting up or a tornado off the coast of Kent, but instead had to listen to his angry producer in his headphones telling him to move on to Drumstx before the entire audience switched off.

'*Drumstx, tell me what first got you interested in this argument between two London kosher butchers?*'

He expected a much easier time with such an established global celebrity, but the singer's whisky-fuelled enthusiasm was evaporating. Suddenly, the man who could rap at a million miles an hour became an interviewee of few words.

'*I like chicken.*'

'*So, we know. But why did this particular song make you want to get involved?*'

'*Like I said … I like chicken. That dude Fogel sounded kinda …*'

Phil was now desperate to finish the interview and years of top-level broadcast journalism had taught him to prompt and probe to elicit an answer, no matter the circumstances.

'*Kind of what?*' he asked, undaunted.

'*Kind of a motherfucker …*'

* * *

The rapid end of the interview and the embarrassed apologies of the entire BBC Radio 5 Live Breakfast team allowed Jack momentary enjoyment. Being called a very rude name by a global music icon was going to be a badge of honour and he was relieved that Lionel's media platform had been dismantled. It was hardly a victory, though. By the time he drove to work, his mood was bleak as he replayed Sonia's final words to him of the previous evening: '*Why should I give a chance to someone who can't be honest about their life?*'

What was his life if it wasn't with Sonia? He could not let this happen, but for now he had to confront a day likely to be a deluge of pressing problems. When it was over, he would formulate his plan for how to make peace.

He began by calling Mike Gibson from the car, fully prepared for bad news in his pursuit of creative success. Mike answered immediately and sounded disappointed.

'Oh, it's you.'

'Sadly, it is, although most days I wish I could be someone else.'

Normally, a bit of banter would elicit a return put-down from Mike. Not today; he sounded like he had caught him at a funeral for a loved one.

'I was expecting my lawyer,' Mike said quietly.

'Sorry to disappoint. Is something wrong?'

'You might say that.' His voice simmered with anger.

'What on earth has happened?'

'Something awful.'

Mike sounded so brittle, and Jack did not know what to say. Ahead of him there was an accident and he had to brake suddenly and join a queue of cars. The sky had turned ominously black, a summer storm imminent, and it promised to be a miserable morning. All he wanted was a smidgen of good news about the one project in his life that fulfilled him, but this now seemed unlikely. He tried one last time to engage Mike.

'You should hear the day I've just had.'

No response.

'You said something had come up? Do you remember you left a voicemail yesterday?'

Jack often wondered if they really were friends or Mike just saw him as a charity case mixed with nostalgia for when they worked together years ago. Perhaps this fragile relationship explained the intensity of Mike's outburst, which accompanied the kettledrum thunder now exploding outside the car.

'I'll tell you what's happened, my would-be Larry David, or whatever great Jewish writer you think you are. I've been accused of "improper behaviour" with a young marketing executive called Destiny. What kind of stupid idiot calls their daughter Destiny? Anyway, she of the stupid name, Destiny, turned my head and I behaved like a prat and now she has the harassment texts to prove it. No one is remotely interested in my version of events, and I have been suspended from my own company. Can you believe it? Twenty-five years of reputation gone like that. What do you care, you're just worried about your stupid treatment for "Widgets". Stick to the chickens, Jack. They're your best bet.'

Before Jack could work out what to say to this tirade, Mike added an unexpected coda.

'Sorry for that rant. It's a tough time, you understand, and I just can't control my anger. The reason I rang yesterday is because in all the mayhem, I did get an email from Channel 4 to say you've got a meeting with Neil Yeats. I thought you'd want to know before I'm sent to Siberia. I'm afraid you'll be doing the meeting on your own though.'

Jack felt guilty now, because despite Mike's personal disaster, it was not all bad news. Finally, he had secured a meeting with the Head of Comedy at Channel 4, and with a bit of effort he could surely find another production company to help him if Mike was no longer available. Sometimes you needed to be expedient in difficult circumstances.

'I'll forward you the details, Jack, and I'm sorry again for what I just said about "Widgets". It's a good idea, I wouldn't have wasted my time with you if it wasn't. Good luck, and I really hope you find what you're looking for. Meanwhile, I must go and save my marriage. Currently, there's more chance of your programme getting made.'

Jack realised the irony of their respective personal situations: both pleading for forgiveness from their partners. Before he could share this miserable coincidence, Mike hung up and he knew they would not talk for a very long time.

* * *

When Jack got to the factory, it was almost ten o'clock, which was very late for him. As he entered, he was aware that his staff were looking at him with a mixture of pity and amusement. A few people tried to give him a supportive nod, and a couple of women even blew him a kiss before dissolving into fits of schoolgirl giggles. Jack was sufficiently thick-skinned not to worry about what his staff thought about him, but he did not enjoy their mockery. All he wanted was everyone to carry on with their work.

Tuesdays were a busy day for killing, often up to seven thousand birds, and Jack made his usual tour of each station in the factory to ensure that everything was progressing as it should before retreating to the calm of his office to deal with the consequences of the previous day. His first job was to check the news and social media to see if he had been vilified further. While the story had been picked up by quite a few papers and news services, the coverage seemed restricted to Drumstx's involvement rather than anything too detailed about his business. He followed various comments threads on Twitter, relaxed about the opinions of random people around the world given they were not likely to be shopping for chickens in Golders Green anytime soon.

Drumstx calling him a *motherf****** on morning drive-time, however, was not going to help the brouhaha go away and so he decided to prepare a statement, just in case. He stared at his computer screen, starting sentences and then rapidly deleting them. Every writing challenge was important to him and even an inconsequential comment to the press quickly became like a commission from a major Hollywood studio for a film script. His difficulty this time was that balancing a vestige of dignity, so as not to offend the kosher authorities, with a sense of humour might reflect well on him and his business. Eventually, he drafted a few lines that struck the right tone.

I am a bit bemused by the attention we have received. Some friendly rivalry between a couple of businesses has bizarrely gone viral. While I would have preferred not to have the global fame, any lover of chicken, like Drumstx, is a friend of Fogel's Chickens. As for the words of our rival's silly song, I can assure our customers that you won't find a better kosher chicken anywhere in London, despite what Chaim the Chicken says. After all, he works for the competition!

Next, he rang his old university friend, Alex Lazarus, for some advice on how to deal with the situation. Alex had sold his parenting website *Primaparent.com* for tens of millions a few years previously and was now a philanthropist and investor. When Alex built his business, he achieved notoriety for a data breach that had required him to give evidence to a parliamentary subcommittee. He knew a thing or two about crisis management, therefore, and would be a good source of guidance. Jack spent five minutes explaining the situation to Alex, who was by the pool of his Mallorcan finca with his family for an extended summer holiday.

'I hope you don't mind the interruption, it's just you're the only other person I know who has been humiliated on the world stage. You'll know what to do.'

'Happy to help if I can. You won't find anyone more unpopular than me, I can promise.'

'So how do I fight back against Lionel? It's bizarre, we even have convergent interests as I still supply his shops with some of their chickens. He's absolutely obsessed with destroying me, however, because he can't get over being humiliated by my grandfather about a hundred years ago. It's pathetic. He's like a nasty blob of chewing gum on my shoe that I can't remove.'

In the background, Jack could hear the laughter of Alex's children playing in the pool and immediately felt regret for his fractured relationship with Natalie. Sonia wanted a child too and this had been an exciting prospect but given everything, it would have to be an immaculate conception for that to happen now. His mind was wandering, and he realised that Alex had been making a long, impassioned speech, which was often the case when asked even the simplest question. Jack hadn't caught a word of what he said.

'Sorry, Alex, bad reception in the factory. Can you say it again?'

'Damn it, Jack, it was one of my better motivational pep talks. All right, you can have the abridged version. Firstly, I thought all digital start-ups were mad, but you win hands down. Kosher butchers are off the scale. Next, I told you not to worry about the PR furore. It always blows over and this one is a classic summer silly-season story that will not be able to sustain itself. I'll give you the number of a great PR person called Louise, who can help you have a quick comms plan to cover all eventualities.'

'Thank you. I knew you'd save the day. If in doubt, phone a squillionaire.' Alex hated being known for his wealth and had not finished.

'Hold on, Jack. You've cut me off in my prime, as they say down the abattoir.'

'There's more?'

'There's always more when I am pontificating. This is the most important part and forms the basis of the class I now teach at business school. I learnt it the hard way from an amoral business partner who I fell out with and is entirely relevant to your dispute with this twat Lionel.' Jack was now entirely focused on what Alex was saying.

'Excellent. I need some smart business guidance.'

'Well, you're going to be very disappointed then. This advice is more basic. What I was going to tell you is: stop being so passive. You must be as big a *bastard* as him. *Bigger* even. *Bollocks* to business integrity. It's time to behave badly, Jack.'

Chapter 26

A few years before, when Jack's stomach had been giving him real trouble, he visited a leading gastrologist in his shabby consulting room just off Harley Street. The consultant was dressed more like a Californian cult leader than an eminent doctor, clad in purple velvet trousers and a baggy white cotton shirt with embroidered flowers. He explained to Jack that most chronic stomach conditions evolved from the inextricable link between the gut and anxiety.

Instead of giving Jack guidance on how to mitigate his discomfort, he lectured him on the impact on our emotional well-being of 'fight or flight' responses to danger. When we were primitive, he told Jack, adopting a stooped neanderthal walk for emphasis, we didn't know where our next meal was coming from or if we were going to be eaten by a prowling lion on the way back to the warmth of our cave after a day's hunting. So, our ancestors developed stress responses to help them survive by becoming momentarily faster or more agile than the threat itself.

Nowadays, he explained, the pressures of modern life trick our bodies into releasing adrenalin and cortisol, which in turn leads to all sorts of debilitating side-effects. Our job is to master these hormones by creating positive energy to turn 'surviving to thriving'. At the time, Jack couldn't have got out of the room quicker, fearing he was going to be taught to levitate, when all he really wanted was a few pills that took the pain away.

Still, when his friend Alex told him to toughen up, he recalled this weird encounter and he resolved to adopt a change in attitude. 'Thriving' sounded much better than 'surviving' and with new-found belligerence, he stared at the antiseptic white walls of his office, deciding how to channel his anger. First, he texted Gadi and Stacey to confirm he would see them the following morning. He was not going to be pushed around and, most importantly, he had planned an early supper with Isobel, who was due to go away the next day for most of the summer. Time to focus on parenting for a bit, given his recent poor record.

Jack called the PR consultant, Louise, who listened to him patiently outline what had taken place. The absurdity of his explanation reminded him he now dwelt in a surreal world in which logic was absent. Fortunately, she was unfazed, telling him that a dispute between a rap star and a kosher butcher was entry-level crisis management. After a thirty-minute chat, she promised him a plan later that day and went off to release his statement to news channels and social media.

He thought it would also be smart to call Rabbi Furstein, who, as a representative of the London Board of Kosher Supervision, could not take his side publicly, hoping nonetheless their deep friendship would secure off-the-record support. The call went straight through to voicemail and Jack started talking, not entirely sure of what he wanted to say.

'Isaac. It's Jack. I would love to speak to you in person, but I'm sure you're very busy being erudite and philosophical somewhere important. I am so sorry this ridiculous spat has got so out of hand and has become world news. I didn't see it coming. I know we're doing the community a disservice by drawing so much attention to ourselves and this was of course not my intention. I wish I could understand what is driving Lionel's anger towards me. I just want to assure you and the Board I will resolve this with as much dignity as I can. You know when we met, you asked me about being alone. I am not. I have ...'

The rabbi's message box was full, and Jack was cut off as he was about to tell him all about Sonia. He had not intended to reveal her existence when he made the call, but as he spoke, for some reason he felt compelled to explain the unfairness of this adverse PR in the context of its impact on his personal life. Perhaps leaving a voicemail was an inadvertent act of confession. After all, his dishonesty to Sonia was as morally deplorable as Lionel's quest for revenge.

There was little time to dwell on these emotions as he received an email from his landlord about the leases for the two shops that needed immediate attention. It was a set of unreasonable demands intended to provoke his fury. The proposed hike in rent would have made it cheaper for him to reopen on Rodeo Drive, and the mysterious Mr Eshtov was also claiming that Jack was in breach of his lease because a few months previously he had started to sell pre-cooked takeaway Chicken Aleppo in his Golders Green shop. Consequently, his landlord now accused him of a change of usage for the shop, claiming the rotisserie counter had become 'an informal dining area'.

He called his humourless, obedient property lawyer and told him to reply with equal aggressiveness. They were still shops, not restaurants, and Jack stressed to his lawyer that concession or mediation was not an option. The need to win was compensation for the pain of Sonia leaving him and he had never wanted to become obsessed with revenge like Lionel, but the last twenty-four hours had made that impossible and all he could think about was different ways to cause him maximum humiliation that would not alert police suspicion. By lunchtime, his new steeliness made him irritable when anyone wanted to ask him the simplest question; he hated being irascible, but consoled himself that even a just war creates civilian casualties.

It was time to call Karen, who had sent a series of strident texts demanding an immediate conversation. He was perplexed by his sister's anxiety that the publicity could possibly impact on her life. She was not even an MP yet, but that had little effect on diminishing her self-importance. No wonder the Conservative Party was so excited to have her in the ranks.

Not having had time for breakfast, he was starving, and thought he had better grab something to fortify him for his showdown with Lady Thatcher. He rarely visited the factory canteen, located in an adjacent portacabin in the car park, and as he opened the door, he was assaulted by the smell of griddled chicken and chips frying in fat, the steam and grease causing his vulnerable stomach to make a noise like a faraway earth tremor. As soon as he entered, the noisy conversation hushed as if everyone had been talking about him. It was strange how uncomfortable he felt around his staff after all these years, almost a reminder that running the business was not quite a natural fit for him. His grandfather would always chat to everyone as he strode imperiously through the factory, and took pride in his ability to recall family detail about everyone.

Grabbing some toast, a cup of tea and a banana, the memory of his *alfresco* lunch with Sonia two days ago in Italian sunshine replaced his hunger with the sensation of deep regret. He returned to his office and, allowing himself ten minutes for recuperation, tried to think what he could possibly still say to Sonia that would soften her anger, but the pain of her loss was overwhelming. Instead, he called Karen to get the conversation over as quickly as possible and hopefully without personal injury.

An echo on the line made her voice sound distant and formal. He realised that they were not alone.

'OK, Jack. I'm putting you on speaker, so the team can be on the call.'

'I wasn't aware this was a team sport?'

'It is when it affects your family.'

'Honestly, Karen, this is not about you.'

She pressed on, indifferent to his protestations.

'I beg to differ. Now, we are joined by Matt, my agent, Kerry, my comms advisor and Damian, my political strategist.'

'My cabinet are all at lunch, so it's just me, I'm afraid.'

'Hi, Jack. Kerry here. Can you tell us how bad you think the situation is vis-à-vis ongoing adverse PR?'

She sounded like a teenager on work experience. Jack had no idea where his hackles were, but they had definitely risen. Last night he had not been able to talk to Sonia on her own and now it was the same with Karen. Why did a conversation with him require outside supervision?

'I appreciate your concern, Kerry, but let me talk to my sister, please. Karen, before I tell the assembled masses what I intend to do, can you please tell me why on earth you're so worried? And any chance of it just being us two?'

There was the sound of whispering and then the phone clicked as it came off speaker.

'OK, Jack. Have it your way. I've asked them to leave.'

There were a few moments of silence during which Jack anticipated an imminent explosion. She kept him waiting a few seconds longer than necessary, adept as she was at controlling an argument.

'Listen to me, now that we're alone. You have caused me huge problems and I despair that you can't recognise why.'

'Please put me out of my misery here. Tell me what on earth you're talking about?'

'All right, dear brother, I will. I know this is a crazy situation even Nostradamus could not have anticipated, but you must understand that my attempt to get into Parliament makes me incredibly vulnerable to attack or ridicule. Yesterday, when I saw the story, I wasn't worried, rather I was concerned for you. You may not believe it, but I am actually rather fond of you.'

'It's nice to be loved. Sometimes, I'm not sure where the next hug is going to come from.'

'Oh, don't be so pathetic, Jack. You don't half like a good wallow in your personal misfortune. Let me continue, as I don't have time to make you a better person. The story was picked up by the *Dudley News* and I have been hounded ever since by some alcoholic hack with nothing else to do. The problem is that he wants to run a story about the prospective candidate's dodgy family business, given I am named at Companies House as a director of Fogel's Chickens.'

'I still don't understand why this is damaging, though. This is a silly news filler because most people are on holiday.'

Karen sighed as if explaining something simple to someone stupid.

'Actions have consequences, Jack. I would have thought that in middle age you might have realised this. I've had to alert Central Office and I look completely unreliable, given you filled in a declaration saying there was nothing that could embarrass me.'

'Well, I hardly thought the potential loss of a shop in Hendon was going to derail your journey to Home Secretary.'

'You idiot. What you don't see is that I have caused them to doubt my candidacy. The local party chairman is angry because they didn't know I was Jewish, and they didn't want anti-Semitism to be a local issue.'

'I'd say it's a pretty global issue, if you ask me.'

'I am not asking you. I have lost control of my narrative because of the stupidity of the story and what it says about me.'

'It doesn't say anything about you. It really doesn't. Isn't it time you were honest with your voters as to your background and be proud of where you come from?'

'What, like you? That's rich coming from the most resentful business owner I know. You'd rather pretend you're a screenwriter than admit what you really do.'

Jack knew that much of what she said was right, but he could not admit that to her and besides, it was intertwined with her self-absorption. The conversation was degenerating to a sibling squabble that could lead to a much deeper and more permanent schism, and he needed to find a way through the acrimony quickly.

'Listen, Karen. Let's stop this conversation now, before one of us says something really nasty.'

'Agreed. Just tell me what you are doing to make this go away. Then I'll go away.'

Jack spent a couple of minutes telling her everything he had done that morning and his resolution not to put up with any further attacks. She asked a couple of questions, but his thoroughness seemed to reassure her. He could not bring himself to update her on the truth about his relationship with Sonia, however, because to admit his failure was a sign of weakness, which was never a good idea to show Karen.

'Can you trust me now to make it go away? I really think the only political damage that can come from this is if you allow your embarrassment to get the better of you.'

'Thank you. Great political advice and I'll consider you for a chief of staff role if one becomes available. For the time being, just get on with your plan. Do you hear that, Jack? I am admitting that I trust you.'

'I do, Karen, and it's the happiest day of my life.'

* * *

After the call, Jack reflected on how all his conversations with Karen were underpinned by uncomfortable levels of passive-aggressive sarcasm, and he wished their interactions could be kinder. Maybe their love for one another was always going to be wrapped in the need for point-scoring. Or were they simply siblings who just didn't get on very well?

He was trying to be more honest in all his family relationships now; Bethany was helping him with Natalie, and he was trying to do the same with his mother and her dangerous marriage to Kurt. Yet the last couple of days had been the most emotionally intense of his life as he grappled to understand his own truth, which seemed basically to cause pain for the people he loved.

His early years were spent trying to assert himself above the expectations set for him. His marriage was built on a vision he could not sustain, and its collapse precipitated years of emotional numbness to stave off his own crushing disappointment. In Sonia, he had found an opportunity to escape this dissatisfaction, but hiding the truth to make her love him had been a misguided strategy. Telling her the truth now was too late.

What was the point of all this introspection and self-discovery if you just ended up alone? Truth was a concept he struggled to understand. He had sometimes stuck to it, and he had also lived for years by not facing up to its importance. What should he do next and which version of it should he use?

Someone must know the answer.

Chapter 27

When she was little, Isobel's nickname of 'Busy-Izzie' reflected her boundless energy and inquisitiveness. While Natalie was a beautifully turned-out princess, her mother's clone, Isobel didn't care what she wore, preferring to chat with grown-ups rather than dress in pink tulle. As she got older, this curiosity became obscured by the fog of adolescent insecurity and Jack's favourite conversation partner became far less forthcoming.

She had changed recently, and her wit and confidence had begun to assert itself ahead of her surliness. Something more subtle was happening; she was re-entering his orbit. As Natalie became unable to cope with who Jack was, Isobel wanted to understand more about him, and why he always seemed so unhappy. She relaxed in his company and her need to point out his ineptitude diminished. Falling in love with Sonia, he had almost been too distracted to notice.

They sat at the top of Primrose Hill looking at the best view of London's hybrid skyline, which blended the sharp lines of modern steel skyscrapers with the squat dome of St Paul's. He remembered taking the girls to this exact spot many years ago and how it had become their favourite place, which is why he thought Isobel would appreciate going there now. She was about to go on a month-long youth group tour followed by a holiday with her mum, and Jack was apprehensive about not seeing her for so long. Right now, he needed all the friends he could get.

The morning storms had cleared, and it was a warm summer's evening as they squeezed between a patchwork quilt of picnic blankets. Jack had brought a hastily assembled supper of bread, cheeses and dips and a bottle of pink champagne, which had surprised sixteen-year-old Isobel, not used to being treated as an adult by her father.

'Are we getting properly pissed then, Dad?' she asked as they clinked their plastic glasses. 'It's just so much quicker if we do shots.'

'Oh, look at *Miss-I've-just-finished-my-GSCEs-and-know-how-to-party*!'

'Well, I didn't learn it from you, did I?'

'No, you're right. Thank heavens you got a couple of genes from your mother, although most of your good traits come from me.'

'Like what? You can save a heap of money on therapy if you tell me now.'

'I'm not sure we have enough time for me to list my virtues. I'll email you when I get home.'

He gave her an affectionate hug and was glad she didn't pull away. He didn't want to let go, which meant her next question was addressed directly to his armpit.

'I've been dying to ask you all day how you felt about being called a motherf***** on the radio by Drumstx. My friends think you're kind of cool now. How did that happen?'

'What can I say? I like *hanging with my homies*.'

'You can start by never saying that again, otherwise I may cancel you.'

'I'd hate that.'

'I'd hate that too. I mean, where else would I get such an over-generous allowance? Do you feel guilty about being a bad parent or something?'

'I am an excellent parent, you're a terrible child. Tell me, though, since we're discussing our feelings so maturely, are you embarrassed that we're being laughed at in the news? Auntie Karen is mortified. She thinks she's going to be excommunicated by the Tories.'

'Would that be such a bad thing?'

'No, but you'll need to tell her. I'm not that brave.'

She clinked her father's glass again. This was proving to be an unexpectedly happy conclusion to an awful couple of days.

'Here's to Auntie Karen ruling the world and sending you to prison.'

'Let's get back to the bigger question, sweetheart. Are you ashamed about what I do?'

Isobel looked genuinely surprised.

'Why would I be ashamed of Fogel's Chickens? Not all my friends are veggies. And the chicken they eat has to come from somewhere, hasn't it? I'm proud you run a business that goes back such a long way in our family history.'

Jack could not believe what he was hearing. He'd been bitter for so long it didn't cross his mind that there could be a different response from the next generation.

'That's great to hear. The business has been like a heavy stone hung round my neck. Well, superglued to it, more like.'

'Yeah, but one day I might want to run it. You never know? Maybe I could take it in a different direction. I love that we own restaurants.'

'I wouldn't have thought for a second that you'd be the slightest bit interested in any of it. I'll get you your own office immediately now.'

'Calm down, Dad. I'm not going to join you yet. You know I really want to be a songwriter. Those piano lessons are going to come in useful, I promise. Still, good to keep my options open.'

Of course she wasn't going to want the keys to the factory just yet; she was a talented musician propelled by idealistic ambition, and her love songs were impressive considering she had never been in a relationship. At the same time, it was enormously comforting to Jack that she wasn't hostile to her legacy and possibly even appreciative of what he did to keep it going.

What he really wanted to find out, however, was how he could repair things with his other daughter. He had inadvertently got swept up by the candour of their conversation and regretted his next question the moment it came out of his mouth.

'It's not the same for Natalie, is it? Why can't she accept me for who I am?'

Isobel's smile disappeared. It was unfair to use her as his proxy and she looked away, weighing up how to respond.

'You know it's not for me to answer that question, Dad. That's why we have Bethany in our lives.'

'I'm sorry. I shouldn't have put you on the spot, it's just you were being so nice. If you speak to your sister about this conversation, please tell her I love her and will be as patient as possible.'

Isobel poured herself another glass of champagne.

'You don't ask much, do you? I think your relationship with Natalie is for the two of you to sort out, *n'est-ce pas?*'

'*Bien sur, mon petit pamplemousse.*'

'That means *grapefruit.*'

'Exactly. I needed to find something to call you since I didn't know how to say "*irritating know-it-all*" in French. Bloody hell, it's tiring dealing with someone as articulate as you. I preferred it when you were monosyllabic. Go on, give me a snort of disappointment for old times' sake?'

'I can get an Uber home if you like, or maybe we talk about something else. How about you warn me about the dangers of mixing with boys before I go on my trip tomorrow, like a proper father should?'

'I'm the last person you should ask about how to have a relationship.'

'Who said anything about a relationship? But since you bring it up, how's your love life going? Why haven't you allowed any of us to meet Sonia? I mean, I wouldn't embarrass you any more than you naturally do yourself. She's made you happy, but you've kept us apart. If she's going to be an important part of our lives, please can we meet her?'

She was right again in her assessment of Jack, and he was immediately suffocated by the miserable realisation this would never happen. Bowing his head, he stared at the yellowing grass and felt the familiar wave of shame rise once more. Like a naughty child admitting guilt to a parent, he mumbled a reply:

'I've got something to tell you, Iz. I've done something stupid. Really, really stupid.'

* * *

'*OMG*, Dad. *OMG*. Did you really think you'd get away with it?'

An excruciating fifteen minutes later, he had explained what had taken place as Isobel sat crossed-legged, elbows on knees and her chin in her hands, staring at him in incredulity.

'It wasn't exactly a plan. I fell in love and got spooked that if she knew my life, she'd run a mile.'

'I am your life, Dad, aren't I? Nat's your life too? Your factory is just the place where you go to work.' Tears of frustration moistened her eyes. How many more people that he cared about could he make cry with his stupidity?

'You're right. I'm ashamed of myself.' It was astonishing to be having such a raw conversation with Isobel, given that six months previously he'd struggled to find out what homework she had. Now she was his emotional confidante.

'How can you be so horrible to such a nice person? And by the way, she's far better looking, which makes it even more remarkable she picked you.'

He had shown her photos from Rome, hoping somehow this would soften Isobel's disappointment. It only made the loss more acute as he stared at Sonia's smile in a variety of happy poses. Exhausted, he had run out of excuses to justify his behaviour but was nonetheless grateful she was still prepared to support him.

'I know I keep asking unfair things, but I don't know how to get her back. Any thoughts? I mean, what's a daughter for if not relationship advice?'

Isobel was getting used now to being asked intense questions by her flailing father, as if sorting out a parent's emotional well-being was the job of every sixteen-year-old. She leapt to her feet and suddenly Jack's love life was no different to the many boyfriend crises she'd resolved on the bus home from school.

'Good thinking. Draft in a professional for this one. I am all over it.'

'I don't need you all over it. I just want a plan.'

What a fool he'd been not to have introduced her to Sonia some time ago, given how much they would have liked each other. He was so busy camouflaging a life that embarrassed him that he had hidden its best bits too. After much pacing, she sat back down with a glint that suggested she had an idea.

'Here's what you have to do. Find a way to show her what's important in your life. How hard can that be? Maybe when you have an answer, you could let me and Nat know too.'

'Wish it was that simple, but what incentive is there for Sonia to be with me? I'm a grumpy git and the last time I can say I was happy was when I was first married to your mum. Look how well that turned out. Let's not forget she runs a vegan café, and I am now famous across the world for killing chickens.'

Before Isobel could reply, their conversation was interrupted by a football landing in their picnic and a boy of about six standing sheepishly by them, looking for its return. Isobel handed it back to him, the interruption allowing her to consider her next piece of advice.

'Stop rambling, Dad. There's no other option than to tell her how you feel and how you are going to change. I can be here for moral support, at least until my plane takes off tomorrow.'

'You're amazingly mature, when did that happen? There aren't many daughters who would help their *no-hoper* father like this.'

'Eye on the prize, Dad, it's not about me. Now get your phone out and get on with it before I ask that kid if I can play football with him.'

It was time, she was right. As he dialled Sonia's number, he smiled nervously at his new life coach and said, 'Ready to watch me get dumped again?'

Before she could reply, Sonia picked up.

'What do you want, Jack?'

Isobel nodded vigorously in encouragement and Jack launched himself into a defence he had no idea how to construct.

'Sonia, hi. I'm not going to ask how your day was, I'm sure it was terrible like mine. I'm sitting on Primrose Hill with Isobel, and I owe you both an apology for keeping you apart. You'd get on so well. Iz has been helping me try to understand myself better. I'm burning with shame for everything I've done. Anyway, I'm not going to ask you to forgive me on this call. I know ... Yes, I'll stop and let you speak ... OK, I understand, yes, yes, OK. Give me time to prove myself, please ... All right ... Can we arrange to ...'

Sonia had clearly hung up abruptly and Isobel moved a few paces back to give Jack space. He looked like he'd been punched in the face as he stared at his blank phone screen, hoping she might call back.

'What did she say? Are you all right?' Isobel asked urgently. Jack was shaking his head, trying to process the brief call.

'I don't really know. She said she couldn't listen to me talk right now. She said that she wishes she'd met you too. And then she finished by saying that I shouldn't contact her for at least six months. What do you think she means?'

Isobel took a long swill of champagne directly from the bottle in a gesture of either commiseration or celebration. She placed a hand on his shoulder and put her forehead on his.

'It means sort your shit out, old man. Sort your shit out.'

Chapter 28

Tracy looked horrified. They were waiting for their mother in the lobby of her new apartment block and Jack had been talking manically about his chaotic last few days in detail. She had listened patiently, absorbing the minutiae of the demise of his relationship, a disapproving frown congealing on her face.

'Really, Jack, you have, as we say in psychiatric circles, made a monumental balls-up of this one.'

'And there was me worried that you'd sit on the fence.'

He was resigned to the justified criticism of his sister, who never sugar-coated an opinion.

'By the way, loser, you still haven't thanked me for my match-making in the first place. I told you you'd get on well with Sonia. My instincts are impeccable.'

'Possibly a bit late for self-congratulation, given you only get paid if we end up staying together.'

'Well, it's hardly my fault you told her you were the next Aaron Sorkin rather than a poultry magnate.'

'Have you got anything helpful to say? I mean, as a psychiatrist you understand how the brain works, don't you? Maybe you can help me understand my behaviour.'

'Except I deal with the elderly and their brains are shrinking. What's your excuse?'

He paused, realising an answer might get to the root of his problems. Eventually, he replied, 'I think it's chronic embarrassment. Is that a clinical condition?'

'No, but it does have a cure. It requires you to stop all the "woe is me" nonsense and stand in front of a mirror, realising who you are. Actually, Jack, why don't you stand up now and turn round.'

'Why?'

'Can you just do what I ask, or I do I have to call up Mum and ask her to give you this pep talk instead?'

The mention of his mother was a sufficient catalyst for him to leap to his feet as instructed and he realised that the wall behind him was a giant mirror that made the lobby seem twice as big.

'OK, doctor, what now?'

'Well, what do you see?'

'A security guard eating a sandwich and the lift door.'

Tracy yanked his arm and made him sit down.

'This might be harder than I thought. We won't do this now, but I suggest you go home and look at your reflection. Ask yourself who you want to be – as a lover, a father, a business owner. It's not as silly as it sounds. Stand and stare at yourself for a long time, repeating the questions until you begin to get an answer straight in your head.'

'And do you think this will help me get Sonia back?'

'How would I know? I've never met her. If she's a forgiving person, maybe. If she can't see herself trusting you again, then quite frankly you're buggered. I hope that helps and who do I make the invoice out to?'

'I am not paying for this stupid advice, but I'll give it a go anyway and stand in my boxers looking at myself in a mirror. I need a new hobby, although I'm not convinced it's a therapy they teach at medical school.'

Tracy had had enough of the conversation. After a momentary silence, she changed the subject.

'Enough of your tedious problems, Jack. Time to deal with our upwardly mobile mum. She must be the only seventy-two-year-old who not only needs a bigger flat but has to find one in a more expensive area.'

Jack leant towards her and whispered, 'Let's see if this flat is up to Kurt's specifications. Apparently, he has a lot of medieval torture equipment that he wants to bring with him.'

'That's our mother. We should be more protective of her if we can.'

Jack shrugged, feeling he would try to be more protective if she would agree to be more loyal. Before he could say anything further, however, Stephanie strode through the front entrance, accompanied by an interior designer carrying a large bag full of swatches and samples. She greeted them with the excitement of a first-time buyer.

'Hello, you two. Are you ready to be knocked out by my lovely new home?'

'Funny you should mention it, Mum, I brought some smelling salts in case I pass out.'

Stephanie, as ever, ignored her son's attempt at humour. The lift arrived and Tracy followed her in. For a second, he thought of fleeing the building to spare himself the excruciating next hour or so. A reluctant sense of duty prevailed, and he rushed to the lift as its doors were closing. Stephanie made no effort to hold them open and he found himself alone in the lobby as it departed without him.

* * *

They sat at the dining-room table while Stephanie fussed over curtain fabrics with the interior designer. Tracy could not have been less interested in the niceties of home furnishings and Jack was disqualified from an opinion because his mother assumed he had no taste. They answered emails on their phones and giggled like children at their mother's inability to choose between the cerulean silk or the apricot linen options.

After ten minutes, Tracy stomped her feet like a child and declared, 'I am soooo bored. She won't even put on a Disney film for us to watch.'

'She'll be with us soon. She just needs to work out the right shade of black for Kurt's study,' he replied with a smirk, unaware that Kurt had entered the room and was moving like a silent ghost to stand next to them. Jack wasn't sure if he'd heard the insult as his face barely registered any emotion.

'Hello, Jack. Hello, Tracy,' he said in a monotone.

'Hello, Kurt,' Jack replied, trying to sound equally indifferent.

'Why don't you join us while Mum finishes up?' Tracy gestured to a chair at the other end of the table from where they were sitting. 'It looks like you're going to be in for a very colourful living room, whichever scheme she chooses.'

He sat down stiffly, and it seemed no one wanted to make the effort of a conversation. Fortunately, Stephanie was showing her designer out and as she closed the door, she turned to them with undiminished enthusiasm.

'Sorry for that. I'm ready for the grand tour. Kurt, are you going to join in?'

He didn't say anything, but his irritated frown suggested his patience was wearing thin. Jack noticed his expression, worrying once more that his mother was making an enormous mistake. Before he could gauge Tracy's reaction, Stephanie dragged them into the master bedroom and was rhapsodically describing its many benefits in excruciating detail. For the next twenty minutes, like reluctant children in an art gallery, Tracy and Jack listened obediently to all her decorating plans and tried to look engaged as she explained the features of every cupboard or drawer she opened.

Eventually, they sat down at the dining-room table, and he knew it was time to ask the difficult question hanging over them for the last few weeks. Once again, an unwanted presence sat next to him in silent judgement, but this time he didn't care what Kurt thought of him. Impatient to get back to work, Jack decided to be as blunt as possible.

'It's a lovely flat, Mum, and you'll make it look great. But can I ask, how are you going to afford to buy it and continue your lifestyle?'

Stephanie bristled and instinctively drummed her immaculate nails on the glass table.

'As you very well know, Jack, we're exchanging contracts on this flat imminently and are here to discuss how I take some money from the business to help me.'

Tracy leant forward in her seat, anticipating a passive-aggressive conversation degenerating quickly into an overt-aggressive one. Even Kurt wiggled his head in a movement that reminded Jack of a zombie stirring to life.

'Yes, of course I know what you need, and obviously we can find a way of doing it through the property arm of the business giving you a loan of some sort. But that's not the question for today, is it?'

'What is it then, darling?'

She only used affectionate terms when she was angry with him. He saw a look of vulnerability as she moved her hand to rest on Kurt's and he remained unresponsive.

'Why should you get extra money that is not really yours? There's a structure to the company, and we all have shares. We take our money in proportion to what we own. And for the avoidance of doubt, I have the largest share, so it's not hard for me to block you, unless you and my sisters outvote me.'

He was relieved to see Tracy nodding vigorously in support.

'I know that, and I'm not expecting some sort of boardroom showdown. You're being ridiculous. Let me ask you the question another way, since I'm not getting younger, and I have finally found true happiness. Are you so jealous that you want to stand in my way?'

Tracy interceded, knowing it would be a fraction less nuclear if the bombshell was dropped by her.

'Ouch, Mum, that wasn't nice, and Jack is not trying to stand in your way. Can we be honest with you?'

'I wish someone would be.'

'The thing is, Mum, as thrilled as we are for you and Kurt, we think that a large flat, a marriage and all the support you give to him leaves you ...'

'Bloody exposed,' Jack interrupted aggressively. Kurt stared at them both with his steel-blue eyes, perhaps deciding which would be the most efficient way of killing them.

'That is just ridiculous. Really. Tell them, Kurt. We are so happy together and I trust him with everything. Tell them, Kurt.' Stephanie's voice was imploring, almost desperate.

'I find this challenge insulting. Your mother is my great love. I shall protect her and support her even if it means taking on her children.'

He gave the table a slap with the palm of his hand as if to emphasise his irritation.

'Mum. We want you to sign a prenuptial agreement with Kurt before we can sort out your finances. That's it. Non-negotiable.'

Stephanie shook her head. 'I appreciate your collective concern, but I do not share it one bit. And it's interesting, by the way, that you have not been joined by Karen.'

'Hardly relevant, Mum, but I assure you we have her support.'

He could have told her at this point that it was her favourite child, Karen, who had hired an investigator to reveal Kurt's concerning past life as a sex pest. But however intense the provocation, the siblings had agreed to withhold the discovery for the time being and only bring it up if the situation became dire.

'I very much doubt that Karen would be happy, but let's move on since this rather hostile conversation needs a conclusion. Of course, there is a very easy alternate option.'

'And what's that?' he asked, not really wanting to hear her answer. There was something about her tone now that suggested she had anticipated how the conversation would unfold.

'Well, I have fifteen per cent of the business, don't I?'

'You know you do.'

'And recently, Jack, you've been given a terrible run-around by Lionel, haven't you?'

'What are you talking about?'

'I spoke at length to Lionel last night. It's hard to just drop our friendship because he's having a dispute with you. And do you know what he's offered?'

It was obvious what was coming but he couldn't bear to hear it articulated. He was spared because suddenly Kurt's face was framed by an unfamiliar toothy grin as he spoke on Stephanie's behalf.

'What your mother wants to say is that Lionel has made a most generous cash offer for her shares. We won't really need you too much after that, Jack.'

Jack couldn't bear to be in their presence for a second longer. It was too humiliating to be fighting with his mother like this. For twenty years he had stood on a noisy factory floor in the biting cold of winter and the searing heat of summer, bombarded by its angry sounds and watching his shoes get discoloured by the blood of thousands of slain chickens. He hated every minute, but he did what was needed and now he was trying to do the same to protect his misguided mother in thrall to a Swedish sociopath. And in the final reckoning, her love was not as strong as her expediency to negotiate with Lionel Gutterman, a man whose mission in life was to make his miserable.

He got up and walked hurriedly towards the door, and was almost on the landing when he turned around and in a measured voice said, 'I'm not sure you've thought this through, Mum, but good luck with everything. I hope it's a lovely wedding.'

Chapter 29

Clucks was beginning its lunchtime trade by the time Jack arrived. Summer tables had been scattered across the pavement and the vibe was much more Tel Aviv than Hampstead. Jack sat inside on his own, waiting to be joined by Gadi and Stacy. He felt numb after his confrontation with his mother but knew he had to regroup for his next difficult conversation.

Having called his PR advisor, Louise, he was relieved that the mayhem caused by Drumstx seemed to be abating. She explained that social media could sometimes amplify a dispute but was also a raging fire that required continued oxygen to make it spread and, fortunately, its supply seemed to be evaporating. The national media had moved on to more significant news and he was now only being chased by the Jewish press, which didn't bother him at all. A morning TV show also wanted him to appear in an on-air confrontation with Lionel, who was no doubt thrilled at the prospect of getting an even more pronounced fake tan in the make-up chair. Jack had no intention of becoming a YouTube clip when he attacked him with a microphone stand, so politely declined.

His challenge was how to manage the expansion plans of Gadi and Stacy, which did not align with his. Their detailed business proposal required committing initially to three new restaurants, two of which were not going to be kosher to increase their customer base. They were also obsessed with launching a chicken sauce and condiments, both in grocery retailers, much like Drumstx was doing in America. The difference was he was incredibly famous, which made generating awareness a tad easier.

In the maelstrom of recent weeks, their plan had made Jack think hard about what he really wanted from his business. Clucks had become an extremely profitable venture, but it had been predicated on him expanding only within a tightly defined kosher marketplace. What Gadi and Stacy wanted was much more ambitious and therefore carried greater risk. He was torn because the logic was sensible, the opportunity significant. He just was not sure he liked them enough to take further risk by their side.

He was still mulling over how to run the meeting when Stacey and Gadi arrived to join him. She was carrying three iced bottles of beer, which she slammed so hard on the table they frothed like an angry volcano. She placed a couple of distracted kisses on his cheeks before sitting down and Gadi wiped his hands on a greasy apron before giving him a similarly awkward fist-pump. Wearing shorts and a black vest, he was glistening with the sweat of his oppressively hot kitchen and emitted a stale odour that Jack doubted was ideal in proximity to food preparation. Stacey was in no mood for social niceties.

'So, Jack. We have finally pinned you down. I know you've been distracted but honestly, it would have been easier to fix up a meeting with the President.'

'I'm sorry, I really haven't been avoiding you, it's just I was away and as you know, there have been a few fires I've had to put out recently.' He took a swig of the cold beer for fortification, given he was about to be attacked.

'I'm here now, and I know I owe you an answer.'

'First our news,' Gadi declared enthusiastically. He was normally laconic to the point of muteness in their interactions, so it must be something significant.

Please let Stacey's visa have expired and she is being deported, Jack thought to himself, and then wondered if he had accidentally said it aloud.

'I thought we were going to tell him at the end?' Stacey asked her husband in annoyance.

'No, we must say now. You tell him.'

Maybe she was pregnant? Jack looked down at Stacey's stomach and she caught his unsubtle eye movement and smiled.

'Sorry, Jack. There is no *bun* in this *pita* oven quite yet. No, we are very excited because Gadi has finally got his own podcast. And not before time.' Jack thought this good news too, thinking maybe the distraction of a media career would be even more helpful than his previous guesses.

'That's marvellous. Tell me all about it,' Jack said, hoping for a few more minutes to work out what he was going to say before the proper conversation began.

'It's called "Better Taste",' Stacey explained, 'and every week a celebrity joins Gadi with a family recipe that they hold dear, and they discuss its significance as they prepare it together. There is a lot of excitement about it, and we have some pretty firm interest from Channel 4 about possibly making a TV spin-off.'

Jack's bonhomie was replaced by an ugly swell of jealousy. Were they actually going to achieve TV success before him?

'Who's producing it for you?' he asked, trying not to sound upset. 'These things cost money and you'll need proper backing.'

Instead of answering, Stacey turned to Gadi and gave him a gentle slap on the wrist.

'I told you not to tell him straightaway. We agreed how we were going to conduct this meeting.' Swarthy Gadi shrank in his seat, chastened.

'Sorry, sweetie, I got carried away.'

Jack was now slightly bemused at the shift in their mood, even though they had just told him about their good fortune.

'Guys, what's going on? All I asked was where are you getting the money from?' Without looking at her husband, Stacey let out an enormous baritone sigh as she gave him another instruction.

'Gadi, would you mind going to the office and bringing Lionel out. I think it's worth him joining us now.'

* * *

Smug.

The word did not sufficiently capture Lionel's expression as he sauntered to the table. Jack wondered if a loud Drumstx track was going to be pumped out of the speakers to make his walk more like a boxer entering the ring. As ever, Lionel seemed to be dressed for a round of golf in Florida with banana-yellow trousers, a strawberry-red polo shirt and a face, of course, of mandarin orange. He again carried his old-fashioned attaché case, the one made of a poor reptile now likely to be an endangered species. Jack marvelled at the incongruity of his appearance to its setting, a modern restaurant.

Jack somehow was not surprised at his presence, the last few weeks having taught him that anything was possible in his life and the more unexpected, the more likely it was to happen. This show-down required him to stay in control, no matter the provocation. He gestured for him to sit down and extended his hand to Lionel, whose palm was like a damp chamois leather.

'Somehow not a shock to see you, Lionel, since you seem to be everywhere I turn these days. I should probably challenge you to a duel.'

'Not necessary, Jack, my boy. I am here to make peace. Rabbi Furstein, I believe, explained the concept of *shalom* to you?'

'But not to you, it would seem from your recent attacks?'

Jack twiddled his half-empty beer bottle for distraction, his plan to maintain his dignity already under threat from Lionel's high levels of odiousness. Seeing the flicker of a triumphant smile on Stacey's face, he decided he should begin his interrogation with her instead.

'I'd love to understand why Lionel is here discussing the expansion plans for our restaurants?'

'And I'll gladly tell you. Perhaps if you had not stalled us for so long, this might not have been necessary.'

As ever, Stacey sounded like she was trying to pick a fight.

'What do you mean?'

'We gave you a plan, hoping that you'd support us, and we wouldn't have had to look for money elsewhere.'

Jack was confused. 'Stacey, have you forgotten that we are not equal partners in this venture and that I own more of the business than you do? You can't quite get rid of me that easily and then join Darth Vader next to you. No offence, Lionel.'

The quizzical expression suggested Lionel was unfamiliar with the *Star Wars* films. Stacey was enjoying a pent-up revenge and was becoming more animated as she spoke, pointing at Jack accusingly as she did so.

'And, Jack, didn't you think we might want to protect ourselves in the event of you not coming to the table? You hardly seemed keen. That's why we met up with Lionel a few weeks back to consider some alternative strategies.'

Lionel was struggling to stay silent, clearly not used to being passive in any negotiation. He interrupted Stacey. 'Do you know, Jack, before we even discussed business, we worked out how we could make Gadi as famous as he deserves to be. If Gadi becomes a famous chef, it's great PR for the business. I don't understand how you couldn't see this. I suppose the last few days show that you aren't as good as me at generating good publicity.'

'Great work, Lionel, I must say. Being a pariah in the rap community has always been my worst nightmare.'

'Can't you just admit that I have won the hearts of our customers?' Lionel seemed to be pushing for Jack to call his victory.

'If you don't mind me saying, Lionel, I think if we asked them, they would probably say you're a bit of a plonker.'

Jack hoped mockery was a good tactic to use on someone with such a craven need for validation and was quite prepared to resort to schoolboy name-calling for a while longer. Stacey, conversely, could sense she was losing control of her agenda so tried therefore to adopt a gentler, more conciliatory tone, even if it sounded unusual to everyone else.

'Gentlemen. Personal insults will not help us resolve anything and we are here today to sort out mine and Gadi's future, so let's discuss things more sensibly, if you don't mind.' She turned to Gadi, who nodded his assent as if under strict instruction only to gesticulate, rather than speak.

'Right. Enough now,' Jack declared emphatically. 'Lionel, you clearly have a deal in mind. You might as well tell me.'

'I do, Jack. In my case, I have a proposal for your business. I think it will be good for you and certainly good for me, Gadi and Stacey. But I think I owe you a little bit of an admission first.'

'Of what?'

'Why this has been so personal.'

Yes, Jack thought, on balance he would like to know why Lionel had tried to ruin his life.

'What is your problem with me, Lionel? I always treated you respectfully in our business dealings over the years.'

'You did, but the problem was your father hated me because Solly saw a talent in me that he didn't possess. And I loved your grandfather, all I wanted was his approval. I would have done anything for him if it had meant I could have stayed in Fogel's Chickens. I had my future mapped out.'

'First of all, none of that is my fault. And as I understand it, Lionel, you were greedy and wanted more than was rightfully yours.'

'You never worked with your grandfather, Jack. Tough as a mobster, but not so strong operationally. I made that place work and deserved more than he was prepared to give.'

'That doesn't explain why you have attacked me so personally.'

'As you know, Jack, your mother and I have become quite close.'

'I can't tell her how to choose her friends. Unfortunately.'

Lionel missed the insult, too engrossed in his narrative.

'She was always talking about how unhappy you are. She feels guilty that she puts so much pressure on you to run the business because she knows how much you hate it. She thinks you wish you could run your life differently and you don't like her. She doesn't know how to help. Apparently, all you really want to do is make TV programmes.'

Jack felt dizzy. He had experienced so many uncomfortable physical sensations in relation to the complicated events in his life, but this was a new one. Lionel had revealed something he would never have believed: his mother understood his unhappiness, even though she was complicit in its continuation. It was a completely unexpected perspective, but still required further explanation. Stacey was now looking like she wanted to clean the restaurant's toilets or be anywhere else rather than listening to these two strange men reveal the causes of their ridiculous war. Jack sought clarification.

'This doesn't make sense. If my mother thought I was so unhappy and turned to you, why have you made it your mission to make me even more unhappy?'

Lionel gave a large stagy laugh, like a poor actor in a bad play.

'That's just it, Jackie boy. She knew you'd never listen to me. So, I decided there was no point being reasonable to get your attention. I decided to be nasty. Very nasty.'

'You succeeded then, Lionel. I think as a result you may have jeopardised your place in heaven.'

* * *

Much to Stacey's annoyance, Jack asked for a few minutes to get a glass of water and some fresh air. He had a lot to absorb and needed to regain his composure. Standing in the July sunshine, he watched congested traffic inch past the roadworks blocking their way, honking in frustration at temporary traffic lights that kept changing. The summer heat was making people short-fused, and irritability washed over Jack like a breaking wave as he tried to focus on the offer that Lionel was about to make for his business. Was it time to consider doing something else, even if it meant succumbing to Lionel's negotiating tactics?

When he returned to the table, Gadi, Stacey and Lionel were engrossed in a deep discussion. As he sat down, they looked shiftily at him, and Jack knew that the husband and wife had most definitely swapped sides. All that was left was to hear their terms for peace.

'OK, Lionel. You win. I think you need to tell me about your proposal without further reference to my mother.'

Lionel put his attaché case on his knees and clicked its two locks. As he opened it, Jack caught a glimpse of a manila envelope and three enormous wads of cash, seemingly all in £50 notes. He wondered what was going on.

'That's a lot of money to be carrying around. You're not thinking of paying me off here and now, are you?'

Lionel looked discombobulated that he had revealed the contents of his case. He took out the envelope, slammed it shut and, in a slightly frazzled tone, began to talk.

'No, Jack, of course the cash is not for you. Some of my suppliers are a bit old school, if you know what I mean. Now, let me tell you my thinking. I've told you I want your shops.'

'On more than one occasion.'

'I was always going to get them from you. Of that there was no doubt.'

'And why is that?'

'Because I am your landlord.' Lionel folded his arms triumphantly, almost expecting a dramatic musical accompaniment from somewhere in the ether. *Da da da der* ...

'What do you mean? I had a feeling you were lurking somewhere, given the ludicrousness of the demands being made.'

'Mr *Eshtov*. Rather clever, don't you think?'

'Lionel, can you just tell me what you are talking about.'

Jack prayed he would stop talking cryptically like the murderer at the denouement of some rubbish whodunit explaining how he got away with the crime.

'You clearly know little Hebrew. "*Eshtov*". It means "Good Man", like "Gutterman", which is German for "Good Man" too. That's how I fooled you.'

'And this is who you want to go into business with, Stacey? You'll certainly learn a few words in a different language.'

Lionel could not cope with these slights any longer and banged the table as petulantly as Kurt had done a couple of hours previously.

'Right, Fogel. You clearly have no respect for me, so this is what I have done. I bought your shops three years ago, knowing that I'd get you out. I am going to buy you out of these restaurants as well, because these two don't want to work with you. They trust me to have deeper pockets and, what with my catering business, we are going to do great things. Bloody great things. So, take this envelope with you and read its contents. I have made you a very fair offer for the parts of your business that I want. I am doing you a favour, after all. You can go write your little TV shows and leave the business to someone who knows what he is doing. Take this and discuss it with your family and you'll realise that you have no choice. And your lovely mother is going to sell me her share anyway, because, as you know, Kurt needs a bigger flat. He doesn't want you to call him Dad, by the way. What an insult that would be to the memory of your blessed father.'

Lionel had walked to the bar counter and was grabbing it to steady himself while Stacey and Gadi sat impassively. He could not tell if they were embarrassed by Lionel's rant or relieved that the endgame with Jack had begun. There was clearly very little further conversation required and he knew he was about to spend a lot of time with his lawyers and accountants.

He got up and said quietly to Stacey, 'I am not going to be pressured into making a stupid decision. You have behaved appallingly in going behind my back before we even had a conversation. That is going to have an impact on what I do next.'

Gadi looked like he was going to say something conciliatory, but the dismissive shrugging of his wife's shoulders prevented him. Jack walked over to Lionel, who had turned his back on him.

'I have your proposal and I will give you my answer when I am ready, after considering the best interests of the Fogel family. Tell that to Chaim the Chicken when you next see him. I'm sure he'll have a tweet he'll want to send.'

He emerged into the bright afternoon and strode towards his car, parked across the road. Switching on the engine, he let the air conditioning blast him with respite from the stifling heat of both the day and the intense confrontation that had taken place. After attempting some yoga-like breathing that to a passer-by may have looked like hyperventilation, he considered that maybe the rancour of the last hour might prove to be a turning point. An unfamiliar serenity bubbled up within him and, to his surprise, his overriding emotion was now optimism for a new chapter about to start that could be more enjoyable. Clichés of bright dawns after dark days filled his head as, for the first time, he saw a possibility of escape.

His joy was short-lived, however, as he suddenly got out of the car and trudged back into the restaurant, avoiding eye contact with Lionel, who was poring over papers with Gadi and Stacy. He'd left the bloody envelope on the table.

Chapter 30

A week later, he sat in Reception at Channel 4, waiting for his meeting with Neil Yeats, its commissioner of comedy. The glass atrium bustled with creative energy and Jack reflected on what it would have been like to spend his career in a place like this, which had always been his dream. Who knows, if he had not given it up, maybe he would have been the person deciding which programmes got made?

He silently rehearsed his pitch for the hundredth time that morning as he was kept waiting. Without the backing of Mike Gibson, it was a long shot, but clearly the script had some merit or there would have been no meeting scheduled. Half an hour elapsed, and he remembered back to the chaos of his early years in production when punctuality was always sacrificed to chaotic spontaneity. Eventually, the lift doors opened and a young woman strode enthusiastically towards him like he was television royalty.

'Jack. Jack Fogel? Hi, I'm Charlotte Casey. So lovely to meet you. Have you been waiting long? How rude of us. The day has been off-the-scale mad. Would you like to follow me?'

She was very young and seemed disproportionately excited to meet him, pumping his hand for a few seconds longer than necessary. They walked to a café area where some chairs and tables were placed by a small counter and a solitary harassed barista was serving a large queue of impatient people. He wondered why they were not going to a meeting room and was perplexed when she gestured for him to sit at a table with only two chairs.

'Can I get you a coffee, Jack? Although you may have to wait a few minutes, so it might be best to push on.'

'No, I'm fine, thank you, Charlotte. I've had so much coffee this morning that one more will make me unable to form a sentence. I was wondering, though, is Neil meeting us here or are we going somewhere else?'

This was not the start he'd imagined, and she looked flustered.

'Oh, I am sorry, Neil has got held up in an important production meeting and has asked me to hear your idea. Did no one text you?'

She was desperately trying to sound upbeat but was hardly convincing and Jack felt a rising dread.

'And what exactly do you do here, Charlotte?'

She smiled sheepishly, realising Jack was going to hear her good news before her own parents.

'It's funny you should ask, because yesterday, I would have had to say "intern", but as of an hour ago, I'm a trainee production assistant. You're my first meeting on my own, how weird is that?'

She sat down and rummaged in her rucksack, eventually producing a leather-bound notebook, which looked to Jack like it might also have been her teenage diary. A few seconds later she pulled out a pen with a miniature purple furry animal linked to it by an invisible chain. Like a fresher at a university lecture, she opened the book and smoothed down a page. It was time for her to justify her new salary, only marginally higher than the minimum wage.

'So, Jack, I'd love to hear all about this idea of yours. What it's about and why should I take it seriously?'

PART 5

PEACE TREATY

Chapter 31

The January morning was freezing as Jack waited on a bench on Primrose Hill for Natalie. He felt the cold these days and wondered if his exercise regime of the last few months was the cause. The pounds had not exactly fallen off, but regular gym work and less chocolate consumption had made him a little trimmer and more energetic. His stomach was not just flatter, it was also quieter and less prone to attacking him with explosions of pain at unexpected moments. He considered answering a few emails. Having been very busy on so many fronts, even a few hours off on a Sunday morning resulted in a pile-up of pressing correspondence. Today, however, was different and he did not want to think about work.

His new-found equilibrium was a result of the improvement in his relationship with Natalie. In particular, the last few months of intense therapy sessions with Bethany had made him confront the nature of his anger. Stemming from resentment, inadequacy and shame, its consequence had been indignation worthy of a disgruntled Old Testament prophet. Bethany had explained how his bitterness made Natalie avoid him for her own protection.

The day was perfect, despite its chill, with a flawless blue sky that could warm even the most curmudgeonly mood. In the distance, he could see Natalie walking briskly up the hill towards him. She seemed carefree, a far cry from her morose demeanour during their many therapy sessions. There had been various permutations of attendees: Jack and Ali with the girls, Jack with the girls or just Jack and Natalie. On one excruciating afternoon, Jack had to pitch up with both his mother and Natalie, which proved as much fun as a tooth extraction by an unqualified dentist with a rusty drill.

He attended every session without fail and obediently followed the instructions he was given. Bethany set him 'homework' to prepare, and he diligently completed these tasks without complaint. He was communicative when asked to discuss his feelings and peppered most of his conversations with heartfelt apologies. There was no epiphany or breakthrough moment for Natalie. Rather, the sessions examined her unhappiness to help develop coping strategies for her combustible emotions. It was a process of self-discovery for them both as he understood how let down she felt by many aspects of his behaviour.

Primarily, he had failed as a father by not being a good enough husband and dismantling their stable family life. He had also undermined his status as an adult role model by hating his job. And finally, his dating ineptitude suggested all men were untrustworthy, just as she was trying to form her own relationships with boys. Jack did not think her version of events fair or reflective of what really happened, but Bethany helped him understand this was not the point. The key to finding balance was living with unpredictability and remembering it is better to celebrate what you have than lament what you think you are missing. The more therapy he attended, the more he appreciated it was not just for Natalie's benefit.

After months of intense conversations, Jack perceived Natalie was softening. First it was the regular text messages. Brief and to the point, she would reply to his enquiries about her life, made easier by her being in the last year of school and applying for university. There were practicalities he could discuss, and he became adroit at asking questions without volunteering an unsolicited opinion.

By the end of the year, he was allowed to meet her for a meal, chaperoned by Isobel. They talked mostly about music, films and television. He remembered Ali castigating him years ago about his lack of parenting patience, prophesying they would never want to chat about culture when they were adults. She was wrong. Because they spent so much time discussing their feelings with Bethany, the only safe topic for these restaurant trips was what's new on Netflix. He loved being able to find common interests, although the girls found his attempts to share their musical tastes utterly horrific.

The morning reminded Jack of his summer picnic at the same spot when he had confided his despair to Isobel. Sonia had told him to stay away for six months, and that period had now passed. His last contact was when he sent a text that simply read:

Let me prove myself and I'll meet you in January to show you who I really am.

At the time, it sounded the sort of statement he needed to make, but in truth he had no strategy to get her back. Since then, he had become immersed in a plan that was nearly ready to be unveiled.

This was the first time he had been alone with Natalie for the best part of a year and his nerves were immediately calmed by the enthusiastic hug she gave him, as if she saw him every day. Rosy-cheeked and breathless, she sat down to explain why she was late.

'Sorry, Dad, for keeping you. I've been with Grandma, cheering her up. She's still in such a mess because of that bastard Kurt. She was very weepy this morning, it was horrible. I really need to ask you something.'

'Anything you want, darling. I'm big on the truth these days.'

She looked at him with a familiar expression of disappointment. 'Why on earth didn't you warn her about him?'

* * *

They walked for an hour in the sunshine as Jack tried to explain to Natalie more about his relationship with his mother. He made it clear that all three siblings had constantly warned her they did not trust Kurt. Natalie was impressed that her Aunt Karen had hired an investigator to uncover the truth about him but frustrated that they did not disclose the alarming findings to Stephanie before her discovery of Kurt's behaviour a couple of months previously.

After Lionel's negotiation for his mother's share of Fogel's Chickens, Jack had intervened and bought her out of the business instead. This had released capital for her to buy the flat in Maida Vale and he had agreed to provide her with an income from the business in perpetuity that would support her comfortable lifestyle with her dubious partner. She was not that happy with the deal, but the siblings presented a united front to remind her that since she had not agreed to a prenuptial, there had to be some protection in place.

Stephanie was planning a guest-free wedding on a cruise of the Florida Keys. The thought of the family being together at sea would have produced a mutiny and they were all enormously relieved that this was no longer required. But just as Jack was beginning to accept that he had done all he could, he received a late-night call from Tracy telling him to get round to his mother's flat immediately. There had been a development with Kurt.

Jack found his mother being comforted by his sisters on the sofa. Her face was contorted with despair and anger, her eyes bloodshot and teary. In her dressing grown and slippers, she looked to him for the first time like an old lady. When she saw her son, she wailed and collapsed in his arms, sobbing uncontrollably. For a few minutes, her children quietly comforted her as Jack waited for an explanation.

It transpired that earlier in the evening, Kurt had left the kitchen to change his shirt, having accidently spilt coffee on it, forgetting his phone on the table. Stephanie had no intention of spying on him, but the text that flashed across the screen was impossible for her to avoid reading:

I have to see you, Kurt. I miss you.
When is she busy? D xx

No detective was needed to unravel the mystery. Stephanie told her children that as soon as he came back in the room, she started screaming at him, demanding an explanation, and was amazed he provided one with little resistance. 'D' was Diane, a fifty-four-year-old living in Marlow whom he had met online. A divorcee whose ex-husband worked for a City law firm, she had no children, a huge amount of money and seemed besotted with Kurt, wanting to help him research his esoteric lectures and support his glittering academic career.

Kurt was indifferent to Stephanie crying and calmly explained that he was sorry but ultimately '*the heart wants what the heart wants*'. Diane was younger and therefore a much better long-term prospect; her finances were substantial and free from the unwelcome intervention of a jealous son. Kurt retreated to the bedroom and after thirty minutes emerged with two suitcases to gather his final possessions from the living room. At the front door, he gave a half-hearted wave, as if passing a casual acquaintance on the deck of a large ocean liner. The last thing she saw as he slid out of her life was the Cartier watch she had bought, strapped tightly to his wrist.

Jack wished he could have found a better way to warn her, but in some ways he was too wrapped up in his own problems. Using his newly acquired therapy language, he observed to Natalie that he had grown up in conflict with his mother because she treated him like a means to a financial end and was clearly emotionally better connected to his sisters. It sounded so obvious now, he wondered why it had taken so many years to process these feelings.

Kurt had destroyed Stephanie, and she feared she would be on her own for the rest of her life. The family rallied together, visiting her regularly as vulnerability softened her demanding nature. For the first time, Jack and his mother were properly talking about the backlog of frustrations amassed over many years. Out of her grief arose an opportunity for him to reset their relationship and in turn, she craved his emotional support. Of course, a few weeks do not repair the damage of many years. Nevertheless, it was a beginning.

This prompted Natalie to ask what he felt about his parents' impact on his own development. He knew she was compiling a dossier against which to judge his own skills as a father, but he didn't mind. It was such a relief to have an adult conversation without constant fear of saying something that would antagonise her. He talked about growing up without a sense of his rightful place in the family. The men wanted him to run Fogel's Chickens. The women didn't care so long as he didn't disrupt their plans.

They strolled to a café and grabbed a table in the sun, which was now beginning its afternoon retreat. How ironic, he reflected, that his separation from Sonia had in many ways precipitated his rapprochement with Natalie. As they sipped their cappuccinos, he changed the subject to address his own future.

'So, Nat, you haven't asked me about Sonia.'

'What's there to ask? Not to put too fine a point on it, didn't she dump you for deliberately avoiding the truth about being a kosher butcher because you worried that as a vegan café owner, you weren't exactly the perfect partner for her?'

He winced in memory of a particularly awkward therapy session several months previously when he had told the whole story. Admitting to your child you have repeatedly lied to someone you supposedly love was not a proud moment. Bethany abandoned professional integrity and sat staring at him with her arms folded in contempt, implying he was an affront to all women.

'I need your help. And Isobel's.'

'What can we do? I think it may be too late to roll out your cute daughters and go on a trip to the zoo.'

'Funny you should mention it, but I do want you to meet her. I need you to keep next Sunday afternoon free, please. I've been preparing something.'

Natalie's expression changed to one of apprehension. It reminded him of when she was little and nervous about doing something physically daring, unlike her reckless tomboy sister. Her fear of heights had somehow shifted to a concern her father might hurt her.

'Are you sure, Dad, it's a good idea for her to meet us when you're not together?'

'Nope. I'm on a mission to get out of the mess I've created. I really love her, Nat, and she needs to meet the two most important other women in my life to finally understand if she can be with me.'

'No pressure, then, for any of us?'

Jack could not think of a satisfactory reply to this valid assessment of his ambitious plan. What a disaster if he jeopardised carefully rebuilt relationships to repair one that he had destroyed, and his thoughts were overwhelmed by the enormity of what he was attempting. The elation of being with Natalie had been replaced by a feeling of dread as he twiddled his spoon in the dregs of his coffee foam, staring vacantly on to the street.

'It's shit or bust, Nat. Shit or bust.'

She did not know if he was talking to her or thinking aloud. It seemed best not to ask.

* * *

Calling Sonia was a terrifying prospect, even though he had planned it with the meticulousness of a Prussian general. Throughout their separation, he had maintained an idealistic belief in the possibility of reconciliation, even though this logic was flimsy as contact between them had been minimal. In his mind, Sonia had not definitively ended the relationship; rather, she had suspended it until she could evaluate his worth with the distance of time. This unfounded optimism produced a chemical release in his brain that persuaded him anything was possible, even if the prospect of his relationship reigniting would be given terrible odds by any decent bookmaker.

He had sent flowers on her birthday with a short message – *Thinking of you. Permanently sorry.* – that failed to elicit an acknowledgement, and had otherwise respected her wish for radio silence. Whenever it rained, he repressed the urge to stand under a lamp post by her café looking forlorn, and knew a sonnet shoved through her door would not achieve much either. His greatest worry was that she would move on without him and the thought of her with another man was too excruciating to contemplate.

He desperately needed to know something about her, but his only channel was via his brother-in-law Clive's tennis partner, who had made the initial introduction. Clive refused to help, telling him he was too old to pass notes in the playground on his behalf. Undeterred, Jack betrayed this intransigence to Tracy, who threatened her husband with a sex strike if he did not help her brother. The next day, Clive grudgingly made the phone call and found out snippets of relevant information. Sonia was fine, it seemed, and focusing on work as her catering business was beginning to take off. Consequently, she barely had time for a social life and seemed unbothered. She was suspicious, apparently, at the nature of the call from her cousin and asked directly if Jack was behind his sudden solicitousness.

He was none the wiser about her feelings, but at least his hope was not eviscerated. By now, he was working every hour of the day on a master plan that was going to show his genuine contrition and help her reconsider him as a potential life partner. The mirror in his bedroom was a collage of rainbow-coloured Post-it notes, a giant to-do list that resembled a clue wall in a murder investigation. For months he had painstakingly worked his way through them individually, imagining how incredible it would be if the sincerity of his effort could be rewarded by Sonia's love. If only.

* * *

She answered his call immediately, her voice guarded.

'Hello.'

'Sonia. It's me.'

'I know it's you.'

'Well, at least you haven't deleted me from your phone.'

'The night is still young. What do you want, Jack?'

'I want to see you if you're free this Sunday afternoon. Two hours of your time. Then you can erase me from your life if you want to.'

'What is there to say?'

It was a question, yet her cold tone made it also sound like a statement of fact. Jack had scripted this conversation in his head so many times that he knew his next few lines by rote.

'Do you remember I asked you for time to prove myself?'

'You must also remember I didn't reply and told you not to contact me for six months.'

'Well, it's been that long and I was hoping we could meet in the bar at the Covent Garden Hotel at three o'clock, if that's OK?'

'And?'

'And I am going to introduce you to my daughters. Then I would like to show you all something.'

'Is it fair to me and the girls to meet like this? You know I would have loved nothing more than to be introduced to them in the summer, but you always wanted to be alone. I assume you were worried that they wouldn't stick to your script.'

To his surprise, her tone changed as if something then occurred to her. She sounded warmer.

'Both girls? Is Natalie talking to you again? That must be a relief.'

'She is, thank God, after endless family therapy. Bethany has just bought a superyacht on the proceeds. It's early days, though, and I'm not counting my chickens.'

'Unfortunate turn of phrase, Jack. And how is the secret abattoir these days?'

'I'll tell you on Sunday. I've made some decisions I want to share. After that, if you never want to see me again, I'll leave you alone. Promise.'

The gap between her answers was gradually lengthening, suggesting indecision, but her voice did not lose its edge.

'What do you expect from me after just six months? Forgiveness? For someone who doesn't like the clichés of a romcom, you're certainly behaving like you think you're in one.'

'Look, I'll not be galloping up on a white horse if that's what you're worried about. My breeches are at the dry cleaners anyway.'

'So why do I have to see you?'

'You don't. You owe me nothing. I owe you a genuine explanation.'

This last assertion made her reflective and Jack refrained from filling the uncomfortable silence with an unnecessary comment. Sonia was clearly weighing up her response, as if it carried with it either a prison sentence or a life of happiness. When eventually she spoke, she still sounded hesitant.

'OK, I'll hear your explanation. Two hours, tops. Just make sure you don't upset your girls in the process. You really are something of a disaster where women are concerned.'

'Thank you for agreeing. I appreciate this isn't easy for you.'

Sonia sighed down the phone.

'No, Jack. You don't make it easy for anyone.'

Chapter 32

They came by cab to the hotel in strained silence. After their encouraging walk, Natalie's positivity had evaporated and even his cheerleader, Isobel, stared out of the window, reluctant to chat. Jack wondered if it was an enormous mistake to involve them in his relationship by introducing them to Sonia like this. Perhaps he was conflating a desire to win her back with his quest to become a better father. It was too late to stop, and he consoled himself this was an act of love, not selfishness.

As they entered, the doorman wished them a pleasant afternoon, which Jack hoped was an accurate description for the next few hours. The bar area was rammed with young families enjoying an indulgent afternoon tea and it was hard to talk over clattering plates and clinking glasses, hardly ideal for such a challenging reunion. Isobel was looking at the assortment of sandwiches and multi-coloured cakes arriving from the kitchen and seemed concerned.

'You have remembered to check they have vegan options for Sonia, haven't you, Dad?'

He had completely forgotten, but surveying the hip people around him, he felt confident there would be something available not cooked in butter or lard. They were all visibly anxious and he tried to distract them by asking Natalie about her university applications. She kept turning away as she spoke, making it difficult to hear her above the din, and Jack wondered how angry Ali would be if she could see Natalie's present discomfort.

The thought of his ex-wife made him change the subject to Ali's new boyfriend. For the first time since their divorce, they were getting on well, particularly after gruelling months of family ther-apy. In one session, Jack had apologised for abandoning their life plans to run Fogel's Chickens and Ali had admitted to giving up on the marriage because of his forced career change. She was now in a good place, having been dating a doctor called Daniel for the last six months. He was a widower with twin boys of ten and Natalie perked up as she described their relationship with surprising enthusiasm, reporting how content her mother was these days.

Jack was very amused when Isobel let slip a misunderstanding that had accompanied their early courtship. Ali had misheard his medical specialism, believing him to be a paediatrician, and was always asking how difficult his job was emotionally, particularly dealing with the worried parents. It turned out he was in *podiatric* not *paediatric* medicine, spending his day looking at misshapen feet and fungal growths. Jack found it ironic that Ali, who had resented his career of gory poultry slaughter, was now with a man whose expertise was the glamorous world of bunion removal.

Just as they were about to discuss the implications of their moving in together, Sonia entered the restaurant and Jack uncon-sciously raised his finger to his lips, as if her arrival should be greeted in reverential silence. This was it: an encounter he had thought about for weeks and months, imagining every possible permutation of reaction and consequence. As ever, his body reacted to the intensity of his emotions and his heart raced so quickly he felt light-headed.

She stood at the front desk, unwinding a long scarf and unbutton-ing her coat, her eyes searching the room for them. Eventually, after some unnecessarily frenetic waving, he caught her eye and she smiled nervously, weaving deftly in between the crowded tables towards them. Her hair was much shorter, sitting just above her shoulders, and he was poleaxed by resurgent desire. They kissed on the cheek awkwardly and Sonia hugged the girls as if they were old friends.

'It's lovely to meet you both,' Sonia began. 'I've heard so much about you from your doting father.'

Jack thought his intestines might spontaneously combust, so sharp was the pain he now felt, her naturalness reminding him of how much he had lost. Natalie turned her back on him to launch excitedly into her own private conversation with Sonia.

'Bit weird meeting you like this, and I'm so sorry we've only been able to do it when Dad *fucked up* so badly. Excuse my language.'

Sonia smiled.

'No need to apologise. It's the right technical term for what he's done. My friends have called him far worse.'

Isobel, fearless and loyal, felt compelled to stick up for her father.

'It's not all his fault. He's had to deal with lots of rubbish recently and I believe him when he says that he didn't want to hurt you or any of us.'

'That may be true, Isobel, but he did, and it's hard to forgive, no matter how wonderful his daughters are.'

The girls looked at each other, unsure if this was the start of a relationship or a one-off farewell, as Jack remained tongue-tied, worried he might be losing control of the afternoon already. Having hoped for an amiable chat about the weather over coffee and cake, suddenly they were discussing his failings before he could reveal the real reason they were there.

He caught the eye of a passing waiter, who recognised his look of desperation and jogged over to them, pad at the ready. No one had an appetite so they ordered a round of tea and coffee, and as the waiter moved away, Jack added, 'Would you mind having these served downstairs?'

'Where are we going?' Sonia asked. 'I've only just got here.'

'The Screening Room.'

Natalie's scowl returned at the news they were going elsewhere.

'We're not watching a boring black-and-white film, are we, Dad? That's so like you, to have a stupid idea when we should be getting to know each other properly.'

'Not quite. I'm going to show you something very important I've been working on for the last few months. It's the most important thing I've ever done. It's for all of you.'

Isobel nodded obediently, while Sonia shrugged.

'Whatever you want, Jack. I promised you a couple of hours and if you think it's important, then that's what we'll do. Having said that, I do agree with Natalie. I'd much prefer to speak to her and Isobel.'

Jack knew it was best not to say anything further, so he simply pointed in the direction of the stairs. As they gathered their belongings, he was unable to hold back telling her what he had been thinking since she arrived.

'I really like your hair. You look lovely.'

It was like praising a stranger, given her non-committal response to the compliment. Isobel was by now fully attuned to his awkwardness and decided therefore to help him out by punching him on the arm in a fit of false pique.

'Don't you like my hair, Dad? Typical. I had it cut last week and you've barely noticed.'

* * *

The pink leather cinema seats had bottles of water and popcorn resting on them. Sonia and the girls entered the room hesitantly and, despite there being at least ten empty rows, chose to sit next to each other at the front, in solidarity for the ordeal that was planned for them. Jack disappeared to the projection room, and the girls quietly munched on popcorn while Sonia read the ingredients on the carton in the forlorn hope they were dairy free.

After a couple of minutes, the waiter arrived with their drinks. It seemed pointless to continue their conversation, so they sipped silently, smiling nervously at one another. The awkwardness did not go on for long as Jack suddenly marched back in and clapped his hands to get their attention. He did not look comfortable, his forehead moist with sweat and his face muscles refusing to co-operate whenever he tried to smile.

'I'm sorry for the mystery. This must feel very strange for you all.'

'What do you reckon, girls? It seems to me a perfectly natural way to meet your ex-boyfriend's kids.'

Sonia's calmness contrasted with Natalie, who was tapping her foot and struggling to control conflicting emotions. Suddenly, she stood up and accidentally knocked over the popcorn, which spilt half its contents on the carpet.

'Dad, why are you trying to make us all so uncomfortable? This is weird, even by your standards.'

She was in tears, which was the last thing he had wanted. Isobel gently pulled her back into her seat and Jack steadied himself. It was time, the culmination of a frantic crusade to prove he was a good person, a caring father and not an idiot. Unable to look at them, he stared at the popcorn on the floor and, in a voice cracking with desperation, revealed why they were there.

'So here it is. I've been very busy, Sonia, since we met, trying to find a way to rectify my actions, and have made a film for you all that explains everything. I really hope you like it.

'It's called "Chicken Wars".'

* * *

The idea had come after his humiliating meeting with Charlotte, the newly promoted intern at Channel 4, who had thought 'Widgets' was a documentary and sat bemused when he earnestly explained it was a sitcom. Fidgeting in her seat, she struggled to know what to say as he outlined an idea she thought would only appeal to her grand-parents. A week later he received a templated rejection and found his overriding feeling to be relief. Having reviewed the treatment, he realised any merit in his writing was offset by its fundamentally old-fashioned style. He was living in the past by hoping to be a writer and somehow his need for creative validation could not be separated from all his other frustrations.

'Chicken Wars' was for Sonia.

By recording his thoughts convincingly, he hoped he could provide her with an honest depiction of how he wanted to live from now on. Created for a limited audience of three people, he wondered if he could produce something of which he might be proud and he set about it with the fervour of a hyperactive zealot, hiring a camera man, editor and production assistant. The crew was slightly bemused by Jack's commitment to this esoteric project, but the money was good and their daily rates unquestioned. The documentary was to be a blend of conversations and interviews, illustrated with meticulously compiled imagery, and he scoured photo libraries, video footage and family portraits to make sure he had enough content.

He also had to persuade people to participate. His sisters and mother thought it odd but agreed, as if apologising for their lack of enthusiasm for his previous creative projects. Gadi and Stacey were less obliging. They had no interest in supporting Jack's mercu-rial request and their relationship by this time had degenerated to contact only through lawyers.

After being ambushed at the restaurant, Jack had made the decision to sell his share in the restaurants to Lionel. He did not want to be their partner any longer and found their ambition and egos unmanageable. The prospect of them working with Lionel was rather exciting to him. They would be screaming at each other within weeks.

Next, he agreed to sell Lionel all his shops, his biggest decision since taking over the business twenty years before. It was made with considerable ease and far less regret. Not just the two that had been in dispute but all five of them: lock, chicken stock, gherkin barrel and all.

He read the offer Lionel handed over at Clucks and laughed at its derisory valuation, at the same time concluding there was only one course of action that would give him peace. Being Lionel's competitor would sustain the feud forever and he would always want to fight over something. By divesting his retail business and just owning a factory, it would allow Jack to do something else with his life.

It was that simple, although predicated on the right commercial settlement, and there followed an intense negotiation to reach an agreement. Jack made it clear he would not entertain a lowball offer. Given Lionel had already told the world he had won the war, he could not walk away from the acquisition without looking silly. A figure marginally below the asking price was agreed after six weeks of complicated conversations in which Jack's financial acuity ensured a comprehensive settlement and a significant slug of capital. After twenty years of hard work, his family had all done very well without having to go through the hassle he had.

Jack wanted to make his final negotiations a big part of the film. When he emailed for consent, he encountered an unrestrained ego willingly courting fame. Lionel was thrilled his triumph would be recorded for posterity and might one day be taught at business schools across the world. He wrote back that he had '*nothing to hide other than your humiliation*' and even suggested he was helping Jack find a new career now that his business was in ruins.

Pre-production coalesced with complex negotiations to divest parts of his business and, for the first time, Jack demonstrated his commercial expertise alongside his need for creative expression. His purpose? To impress a former lover, earn the respect of his children and prove he was not an idiot through the extravagance of this self-funded documentary. What was odd about that?

Chapter 33

CHICKEN WARS
A film by Jack Fogel
Dedicated to Sonia, Natalie and Isobel ...
... and the millions of fallen chickens

Scene 1

Willesden Cemetery on a blustery October morning, eddies of fallen leaves blowing around the rows of graves. There are rapid cuts between stones and large mausoleums of well-known Jewish families, leading rabbi, long-forgotten communal leaders. Jack stands by a gravestone and as the camera focuses, we see it is his grandfather Solly's. Prominent on the stone is a quote from Deuteronomy:

Do not be afraid, do not panic, and do not be broken before them. For your God is the One who goes with you to fight for you with your enemies to save you.

Staring at the camera, he outlines the film's purpose.

'I am Jack Fogel, forty-seven and divorced. I run the largest kosher chicken business in the UK. Not much of an accolade, but it's the only one I have. I have two daughters, two sisters, a mother. I was recently in a relationship that meant everything to me. I didn't tell her about my business because she was a vegan and I thought it would prove a dealbreaker and when she found out, it ended. Can I be forgiven?

'I have been in a war with myself since I was thirteen, when my grandfather told me that I was going to run Fogel's Chickens when I grew up. Even though I always wanted to do something else, I knew deep down that I couldn't escape its pull, especially when he gave me the key to the family abattoir for my bar mitzvah. From that moment, I have been fighting battles with everyone, but particularly myself. And the result? Only my perpetual confusion and broken relationships.

'This is my attempt to discover the truth.'

* * *

Scene 2

Jack and Rabbi Isaac Furstein are sitting in the classroom of their old school. The room is a mixture of tatty, peeling paint and old wooden chairs with new technology of a laptop projecting on to a whiteboard. The camera focuses on the screen:

King Solomon School welcomes its esteemed pupil Rabbi Isaac Furstein and his friend Jack, whom no one remembers.

Rabbi Furstein lifts his yarmulke and scratches his head before putting it back on. Staring at his immaculately manicured hands, he turns to Jack:

'When you told me you wanted me for a film role, I was hoping for a more glamorous location.'

'Your riders were too demanding. Do you know how hard it is to create a statue of a swan made of chopped liver?'

'Jack, my car is on a meter outside and we rabbis can't afford to waste our money. Why have we returned to the scene of some of our most boring lessons?'

'I am on a voyage of self-discovery, and I thought this would be a good place to ask you a question, given you have known me for over thirty years.'

'I try not to admit this in public. Now, what's your question?'

'A simple one. Is it ever OK, as a Jew, to tell a white lie? My grandfather positively encouraged me to believe it was necessary. When I told one to Sonia, somehow she did not share this view.'

'Do you want the official Talmud version or my personal opinion?'

'Let's start off official and if I don't like the answer, you can tell me as a friend what you really think.'

Rabbi Furstein stretches his arms as if about to do some yoga and then stands up as if unable to dispense wisdom in a sedentary position.

'Well, let me start by informing you that the official view is we should not lie. There are many instances of this being unambiguously articulated. It says in Leviticus: *Do not steal, do not deceive and do not lie to one another.* You probably do all three, sometimes on the same day.'

'Thanks for the heads-up.'

'But I think you are asking me a different question. I think you want exoneration for misleading your girlfriend because somehow you thought it was in both your interests and you want me now to help you make her understand you behaved expediently rather than badly.'

'Something like that.'

The rabbi begins to pace the room as if teaching an invisible class. He seems to need a bigger congregation.

'Let's start with a small incident from the Book of Genesis, when an angel tells Abraham and Sarah, who are respectively ninety-nine and ninety, that they will have a baby. Sarah laughs to herself about the prospect given their unlikely ages. But in the next verse, the Almighty, who is all-knowing, so aware of Sarah's response, has a catch-up with Abraham and doesn't mention her reaction, as our sages tell us, to avoid upsetting him with his wife's unflattering description. This is perhaps the first example of doctoring the truth to minimise the pain caused. What do you say to that, Jack?'

'Seems like a bona fide "white lie", even if it is also gynaecologically unlikely.'

'So, you might say from this incident that it is permissible not to relate the whole truth, even if it conveys a false impression?'

'Vindicated at last!'

'Easy, tiger, you can't think the centuries of scholarship will make it that easy for you. There's a tractate in the Talmud in which the question is asked what you should say when you see a bride. One rabbinic school, the House of Shammai, says you should describe her as she is. Quite literally warts and all. The contrasting view, from the rival House of Hillel, is that you should describe her as beautiful, no matter if this is not the case. It's a conundrum – calling her beautiful and graceful when she is neither is clearly a falsehood, which we are meant to avoid. Conversely, we are also taught to be pleasant, so why talk bluntly and upset someone? Which do you think is right?'

'Isaac, my kids are watching this. They'll be appalled at how sexist the examples you've given me are.'

'I don't write this stuff – I'm just paid to interpret it. Now, how do you think this relates to your situation? Fogel, Class 4C. Your answer, please.'

'I was hoping you'd tell me, sir.'

'Disappointing, Fogel. Disappointing. Let me help you. Did your withholding the truth save Sonia from pain?'

'I don't think so.'

'Did it spare her feelings?'

'No, it made her more upset.'

'Did you do it for her benefit or yours?'

The camera is now focused on Jack's face. It is contorted with discomfort, as he considers his answer. There is a shot of the clock on the wall showing the seconds ticking away.

'No, I did it for my own sake, not hers.'

'Then I suggest it's time for you to respect the truth a little bit more as far as Sonia is concerned. What you did was wrong.'

'Is that you or the Talmud speaking?'

'It's your friend who sat in this room and watched your teenage conflicts turn into adult turmoil. It's not that complicated, and you don't need to find the answer in the scriptures. If you want Sonia to love you, step out from behind your resentment and remember you're an impressive bloke.'

'Do you think I'm impressive?'

'Well, more than Barney Green who used to sit at that desk over there. He's in prison now.'

* * *

Scene 3

Jack is in his factory; it is late at night and practically deserted. The conveyor belt and machinery are stationary and in the background a couple of workers are hosing the floor. The camera tracks a lengthy shot of the empty building. We see the closed doors of giant freezers, an industrial kitchen with pots and pans, and lengthy runs of stainless-steel work surfaces. Its emptiness makes it impossible to tell that this is an abattoir. Jack continues to address the camera.

'This is my place of work, where most days you will find seventy industrious people shouting over the metallic symphony of this machinery in full operation. When I left university, I was hoping that BBC Television Centre or the James Bond Stage at Pinewood would be where you would find me building my career. I got that one wrong.'

Jack's voiceover continues over a montage of imagery from the food industry. Kosher meats and cold cuts are interspersed with shots of the latest meat substitute products. We see footage of cows being milked dissolving into shots of endless rows of cartons of dairy substitute, from almond milk to hemp milk. We cut to scenes of families gathered around traditional roast dinners intercut with vegan and vegetarian street fairs and festivals.

'It's odd because I am not religious, if not something of an atheist, and yet my life is governed by Deuteronomy, Chapter 12, which contains the verses in which Jews are given the instruction to kill animals in a specific way to make them fit to eat. It's called *shechita* and the kosher food industry is now worth $25 billion globally. To give you some context, the vegan food market is estimated to be worth slightly more, at $29 billion. There are approximately 79 million vegans in the world but only 15 million Jews. That's a lot of kosher chicken consumption per head when you think about it.'

Jack is in his office. We track the bare walls to discover that a framed certificate of his kosher licence is hung adjacent to several pictures of his girls as small children and then young adults. We see a few spreadsheets on his desk and the camera focuses to allow us to see orders from his farmer suppliers for live birds and production schedules for their killing.

'My grandfather was right when he told me that the business could sustain the Fogel family for many years to come. And yet, is it right to carry on with an antiquated process slaughtering innocent animals? Should we eat meat at all? Should I make a living from it? Should I be proud or ashamed?

'I have just lied to a woman who I fell in love with, because I was unwilling for her to consider that what I do could be part of who I am. I wish I could walk away from it all, but it's just not that easy.'

* * *

Scene 4

The animated Chaim the Chicken appears on screen singing 'Ain't nobody here but us chickens'. It has had over 400,000 views on YouTube. A succession of images outlines the conflict with Lionel: Chaim standing outside his shop handing out leaflets, aggressive ads in the Jewish press, screenshots of Chaim's Twitter feed, Drumstx's tweet and its global response, national newspaper articles. The gamut of its absurdity. Jack's voiceover accompanies the montage.

'In 1988 my grandfather fired Lionel Gutterman. I was only fifteen at the time and little did I know that one day, I would be the focus of his revenge. The cliché says it's a dish best served cold. Lionel left it so long it was completely frozen. I could spend the rest of my life trying to understand his motivation or the greed that drives him forward. Instead, I have decided to resolve the conflict.

'Since my grandfather caused my problems today, I have asked myself is there anything I can learn from how he would have approached the problem. Of course, if it had been him, Lionel would have been in hospital, pressing charges for the physical assault he had suffered.'

A series of sepia-toned photos now illustrate the life of Solly Fogel, husband, father, businessman, communal figure, provoker of fights and opportunist. Black title cards with white text punctuate the images, like a silent movie, to tell his story.

In 1925 Solly started transporting chickens, even though he did not have a licence.

In 1956 Solly visited New York to discover the new technology of a plucking machine.

In five minutes and a dozen titles, we learn the history of Fogel's Chickens and the unorthodox way in which it was built.

'I want to be a good man and behave properly, but sometimes you must be prepared to act with a little guile and mischief to win. That's not how Solly would have put it, but it's a more palatable version of the many life lessons he freely dispensed. I have realised that I can do this my own way and make my family proud at the same time.'

We see Jack's shops, bustling with loyal customers filling baskets with a freezer load of different meats.

'The legacy of my grandfather and the lunacy of my rival has helped me realise a simple truth.

'I like chicken.

'I like its taste.

'I can reconcile myself to its production and its role in the food chain. If you think killing animals to eat them is cruel, which is totally understandable, then nothing I can do to explain our methodology will change that belief.

'For me, my business is a link not just with my family's immediate past but also with the many generations of Jews who have for some reason followed the instructions given to them two thousand years ago. I can't explain it more. It's just who I am.

'The past few months of being immersed in a feud has made me realise something else hardwired into my existence. This is my business. It provides for my family. I will not abandon it yet. The more interesting question is: what sort of business do I want to run?

'After weeks of negotiation, I have decided to sell my shops and restaurants to Lionel and start living differently. I have one last conversation with him over a coffee to finalise our new arrangement, which he has kindly agreed to let me film.'

* * *

Scene 5

We are in Yoffee Coffee, the café where Jack first met Lionel months ago to be told of his destruction. They are seated opposite one another with coffees and a few legal documents spread across the table.

'Thank you for coming, Lionel.'

'It's about time we had this conversation, so I am glad you called. Always good to clear the air. Where should I look, by the way, I want to make sure you get my best side?'

'Let's chat naturally and pretend we are not being filmed.'

'Whatever you say, Alfred Hitchcock.'

Lionel slurps his cappuccino. We watch them converse amicably in the fast-forward of a time-lapse. They seem to be relaxed, almost enjoying each other's company. Minutes pass. Lionel's coffee cup is empty. Jack leans forward to ask a question.

'One more thing. I'm just wondering, now that all the paperwork is signed, if you are pleased with yourself? Has it been a good few months' work?'

Lionel taps his spoon on the cup like a judge banging a gavel to deliver a summing-up.

'I am quite frankly delighted. I've bought your shops and restaurants and will make more money than you ever did. You know, Jack, you never really understood the humiliation I felt because of your grandfather. It made me so bitter, I think it may well have ruined my first marriage and made me a very difficult person to be around. So yes, since you ask, the satisfaction of battering you into submission is rather hard to contain.'

'But, Lionel, do you really think it was a decent way to behave?'

'Decent? There's no prize for decency. I'm running a business, not a charity saving lives. You are very naive. In fact, the only thing I learnt from your grandfather is that sometimes your tactics need to be brutal.'

'And do you know what I learnt from him?'

'What's that?'

'That if you have a terrible enemy, it's OK to be a bastard in return.'

'What are you talking about?'

'I've been chatting with my family and we all feel that *Zeyde* Solly would be livid if he thought you had won. He'd expect more from me.'

'But I have won, you *potz*.'

'In which case, you won't mind that I've decided to use all that money you've spent on buying me out on something worthwhile.'

'I'm not following you. What have you bought?'

Jack waits a second for dramatic effect. There is a sound effect of a drum roll and the frame freezes on Lionel's apprehensive expression for a couple of seconds. The camera switches to Jack, who is doing his best not to smile.

'Thornstein's in Manchester. I believe you know the business.'

The camera returns to Lionel's face, its Jaffa-orange sheen growing redder.

'But that would mean you own *all* the kosher abattoirs in the country?'

We cut to Jack and Gary Thornstein, the seventy-year-old son of the founder, signing the sale and purchase agreement in a dingy office in the Manchester factory. A bottle of Prosecco is opened after they shake hands. We see a shot of the factory interior, also at night. It is large but clearly in need of modernising.

'It would, Lionel. You catch on fast. And wait a minute? You own most of the kosher butcher shops and two kosher chicken restaurants. That means you'd have to buy all your chickens from me. What a stroke of luck for the Fogels. Don't worry, my friend, I'll make sure you're looked after properly. After all, my family goes back a long way with you.'

'You think you're really clever, don't you.'

Lionel jabs a finger aggressively towards the invisible camera lens. He is scowling.

'Since you ask, I am indeed feeling very pleased with myself. Almost as smug as you were a few seconds ago. It's all change. You are now my largest customer, and I am your only supplier. Life is going to be so much simpler now that if you need a kosher chicken, you will have to come to me.'

Lionel cannot contain himself any longer. Like an actor hounded by a merciless throng of paparazzi, he pushes the camera out of his way as he gets up to leave.

'Enough of this nonsense. And turn that thing off now. If you make this conversation public, I'll … I'll …'

'You'll what, Lionel? Set Chaim on me?'

'I'll slit your throat like a chicken.'

The camera captures Lionel's petulant shove of a waitress carrying a tray of hot chocolate as he stomps towards the door.

* * *

Scene 6

We are now in Tracy's house. The siblings are sitting around an enormous farmhouse kitchen table, empty except for a vase filled with drooping white tulips. Tracy and Karen are sitting next to each other and address the camera like newsreaders. Tracy begins:

'I have been asked by my brother for an assessment of who he is and some advice to him on how to behave moving forward. Sonia, I'm sorry my brother hurt you. If you want my professional opinion, he suffers from that rare psychological condition called "chronic but reversible emotional incompetence".

'He's very talented, funny and kind. He has provided for us all for years and has a sense of responsibility to his family that is exceptional. He just needs to be a little less useless at admitting his feelings to the people who love him the most. He can come across as a bit of a victim when in truth he is really something of a hero.

'And, Sonia, although we have not met, just because you are vegan, there is nothing wrong with loving a man who makes money from the kosher chicken trade. Different outlooks make for more exciting relationships. I hope you forgive him.'

Next it is Karen's turn. She tries to smile, but it seems more a grimace of irritation. However, she delivers her short speech as if addressing a crowd of would-be voters, with confident self-assurance.

'This is the last ridiculous thing I am going to do for my idiot older brother. Now listen here, Sonia, the vegan café owner who Jack is pining for so much that he's making us participate in his elaborate apology. You are most definitely too good for him but let me make the case for giving him a second chance.

'When I look back at growing up, we were very mean to him. All he wanted was support for some nonsense or other he was writing. Instead, we mocked him and then when he followed his dream, we dumped the family business on him so we could carry on with our own lives. No wonder he's made a mess of every relationship ever since.

'But I tell you what, Lady Nut-Roast, despite the grief I give him, I could not love him more. And do you want to know why? Of course you do, since you're probably handcuffed to a cinema seat having to watch this rubbish. He's the most loyal bloke you will ever meet. He will support you for eternity, irrespective of the sarcastic abuse he receives. He is a veritable *mensch*, and you could do far worse.

'So, for heaven's sake, stop making inedible salads from things you've found on the forest floor, and give him another go. For all our sakes.'

* * *

Scene 7

Jack is sitting with his mother in her new flat. The walls are bare, the detritus of the decorators clearly visible. Stephanie is dressed casually in jeans and a cream cashmere sweater, a cigarette in her hand. She is fidgety and uncomfortable.

'Is this absolutely necessary, Jack?'

'I want to show Sonia and the girls who I really am and you're a vital part of the equation.'

'I'm not really sure why we have to do this now, given I am trying to recover from Kurt. Turning up with a film crew to ask questions about if I've been a good mother is not that helpful.'

'I'm sorry, I know how hard it must be in a new flat now on your own.'

'How can you? You got divorced years ago.'

'I'll let that one pass in the spirit of truth and reconciliation. I'm here because I have something important to ask. Forget the camera.'

'It's not the bloody camera. It's the two strangers holding the equipment I could do without. Please let's get this over and done with. What's your question?'

'What I want to know is, why do I feel I have disappointed you?'

Stephanie stubs out the cigarette in the overflowing ashtray by her.

'Disappointed? What makes you think you're a disappointment?'

'You've never seemed to enjoy my company like you do with Tracy and Karen. I felt I was something of an irritation. All you cared about was that I ran the business.'

'That's not true, Jack. It's just complicated.'

'How is it complicated? You either want to spend time with me or you don't.'

'This goes back to your grandfather's behaviour years ago.'

'What are you talking about, Mum?'

'Do you know how much he loved you? Adored everything about you. Thought that you were a brilliant boy with a tremendous future.'

'Well, I knew for some reason he saw me differently to the girls.'

'That's an understatement. He thought if they didn't know how to pluck a chicken blindfolded, they would never find a husband.'

'That's not my fault.'

'Maybe not, but your grandfather treated you as if you were so much more special than anyone else in the family, which irritated me enormously.'

'I don't want to sound ungrateful, but that was an unfair burden to put on me.'

'Well, you need to blame your father, not me.'

'What do you mean?'

'Oh, Jack, you have no idea how unlucky you were.'

'Unlucky. Do you mean when Dad had his heart attack?'

'No, way before then. Solly realised you hated the business as he watched you become a teenager with different interests. It broke his heart, but he loved you so much that he was prepared to free you from the responsibility of taking over. Why do you think Solly made Lionel his protégé, not your useless father? He was meant to run the business, rather than Phil. Lionel was your means of escape.'

'Do you mean, if Lionel had not got greedy, I could have been spared the miserable last twenty years?'

'It was your jealous father's fault. He lied to Solly with lots of rubbish about Lionel planning to get an outside investor to oust him. No wonder Lionel was bitter, he was heartbroken that he never had the chance to tell his version. I think he admired your grandfather more than anyone. We're not meant to speak ill of the dead, but for your father an exception can be made.'

'Is that why you've been on "Team Lionel"? Are you friendly with him because you feel sorry for him?'

'*Was* friendly, Jack. *Was.* Not any more. Even your cruel mum can now see he crossed a line. This stupid vendetta can't be excused. Not that he cares. He was only inviting me round for all those games of bridge to get up your nose.'

'Well, it worked, he got so far up my nose he even overtook Kurt. It drove me mad that you had some weird loyalty towards him. But why are you telling me this now?'

'For one thing, you've brought a film crew round to interview me, so I was assuming you'd want to know.'

'I am reeling that my life could have been different. Anything else I should know?'

'Only that after Lionel, Solly made me promise I'd persuade you to take over, whatever the circumstances, from your dad, who made the decision for you by dropping dead. We all got what we wanted, except you. I'm sorry if that's a bit selfish.'

'You could have just once said something supportive?'

Stephanie lights another cigarette but leaves it burning in the ashtray.

'You're right. I am very proud of you, Jack. You are a wonderful son and father. I'm sorry for not telling you this before.'

'Can I get it in writing?'

Stephanie smiles and wipes a tear or a bit of dust from her eye. She takes a long drag on the cigarette, exhaling a ring of smoke that slowly disperses.

'Now, darling, enough self-indulgence for one morning. Tell me about what's happening with Sonia. Is there a chance she'll forgive you?'

'I suppose it depends on how well I edit this film.'

'You really were very silly to be embarrassed about what you do, although I'm not surprised you didn't tell her the truth. I'm not sure you recognise it.'

'What do you mean?'

'You were always destined to be a great success as a kosher butcher. You're a natural. I may not have looked interested, but we've watched what you've done with admiration. I'm not that convinced the same would have been true for a TV career. You were such a pretentious teenager, and I must tell you, some of your ideas back then were appalling. Maybe the truth is Fogel's Chickens saved you from a frustrating career of mediocrity?'

Silence. The cameraman off screen can be heard.
'Shall we cut, Jack? Is that a good place to stop?'

* * *

Scene 8

A black screen. We hear footsteps approach. A yellow glow seems to be getting brighter from the right-hand corner of the screen. A figure comes slowly into focus. It is Chaim the Chicken, animated in a similar fashion to before. We hear a burst of Merle Haggard's 1994 song, 'Set My Chickens Free'. For twenty seconds, Chaim performs a manic dance, a mixture of line dancing and a hora. The music fades. Chaim speaks, gesticulating with his wings. It is Jack's voice we hear.

'That dance of love was for you, Sonia. Maybe that was my mistake all along? Chaim has done some ridiculous things to hurt me but has never shown me a moment's shame for who he is. This film has been me embracing my inner Chaim. I like myself a bit more now. I hope you can too. And I should warn you that I have learnt all the steps to that dance, which I will perform in your café every day until you change your mind.'

THE END
(Or maybe the beginning?)

Chapter 34

The lights went up in the screening room and they said nothing, each lost in impenetrable thoughts. Jack was unsure what to do other than some vigorous praying as Sonia asked to be left with the girls to talk about what they had watched. Like an expectant father, he paced outside the room, veering emotionally from fear that he'd done something wrong to pride at how good the film looked on the big screen. After five minutes, Isobel called him back in and, to his dismay, Sonia was putting on her coat and scarf. She spoke very quickly.

'I'm going now. We all agree it was an amazing thing that you've produced. I now understand what you've gone through and I've even got to meet your family, although perhaps not how I'd hoped. But surely you don't expect an immediate pardon just because you've gone to such great lengths to explain yourself? It doesn't work like that.'

The girls looked awkwardly at their father for guidance, their supportiveness dampened by Sonia's clear discomfort. He didn't know what to say, in case his efforts ended any chance of reconciliation. Tentatively, he stepped towards her, but she backed away, unwilling for physical proximity. He mumbled a few words, trying in vain to sound calm.

'I understand.'

'I'll call when and if I am ready. No promises when.'

It was hardly encouraging, and Sonia was half out the door.

'I'll hold off on Episode 2 then, shall I?'

* * *

The following weeks were like waiting for exam results, not sure if you've done enough revision to pass. Jack knew he had to get on with things without living in thrall to every text alert, hoping that it was from Sonia. At the same time, he had to build a new life in case she never called.

Having put so much effort into selling his retail business while producing 'Chicken Wars', his life had changed dramatically. In buying the second factory, he acquired its manager, a highly competent deputy, to oversee production across both sites, freeing him from many responsibilities. Jack now had a comfortable pension without the disparate hassles he had endured for years. He had his liberty, but potentially to be enjoyed alone.

As he waited for Sonia's verdict, he retreated to the security of his family. A few days after the screening, he showed his mother the film, trepidatious she would hate her lighting or think it another of his creative follies. While slightly bemused by his oblique approach to an apology, she was too consumed with rebuilding her life to offer a critical assessment. Jack realised his role as a son was now to support her unconditionally, without wishing she could behave differently towards him. There followed frequent restaurant trips where he listened to her misery without trying to throw in some of his own.

He tried to be a present and attentive father. With Isobel, it was easy. She was happy to talk openly and remained unwaveringly loyal, even discussing with him if there could be a Fogel's Chickens 2.0 that they might one day run together. He could not imagine what sort of business this might be, but knew that somewhere in heaven, Solly would be thrilled at the prospect of his legacy continuing, before inevitably punching a passing angel who did not agree.

His relationship with Natalie was better but not perfect. On the positive side, they put sessions with Bethany on hold, given how openly they could talk with each other most of the time. Natalie was mercurial in mood, however: sometimes she competed with her sister to be his favourite, other times she dismissed his opinions as reactionary, even if he tried not to offer any. On the surface, normality had resumed, but he constantly worried it could disintegrate when not expected.

One night, he invited Ali and the girls over to play her the film. When it finished, she was visibly moved and wrapped him in a spontaneous hug. The girls did not know how to react to their mother's unexpected emotion. Now that she was in her own happy relationship and less irritated by his failings, perhaps she could be more objective about his attempts to repair his relationship?

'It reminds me of the Jack I fell in love with, who had romantic dreams of being creative and different. When I look back, I was so wrong not to respect the other part of your life you couldn't ignore. You are someone who will always do what is right, not necessarily what is easy. That's your truth and if Sonia can't see it, I will drive round there myself and personally kick the shit out of her until she takes you back.'

* * *

They sat in the crepuscular light of Karen's new House of Commons office. Enjoying the novelty of her election success, the siblings drank tea in discoloured china cups from a chipped teapot that Karen inherited from the previous incumbent, along with a comfortable majority.

Jack showed them 'Chicken Wars' on his laptop and Tracy was intrigued by Lionel's violent reaction.

'Were you worried for your physical safety after he threatened to slit your throat? Full credit to him, though, for offering to make it a kosher killing.'

'Scared of Lionel? He'd be too afraid of getting blood on his immaculately pressed slacks. However, I'm pretty certain he's not going to invite me over for supper for quite a while yet.'

'And why's that?'

'It's all to do with HM Revenue and Customs.'

'Do I want to hear this?' Karen interrupted. 'I'm a Member of Parliament now, in case you haven't heard, and I don't want to be involved in anything to do with tax avoidance. I mean, you didn't make my campaigning easy, Jack. I got followed by a man dressed as a chicken to most of my hustings, a nutter who read the story and thought it would be amusing to make strange clucking noises every time I spoke. It wasn't funny.'

'Don't worry, baby sis. There's nothing to fear. I merely phoned Lionel to tell him that I'd seen a vast quantity of cash in his brief-case, which was apparently how some of his old-fashioned suppliers prefer to be paid. I made a few enquiries, and what do you know, naughty Lionel has been trying to avoid a hefty tax bill. It seemed only sensible to tell him that if he behaved badly again with me, I'd consider an anonymous tip-off to the revenue.'

Karen shook her head.

'That's blackmail, Jack. You need to be careful.'

'I'm not going to do anything, but it's made him vulnerable, and Lionel got the message that we just need to carry on with our businesses without continually fighting. That's all I want. Peace at all costs.'

'Any more physical threats after this?' Tracy asked while aiming an invisible gun at Jack.

'He was more concerned that this film is never released.'

'He's not the only one.'

'Of course it won't be broadcast, Karen, who'd want to watch it?'

Tracy looked puzzled.

'Let me see if I've got all of this clear, Jack. You sold half the business for a good price and reinvested it in buying another abattoir so that you can control supply to Lionel, and you have the added insurance of his dodgy accounting to protect you from any mad scheme he comes up with next. Well done, you. And you've made a film of these events with a lot of pontificating on the nature of truth. This confused shrink has only one question, if you don't mind me asking?'

'Fire away, doctor.'

'How on earth is this going to help you get Sonia back?'

* * *

Jack kept Sundays free, knowing it was Sonia's day off and the only time she might be able to see him. Like a doctor on call, he remained available to drop anything and rush to her, but the emergency never materialised. He had waited six months, and now after the film screening, another couple elapsed. They could have practically had a child together in that time. Instead, there seemed little left of their relationship other than his dread that it was over.

A mild winter had led to an early spring. Hampstead Heath was graced by daffodils and snowdrops heralding brighter times as Jack walked with the girls on a Sunday morning. Unseasonably warm sunshine had brought out the hordes and the three of them weaved between the dogs and toddlers as they discussed the weekly roundup of their latest TV viewing. As they stared in admiration at a few hardy individuals bravely enduring the chill of the swimming lakes, Jack's phone vibrated in his pocket, and he fumbled for it urgently as if the text would self-destruct if not read immediately. It was finally a message from Sonia.

Please come this afternoon to the café if you can?
2pm ok? S x

He showed the screen to the girls, who stood either side of him clasping an arm each in a show of solidarity.

'This is it, Dad. She's coming back to you. I can feel it.'

'I hope you're right, Iz. There's only so long I can live in limbo.'

'Can you be arsed to go?' asked Natalie, trying to make him smile. She felt his arm stiffen in her grip.

'I'll swing by for old times' sake. I don't know why I'm joking about this – I think I may throw up now, I feel so nervous.'

Isobel gave him a gentle slap on his cheek, nothing more than a tap.

'Pull yourself together, man. You need to live up to the promise you showed in your film. You're Jack Fogel. You're like the mirror in "Snow White". You say it as you see it.'

Jack nodded as he looked from daughter to daughter.

'Any advice from you, Nat? All help gladly received.'

Natalie looked like she'd been asked to solve a complex problem. When she spoke, she sounded very earnest.

'Absolutely no jokes, Dad, and let her do all the talking. Otherwise, you're good to go.'

* * *

Jack hoped he wouldn't be confronted by Sonia's truculent chaperone, Alexandru, when he arrived. Fortunately, she was alone, greeting him with an inscrutable peck and very little encouragement that things were going to turn out well. It was eerily quiet, the chairs stacked and tables bare, save one in the corner covered in spreadsheets, an open laptop and the remains of a half-eaten lunch. As he sat down, Jack noticed a printout of flight options from a travel website. Sonia grabbed the sheets of paper before he could study their contents, stuffing them in a rucksack by her chair.

How ironic that his fate was going to be sealed in this vegan café, having just expanded his chicken business through the purchase of another abattoir. Sonia had evidently been doing some bookkeeping, and when he sat down, Jack also noticed various boxes of new crockery in the process of being unpacked next to the table, while patches of paint were daubed on the wall, with exotic names like 'Tuscan Mint Juniper' written underneath. Everything looked in transition and his stomach reacted to this uncertainly with an unwelcome series of stretches, pulls and kicks.

Sonia popped into the kitchen and returned with two mugs of black coffee. She seemed jittery as she sat down.

'You'll have to make do with black as I'm not wasting any of my oat milk on you, only to see you pull a face.'

'Cold and black is better than having it with that revolting stuff, don't you worry. However, I was hoping today wouldn't be a discussion on the best dairy alternatives. Please put me out of my misery and tell me what you're thinking. Do we have a chance to start again?'

'There's always a chance, Jack, but you've made things rather complicated.'

'What do you mean? I thought I did a good job editing the film to state my case.'

'You did. It was marvellous and if there's a BAFTA for "Best Kiss-And-Make-Up" documentary, you are sure to win.'

'And yet, we are not kissing?'

'No, we are not.'

Jack wanted to take her hand or stroke her face.

'Then tell me. Will you take me back? Nothing has changed about how I feel for you and how much I love you. I can't put it more clearly than that.'

Sonia frowned.

'No, you can't. It's just not easy to forget the hurt, despite your elaborate apology. The consensus among my friends and family is that I would be insane to forgive you. They're considering starting a petition if I do anything stupid.'

'Mine, as you know, tried to help change your mind by appearing in my film. You'll be glad to hear, by the way, that Nat and Isobel have threatened to put themselves up for adoption if I come back from here single.'

It was so strange to be bantering like an established loving couple and yet Sonia's body was rigid with tension.

'They are wonderful. We'll get on brilliantly given the chance. They seem less confused by "Chicken Wars" than I was. I mean, what was I meant to think? No one has ever dedicated a documentary to me. I loved the bit with Chaim at the end when he sang me a song. That was sweet. It must have hurt when your mum told you that you were a better butcher than writer.'

'She's probably right. It wasn't meant to be complicated to understand. Basically, the realisation is that lying to you has taught me to stop lying to myself.'

'Anything else?' His first answer was clearly not enough.

'I suppose I am proud to be in the chicken business, and it provides a bloody good life for those that I love. I'm a decent bloke who wants to improve myself and paid a fortune to a film crew to help me reach that conclusion.'

She still looked unhappy.

'What's wrong, Sonia? A grimace was not the reaction I was hoping for.'

'Look, I'm delighted you've worked it all out, it's just your little voyage of self-discovery has had an effect on me.'

'Good or bad?'

'Different. It's unsettled me. I'm not sure what I think about anything any more.'

'What do you mean?'

'Well, look at the café. For the last few weeks, I can't decide if it's really worth the effort, and I'm completely uncertain what to do next. The catering business is going very well, but I need some investment so that I can expand it. I think I may need to do something different; I just don't know what.'

'Is that why you want to change the colour of the walls?'

'Yes, a bit superficial, I know. Two days ago, I just got carried away and ordered all this new crockery that we don't need and now I think I want to send it back. And when you came in, I was looking at my accounts to work out if it was worth selling the whole shebang anyway. When you got rid of your restaurants because you didn't like your partners, it made me wonder if I still want to be in business with Alexandru. He's very loving and all, but he can be a moody nightmare to work with. I'm blaming you for unsettling me.'

'You love your café, don't you?'

'I do, but maybe this isn't right for me in the long term. You know, I always wanted to be a psychotherapist. Did I ever mention that? I think I'd be very good. I've looked at courses, but it'll take ages to qualify. Maybe now is the right time. What do you think?'

Jack had no recollection of talking with her in the past about retraining and, given the intensity of his own family therapy sessions, he was sure he would have tried to dissuade her. She seemed overwhelmed with life decisions more significant than the state of their relationship.

'Where did all this come from?'

'Your stupid bloody documentary. Rather than helping me understand you better, it has made me doubt myself more than ever. It's all very well for you to find your truth and commit it to celluloid, it made me lose mine at the same time.'

'Blimey. I wouldn't have bothered with all the early-morning starts for filming if I knew this was going to happen.'

Jack was flummoxed by her reaction. His film was intended to eliminate her doubt, but it seemed to have exacerbated her indecision.

'So what if you sell the café and study for a new career? I'll be there for you, whatever you decide. You can be a vicar or a cat burglar just as long as we're together.'

Sonia had her head in her hands and emitted a strange wail of frustration. By now, Jack realised she had invited him over not to give him her decision but to share her turmoil. He put his hand on her shoulder and stroked her back. For a few seconds she seemed to welcome his touch, before sitting up sharply. He still had one more thing to ask that was troubling him.

'What's with all the different flights I saw on that sheet you stuffed in your bag like a stolen document. I'm very good at reading upside down and it seems you are also going on a big journey of some kind. Where?'

'That one is much more complicated.'

'Surely you don't want another gap year?'

Sonia avoided his gaze.

'No more jokes, please. This is the biggest decision of all, and it's been tearing me apart. I'm planning a trip to the States to find out about surrogates and sperm banks. Meeting your gorgeous girls confirmed for me I want to have a baby and that you are a great father. It's just I am unsure how long we need for me to fully trust you and I think I want a child, and soon. I know you have tried to correct everything, but maybe it's all still broken?'

Jack's stomach performed a few Braxton Hicks contractions in response to her last admission. If she wanted a child on her own, then she did not want to be with him. Simple as that. The subject of children had never scared him during their brief time together, quite the opposite. He understood that being with Sonia meant creating their own family unit, whatever that looked like, and his mind had been filled with excited thoughts about new beginnings. Now she was considering alternative plans.

'You know, I'd love to have children with you. I've told you that. We could be so happy if you'd just give me the chance.'

He saw the indecision in Sonia's eyes.

'I know you mean that. A large part of me would love to be with you too. It would make everything so much simpler.'

'And better, that's the most important bit. Stay with me, Sonia. Have a child with me. Be happy with me.'

How much more clearly could he put it, and he now knew that her tumult was because such a strong part of her wanted to come back. But not yet.

'I wish I could forgive you for everything. I've realised that I don't care about your business if it means being happy.'

'That's a start. So, what's stopping you?'

'Because, Jack, just because you made a film for me, how do I know you won't lie to me again?'

'What is there to lie about any more?'

'Nothing, I suppose. But my answer to you is still *maybe*. My whole life feels like a series of options to consider. "Chicken Wars" answers your questions, not mine.'

She had a point. You couldn't resolve heartbreak just because you filmed and edited a convenient narrative and he'd run out of ways to persuade her. The film had not gone as intended. It explained everything about his life while making her question every aspect of her own. He leant forward and rested his forehead on hers. There was a long silence, punctuated only by the sounds of the traffic outside. Without thinking, he kissed her tenderly on the lips. She shut her eyes and kissed him back.

'I need more time, Jack. I really do. Can we just see what happens? I do love you, but we'll have to find out if that is enough.'

'What choice do I have?'

She did not reply.

Chapter 35

As Jack left Sonia's bed several hours later and returned to his car, the spectacular sunset was a reminder that the day had been both beautiful and confusing. He could not define the unfamiliar blend of emotions he now felt after an afternoon spent reunited physically with Sonia, but without any clarity on their future. During the journey home, he grappled with the dissatisfaction of their parting, repeating the phrase he had said to her earlier as if it was his new personal mantra.

What choice do I have?

Those were the words he had used to the family lawyer, Mr Gledhill, when he agreed to take over Fogel's Chickens more than twenty years previously. Then, he was overwhelmed with resentment and bitterness at the change in direction he was compelled to take. Now, he had resolved all his battles just as Sonia was beginning new ones of her own and it seemed unfair that he was again going to be denied free choice. He desperately hoped she would consider him an ideal partner and parent and not go to America in search of an alternative. After all, the truth was, she loved him. Even in her anger, she had never stopped. She just didn't know if she wanted to be with him.

Later that night, buoyed by their partial reunion but exhausted by the despair of its ambiguity, he slept fitfully. When he awoke, the sunshine had been replaced by drizzly greyness. A new working week. Another week without Sonia. More chickens to be killed. More dinners alone. The harsh truth was, his new-found self-awareness had done very little to improve his prospects.

His daughters were anxious to find out what happened and had tried to reach him. It was too complicated to explain quickly, and he did not have the energy as he struggled out of bed and into the shower. They would have to make do with his promise to call them later for a proper conversation. To his irritation, they must in turn have told their aunt about his visit to Sonia, as Tracy had also texted him from New York, where she was speaking at a conference. He certainly did not have the resilience for her well-meaning advice, so he replied with enough detail to keep her in the loop while shutting down communication for the time being. '*We laughed, had a cuddle and resolved nothing*' was his summary of an afternoon that was either a reunion or a farewell.

Jack made himself a breakfast of coffee, porridge and fresh fruit with a dollop of expensive date syrup that Sonia had bought him a lifetime ago from a vegan food fair. His improvement in health of recent months had been accompanied by a dramatic change of diet, another gesture of solidarity with her lifestyle that was apparently all for nothing.

Normally, he was starving in the morning, but all he felt was a queasiness resulting from uncertainty. Sipping his coffee slowly, he wondered at the point of going into work in such an emotionally fragile mood. They would cope without him, and by now what he wanted to do was yomp across Hampstead Heath avoiding eye contact, while feeling properly sorry for himself.

He called his assistant to tell her he was not going to be in for a couple of days, which once would have aroused suspicion or concern. These days, other people could make decisions for him. Indeed, the unquestioning acceptance of his absence was a reminder that time stretched in front of him like a bleak desert highway. What was going to be his new purpose if Sonia kept away? He certainly didn't want to have to make another documentary to find out the answer.

What choice do I have? he said to himself once more, realising that being passive was not his only course of action. Maybe he did have agency? After all, Sonia had given little direction as to how they should behave from this point on, and their parting had been affectionate without ground rules for further communication.

Emboldened, he washed up his breakfast dishes and wiped the kitchen surfaces energetically with bleach, as if germ elimination was somehow a sign of a fresh start and a reminder to keep going with the new spirit of openness. He grabbed his phone and began to type a text, the words tumbling out effortlessly.

> Morning Sonia. I had a wonderful if inconclusive afternoon with you yesterday. I have been thinking overnight and realised that maybe I had to tell a few lies to find out the truth. Can we move on now? I am not going anywhere without you and will wait for you to make up your mind, however long that takes.
> Hurry up though, I am not getting any younger. x

Satisfied with the message, he went to the bathroom to prepare for his mind-clearing walk, unfazed by whatever was going to happen next. When he heard an incoming text, he did not rush to his phone. He finished his ablutions and calmly picked it up, relieved it was Sonia rather than a farmer discussing a problem with a poultry delivery.

> Never mind that rubbish, what are you doing Wednesday evening? I've got an engagement party in Hackney to cater and my favourite waiter has dropped out. Consider it a trial shift. x

Acknowledgements

Kosher chickens are not in my blood, but romantic comedies are an integral part of my DNA. Indeed, my initial idea had been a story about business rivalry in this unusual milieu, but I realised quickly that was not going to be enough for me. My sentimentality is boundless, and I wanted to write about finding love amidst a clash of beliefs and food choices.

I must start by thanking the Grossman family for providing the inspiration for the novel's setting. Antony Grossman is a highly regarded corporate lawyer and one of my dearest friends. He is also my stoic companion on regular trips to White Hart Lane to watch Spurs underperform and for many years we were accompanied by his much-missed late father Bernie. So began my induction into the world of kosher chickens and its unique business challenges.

Antony's beloved grandfather Issy founded Lewco-Pak chickens, a wholesale business, nearly eighty years ago, and Bernie ran it with other family members after Issy passed away. In the car to the match, I used to listen to all sorts of weird discussions about the issues they faced. Bernie would get irritated with me for my poor driving and call me *potz*, a Yiddish word for *fool*, each time I took a wrong turning. It is still my affectionate moniker amongst the family. Today, the business is run by Antony's talented brother Stephen, who has added a series of very successful shops to the operation.

The character of Solly is based on Issy, who wrote a charming autobiography, *Ain't No Use Sitting On The Fence*, in 1994, and I have lifted some of his experiences directly into the early scenes where Jack has his inheritance explained to him. I cannot thank Stephen enough for taking time to show me around the factory and explain in detail how everything works as well as enthusiastically agreeing to sell this book in his excellent Silvermans shops, to date an impenetrable retail outlet for more high-profile authors. In return, can I just say you won't find better kosher meat anywhere in London and the fresh salt beef sandwiches on Sundays are unbeatable.

Chickens can be funny. By bizarre coincidence, when I explained the plot to Stephen, he told me that when starting out in the business at seventeen, he once lied about what he did and pretended to be a trainee lawyer to impress a girl. Antony has regaled his friends for many years with unlikely stories about his relationship with the business. He has driven into hedges delivering kosher turkeys at Xmas and has never recovered from failing his Cambridge interview in 1981, when he bemused three law dons by answering a question about a trespasser's right of redress with a comparison to chicken licenses.

Thanks once again to the wonderful team at whitefox publishing, John Bond, Rosie Pearce, Laura Lees, Jenni Davis, Chris Wold and Claudia Besant, for all their guidance and creative input in helping me improve this book and publicise its arrival. Thank you to Dan Mogford for the brilliantly simple cover that has brought the idea to life.

To all my close friends, your support and enthusiasm for my writing projects encourages me that I do have an audience of at least a few people. To my children, Sophie, Matthew and Jake, I want to say something nice because you'll be irritated if I don't mention you. Here you go: you all have lovely teeth. Finally, to my perfect wife Hannah a massive thank you for your unstinting love and support. You had to listen to me read out dialogue of a character going on a date and flirting with another woman and remain calm. Those noise-cancelling headphones do come in useful sometimes.

January 2023